RAVEN IN THE RUNES

ᚠᚱᚲᛊᛏᚷᚹᛈᛁᛟᛉᚾ

A NOVEL

by
Laine Stambaugh

Book II: The Heart Stone Trilogy

Write: lainestambaugh@gmail.com.

Published by Ingram Spark
1 Ingram Blvd.
La Vergne, TN 37086

ISBN: 979-8-987612-2-6
ISBN E-Book: 979-8-987612-3-3

Library of Congress Cataloging in Publication Data:

Cover design by: Sana Asghar
Interior design by: MyRemotePro on Fiverr

Printed in the United States of America

**Parmata
valdu
bilara!**

(*Knowledge is Power*! in Delsiran language)

Part I: RAIDHO

(The Journey)

1

ᚠᚱᚲᛋᛏᚷᚹᛖᛚᚱᛪᚾ

Northwest Alba (Scotland)
MacAoidh Stronghold
Summer, 1153 A.D.

Eilidh ran a clean cloth over the blade of her sword. The thick and humid air in the courtyard gardens seemed to vibrate with tension as she awaited her brother, Gregor's, return with a new sword he wished to test. While she waited, she enjoyed the view of the bay from high atop the promontory where the MacAoidh stronghold sat. Not a cloud in the sky hinted of summer rain, which would bring welcome relief and cooler temperatures. She wanted to resume their swordplay, but she was suddenly filled with a nagging sense of foreboding. And not just about the weather.

Impatient, she paced back and forth along the path bordered by tall hedges. Despite her angst, she savored the freedom of wearing a man's tunic and hose that she'd borrowed from Gregor for this exercise. Frustrated when he didn't appear, she returned to her original spot and slashed her sword through the air for practice.

It was no secret that all four of her brothers were excellent swordsmen. And whatever they excelled in, so must she. If only she'd thought of gaining self-defense skills earlier, she could be a master swordswoman by now.

Eilidh yawned. She hadn't slept much the past few nights, and her instincts were telling her that time was running out – but for what? And how could she be prepared for the unknown?

Tired of waiting, she plopped down on a bench and inhaled deeply. As she did, things began to swim about her, coming in and out of wavy focus. Alarmed, she glanced around. Although it wasn't the first time this had happened, it had been quite a while since Eilidh had experienced one of these images, but she recognized the feeling of lethargy settling over her. She'd been nine when Grandmother Marsaili explained that a few women of the MacAoidh bloodline had inherited the ability to see the future, and for some, like Marsaili and her mother, they could see the past, as well. As a result, Eilidh's parents had no choice but to wisely defer to Grandmother Marsaili in these matters.

Eilidh glanced up at the sky. Still no rain clouds. She wiped her damp brow and pulled her tunic away from her chest where the fabric stuck to her skin. After a few moments of slowly breathing in and out, she regained her sense of awareness. While her vision returned to normal, she suddenly felt her stomach lurch at memories that she'd long since buried.

She stood up quickly and marched toward the opening in the hedge that led back to the castle, refusing to allow the nightmare to ruin her day. It had been three years since "The Incident." The power it held over her should have lessened over time, shouldn't it? And yet, she still felt the shame of a naïve girl thinking magic could chase all her shadows away. The incident had taken place during her thirteenth summer ... when everything changed. If only Grandmother Marsaili had been well enough to have attended that clan gathering and remained by Eilidh's side.

Eilidh paused at the opening to the hedge path. She swiped at the gathering tears and straightened her shoulders when she saw Gregor coming towards her wearing a big grin.

Every once in a while, Eilidh wished she had been born the fifth son. If so, she could wield a sword in her own defense, if the situation called for it, without worry that her mother would consider it an unladylike pursuit. All of her brothers were trained as warriors, in case of an attack, so the clash of swords nearby was not unusual. If she had to do this in secret, as she had when her grandmother had taught her to read and write, then so be it.

"You ready?" Gregor called, removing his sword from its scabbard.

Without further ado, they resumed their earlier parry and thrust of swordplay. For the next half hour, while she concentrated on the techniques she'd learned that afternoon, Gregor surprised her with a counter-move she hadn't seen before. She winced as the sharp tip of his blade grazed the back of her hand.

Gregor pulled back when he saw the spot of blood, his dark brows creating a deep furrow on his tanned face. "Did I nick you?"

Eilidh inspected the small cut. "I'll live. Keep going." She wiped the trickle of blood on the old braies she'd borrowed from him for the exercise. "Show me how to make that move."

Gregor checked the tip of his blade, a wry grin showing how much he appreciated her ability to bounce back and not give in to tears like most young ladies her age.

He laughed. "Heaven forbid I should know something you don't."

Eilidh and Gregor had always gotten along well, even though their mother referred to Gregor as the "mischief maker." Eilidh rather admired that about him.

"You know I won't give up until I can win," she responded.

He laughed and wiped his blade tip. "Why am I not surprised?"

Eilidh glanced at the hilt of the sword given to her by Grandmother Marsaili shortly after Eilidh celebrated her name day last autumn. Her mother was appalled, considering the sword an inappropriate gift for a lady whose father was clan chief, meaning her daughter must marry well and cease imitating her brothers.

Both Eilidh and her grandmother shared Raven as their spirit guide, so there existed a unique bond between them. And when Eilidh found trouble -- and she usually did -- Grandmother Marsaili was always the first to defend her and convince her parents their daughter meant no wrong.

As for the sword, Grandmother referred to it in Gaelic as *Fitheach*, due to the hilt bearing the engraved image of a raven in flight, wings outstretched as might be seen from above. Supposedly, it was created by the Goddess of the Moon, and was given to Eilidh's grandmother when she was forced to flee her home and Druid family to travel north to MacAoidh land.

"It's too hot and miserable to continue." Gregor motioned to a nearby bench in the shade where they could cool down before going inside.

Eilidh's personal servant, Muire, who had been standing in the background watching the pair, appeared with two mugs of cold water from the well. "I thought you might like a refreshment on this uncomfortable day."

"Perfect timing." Gregor gave a nod of thanks and drank nearly half the contents in one gulp.

Eilidh, grateful for Muire's thoughtfulness, said, "Thank you, Muire. You always seem to know when we need a drink. How do you do that?" Eilidh took a long, refreshing sip.

"It's obvious. When the clash of swords and cursing stops, it's time for water," she replied with a grin.

"Sassy lass." Eilidh smiled wide, having known Muire since she was seven — the sister she wished she'd had.

As she watched her friend retreat to the tower, she wondered how Muire could bear each day since her husband had died of a short illness the previous winter. Unable to cure Fearchar, Muire's husband, poor Grandmother Marsaili had been beside herself.

Left a grieving young widow, Muire would have been all alone at nineteen, if not for the MacAoidhs. And yet she never grieved around the family. Still, she was not quite back to her typically optimistic self.

Eilidh knew she would do well to follow Muire's example and display an unshakable confidence to the world, if she was going to stay put and be able to embrace her passion to pursue knowledge.

Eilidh closed her eyes and concentrated on the sounds of bees humming nearby. Red squirrels raced up the bark of a tall pine, chattering as they climbed. A raven caw drew attention, and Eilidh's eyes flew open.

That was when she spotted their servant, Bothain who'd been with the family since long before Eilidh was born. He approached the two siblings in their hedge hideaway and bowed respectfully, revealing a rim of hair not unlike a priest's tonsure.

"Pardon the interruption, Mistress Eilidh, Master Gregor, but your father requests the mistress's presence ... immediately."

Eilidh glanced down at her and her brother's old clothing. "What perfectly awful timing. I must change." She jumped up and grabbed her sword and shrugged at Bothain. "Oh, bog feathers. Tell him I was outside searching for plant roots and will come as soon as I can."

Bothain nodded, despite the white lie.

She grinned and shot off for a side door into the tower, praying not to be seen. How wonderful to run without the encumbrance of a long skirt! Even so, she tried not to upset her parents on a recurring basis with behavior unbecoming a lady ... if possible. She slipped inside the doorway without being seen, then raced up the stairs and made it to her bedchamber. Fortunately, Muire was busy elsewhere. She placed *Fitheach* in its scabbard and buried it in her trunk, under her clothes. Then she removed the borrowed tunic and hose and stuffed them inside an empty basket.

She quickly washed away the dirt and blood and then donned a blue-gray gown she knew her mother would approve. Afterwards, she tried tying the laces on the side that held the gown closed, but gave up when she couldn't quite reach all of them. At least she would appear decent as long as she didn't raise her arms. As soon as she finished meeting with her father, she would find Muire and ask her to complete the job.

She hoped her father's summons was for some minor infraction and not the sword fighting lessons. There was no point in owning a sword if she didn't know how to use it. And she refused to give up *Fitheach* or hang it on the wall to gather dust. She had plans for getting to know the weapon, which Grandmother Marsaili insisted possessed magical properties she must learn to use if she wished to achieve her destiny.

When she passed through the great hall, she found her father at his desk, hands behind his head as he gazed at the ceiling. She quietly seated herself on the other side of the table piled high with documents, quill pens, pots of ink, and a stamp that represented the MacAoidh chief's seal. Eilidh glanced at the documents pile, wondering if there was anything of interest.

Her father sat forward, eyes growing round as he rested a hand upon the stack of documents. "You look like you've been exercising in the sun. Have you and Gregor been practicing with swords again?" He frowned, which was most unusual. He was a man who liked to laugh and share in the fun with his children. But that wasn't always possible, not when his wayward daughter refused to settle down and marry.

Eilidh exhaled, glad she'd cleaned up and changed.

"You appear out of breath," said her mother, appearing in the doorway. "A lady walks slowly, and doesn't work up a sweat like men."

Eilidh looked down at herself and winced, deciding to keep Gregor and the swords out of the conversation. She ignored her mother's comment and instead turned to her father. "You summoned me, *Àthair?*"

"We have something important to discuss with you."

Eilidh watched as her father's twinkling eyes followed her mother, who was dressed in a fern-green gown that complemented the thick auburn hair piled high atop her head. She set a fresh mug of ale on her husband's desk, then waved a slender hand at Eilidh. The expressions on her parents' faces told her all she needed to know. They wanted to discuss The Marriage Matter. She slumped in her chair, trying to look invisible.

When her father didn't immediately speak, Eilidh heard her mother gently clear her throat. "Eilidh, are you alright?"

Eilidh sat up and glanced around, wishing she could run off and join a convent. "I'm fine. It's just ..."

Her father took two long sips of ale, then set the mug down. He'd been a handsome man in his youth, his fair complexion now ruddy from time spent outdoors in all sorts of weather. Usually known for his ready smile and hearty laugh, he rested both forearms on the desk, suddenly appearing tired and defeated.

"Eilidh, I'm not going to repeat what I've said over the past two years about you scaring off your suitors. That was then. This is now. You have lived with your family for almost seventeen years, safe and protected. But you are more than old enough to be a wife and mother. I wouldn't be doing my duty to provide for your future if I didn't find the best man possible for you to wed."

Eilidh's throat tightened.

Her father paused as her mother rose and placed a hand on her arm.

"Eilidh, we love you dearly, but you've frightened off every suitor we've invited." Her mother shook her head sadly. "There are no more decent unmarried men left in *Srath Nabhair*. We must look beyond our borders, and that may take some time."

"We want you to feel fulfilled as a wife and mother, to have grandchildren and a pleasant life. But we've run out of options with your lack of cooperation," her father added.

Would her parents send her away to some far-off land where she'd never see her family again? Just like what happened to Grandmother Marsaili all those years ago? She choked back a sob.

"Eilidh, as your father said, we only want you to be happy." Her mother pressed her lips together.

"But I'm happy *here*."

Her mother stood and gently lifted Eilidh's chin. "Come, *nighean*. Let's go and discuss what new gowns you might need for meeting your new suitors."

"I don't care about new gowns. I want to stay where I am."

Eilidh knew she sounded childish and petulant, but she couldn't accept this major life change being forced upon her. Not without a fight.

"Eilidh, go with your mother. That is the end of it. For now." Her father gave her that stern look that told her he meant business, but then his face softened. "Who knows? You may be surprised to find a man who has a lot in common with you."

With that, he bid her farewell and Eilidh followed her mother to Eilidh's bedchamber. Once inside, it suddenly occurred to her that just the thought of leaving her grandmother, her *seanmhair*, caused the back of her throat to ache.

"I'd like to check in on Grandmother now, if I may."

Her mother nodded. "That would be fine. Meanwhile, no sword practicing between now and your next meetings with

Her grandmother nodded, then lay her head back on the pillow as her cough subsided. For now.

2

ᚨᚱᚲᛊᛏᚷᛈᛗᛚᛉᚾ

As Eilidh observed her parents and brothers in lively conversation at the supper table, she remained uncharacteristically silent. Grandmother Marsaili had retired to her room, which worried Eilidh. So, instead of trying to compete for attention amongst her brothers, Eilidh focused on what she might include in a poultice that evening to help her *seanmhair* sleep through the night.

The warm, humid weather made her feel listless and she had no appetite. She pushed her food around on her plate, sad to think that Grandmother may be destined for her journey to the Otherworld sooner than any of them would have expected. Eilidh narrowed her eyes at her brothers in resentment. They weren't as close to Grandmother as she was, so wouldn't feel the loss. *Seanmhair* had taught her everything worth knowing.

As for the marriage matter, the other situation weighing her down, she expected her brothers surely must have heard the news. And yet, not one of them expressed sympathy that she was being forced to marry a stranger and most likely to leave the region. It seemed that they could care less who she married, just as long as she was someone else's responsibility. Men were happy, simple creatures, Grandmother liked to say.

It just isn't fair.

But then, something her father said quickly caught her attention and she set aside her worrisome thoughts. She picked up her tea mug and took a sip, trying not to show too much interest. "You're going to take horses to auction in *Inbhir Theórsa?*"

"Aye. I will set out early tomorrow. Padruig and Gregor will come and help with the horses." Her father smiled at her, then reached for the last piece of roasted venison. "You want me to bring you anything, my sweet lass?" He tore off a piece of meat and chewed with enthusiasm. "Ribbons? Lavender soap?"

Padruig and Gregor were attempting not to break out into laughter.

"Aye, she could use some scented soap to cover up the sweat from wielding a sword," Gregory said, with a chuckle.

Leith gave him a sharp look. "Let her speak for herself."

"I need nothing," Eilidh said, her voice small.

"Well, that's enough talk about unmentionable topics at the supper table. You lads will want to get a good night's sleep to be ready to go with your father early in the morning." Her mother smiled sweetly and turned her attention to her husband.

A strange thought made its way to Eilidh's confused mind. Was it possible she'd been too hard on her mother? That she loved and protected her daughter in her own way, every bit as much as her grandmother? Eilidh wondered if she'd missed that while focused on her grandmother.

For a moment, Eilidh nibbled her lower lip, as she gathered courage. She squared her shoulders. "May I please go with you to *Inbhir Theórsa?* I won't embarrass anyone or get in the way. I'll sit, quiet as a mouse. I promise." She angled her hands as if praying. "Please, please? I need to get out and see people my own age, *Àthair.*"

"We'll be too busy with the horses, Eilidh. This is a business trip, not for pleasure."

Her mother heaved a sigh and glanced at her husband. "On the other hand, if we both accompany you, I can take Eilidh to a seamstress in town and have her fitted for new gowns." She seemed to perk up. "We could make a day of it, and stay the night at an inn. Would you like that, Eilidh?"

Eilidh's breath caught. Nothing could be more unappealing. But it was better than staying home and fretting over meeting a new group of suitors. "Um, aye, *Màthair*. That would be fine. As long as *Seanmhair* is doing well."

"Of course," her mother demurred.

Her father shuffled his feet, looking down at the stone floor. "Hmph. Hadn't thought of that." He rose from the dining table and scratched his beard. "I suppose that can be arranged. Gregor can drive the supply wagon. Leith and I will herd the horses."

"I can help with that!" Eilidh volunteered, not wanting to ride in a bumpy wagon the whole way with her mother.

Her mother's lips pressed together in a straight line. "I don't want you smelling like a horse when we visit the seamstress."

"She's got a good point," said Gregor with a grin.

"There are worse things than smelling like a horse," Leith said with a thoughtful look at Eilidh.

What was with him today? He'd promised her he wouldn't tell a soul.

She sat up and tossed her long coppery locks over her shoulders. "I will wash up with rosewater as soon as we check into our bedchamber," Eilidh offered, not wanting her brothers to ruin her plans before they even left home.

"Hmmm. We won't have time for silliness," her mother insisted.

"Of course," Eilidh agreed readily. This would be the fastest fitting ever, she promised herself.

"Well, I suppose ..." her father started to say.

Eilidh jumped up and hugged her father, then made a point to place a gentle kiss on her mother's cheek. "*Tapadh leat*. Thank you! May I be excused now? I wish to prepare a poultice for Grandmother's cough."

"Your grandmother must be feeling somewhat better since this afternoon. I thought I saw her head out to the garden. It's still sunny and warm out." Her mother smiled and waved her away.

Eilidh nodded. Perhaps they would have time for that important conversation Grandmother had only hinted at earlier.

After a few moments, she discovered Grandmother Marsaili enjoying the warm sun as she sat facing the bay with her eyes closed. Her skin appeared a bit rosier than that morning. Eilidh's shoulders sagged in relief. Now she wouldn't need to feel guilty if she was gone for a day and night.

Her grandmother's thick coated, long-haired white cat, Fenella, lay sleeping on the bench beside her. When the cat saw Eilidh, she made a chittering sound, as if pleased to see her. She rose and stretched, then jumped down and rubbed up against Eilidh's legs.

Eilidh smiled. "Such a smart cat." She was the only person in the family, besides Grandmother, who Fenella allowed to pet and hold her. Fenella gazed up at her with mysterious golden eyes.

Not wishing to interrupt her grandmother's reverie just yet, Eilidh observed her fondly as she knelt and caressed the friendly cat. No one in the family understood nor defended Eilidh as well as her beloved grandmother, who refused to hide her intelligence in front of men, including her son, Eilidh's father, and his two younger brothers. *Seanmhair* felt it her duty to teach Eilidh to read and write, though she'd kept it secret for a long time—that is, until Eilidh demanded more and her father had learned of it. But Eilidh's father would not budge on hiring a special tutor for his daughter, a practice which he frowned upon. Regardless of his views on educating women, Eilidh had experienced a view of the world that had expanded far beyond the borders of the stronghold, thanks to her grandmother's dedication.

Eilidh rose and Fenella gave a disapproving meow.

Grandmother opened her eyes. "Ach, *ban-ogha*." She glanced up and regarded Eilidh for a moment. "You look troubled. Tell me." She patted the now vacant bench beside her.

When Eilidh seated herself, she felt the calming warmth left behind from Fenella's body. At peace beside her grandmother, she inhaled deeply of the sea air.

"*Màthair* and *Àthair* are insisting I meet more eligible men. *Àthair* says I must marry soon." She clasped her hands in her lap. "But I can't do what they ask of me, *Seanmhair*."

Eilidh wiped a lone teardrop as her grandmother opened her arms wide.

"Come here, my dear."

Eilidh leaned into her embrace for several moments, her touch soft and familiar as she patted Eilidh's back. "Ach. That again."

Eilidh sniffed and nodded. "I want to be a healer who travels wherever I am most needed, always learning, like the Druids." Eilidh's chest felt tight. "I don't wish to marry. Show me how to convince *Àthair* of my destiny." Eilidh's lips trembled.

Grandmother Marsaili let go of Eilidh and sat back. "You sound a lot like me when I was your age, *ban-ogha*. I was forever testing the boundaries, and it didn't always end well."

And yet, after a brief reflection on her life, a smile blossomed on *Seanmhair's* tranquil face. She had few age lines, if any, which Eilidh thought interesting, considering she was nearing sixty winters. Her white hair, typically tied back with a leather cord, was loose today, falling about her shoulders, while her eyes sparkled at her granddaughter's words. The familiar and soothing scent of her grandmother's rosewater tickled Eilidh's nose and reassured her all must be right with the world.

"You will not forget what you have learned here, even if you leave home to marry a man from another land. Knowledge is power, *ban-ogha*. We share that passion to learn." She squeezed Eilidh's hand in reassurance. "I will teach you all that I can as long as I am able, but you must begin to forge your own path. You can accomplish much, and you will influence the lives of your daughters and their daughters for many generations to come. But you will need to work hard and stay focused. The Goddess has special plans for you, *mo chridh*, my love. You have a *special* journey to make in order to reach your destiny."

Goosebumps rippled along Eilidh's arms. "I do?"

Her grandmother kissed her cheek fondly. "You are chosen. Of course you do."

"And when does this journey begin, *Seanmhair*?"

Her grandmother framed her face with her hands and smiled almost sadly.

"*Ban-ogha*, my lovely and fierce granddaughter, it has already begun."

3

ᚨᚱᚲᛋᛏᚷᚹᛖᛗᛚᚱᚢᚾ

Torleik wondered why he hadn't met someone like Hilda to be his wife. With her cheerful, yet calm temperament, she clearly loved children. She and husband Borgny had three already. Whenever Torleik was in *Thjorsá* on business, he made it a point to stop and visit the daughter of his father's friend back in *Nord Vegr*. A few years older than Torleik, Hilda ran a small but profitable ladies' tailor shop. Each time he entered the shop with its brightly colored fabrics, the aroma of lavender was the first thing he noticed. Consequently, he didn't actually mind when Kelda gave him the task of purchasing fabric and thread when he was in town.

Hilda was one of his few female acquaintances in the area, and he had to admit he liked taking advantage of the opportunity to converse in his native Norse, rather than the dialect spoken on the island. She was married to an outgoing brewer and tavern owner, Borgny, originally from Oslo. Torleik and he had become fast friends.

Full of personality, Hilda made a point of teasing Torleik about a big, strapping Norseman stepping inside a ladies' clothing shop, which always made him laugh. Worth the trip alone. She also knew of his frustrating search for a wife.

Before he stepped inside Hilda's shop on that day, however, his eye was drawn by a notice posted on the wall of the shop. He pulled it off the wall and scanned it quickly.

"What's that?" asked Hallkel.

His best friend from Torleik's home town, Hallkel had accompanied Torleik from *Nidaros* to the Orkneys. He'd met a friend of Hilda's and fell head over heels in love for the first time. Torleik had never seen Hallkel smile as much as he did those first few months. But when Alana and Magaidh fell ill with fevers and died, poor Hallkel was devastated. He fell into a deep cavern of grief, and it wasn't long before Torleik heard the news and rescued Hallkel, bringing him to *Meginland* and making him a partner in his horse business. Eventually, Hallkel came out of his hole, but for a long time, he didn't smile much.

He was good with children, and Torleik's four-year-old son, Atli, spent much time in Hallkel's company. Hallkel was patient and tried to answer the many questions the boy asked. Therefore, Torleik felt comfortable leaving Atli with Hallkel if he needed to leave the farm for some reason. But the boy was a handful. Torleik needed a mother for Atli who was not only patient, but willing to take charge and provide consistency with behavioral issues.

Hallkel peered over Torleik's shoulder at the notice. "An auction."

"*Ja*. Looks like there's a horse auction this afternoon." Torleik glanced up at the sun to gauge the time. "We're almost done for today, so why not stop at the auction and see what new breeding horses we can find in *Alba*, once we're through shopping?"

Hallkel grinned, the dimple in his friend's chin always a surprise to Torleik. "Sounds like the perfect end to our trip."

Torleik nodded, then folded the notice and stuck it in his pocket. "Let's finish running Kelda's errands and then head for the stables."

They quickly entered the shop. No other customers were present. Hilda sat in a chair behind the counter, humming while she worked on a bright green gown. She looked up and smiled. "How good to see you two."

Torleik, typically not much of a talker, grinned and gave her a hug. "Good to see you." He glanced around the shop with interest, as it was packed with bolts of fabric in colors, from bright orange-red, to soft pastels, like a butter yellow and a blue the color of the sky in summer.

"How goes your search for a mother for Atli?"

She'd switched from a rough Gaelic to Norse, and he gave a grateful nod then glanced at Hallkel, who was examining a completed gown made in a practical gray wool with white trim.

"I think I must abandon my search for now. I've had no luck in *Orkneyjar* ... or *Thjorsá*." Torleik heaved a sigh.

"You mustn't give up hope. You are a good man, Torleik. The right woman for both you and your son is out there."

Hilda went back to folding fabric as she rarely stood or sat still.

He grunted, his typical response when he didn't know what to say. "Kelda wants enough fabric for two gowns. Please."

"Colors?"

"Just something practical and affordable."

"Hmph." She turned and pulled out a nice dark green wool, then a bolt of light grayish-blue linen. "The dark for cooler days, the light for when the sun is shining."

A widower for two years, Torleik had no desire to become too knowledgeable about ladies' clothes' issues. He couldn't wait to hand such a task over to his wife. He waved a hand and reached for his coin purse at his waist. "Those colors should be fine. You know how much fabric Kelda needs."

"Is she well?"

Torleik watched as she measured, then cut the green fabric using precise motions. "She's fine, as far as I know."

"And Atli? He must be growing up quickly."

Hilda wrapped the cut cloth, then added some matching thread and a needle. She then reached for the gray bolt of cloth.

"He gets into mischief. It's hard to get much work done. That's why I'm impatient to find someone soon."

She glanced at him with an odd smile.

"What? Am I expecting too much?"

Hallkel finished his inspection of ready-made clothes and returned to Torleik's side. "I don't think it's reasonable to bring someone home and expect her to be perfect the first day. These things take time. You need patience."

Hilda handed Torleik the second package and grinned. "He knows what he's talking about. Listen to him, Torleik."

Hallkel was not one to share his personal details. Hallkel was not one to share his personal details. However, he'd been married once, so perhaps he did know a thing or two about expectations for a successful partnership.

Torleik paid for the packages Kelda had requested.

Then Hallkel turned to him and said, "I'll meet you at the auction."

Torleik said a hurried goodbye to the pair then left, dropping the packages off in their room at the Gray Goose Inn and Tavern near the harbor.

Relieved to have completed his tasks, Torleik headed for the public stables on foot, where the auction was to take place. And yet, he balled his fists, more frustrated than ever because he couldn't find a wife he could stand being married to for life. Was there something wrong with him? Or, was he going about this all wrong?

He couldn't help but compare every woman he encountered to Ulla, his first wife, and Atli's mother. Beautiful inside and out. The perfect companion and partner.

4

ᚠᚱᚲᛋᛏᚷᛈᛗᛚᚷᚾ

As it turned out, Eilidh's grandmother, Marsaili, seemed better that morning, her coughing having lessened. Greatly encouraged, Eilidh threw a few last-minute items into her traveling bag that also held a change of clothes for the return trip back. Excited, now that *Seanmhair* was out of danger, Eilidh watched her father and brothers tie ropes to link several horses so they would stay together on the trip. A few were young and had never traveled anywhere else. Confused, they put up a struggle, their cries deafening.

Perhaps she'd leave the horses to the men. Instead, she could please her mother by riding with her, and at the same time, keep her outfit free of dirt and ultimately smelling like horses. Although she loved that unique blend of hay, horse manure, and horse hide, whenever she entered the barn, she kept that little tidbit to herself. Her brothers would tease her endlessly if they got a whiff of that.

Although early, the bailey was bustling with life as Eilidh observed the community of artisans, shopkeepers and service providers who lived within the walls of the stronghold dedicated to Clan MacAoidh. She went in search of her mother, who was waiting on a bench several feet away from the stables.

"I thank the Lord today is cooler," Eilidh's mother told Eilidh as she waved at her husband almost gaily. "Are you excited about the new gowns?" Her mother eyed what Eilidh wore and shook her head. "I've always loved that light shade of green on you, but it looks almost threadbare."

Eilidh glanced down and fingered the material. "It's fine. I rarely go anywhere anyway."

"And I would swear you are still growing. You're already taller than your grandmother and me. You simply must have new gowns that fit you properly to impress your suitors."

Eilidh winced, relieved when her mother turned her attention to Eilidh's father. She needed to accept that her parents would never give up on marrying her off to a stranger. This was meant to be a day of distraction from all that. She sighed as she prepared for the journey. Besides, she should be grateful for new gowns with hems that covered her feet. *Màthair* was right about that.

***

Geirolf usually passed his time haunting the Crusty Crab, a tavern directly across from the harbor that attracted a rougher class of men. Seamen. Warehouse workmen. Construction workmen. Farmers. Livestock breeders. Men like himself who would do anything for money.

He was searching for one man in particular that night. He'd heard he was in town at the moment, so Geirolf's unplanned arrival couldn't have been more perfect.

He hadn't been there long when he caught a glimpse of Torleik Sorensson from his old hometown of *Nidaros*. Immediately on alert, he used the crowd as cover as he inched closer to Torleik and his friend, Hallkel, who were in conversation with a man behind the counter. Geirolf took another step closer and managed to hide behind a heavyset man sitting on a barstool. The big man's clothes were black with soot, and Geirolf could see where sweat had dried that must have run down his face like rivulets from a stream. The man's bare arms revealed burn marks made by a hot iron, which helped in identifying his occupation as a blacksmith.

Geirolf was a great observer of small details. He'd need that particular skill if he was to best Torleik, that hypocritical snob. Geirolf had heard from various sources that Torleik had started a horse breeding business in *Orkneyjar*, as well as become a farmer. Supposedly, Torleik was in town searching for a wife. He wondered if Torleik had found that bride yet. He hoped so. He had big plans for her, whoever the lucky girl turned out to be.

However, as the night grew late, he saw Torleik and his friend leave the Gray Goose tavern and enter the inn side of the establishment.

With a sly smile, Geirolf stepped outside. He needed to make plans for the next day.

5

ᚠᚱᚲᛊᛏᚷᛈᛗᛚᛟᚾᚢ

By the noon hour, as Eilidh tried on one gown after another inside the small dress shop, she decided that trying to please her mother was a lot harder than she'd expected. It wasn't that she complained about her daughter's lack of interest in being measured for new gowns. But Eilidh suspected that her lack of enthusiasm for ladies' fripperies disappointed her mother greatly. After bearing four strapping sons, her mother had probably been desperate for a sweet, quiet, and obedient daughter to make up for the boys.

As they left the shop with their packages and walked to the inn, Eilidh wondered if Grandmother Marsaili ever found it a challenge to raise three sons, having no well-behaved daughters to provide a calm within the storm.

They dropped off their packages in their room at the inn, then proceeded to the tavern next door to enjoy a quick midday meal before attending the auction where their Highland ponies would be sold. And Arabel, Nairna's filly. The thought sent her stomach plummeting. She had known the day would come when she must part with the horse, but now that it was here, it had her stewing. Better to concentrate on what she *could* control.

Hopefully, the horse would be gone by the time she got there so she wouldn't have to face that awful moment.

She turned her attention to the tavern. Female customers, some with young children clinging to their skirts, mixed with businessmen and other professionals, so Eilidh felt safe. She was starving after standing and holding up her arms for so long, but the lady who owned the shop, a young woman named Hilda, had made it bearable as she kept up a constant chatter, despite her heavy Norse accent. Anyone who could make Eilidh laugh under those trying circumstances, was a special person, indeed.

As Eilidh and her mother waited for their order, her mother reached across the table and held Eilidh's hands. "Are you excited about the gowns we decided on? That blue fabric, the color of ripe blueberries, should be lovely with your features. As should the forest green."

Eilidh examined her short fingernails. "Thank you, *Màthair*, for letting me choose a color on my own."

"You're most welcome. I look forward to seeing how you look in raspberry, since that was your first choice." Her mother had flinched when she said that and looked away.

Eilidh had been pondering if now would be a good time to tell the story behind why she was so adamant about not marrying. Guilt was starting to build up. Guilt for preventing her mother the pleasure of planning her daughter's special day, sharing in the joy as mother and daughter. Guilt for not trusting her mother with her secret. Guilt for wanting to determine her own future, whether she lived alone or not. But it was *The Incident* that haunted her. The longer she held this secret inside, the larger it seemed to grow. Even Leith appeared weary of being the only witness to her humiliation.

A serving woman of middle years and grumpy temperament delivered their aromatic bowls of thick, creamy potage with vegetables, mushrooms, and bits of chicken. She placed a basket containing fresh oat bread and a plate of fresh butter in the middle of the table with a thump. Then the woman wiped her nose on her apron and moved on to the next table.

Despite all that, Eilidh said, "Mmm-mmm. This is really good!" She dug in with enthusiasm, not waiting for anyone. With brothers, it was grab and eat at their table, or else miss out on something you'd been thinking about all day.

"Sit up straight. And don't slurp your soup, daughter." Her mother leaned forward. "You should always employ your best appearance and manners when in public. You never know when the right man will walk through that door."

Eilidh glanced at the open door, imagining the drunken customers come nightfall. The floors and tables had been cleaned, but still reeked of ale. She wrinkled her nose. "You think I would meet the perfect man in *this* tavern?"

"Don't be impertinent, dear. I'm afraid you've been ruined by those four rascals I gave birth to long ago."

Surprised that she was actually enjoying herself, Eilidh remained silent and finished her soup so they could see the rest of the auction. She hoped her father's special Highland ponies did well with nobles and landowners, men who could afford to train and keep them in luxurious green pastures. Especially Arabel.

As they set out for the stables, a cold breeze blew right through Eilidh, and she pulled her shawl tighter, narrowing her eyes against the chill. *Seanmhair* would say it was a bad omen when a cold wind came from out of nowhere on an otherwise pleasant day.

When they arrived at the auction, Eilidh was surprised to see a few horses outside the stable. She glanced around for her father or brothers. When she saw several people coming and going from the public stable, she started that way.

"Eilidh, wait. Where are you going? We should wait for your father to come find us. I hate to interrupt his business."

Eilidh had never seen her mother act so timid before. It was a confusing sight. "If you wish to wait here, please do. I am going to go inside and check on Arabel. I'll be back shortly."

She felt confident around horses and the people who raised them. She wrapped her gray shawl a bit tighter against the cool breeze. So far, the trip had been rather tedious. Her belly may be full, but her muscles ached from standing still for so long at Hilda's. She looked around for Arabel, relieved when she didn't see her sweet girl. At least she wouldn't have to face a sad goodbye.

The stable was oddly quiet. Where were the half-a-dozen horses her father brought to auction? It couldn't be over already, could it? She and her mother hadn't dallied for long at the dress shop, nor in inhaling their meal.

When she glanced around, she saw neither Gregor nor Leith, but she did hear what sounded like her father's voice. He stood just outside of a stall door, holding Arabel's reins.

Unlike her mother, and thanks to her brothers as role models, Eilidh had no problem interrupting. However, when she got a good look at the two tall, handsome, Norsemen in conversation with her father, she sensed something was different. They clearly were discussing horses, for the two men kept admiring and running their hands over Arabel's sleek chestnut coat. The filly tried to shy away, but her father held her reins tightly.

Eilidh cleared her throat, staring in awe at the image of the handsome men and the anxious young filly. *Her* filly. She had raised Arabel from birth, watched her grow strong and confident.

At that moment, her father looked up and saw her. He waved a hand and beckoned her over. Eilidh's scalp prickled at the two strange men, and yet, she took one slow step at a time until she finally stood before her father.

"This is my youngest, Eilidh. Daughter, these gentlemen are from Orkney. This is Torleik, a horse breeder, and his associate,

Hallkel. They've traveled a long way from the isle of *Meginland*. They're considering the purchase of our little filly."

Eilidh acknowledged their polite nods, even as her stomach began to churn. She glanced away, unable to focus. "Where are the other horses? Is the auction over already?"

Her father grinned and nodded, like a proud lad. "Aye, the sale is over. Every horse was purchased, except for the filly here. She hasn't behaved herself properly today, and spooked several potential buyers. She clearly needs more training and attention. Perhaps she'll be ready *next* spring." He glanced at the two men. "We leave at first light. You'll need to make your decision by then. We'll be heading west to *Tunga*."

A groundswell of hope filled Eilidh at the thought that her horse wouldn't be sold and that they would have another year together. She scratched under the filly's chin for a few moments, and Arabel stopped struggling. When Eilidh spoke softly to her as she ran her hands over her back, Arabel responded by resting her soft muzzle in Eildih's hand and heaving a great sigh. Tears gathered in the corners of Eilidh's eyes to know that the horse's fate hung in the balance.

"See how she responds to a gentle hand?" her father said. "I'll bet you'll have her smoothed out and eager to please in no time."

Eilidh couldn't stop sniffing. She reached in her pocket for a kerchief.

"She does appear docile right now. Hallkel is known for bringing problem horses around, as well. It's a gift, gentling an anxious animal enough to trust you." Torleik turned his ice blue eyes on Eilidh, as if suggesting she was special, as well.

"Perhaps we should reconsider making an offer," the older Norseman said to his companion. "If she gets feisty again, I can handle that."

Torleik's eyes never left Eilidh's green eyes, though he responded with a nod and a smile to his friend. "That's true."

Distressed at the thought of Arabel going so far away with these strangers, Eilidh turned her back to them so they wouldn't see her tears that she was now shedding freely. Would they treat the filly kindly, and not lash her when she misbehaved?

She gently took the reins from her father and led Arabel into the empty stall. While she provided fresh water and oats, she could hear the men speaking in low voices. She spent as much time as she could with Arabel, but then knew she should leave and let the men negotiate. Stomach clenching, she said a heartfelt farewell to the horse, then realized she'd forgotten her mother waiting in front of the stable. She would receive an earful for that, but when she left the stable and looked around, she located her mother sitting on a bench talking to her brother, Leith.

Eilidh felt her scalp prickle.

Surely her brother wouldn't divulge her secret after all this time.

Would he?

Eilidh watched as her father put an arm around the shoulder of the Norseman called Torleik, while she followed in silence. Without a thought for her, they laughed and continued their discussion as they entered the closest tavern to celebrate the purchase of Arabel.

6

ᚠᚱᚲᛊᛏᚷᛈᛗᛚᛩᚾ

Eilidh couldn't face her mother and brother, Leith, just yet. Instead, she quietly slipped down a narrow street so she could figure out what to do while walking the small port town, and to mourn the loss of her beloved Arabel. No longer interested in peering into shops nor admiring outside vendors selling their goods and produce, she kept a hurried pace until she reached St. Peter's Church, then circled back and returned to the harbor the way she'd come. She recognized Hilda's clothing shop with a feeling that could only be named as longing as she passed it. Maybe, deep down, a small part of her wanted to marry a kind man someday, and raise children she could teach whatever they wanted to learn, whether they be boys or girls. But how could that possibly happen in an arranged marriage where she barely knew the man?

By the time she reached the spot where she and her mother had begun the day near the harbor, she still hadn't come to grips with the loss of Arabel, nor a plan for what she was going to do about being forced to wed. Furthermore, what if Leith had spoken to her mother about The Incident? Thankfully, Leith and her mother were nowhere in sight, so Eilidh sank down onto a bench that overlooked the harbor, a few steps from the tavern where her father had disappeared with Torleik and Hallkel. As she chewed on a fingernail, she wondered if telling her parents about the incident would result in them calling off plans to find her a husband. As painful as it would be to tell the story, perhaps it was time to explain to her parents how dramatically her life had changed that day in the woods. Even now, her body began to tremble at the thought. She wrapped her shawl tighter around her.

If Leith had indeed informed her mother about what happened at that last clan gathering Eilidh had attended, she would most likely believe Leith's story. As the second-born son, he was very serious and kept to himself. Consequently, he was not likely to be next in line to be named clan chief when his father died. That is, not unless something happened to Friseal, the practical and responsible son who spent a few months each year with Clan MacAoidh and the rest with his wife's clan, the MacLeods. That allowed him to stay informed and ready to help both clans, if needed.

With that understanding, Leith pursued his own interests, though he was a very private person. He disappeared for weeks at a time, then returned with no explanation. Eilidh's vivid imagination tended to make up stories about her brother's mysterious activities. Her favorite story was that he was a warrior who traveled the land on his battle-trained steed, fighting for kings and princes, charming beautiful ladies, becoming rich in the process. Her late Great Uncle Luthais, married to Grandmother Marsaili's twin sister, Davina, had taken a similar path, and done well enough to eventually afford a large tract of land and cattle.

After some time, Eilidh realized her thoughts were all jumbled. She needed to focus on what she was going to do if her parents went through with lining up more potential suitors. Either tell them ... or don't. Her head began to throb and she hugged her shawl tighter, then closed her eyes for a few moments.

She could hear the seabirds above, already on a quest for fresh fish as they squabbled with each other on the ground, while others soared high to prepare to dive. Not much time had passed when she was rudely interrupted by a man's voice.

"If it isn't the little bitch of *Srath Nabhair*, Eilidh of Clan MacAoidh, herself. And all grown up, by the looks of you."

She opened her eyes and felt a cold sweep into her bones that didn't come from the breeze sweeping over the harbor and bringing dark clouds along the way. The voice was familiar. Perhaps a bit deeper, yet the same raspy voice that sent fear cascading through her.

"Bennett Sutherland," Eilidh said, her voice breathless. She rose from the bench.

Run!

Before she could move, he grabbed her arm.

"You remembered."

He wore that same aggravating smirk. A sick feeling bared down on her, freezing her. As she stared back, she realized he'd grown into a young man and had filled out accordingly. And yet, he was no taller than she, making him appear stocky and solid. It was apparent he was attempting to grow a mustache, but he wasn't making much progress by the looks of the thin ginger colored hair beneath his nose, the color hair native to his clan. His hair was cut a bit short, making his face appear wider, but he was still the same bully he'd been three years ago.

For three years she'd agonized over this man. She swallowed back the bile that threatened to spill out into a scream.

"I happened to be in a tavern earlier and saw two of your brothers. I overheard them say you're entertaining suitors for marriage ... after a long break."

Her mouth dropped open at his words. Quickly, she regained her composure. "That's none of your business. Now, away with you! I don't wish to speak with you."

"Well, I haven't yet finished with you, princess."

With a grip that shouldn't surprise her, he pulled her out of the public square and into an alley filled with cargo boxes waiting to be unpacked. Eilidh struggled to break free, but could only squawk until he grabbed her by the throat and silenced her with a look. Her body felt as if it was turning into ice, limb by limb. She was all alone. No one would come rescue her this time. She had to fight back.

"Why are you doing this? I've done nothing to you," she said, trying to reason with him.

Bennett took a step back and let his eyes roam up and down her body, his lustful intentions clear. A small smile appeared. "You've grown up to be a beautiful woman, Eilidh MacAoidh. I think I will throw my hat into the ring as a suitor for your hand in marriage. Your parents might find it very useful to have a son-in-law who is a Sutherland."

Eilidh shuddered. She'd hoped he would apologize and say the incident that occurred three years ago had been a mistake perpetrated by young lads scratching their itch. But that was not his intent, she could see clearly now.

I am such a fool.

"Aye, I like that idea. Marriage to the lovely Eilidh, who was finally captured by a prince. What do you say, my love?"

"You're a sick fool to believe that's even possible, Bennett Sutherland." She glanced at the street to her right of the entrance to the alley. If she could just get to that spot, someone might see her and offer assistance.

While her focus on him wavered, Bennett used that moment to attack. He shoved her against the wall, hands groping her, then reaching around her neck.

"A sick fool am I?"

With arms raised to hold her in place, the sleeve of his tunic slipped down to reveal his right forearm. At first, Eilidh thought it was a tattoo, but when she realized the flesh was a red and puckered scar, her breath caught.

"Aye, you remember our time in the woods, don't you?"

"You attacked me!"

"You didn't fight it, my lovely."

"Stop calling me that!" Eilidh twisted and turned, but caused only more bruising.

Eilidh screamed, wishing she had Fitheach with her at this moment. She would run him through, at the very least. She had vowed to never be vulnerable again. How could she have been so unaware? She must always be on guard.

A man in a dark cloak appeared at the entrance to the alley. "Did I hear a lady's scream?"

Bennett clamped one hand over her mouth, the other holding her against the wall. Eilidh attempted to move her head up and down, her eyes growing wide.

"This won't do at all," said the darkly clothed man, who surprised Bennett with how quickly he moved.

The man seized Bennett from behind, holding a knife to his throat. Bennett quickly released Eilidh, her breathing coming in short bursts as she stepped to the side, out of his reach. The stranger turned his gaze to Eilidh and gave a teasing look. "Would you like me to dispatch this man, young miss? What is your pleasure?"

Eilidh couldn't even look at Bennett. She shrugged off the niggling feeling that she knew how he got that scar. Something she must look into.

"I suppose we should let him go. I don't want anyone else to get hurt," she said, still panting and out of breath.

"You just wait until my father returns from his business in the east," Bennett rasped. "He will kill you ... slowly, MacAoidh."

With fire in his eyes, her father appeared at the head of the alley. He stepped toward the dark-haired man, who struggled to keep Bennett from escaping.

"Well, you can tell your father how we keep a cursed Sutherland man from assaulting our women." Her father punched Bennett's mid-section, then his head, then back to his ribs. For a moment, Bennett appeared as if he would pass out, but he dropped to his knees instead. Eilidh's father yanked Bennett up by the collar. Bennett managed to shake off her father's big, work-worn hands.

Breathing hard, her father turned to Torleik, who along with Hallkel, appeared at his side. "We need to tie this man up until the authorities arrive."

Eilidh watched with relief as Torleik ran back to where he'd left his horse, then returned moments later with a rope from his saddle bag. He and Hallkel made quick work of tying Bennett so tight, he would never escape. All the while, Torleik's gaze shifted back and forth between Bennett and the other man. Did they know each other?

A couple of strong-looking men from the docks stepped through the crowd that had now formed and spoke to Torleik directly. "We'll take the prisoner to the jail and out of your way."

Torleik gave a quick nod, his face grim. "Thank you." He then glanced at Hallkel and must have communicated silently that he wanted him to accompany the two men and the prisoner ... just in case Bennett broke free along the way. For all Eilidh knew, the three strangers were in league together to profit in some way. A kidnap ransom?

When Hallkel departed with the other men, Eilidh regarded Torleik as he turned his attention to the man with eyes so dark, they appeared black.

"What in Odin's name are you doing here, Geirolf?"

7

ᚪᚱᚳᛋᛏᚷᛈᛗᛚᛦᚾ

As Eilidh waited in front of the Gray Goose Tavern and Inn, she wondered what Torleik and the charming man who'd rescued her from Bennett Sutherland's attack were saying in voices they attempted to keep low. Their faces were red, their gazes intense. Something dangerous simmered in the air.

All Eilidh knew was that with Bennett out of the way for the moment, she could breathe again. She turned to her father. "*Athair*, what will the authorities do to Sutherland? Will he go to prison?"

"They will do the right thing, *nighean*." He hugged her close. "I will make sure that he doesn't go free after attacking you. There is no excuse for that kind of behavior. Even a Sutherland cannot bend or break the law and get away with it." Her father released Eilidh and held her at arms' length to inspect her clothes. "Did he hurt you?"

Eilidh was about to brush off the encounter in her usual manner when Leith and Gregor appeared, walking towards them with their horses trailing behind. Both wore somber expressions as they sized up the scene.

Leith settled his gaze on Eilidh with his brows arching upward. "We heard there was a bit of excitement here. Is everyone alright?"

"I'm fine." Eilidh turned to the dark-haired man who'd saved her and held out her hand to shake his. "I don't know who you are, but thank you for coming to my aid."

He bowed with a flourish, and took hold of her hand. Inclining his head again, he placed a kiss on the back of her hand and glanced up, dimples appearing in his cheeks. "It's what any gentleman would do. Geirolf Sveinnsson at your service. Most recently a citizen of *Nidaros* in *Nord Vegr.*" He fixed Torleik with a glance she couldn't read. "Also the home of your new acquaintance, Torleik Sorensson. Like him, I'm here to start a new life."

Torleik grunted an acknowledgement, lips pressed thin and his icy blue eyes narrowed.

Geirolf let go of her hand. "Alas, as much as I would like to continue our pleasant conversation, I must leave you now to take care of business. Perhaps we will meet again soon."

Eilidh blinked once, twice, and he was gone.

Hallkel muttered something under his breath as he watched Geirolf walk away. Eilidh got the impression Torleik and Geirolf were not exactly friends.

"Eilidh, boys, I need to return to the Black Swan Inn, where we are staying, to see how your mother is doing," her father suggested. "She had one of her bad headaches, I'm afraid. Are you coming, Eilidh?"

Eilidh turned and waved to Torleik and Hallkel. "It was nice meeting you. I hope you enjoy riding Arabel. She's... special."

Torleik nodded politely and a tiny smile appeared. "Thank you. I'm looking forward to becoming better acquainted with Highland ponies." Torleik held his hat in hand and shifted his feet, as if he wanted to say more.

"I'll be just a moment," she told her father. "You go on." For some reason, Eilidh hesitated to follow her father and brothers as they headed the few blocks to the inn where they'd been staying. To Eilidh's surprise, Torleik wore a grave expression when she turned to face him.

"Mistress Eilidh, if you happen to see Geirolf again, run as fast as you can. He's dangerous and unpredictable."

Eilidh crossed her arms over her chest, finding his words hard to believe. After all, the man had just saved her life. "Dangerous and unpredictable? I thought he was polite and a gentleman."

Torleik cocked his head for a moment. "He's been accused of several murders back home. That's why he fled *Nord Vegr*."

Her mouth dropped open as she glanced at Hallkel for confirmation. He gave a quick affirmative shake of his head.

"Since your father and brothers aren't in sight, I will walk you to the Black Swan Inn," Torleik said, stepping forward to offer his arm like a gentleman. And yet, his pale blue eyes seemed to be judging her.

Eilidh scowled. How dare he think her foolish? On the other hand, she had no cause to be rude to one of her father's new customers.

"I thank you for the offer. But I can get there on my own."

She didn't wait for his response, as she made her way to the inn. After a few blocks, she crossed the street when she reached her destination. As she turned her head, she realized Torleik had followed her, keeping her in his sights, as he ducked behind buildings and vendors' carts.

Stubborn man.

***

"Stubborn lass," Torleik murmured from behind a vendor's cart full of vegetables as he watched Eilidh enter the inn. Her brothers' two horses were tied to the front post. Curious, Torleik wandered over to take a closer look at the MacAoidhs' horse breeding results. A few moments later, Hallkel approached as Torleik admired the larger stallion.

"I figured I'd find you here."

"Foolish girl wouldn't let me walk with her to the inn. I had to follow so she wouldn't see me." Torleik shook his shaggy blond hair. "She doesn't understand how men like Geirolf can harm her. Larger towns are more dangerous, as she just experienced with that man who attacked her. And Geirolf posing as her savior? He's up to something."

Hallkel turned him away from the horses and they started to walk slowly in the direction of the harbor. "Do my eyes and ears deceive me? Or did you just speak *six* whole sentences ... all regarding that beautiful young lady. Is that a spark of interest I detect?"

Torleik gave him a disgusted look. "Of course not. I will be faithful to my Ulla for the rest of my life. Any marriage will be a marriage of convenience."

"How does that sit with Atli? Does he know there will be no brothers or sisters if you bring home a new mother for him?" Hallkel sat on a bench that faced the Black Swan Inn and the great northern sea beyond it, then rested his arms along the back of the bench.

Torleik's gaze returned to the inn's entrance. "He doesn't need to know that ... yet."

Hallkel pulled a small wooden toy and a knife from his leather pouch and resumed carving where he'd left off the previous evening. "So, you made sure Eilidh arrived here alright. So, why are you still here?"

Torleik swallowed. "I don't know why." His stomach clenched. "I want to know that her family leaves town immediately and gets her safely away from Geirolf."

"So you're going to just sit here and watch?"

Torleik shrugged. "Maybe. Though, I must sleep to be in shape to sail early." He grunted again, knowing Ulla would have called him "cranky" about now. He coughed and stood. "It wouldn't hurt for the MacAoidh clan chief to hire more security to guard his family."

A snapped twig behind drew their attention as Èoin MacAoidh emerged from a narrow pathway leading down to the sea. He nodded in greeting, though it hadn't been long since they last met. "Funny you should say that, Mister Sorensson. I just hired two men who've been seeking employment in security. They're English, but have experience guarding important people and places for very important men – dukes and earls, I believe Edgar said."

Torleik and Hallkel nodded in unison as Eilidh's father regarded them with a somber look.

"That's good. I will rest easier," said Torleik.

Hallkel gave his friend a strange look, making Torleik wonder if he'd said too much. He wished he had Ulla by his side. She always knew the right words to say in any situation.

"Torleik, may I speak with you ... privately?" Eilidh's father inquired.

"I will go check out preparations on board ship, then return to our room at The Gray Goose," said Hallkel, quickly packing up his carving project. "Nice meeting you, sir."

Èoin led Torleik inside the Black Swan, and seemed glad there weren't many customers this early. They quickly found a table in the corner. Once orders were placed, Eilidh's father leaned his elbows on the table.

"When do you sail for home?"

"Early, on the morning tide."

Èoin grinned widely. The etched lines bordering his mouth and the corners of his eyes indicated a man who liked to laugh and celebrate the good things in life.

As they sat at an empty table, Eilidh's father settled back. "Since we first spoke this morning, an interesting idea has been developing inside my head," he said, pointing to his dark hair showing some gray. "I have a proposal for you that may be to everyone's benefit. This won't take long, as I know you wish to return to your ship."

Torleik shrugged as their mugs of ale were delivered, and he glanced up to see the now familiar trademark grin return to Èoin's face.

For some unknown reason, the hairs stirred on the back of Torleik's neck.

8

ᚨᚱᚲᛋᛏᚷᛈᛖᛁᛒᛟᚾ

Two weeks had slipped by without incident since Eilidh's trip to *Inbhir Theòrsa*. Although glad to be where she could keep an eye on her grandmother's health, she hadn't slept well the previous night due to wind and rain that lashed at the window shutters. She rolled out of bed and groaned at her lack of energy.

As she washed and prepared for the day, it occurred to her that Muire hadn't yet appeared with her morning tray. No wonder her stomach growled.

She pondered the notion her parents had been acting strangely since their return. Her brothers must be in on the intrigue, as well, for far too much whispering was taking place, only to cease immediately when she entered a room. Not another word had been said about inviting more suitors to offer for her hand in marriage, which seemed suspicious. On the other hand, she didn't have to explain about Bennett Sutherland, had he followed through as he'd threatened. She didn't ask what happened to him, and no one offered information.

One last bit of suspicious activity had failed to escape her attention. It seemed that at least one of her brothers, or one of the new English guards her father had hired in *Inbhir Theòrsa*, tagged along if she left the castle now, even to gather herbs for Grandmother Marsaili. She must speak with her father and tell him she felt perfectly safe in the isolated castle and in the hills where the only living beings she came into contact with were wandering sheep.

When she dressed for the day and went downstairs, she found servants rushing about, studiously avoiding her eyes whenever she stopped to ask what was happening. They mumbled something she couldn't understand, then hurried off. Had her parents invited a special guest? Maybe she was wrong about them giving up on finding her a husband, and several candidates were scheduled to arrive that very day.

Frustrated that she couldn't go dashing to her refuge in the hills due to the rain, Eilidh went in search of her mother. Unable to locate her, she climbed the stairs to approach her grandmother's bedchamber, down the hall from her own. The door was closed, so she suspected her grandmother was still sleeping. But when she placed her head against the door and listened, her grandmother's coughing sounded worse.

Eilidh knocked briefly and entered to find her grandmother sitting by the window, watching the rain outside while cradling a warm mug of tea. She'd wrapped her warmest shawl around her frail shoulders as she viewed the garden below.

"*Seanmhair*, that window may be too drafty for you to sit so close. How are you feeling? Did you keep that poultice on overnight?" Eilidh stepped closer to help her grandmother stand.

Grandmother would have none of it. She waved a hand for Eilidh to stop. "Ach, I'm fine, *ban-ogha*." She sipped her tea and looked out the window again. "I suppose you're wondering what is going on downstairs with all the rushing around?"

"Aye. But I couldn't locate *Màthair*. Or Muire, for that matter. Do you know what's happening? Are we expecting a guest?"

Grandmother Marsaili coughed for a few moments, then sipped her tea. "Ach, I don't know about that. You'll have to ask your parents. They don't always tell me what's taking place. On purpose, I think."

Eilidh knelt at her grandmother's knee. "I'll bet they are trying to handle things so you don't worry. If you worry, you may become ill."

Her grandmother nodded. "I suppose that's possible."

Eilidh retrieved the used poultice from the bedside table and sniffed, then set it aside to take downstairs and wash. "Did adding Coltsfoot help at all?"

"Perhaps a wee bit. Don't be discouraged. As a healer, you must know that not every treatment responds the same in each person."

Grandmother resumed her coughing, which lasted a few moments.

Worried, Eilidh waited patiently and poured her grandmother more hot water for tea after checking her forehead for fever. Finding none, she sniffed the mug and recognized chamomile, always helpful for sleep. To that, she reached into a pocket and pulled out a dash of marjoram to help relax her sore throat muscles.

Eilidh's stomach suddenly growled just as the voices downstairs grew louder. "I must find one of my parents to learn why all the noise and upset. You drink your tea and then take a nice, long nap. I'll be back to check on you."

Eilidh left her grandmother, stopping in her bedchamber to grab a shawl, but when she stepped inside, Muire and her mother were packing trunks with what appeared to be most of Eilidh's personal belongings. That included the three new gowns her mother had insisted she be fitted for, all hanging over the wardrobe door, a rainbow of color compared to what she usually wore.

Her stomach lurched.

"What are you doing with my things?" She reached for one of the gowns. "*Màthair*, you must tell me what's happening and why the castle is so full of whispers and secrets that everyone seems to know, except me."

Her mother wrung her hands and put an old gown on the bed. She hesitated for a moment too long.

"Mother, what is going on?" Eilidh waved a hand to encompass her personal things scattered about the bedchamber.

Her mother heaved a big sigh. "Your father is going to explain everything at the midday meal. An invited guest will be joining us. He will make things clear for you." She resumed inspecting and folding clothes while Eilidh stood speechless. "We thought it wise to get a head start on the packing, so we don't waste precious time."

An odd tingle raced down Eilidh's arms, ending at the very tips of her toes, as she stood rooted to the floor like a huge oak tree.

"He found someone to marry me, didn't he?"

Eilidh sank to the bed, defeated at last. What if the man her father had chosen was Bennett Sutherland, from one of the wealthiest families in northern *Alba*? Or the smooth-talking man with black hair and eyes? Geirolf. The man Torleik had tried to warn her about.

She experienced a lightheadedness, and nausea began working its way up her throat. "I'd rather go to the convent in England. Will I not be given a choice?"

Her mother must have anticipated her daughter's strong reaction, for she turned to the servant. "Muire, bring a tray of food so Eilidh may break her fast. I fear she's a bit slow this morning."

Muire seemed eager to leave the two women alone.

Eilidh felt the ground beneath her feet tremble ... or was that her legs that shook so hard?

Had her father sold her off to the highest bidder — like the horses? Stunned, she fell onto the bed and wept.

9

Once Muire had her calmed, she insisted Eilidh bathe and wear one of the new gowns delivered from *Inbhir Theòrsa* in which to greet the special guest who had been invited to the midday meal. Eilidh went through the motions, but she found no joy in it. Her father wouldn't divulge the name of that guest ahead of time, which left her nursing her suspicions.

Bennett Sutherland. It only made sense. Without a doubt, he would be the wealthiest of any local man asking for her hand in marriage and he *had* made his intentions clear. But would her father really give her over to him after what he'd witnessed?

As Eilidh responded to Muire's instructions to hold her arms up so Muire could secure the side ties of her gown properly, she tried to consider the reasoning for selecting Bennett but couldn't fathom it. First of all, her father had always treated Eilidh like a gem of rare value, being the youngest and the only girl child. Therefore, would he truly disregard her feelings and choose the man with the most money? She wouldn't have thought so ... unless he was suffering financially. A weight settled on Eilidh's chest.

Father and Padruig oversaw financial matters, but she couldn't recall hearing recently about expensive repairs or new buildings or equipment needed. The horse breeder's market had been robust this past year, as had the sheep and cattle markets. Was her family in need of an infusion of money that might come in the form of Bennett paying an amount equivalent to her dowry?

She shivered at the thought of being married to that dangerous bully, even if he was the richest man in *Alba*.

"Are you cold from the bath, mistress?" Muire reached for a shawl and draped it over Eilidh's shoulders. "You can wear this while I fix your hair." She began humming an old song from long ago. On her hands and knees, rummaging through items in Eilidh's roomy wardrobe, Muire grabbed something and pulled it out to make sure it was what she sought. "Here we go. I thought these light-colored leather shoes with the bows would look nice beneath the blue gown." She helped Eilidh slide into them.

Eilidh stood and glanced at herself in a mirror propped against the wall of her bedchamber.

"It fits you perfectly, mistress. That lady, Miss Hilda, did a fine job."

Eilidh regarded herself and gave a reluctant nod. "I hate to say it, but *Màthair* was right about this fabric and color. She says it reminds her of blueberries in summer."

"Aye. That it does. Now, come sit and I will fix your hair. Madam Giorsail suggested I pin it up."

"I prefer it down."

Muire stood there holding the hairbrush and tapping the toe of her left shoe on the stone floor as she considered her options.

Eilidh smiled sweetly. "You can please my mother, or you can please *me*, your mistress – and friend."

"I see you're in a feisty mood ... mistress ... meaning no disrespect." Muire focused on Eilidh's long, coppery locks. After a few moments of brushing and combing out tangles, she sighed. "I suppose I could compromise and braid your hair in one thick braid down your back. Would that be acceptable?"

"Aye, that's the solution."

"Do you know who the guest will be?"

Muire couldn't help herself. She was such a bubbly and extroverted young woman who liked to know everything that affected her mistress. But there were times Eilidh would have preferred a bit more restraint on Muire's part.

Eilidh gave a casual shrug, as if everything was under control and her stomach was not already churning. "They won't tell me beforehand, but I have my suspicions. I think, perhaps ..." She looked away, unable to say Bennett's name.

"You know the man's name?" Muire encouraged her to speak.

"It's probably a Sutherland."

"Ach, don't say it! Your father would never do that to you!"

Muire gathered her mistress in her arms and soothed her as Eilidh let a flood of tears roll down her cheeks once more.

She would be subject to obey her husband. And if the man was a Sutherland, she doubted it would be a good life, where he left her alone to her studies and to her healing practice. If only she'd told her mother about Bennett's original attack. She stood and swiped the tears from her cheeks, a new thought emerging.

"I wonder if it's not too late – if I tell *Màthair* before he arrives."

Muire finished the braid, tied it in a blue cord the same blue as Eilidh's gown, and let it fall down her back. "Tell who what?"

Eilidh realized she'd spoken out loud. She took one last glimpse in the mirror. Satisfied that her looks would do, she turned towards the door.

"I don't have time to explain right now. I'll fill you in later when I've got it all figured out." She hugged Muire briefly.

Muire's brown eyes grew wide, but she said nothing as her mistress hurried down to the great hall.

As Eilidh went in search of her mother downstairs, she could smell the wonderful aroma of roasted meats and seasoned vegetables coming from the kitchen but today they only made her feel queasy. She found her mother making minor adjustments to the place settings, as Eilidh counted eight of them. Leith was in *Inbhir Nis* on business, so that left the two youngest brothers in attendance. Six spots for her family, if Grandmother came down ... and one for Bennett. Who was the eighth seating for? Perhaps one of Bennett's brothers or friends?

Eilidh inhaled a deep breath, refusing to allow her mother to see how wretched she felt. Instead, she took a step closer to the dining table and forced a smile.

"*Màthair,* what do you think of my new gown?" Eilidh asked to break the silence.

Her mother turned, appearing startled. She accidently dropped an eating utensil on the floor with a clang. "Oh, my. I didn't know you were ready yet. Let me see." She stood back and regarded Eilidh from every angle. "How lovely you look in that shade of blue. I knew that would look elegant on you. I must consult with Miss Hilda again in the near future. She's quite talented."

Eilidh fingered her soft linen skirt, summoning her courage to tell her mother about The Incident – and why she didn't want to marry ... *any* man. She glanced around to be sure no one would be standing close enough to overhear what she said. It was almost impossible to find any privacy in an active castle keep.

"Aye. I must say, I'm very pleased with Miss Hilda's work, as well."

Her mother turned away to finish the last small adjustment. She clearly wanted to make a good impression.

"*Màthair*, I must tell you something about any plans to marry ..."

A loud knock sounded at the front door.

Before her mother could respond, Eilidh's father opened the main entrance door, then ushered in their guest. Panicked, Eilidh quickly slipped out the side door that led to a separate kitchen across the way in a stone building. If she moved quickly, she might be able to stay hidden in the kitchen until their guest left.

To her dismay, the first person she encountered was her brother, Gregor, coming from the direction of the tower road. He'd clearly bathed and his clothes appeared clean, his light brown hair still damp, the ends curling upward as they dried.

He stopped in front of her, blocking her path to the kitchen. "Where are you headed?"

"Oh, um ..." She reached for her braid and ran her hands over the soft texture. "I told the cook I would help with–"

Gregor reached out and grabbed her shoulders, physically turning her back toward the house. He pushed her gently toward the main entrance. "The cook doesn't allow you in the kitchen since you accidentally scorched the oven."

"That wasn't my fault. I told everyone ..." Eilidh sighed, her head hanging. "You're right. I did ruin her pan. I've been searching for a replacement every chance I get."

"Meanwhile, our parents are going to a lot of trouble to make sure you have a good life and are taken care of. You should be grateful, not afraid. It's your duty–"

Eilidh stopped just outside the entrance and placed her hands over her ears. "I know it's my duty. I just don't like the idea of being sold off to the highest bidder to a man like Bennett Sutherland. Father has betrayed me. He won't even tell me *who* the special guest is."

"Well, now's your chance. Let's just go inside and you can ask all the questions you like." Gregor escorted her through the door.

Eilidh glanced up to see the backs of her father and two very tall men not far from the door. But neither stranger had ginger hair, nor the solid bulk of a man who didn't appear to exercise much. Eilidh gasped, wondering if this was a trick.

At the small sound she made, the slightly taller man turned and acknowledged her with a polite nod. "Mistress Eilidh. It's good to see you again."

Her father stepped up. "Eilidh, you recall meeting Mr. Sorensson and his associate, Mr. Gunnarsson in *Inbhir Theorsa*?"

Torleik. And the other man, his good friend, Hallkel.

Eilidh gazed at Torleik in confusion, then quickly gathered herself together. "Ach, you came to report on Arabel's training?"

Torleik shifted his weight from one foot to the other. "If you would like an update, then Hallkel can fill you in. But–" He glanced at her with raised brows that were darker than his shaggy, blond hair, then turned to her father.

Before Eilidh had a chance to assess his meaning, her mother took charge and told everyone where to sit at the dining table. Gregor and Padruig appeared out of nowhere, and quietly seated themselves as they nodded to the visitors with relaxed expressions.

Eilidh's chest tightened, as she willed herself not to faint in front of these two brawny men.

10

Torleik didn't smile much, Eilidh was quick to notice. In fact, he appeared as if his shoulders were weighed down with the worries of the world as he sat at the midday meal. She glanced at her father sitting at the head of the table, and wondered why he let the conversation around the table continue in such a casual manner. The men spoke of horses, mainly, including progress made with the filly Torleik had purchased from her father. Not once did anyone mention marriage.

Pleased Grandmother Marsaili felt well enough to join them, Eilidh watched as the matron of the manor listened closely to everything, her sharp hazel eyes missing nothing.

Finally, as the meal came to an end, Padruig and Gregor excused themselves, returning shortly with two bottles of French wine, along with empty goblets.

"Why are they serving wine ... after we've already finished?" Eilidh whispered in her grandmother's ear. "I don't understand."

Grandmother squeezed her hand under the table. "Wait and see what your father has to say. Trust him, *ban-ogha*."

Eòin MacAoidh was dressed in a fine green tunic, black hose, with a gold chain belt encircling his waist. Dashing black leather boots displayed legs that were still in good shape. As Eilidh glanced back at her mother, she noticed that she also looked elegant in a pale green linen gown, with simple ivory lace to decorate the sleeves and neckline. Conservative, not flaunting their wealth in any way.

Once everyone had a glass of wine in hand, her father raised his goblet to propose a toast. "This is to wish our daughter, Eilidh, a happy and long life with ... Torleik, as they begin a new life in the Orkneys as husband and wife."

The room fell silent. Eilidh stared at her father as if she didn't know him. She could feel her grandmother's hand on her arm, and she saw her mother wince as she looked to her husband.

Eilidh felt nausea forming in her stomach ... along with rising anger. This could not be happening. She set her glass on the table, stood, and placed hands on hips. "No one has said a word about marriage since we returned from *Inbhir Theòrsa*. You can't just make this announcement without consulting with me." She turned away, her heart racing. "I'm not going anywhere. I told you I want to remain unmarried, continue to practice as a healer, and continue with my education. That's all."

Her father nodded as if he understood. "Eilidh, after getting to know Torleik and hearing about his farm, I think you would be very happy there. He can keep a close eye on you and protect you from people like Geirolf. He has all kinds of farm animals in addition to horses. And Arabel will be there."

Eilidh fought back tears. "You would tempt me, try to rip apart my life with family and friends for ... horses and goats?"

Gregor snorted. "You're being overdramatic, Eilidh. He has ducks and geese, as well."

His mother gave him a disapproving look. "Gregor, behave."

Torleik rose from the table, still holding his glass of wine. "*Ja*, it is a simple farm to produce both food, and to breed and train horses." He glanced around the great room, noting the sumptuous tapestries on the walls and carpets on the floor in rich tones of burgundy, green, gold and black.

Eilidh narrowed her eyes and faced her father. "You will send me off to be a farmer's wife? Is that my punishment – to marry someone outside the clan?"

"Eilidh, that's enough of that." Her father growled. "I proposed this union for two good reasons. You need protection from men like Bennett and Geirolf, so it's best you leave *Alba*. Torleik needs a mother for his young son, Atli. He is willing to agree to a marriage of convenience so you both get what you want. You may continue your healing and studies. He can keep the memory of his late wife in his heart and provide a mother for his young son. A simple arrangement."

Torleik stood next to her father and nodded. "If you have concern about a legal marriage ceremony, I would suggest we have a handfast ceremony as soon as we arrive on *Meginland*. My housekeeper, Kelda, can perform the ceremony."

Eilidh stared, her mouth hanging open. Could this get any worse?

"The handfast is an ancient tradition in Norse lands, and is valid for a year and a day. It is accepted by the Church as legal. After that year and a day, we must make a decision to stay together and have a Church ceremony, or part and go our separate ways." For the first time, he glanced directly at Eilidh. "If you wish to return here to your family at that time, you may do so without judgment. I would provide financial support and an escort for your journey ... if that is what you decide."

Eilidh felt the blood drain from her face.

"It's a very flexible system for countries where weather is brutal and priests are hard to come by," added Hallkel. That's why the Church goes along with the practice. It's an ancient ritual, but still relevant in most modern northern lands."

Eilidh sank back onto her chair, thoughts careening while visions filled her head. Bennett, his filthy hands on her body. Up until now, she'd always felt loved and protected. For the first time in her life, she felt totally helpless and vulnerable. She squirmed, but then she envisioned the slick image of Geirolf – the murderer. Black hair, black eyes, black heart. And such a charming smile. He was the snake. Bennett, the buzzard.

She gazed at Torleik, searching for something warm and welcoming in his expression. Instead, his ice blue eyes showed only a calm and dispassion for her and their impending marriage.

Still, Torleik might never love her, and he might not be the best communicator, but he *did* love his late wife. Wasn't that more acceptable than the other options? At least, she knew a few small things about him now, which was more than she'd started with.

"Tell me about your young son."

His blank expression quickly transformed into a huge grin. "He has seen four winters. He's outgoing and playful. He learns quickly, and is very curious about the world. He's also very active, but a good boy."

Eilidh smiled at his description. "His mother ...?"

Torleik winced. "Atli was not quite two when his mother died, so he doesn't remember much."

If there was one thing she knew a lot about, it was little boys. Granted, her brothers had all been older than Eilidh, but she'd seen them go through most of the phases a boy experienced in life. She smiled back at Torleik, appreciating his love for his family. That made her think he was a good man, and, perhaps, that was as good as it might ever get.

She straightened to her full height, feeling considerably more sure of her response.

"I agree to enter into a marriage of convenience with Torleik ... for a year and a day. I can't guarantee what happens after that."

Torleik nodded. "I agree to this arrangement." His shoulders relaxed visibly. "We sail on the morning tide from *Theorsà* the day after tomorrow, to allow you time to pack things you wish to bring. I go now, to prepare the ship for cargo."

Eilidh gulped and watched her father walk out the front door with Hallkel and Torleik, her future husband.

11

ᚠᚱᚲᛋᛏᚷᚹᛗᛚᛟᛉ

Grandmother Marsaili beckoned to Eilidh from where she hovered in the doorway. "Come in, *ban-ogha*. Come in. I suppose you wish to discuss your handsome new groom-to-be?"

Encouraged that her grandmother appeared wide awake and wasn't coughing, Eilidh entered and stood in front of the window looking out. "I admit, I'm still shocked and disappointed *Àthair* didn't include me in their conversations. As if I didn't matter." She heaved a sigh. "Did you know about his decision before the toast after dinner?"

"In the end, my sweet, you left your parents little choice. Your father did the best he could, given the circumstances."

Eilidh slumped on the bed and ran a hand over the ancient quilt, taking comfort in the faint hint of rosewater that would always remind her of Grandmother Marsaili's presence. She folded a corner of the quilt. "I never meant to cause so much trouble for you or my parents, *Seanmhair*."

"I know you didn't mean for any of this to happen. Perhaps this is all part of the journey the Goddess has planned for you."

Eilidh's emotions swelled to the surface, whirling in every direction as they crashed against each other, competing for attention. "I sound like a child, I know, but I want to plan my *own* future."

Grandmother rose from her chair and retrieved a hairbrush from the nightstand before sinking down on the bed next to Eilidh. She slowly began to undo the braid, which was half-loose anyway. She then used a brush to smooth the strands, her touch surprisingly gentle.

"You were still quite young when your mother began her search to find a good husband for you. I'm sure it was overwhelming."

Eilidh wondered, not for the first time, if Grandmother knew about Bennett and the other boys that day of the clan gathering. She certainly had an uncanny way of discovering what bothered her granddaughter. The Sutherlands had power and influence. It would be Eilidh's word against theirs if the deed came to light. And everyone knew she had rejected each man who came to ask for her hand in marriage. Did she deserve punishment for causing so much disappointment and anxiety over the years?

"*Seanmhair*, I need you to know I'm not trying to be difficult. I had ... an experience a few summers ago ..." She swallowed, seeking courage. "It made me cautious around strange men. *All* strange men."

Grandmother stilled her brushing and pressed a hand to Eilidh's shoulder. "I understand the fear in your heart, but I believe Torleik is the one you can count on to keep you safe from future harm."

"He doesn't seem to like me. He almost never smiles."

"With a son so young, and workers counting on him, I imagine he has a lot weighing on his shoulders."

There were times when her grandmother's calm demeanor made Eilidh want to scream. "Am I capable of helping raise a son?"

"I suspect your parents wouldn't have agreed to the marriage if they didn't believe you could learn how to be a good parent. And

Torleik is trusting you, a stranger, to replace his beloved wife as the boy's mother."

"I hadn't thought of it that way. He must be nervous about my skills, as well."

Grandmother Marsaili scooted awkwardly off the bed and put away the hairbrush. "I think Torleik has a good heart, although it may seem cold at the moment. That's just grief because of the terrible loss he has suffered. That means he feels emotions deeply."

She caressed Eilidh's cheek, but all Eilidh could think about was how the back of her throat ached at the realization she may never see her grandmother alive again, once Eilidh sailed away with Torleik.

"He obviously loves his son. His heart will be opened as he gets to know you, and he will come to love you, as well."

"You think so? Did you see that in a vision, *Seanmhair*?"

"I don't need to be a seer to know you will thrive in your new life if you give it a chance."

Eilidh hugged her grandmother tightly, but was alarmed at how frail she had become.

Grandmother gripped Eilidh's arm to get her attention, then pulled back to look at her. "Just keep in mind that good parents are not born knowing what to do. It will take many successes and failures to become a wise mother. Be patient with your husband, with the wee boy, and most of all, with yourself, *ban ogha*. All will come together as it should if you are patient."

"I will try." There was that word again. *Patience.*

Grandmother gave a nod of approval and then pointed at the floor of her wardrobe. "I have something to give you before you leave, and I need to explain a few things first. Can you reach for that large package at the bottom? Be careful, as it is very old and dear."

Eilidh knelt and lifted the package. "It's heavy. And looks very old, indeed. Where should I put it?"

Her grandmother made a spot for it on a side table. Once they were seated next to it, Grandmother pulled her shawl tightly around her and inhaled deeply.

"When I was just about your age, I was given the sword, *Fitheach*. Before I left the Druids, I had a strange feeling that I may never return to my Druid home. I was right. You've learned how to defend yourself with a sword. Now, it is your turn to have *Fitheach*. I'll tell you about its magical side. It is an unusual weapon in many ways, but mainly because it was infused with Druid magic to use when certain situations call for extraordinary measures for healing or protection. It is like having a direct, personal connection to the Goddess."

"You never told me about a goddess connection before."

Grandmother gave a low chuckle, which caught in the back of her throat and made her cough deeply. Eilidh popped up and brought her some hot tea. After several moments, Grandmother was ready to continue.

"It wasn't necessary that you know all the details until your time came to serve the Goddess of the Moon."

"I'm chosen to serve the Goddess because of the birthmark behind my left ear? The spiral?"

"Aye. That's the truth. I see you have listened to some of what I've taught you about the Old Ways." She set her tea aside. "Now, where was I? Ach, before I made that journey north, our Druid leader, Achaius, told me of a vision *he'd* received from the Goddess when I was still very young. In that vision, I received the charge to 'save the Druids from extinction'. In essence, my challenge was to find a new home for my Druid family, an isolated spot of land where they would have almost everything they needed at hand, and they would have the protection of Clan MacAoidh for those who would do them harm. Christians wanted

Druids to disappear quietly, like the way of the Picts. For the time being, they are safe from that." She looked down and clasped her hands. "In that event, we would awake one day, and find that our people had simply vanished from this world – exterminated, like rats."

Eilidh reached for her grandmother's hand and squeezed gently. "But you *succeeded*, *Seanmhair*. That is how the Druids came to live on MacAoidh land, aye?"

Grandmother smiled. "Aye. And so I completed my charge. During that time, the Goddess came to me and instructed me to pass along the next charge to my first female descendent." She shook her head and laughed. "As you know, I had three boys, no daughters. I had to wait for *you* to be born, Eilidh. And now the time has come for you to receive instructions for how to complete your charge. It will take us another step closer to the future the Goddess envisions for women and others who are invisible or unheard in this world."

"How can I do that? I'm just a female."

Grandmother leaned forward, her face eager. "I thought the same thing when I was told of my charge. Those female descendants in the MacAoidh family line who possess the spiral birthmark on their necks will play an important role to better the lives of all women. The chosen daughters will accomplish this by becoming educated, which, in turn, provides them with more choices in their own lives." She gave Eilidh a pensive look.

Eilidh digested this new information for a few moments. She'd always known she was destined to accomplish something important, having grown up believing in her grandmother's predictions. She just hadn't expected her mission would take place so soon, nor just as she was being forced to leave her homeland. "*Seanmhair*, this charge sounds important and excites me. However, this is happening to me the same way as it did to you – as I leave to start a new life elsewhere."

Grandmother slowly eased up out of the chair and stood facing the window, hands pulling the shawl tight against a brief chill. "Aye, the very same time in our lives. I had no clue I would find a twin sister I knew nothing about, find my birth father and learn he was a nobleman, or marry a man who would become a clan chief. And then, accomplish the task to 'save the Druids from extinction'. It was daunting, to say the least."

Eilidh remained silent for a moment to respect her grandmother's memories. But then, she was determined to say what was on her mind. "What is *my* charge? I worry I cannot accomplish this with everything else I must learn. If I marry and move to a new place, I must learn how to be a good wife and mother, manage a household, learn new customs and practices, and probably things I haven't even thought of yet. I can't do this important task on top of that, *Seanmhair.*" Eilidh's head felt like a ripe melon about to burst, if one more thing was added to her list of new responsibilities.

Grandmother's shoulders dipped as she kept her back to Eilidh and gazed out the window. "The Goddess knows what she's doing. You must trust her. You will have a long and difficult journey ahead of you, as I did. But you will arrive at the place where you need to be, eventually. That is your destiny, and you cannot put it off for later."

Grandmother sighed deeply. "You can do this, *ban-ogha*. I have no doubts. You have made a good start to your mission by studying well and by learning how to defend yourself with a sword. Now you have *Fitheach*. Before you leave, I will teach you how to access the magical properties within the sword. You will need to protect yourself and perhaps those you love. You must be prepared."

Eilidh had heard her grandmother's tales of using magic to save Grandfather Niall, Great Aunt Davina, and Great Uncle Luthais, but it never occurred to Eilidh that those same abilities might be available to her, one day. Eilidh took stock of her grandmother. She was a "special" being. Everyone knew that. She exuded a mystical power, perhaps because of her years of experience and her advanced age. Eilidh's pulse quickened. Could that be *her* someday?

"But, *Seanmhair*, what is *my* mission to complete?" Eilidh repeated the question, frustrated that Grandmother kept side-stepping the matter.

Returning her focus back to the present, Grandmother gazed at Eilidh, her hazel eyes intense with a light Eilidh had never seen before. Grandmother dusted off the top of the package on the table and pulled out a large stack of vellum paper, loosely bound with leather strips.

A book?

"As you know, my birth mother, Saraid of Clan Macafie, was quite young when she was wrongly accused of witchcraft. She'd seen a vision and heard from the Goddess that she would die young. She also knew she would bear twin girls while imprisoned, so prepared a few gifts she called 'Legacy Gifts,' for her daughters – me, and my twin sister, your great aunt Davina." She cradled the odd-looking book with reverence.

Eilidh narrowed her eyes at the dust rising from the battered leather covers, from which she detected a strange scent she didn't recognize, and yet ... she did. "What's that smell?"

Grandmother smiled indulgently. "The smell of time. Of progress. Of women waiting for their chance to make a mark in this world." She set the collection of loosely bound pages on the table and opened to the first page, which contained a title, written in Gaelic, Greek, and a language Eilidh could not identify, though it perhaps resembled Latin.

"What's that word? *Del-si-ran*? I've never heard of that."

"Your great grandmother Saraid was imprisoned for nine months so she could give birth before she was hanged. During that long wait, she created this language, with the intent of using it for women and girls to learn how to read and write without discipline or reprisal from the men who control their lives."

Eilidh's heart raced. "To start a rebellion against the men?"

"Oh, goodness, no." Grandmother shook her head and rested her wrinkled hand on the book cover. "To set a spark in the minds of females, showing them they can do much more in life, if they so choose."

Eilidh paused as her heartbeat returned to normal. "What am I supposed to do with it?"

Grandmother gingerly turned a page that appeared as if it contained an alphabet of some sort, along with pages of instructions. "Your charge is to create a more durable form of paper that will endure through the generations, then copy the words contained inside on the new pages and bind the finished copy. By the time you have completed your task, you will have absorbed the language and understood it enough to teach others. But you must heed this warning: *only females* can know of this language – pronounced Del-SEE-ran, from what I could determine. This language will be the key that allows us to complete the dream the Goddess has for an enlightened future for all women.

Her grandmother placed the book carefully in Eilidh's hands. When Eilidh hefted the weight, she was shocked her grandmother had managed lifting it so easily.

"As for you, *ban-ogha*, it is vital that this book be passed down to our female descendants. It's a grand dream, and completing your charge may require much work and sacrifice on your part. Each journey is different."

"I still don't understand why this book is so important, *Seanmhair.*"

Grandmother smiled indulgently. "When you are settled in your new home and ready to begin, I have provided instructions inside the package, which will be carefully packed in your larger trunk. Eilidh, you must promise to guard the *Book of Delsiran* well. As I said, Delsiran will allow females to communicate with each other secretly and safely, and is now your responsibility."

A chill raced down Eilidh's spine as she fingered the materials used to hold such important words – words she'd never seen before, written in a neat hand on thick pages made from dried tree bark.

Eilidh shut the book, her heart sinking. "I promise to guard it, but it's faded. Where do I find vellum for paper? What if I make a mistake in transcribing?"

Grandmother smiled mysteriously and seemed to glide toward the bedchamber door. She adjusted her shawl tighter. "You are an intelligent young woman. You will take the book with you when you marry Torleik. He is part of your destiny, so will be with you along your journey. You will know what to write when the time comes. And after your charge is complete, you will wait for the birth of your first daughter. You will know when it is time to pass the book on to her."

And then, *Seanmhair* slipped silently out the door, leaving the subtle scent of roses in her wake.

On the one hand, Eilidh felt excited and full of wonder that she had been chosen for such an important task. She'd always wanted to do something specific to improve the lives of girls and women in some way, but thought herself too timid. Perhaps the Goddess of the Moon saw the strength and determination she nurtured deep inside. Either way, she set the book inside a trunk and wondered if she would make a good teacher. That would be another set of skills to take on.

Eilidh sank onto her bed and sighed, feeling as if she'd run and lost a race that day with one of her brothers.

12

ᚠᚱᚲᛋᛏᚷᛈᛗᛚᛟᚾ

Torleik's Norse ship was hard to miss. As the only longship in the harbor, and therefore the only one with a mythical creature on the prow, it caught Eilidh's attention. Torleik was on board, giving orders, so she was grateful for Hallkel's company, since her family had delivered her and her trunks, said their goodbyes, and returned to the MacAoidh keep. Eilidh didn't blame them for not wanting to linger. Besides, it gave her some time to consider what changes she would need to embrace as she started a new life in a new land. She had vowed to be positive and make the most of each day, as Grandmother Marsaili had advised her. "Be your own true self," her grandmother had said, giving her one final hug for the journey ahead. "You are strong. Now, you must practice wisdom."

A lump formed in Eilidh's throat at the memory. She would miss her grandmother's amazing wisdom, most of all.

Tamping down the sadness at having to leave her grandmother and the only home she had ever known, she gave the ship her full attention. She appreciated the clean lines and shape, then pointed at the prow. "Is that a dragon?"

Hallkel grinned. "It is, indeed. Our ancestors were raiders and explorers. Torleik wanted to capture that fierce spirit of adventure on his ships." He glanced at her. "Have you ever boarded a longship before?"

"No. Never. I've only been on small row boats when fishing with my brothers off the coast."

"He drew in a breath, brows lifting. "You fished with your brothers?"

"Aye. I wasn't a very good fisherwoman, however. My brothers told me I kept scaring away the fish by talking too much."

Hallkel chuckled at that. Eilidh felt a spark of hope for the day she could make someone laugh.

"I think you'll enjoy this voyage if you're not prone to seasickness. I can point out the highlights as we pass by, if you like."

"That's very kind of you, but I imagine you have more important things to do."

Eilidh didn't tell him she carried fresh ginger root in her pocket in case of the dreaded seasickness, a thoughtful last-minute gift from her grandmother.

Torleik was rushing from bow to stern, shouting orders to his crew, checking instruments, sails, and equipment. For a moment, Eilidh wondered if he'd forgotten her until he eventually stopped to wave. But he didn't linger for long. Hallkel explained that Torleik had wanted her to stay on shore until the last minute, so she could be more comfortable.

After a few moments of watching Torleik and his seamen, she wondered if it would be a difficult voyage with rough seas. A twinge of unease made her look away from the water.

"How long will the voyage take? Will we arrive today?"

He paused to look at the sky. "If the weather remains fair, and we get enough wind in our sails so we don't need to rely on oars, I think we should arrive well before the sun goes down."

Eilidh nodded her understanding, but her enthusiasm dipped at the notion of such a long voyage across the water. She wanted to see her new home and meet Torleik's son and the people who worked for him. It was a silly thought, but she hoped they would like her.

Hallkel straightened his long frame. "Torleik is waving me over to the ship. I must help with the final details. Would you rather come with me in a rowboat now? Or wait a bit longer, and I will return for you." He narrowed his eyes and shouted something to one of the seamen. "I should warn you. Some of the men remain superstitious about not wanting females to sail with us. They believe it's bad luck. Don't let that bother you. Torleik would never allow harm to befall you."

Eilidh's cheeks heated quickly. "I see. I think I'd prefer to board the ship now so you don't have to make another trip to shore and back."

Hallkel nodded, running a hand through windswept hair that must have been blond at one time. Now, glimpses of white and silver mixed in, yet Eilidh thought it made him appear distinguished. She suspected Hallkel might be popular with the ladies once he flashed that dimple in the center of his rugged chin.

"It's not a bother. But I know Torleik is anxious to get going. We will have food and water aboard, and Torleik brought extra blankets to keep you warm and dry if it rains."

"That was very thoughtful of him." She wondered if Torleik thought she needed coddling, like a child. She sniffed at the incorrect assumption and followed Hallkel to the rowboat waiting for them.

A brawny seaman was at the oars, and as soon as everything was loaded and Hallkel had his long legs folded inside the boat, they set out for the ship, anchored in deeper water. Eilidh looked back at the shore and felt a sense of apprehension. But no, she would not dwell on thoughts of leaving *Alba's* soil or never again setting eyes upon her brothers, Muire, her parents, or her horse, Nairna, whom she'd ridden since she was a little girl. But what concerned her most was not knowing how Grandmother Marsaili was doing. She'd persuaded her mother, Muire, and her grandmother's personal servant, Marta, to learn about ingredients for the various teas and potions to help her grandmother keep her lungs clear. But Eilidh knew, in her heart, it wouldn't be long now.

They arrived quickly, the rowboat brought as close as possible to the ship. Eilidh saw no ladder, so when Hallkel grabbed her from behind and lifted her up, she felt as if she was dangling over the water. Never comfortable at sea, she tried not to panic. When strong arms bearing strange tattoos lifted her up and over the side of the longship and set her down, she felt such relief. She looked up ... into Torleik's ice blue eyes.

"Are you alright, miss ...?"

Eilidh realized she was still holding tight to his shoulders. She quickly let go and adjusted the travel bag she'd brought with her.

"Ach, I'm fine. I will be ... fine."

"You're afraid of water?" He arched his brow.

She straightened her spine and stood tall, yet still had to bend her head back a bit to look into his intense eyes, now a darker blue, if that were possible.

"I am *not* afraid of water," she hissed, so no one would hear. The boat shifted, and she grabbed his arm.

"Perhaps we can get you settled so we can be on our way," said Hallkel, indicating she should follow.

Eilidh took one last glimpse of Torleik and noted a small smile on his lips. She lifted her chin and almost ran into Hallkel, who had stopped in front of the wooden seats for oarsmen, which filled the interior, for the most part. She sank down onto the spot chosen for her, which she could tell right away would block wind and rain, should it come to that. A breeze caressed her face as she looked up and saw the sun was still shining down on her this warm summer day.

Hallkel knelt while she found a place to store her bag.

"When we reach a stretch of smooth sailing, the cook will bring out a small meal, if you are hungry." He smiled and regarded her until someone shouted his name. "I need to finish my duties." Touching his forehead politely, he turned and headed for the bow, where Torleik was addressing his men.

Uninterested in what the men were discussing, she stood and stretched her muscles, probably for the last time before the journey got underway.

For a short while, Eilidh was content to observe Torleik as he moved around the longship, checking the sail and the mast. He then disappeared. She assumed he'd stepped down into the cargo hold, which made her wonder how they would load and unload large animals if the ship had to be reached by rowboat.

A loud encounter drew her attention across the square to the sorry-looking tavern in need of a good coat of fresh paint. A lopsided sign hung by one chain, declaring the tavern was named The Crusty Crab. A man dressed in black stared back at her, but she couldn't see the details of his face.

There was something strangely familiar. When the man pushed back the hood of his cloak, Eilidh thought she would lose her breakfast. She would know that smug smile anywhere.

Geirolf.

She dipped her head and pulled up the hood of her cloak as a sense of dread made its way around her stomach. Nauseated, she reached for the ginger root in her pocket. If what Torleik said about Geirolf was true, she'd do well to listen to him. Still, she couldn't resist one last peek at the dock.

Should she tell Torleik about Geirolf before they left? For a moment, Eilidh felt the old helplessness and fear rise up and take control. Torleik was clearly working as fast as he could. She would hate to delay their departure if it wasn't Geirolf, after all. Her heart raced as she tried to focus.

Seamen began to take their places, and the flat benches were soon almost filled. Eilidh hoped they wouldn't need all those strong arms to row the ship if wind failed them, and yet, it was comforting to know they had enough men on board ship to make a difference, if needed.

Eilidh could see Torleik make his way towards her, so she couldn't help fussing with her cloak and grunting at the buttons that refused to cooperate.

This is it. I'm really leaving Alba.

"Dear Goddess, and Lord God, please don't let me drown," she whispered, having divided her loyalties for years.

"Are you settled in, miss ...?" Torleik paused, his eyes on the navigator.

"You might as well call me Eilidh. And I will call you Torleik. I think it will be easier for both of us."

Torleik gave a quick nod. "I will return to give Hallkel a break after we reach open sea."

Once Torleik left her side to guide the ship out of the harbor and then to open sea where the sail could be raised, she turned her eyes back to the tavern across the square, wondering why Geirolf was following her. What did he want from her?

She took her seat and shaded her eyes as she looked up at all the seabirds above them, squawking, fighting for fish, and scrounging for a meal. Inhaling a deep breath of fresh sea air, thick with salt and brine, she worried her hands together as she began her first real trip outside of *Tunga.*

***

Geirolf sat alone at a table inside The Crusty Crab, thinking how he'd come so close to having everything he wanted back home. Money. Influence. Power. But he'd been wanted by the local authorities all over town in *Nidaros* for unpaid debts, on top of being a main suspect for several criminal activities, including a murder or two.

He snorted into his empty ale mug as he listened to the hum of voices around him. He'd almost taken the MacAoidh lass away from Torleik's side two weeks earlier. And now, Torleik was back – and was supposedly marrying the feisty lass. Geirolf had spotted Torleik and Hallkel entering The Gray Goose with an older man earlier that evening, so he'd hung around outside for a while. While he wasn't intimidated that The Gray Goose attracted a posher clientele than The Crusty Crab, he occasionally stopped by to see if the talkative tavern owner had some juicy gossip to share. Especially as he and Torleik seemed to know each other from *Nord Vegr*. A place Geirolf could never return to, lest he be arrested.

Geirolf growled into his drink, the yeasty aroma wafting up at him. He and Torleik had known each other since they were lads, but that damn son of a famous shipbuilder had always looked down upon the son of a textile dealer. When Geirolf's own cursed father had disowned him for his misdeeds, he felt certain Torleik had testified to authorities, gladly telling lies to get rid of him. After that, Geirolf had spent time wandering other large towns and cities in the north, but never found a new way to fleece the fools who flaunted their wealth without Geirolf getting caught. When he learned that Torleik and his close friend, the runecarver, Hallkel, were moving to Orkney, it was an easy decision to follow them and find a way to ruin Torleik's life.

"Another mug of ale?" the waitress called from the bar.

Geirolf nodded. By strange coincidence, Geirolf had heard that Torleik's wife had died suddenly back in *Nidaros*, leaving a small boy for Torleik to raise alone. Eventually, Torleik came to the conclusion he needed to find a new mother for his young son. But when Torleik's search was unsuccessful within the northern isles, he'd expanded his quest to *Alba*, targeting the northern seaport town of *Thjorsá*.

Glad this was a place to catch up on the latest gossip, Geirolf fingered the textured ceramic mug with a sigh. Things started to fall into place for Geirolf when he'd overheard that the clan chief, father of Eilidh MacAoidh, was actively seeking a husband for his only daughter. And not only was she wealthy, she was said to be a vision of beauty. When Geirolf heard the lass came with a substantial dowry that would cover the debts he owed, he continued to lurk about, trolling The Gray Goose for more details about the woman. When he realized Torleik and Hallkel were sitting inside the crowded tavern and seemed to know the tavern owner, Geirolf wondered what was happening. They'd been joined at their table by an older man displaying a wide grin and carrying three fresh mugs of ale.

"Aye, MacAoidh," a patron at the bar had teased the older man, "I hear you are finally getting your daughter married off – to a Norseman." He gave a hearty laugh and patted the old man on the back.

Geirolf took a long swig of his ale, and wiped his mouth with the back of his hand at the memory. Just then, the waitress delivered a second ale, which he lit into as he recalled the man's words to MacAoidh. At the time, Geirolf figured that had to be the father of the wild heiress who kept running away when suitors came to call. He had moved stealthily so he could stand as close as possible to hear what the three men were discussing so seriously. And then, he experienced his first surprise of that day.

"I'm just so relieved the search is over," Torleik had said. "Atli needs a mother around to teach him and discipline him when he does bad things. He's too much of a handful for my housekeeper."

The MacAoidh chief nodded his head, as if he understood. "My Eilidh was a wee bit of a troublemaker in her youth as well."

Torleik and Hallkel guffawed.

MacAoidh shrugged. "But now, Eilidh is a grown woman who can fill the role of both wife and mother. That's good, aye?

She can help you both feel more like a family. Eilidh is a cheerful, but curious young woman. When she feels she is right, she is determined to prove it. She learned *that* from her brothers."

"Sounds like someone else I know," said Hallkel.

Torleik laughed, but said nothing.

Geirolf digested all this information, then quietly slipped out of The Gray Goose.

Would this information provide an opportunity to finally destroy his nemesis once and for all?

He tapped the rim of his mug with his thumb, thinking. He wanted what Torleik had. And that now included Eilidh MacAoidh. It was his bad luck that when he saw his opportunity to grab the girl on the street a few weeks ago, that chance had fizzled and dried up, due to Torleik's intervention. Geirolf was also savvy enough to know Eilidh had several bloodthirsty brothers, with advanced weaponry skills, keeping an eye on the girl.

Geirolf wasn't the least bit tired, so he made his way out of The Gray Gull as his two last coins jingled in the pouch at his waist. He scowled at the realization. It was going to be a long night.

I just might need to go to Orkney to get my revenge against Torleik.

13

ᚨᚱᚲᛋᛏᚷᛈᛖᛁᛟᚾ

Torleik briefly introduced Eilidh to the crew as his soon-to-be wife. Enthusiastic congratulations made the rounds, and it was apparent to Eilidh that Torleik's men thought highly of him. But then Torleik got right to business, clearly missing his young son and anxious to get home.

As they slipped slowly out of *Thjorsá* harbor, Eilidh had time for one last look. How desperately she wanted to be wrong that the man dressed in black on shore was Geirolf.

Her heart raced and she looked around anxiously for Torleik, but he was scrambling with crew members to check ropes that required securing. She would never want to embarrass him in front of his men by drawing attention to her fears.

Instead, she tried to make herself comfortable on the hard plank bench. As much as that was possible. To distract herself, she began to take in the sights and sounds of a new world opening up before her. Birds she hadn't seen before. Huge fish leaping up out of the water. Farms dotted the opposite side of the harbor bar, the last point for them to clear before they entered the open sea. A sudden tremor shot through her that she was about to leave this land behind her and go where nothing would be familiar. Then she looked down at the water below and it was as if a shadow had covered the sun. Eilidh felt her scalp prickle, as unwanted childhood memories pushed their way inside her head. She hadn't given it any thought in a long time, but as she faced the ocean expanse ahead of them, she recalled the one close call she'd experienced with deep water. It had been a long time ago, but still caused her to shudder.

She had just reached seven winters. Gregor had been telling her stories about the giant sea monster, Nessie, who inhabited *Loch Ness*. Then, Padruig got into the act, and regaled her with tales of Nessie's sister, Bessie. And Bessie lived in *their loch*! Eilidh insisted the boys take her out in a rowboat on the big *loch* not far from the castle. Like the cold sea she sailed upon today, the *loch*'s water also had the deep blue appearance from above.

As the sun approached midday and there was still no sign of Bessie, Gregor suddenly stood up in the rowboat and pointed to the murky depths below, shouting, "Look! I see Bessie!" His motions caused the boat to rock dangerously.

"Where? Where is she?" Eilidh called out, standing up. She had so wanted to be the first to spot Bessie.

As Gregor shifted his weight, which caused even more rocking, Eilidh lost her balance and without realizing what was happening, she tumbled into the *loch*. Her brothers did their best to rescue her, but Eilidh panicked, holding onto the side of the rowboat and screaming that Bessie was right beneath her and nipping her on the legs as she kicked. Gregor finally got her to calm down, and he and Padruig pulled her aboard. Padruig wrapped her in an old fishing blanket and rubbed her arms to warm her up.

When they returned home, her mother had punished the boys for putting their baby sister in such danger. Meanwhile, Eilidh tried to defend her big brothers. They always looked after her. Besides, it had been *her* idea to go out on the *loch* in a rowboat.

It wasn't their fault she'd fallen into the water and never found Bessie.

Eilidh closed her eyes, trying to dispel the memory, then quickly opened them. She wished Torleik would stop by and say something. Something to persuade her she wasn't making a huge mistake by so easily trusting this stranger with her life.

For a few moments, she watched as Torleik moved quickly from one station to another, checking on the sails and navigation equipment as they approached the last land obstacle. Eilidh tried to relax and decided she would wait until they were on land again before mentioning Geirolf. Likely, they could do nothing, anyway. Geirolf was free to go wherever he wanted. And she hated to appear weak or a complainer the first day of marriage, especially in front of Torleik's men. She was determined to be self-sufficient and solve her own problems.

As the ship emerged from the relative safety of the small harbor and reached the open sea, the sails were raised and immediately filled by a cold gust of wind from the north. The men eased up on the oars and the ship picked up speed. Eilidh's stomach tightened as she glanced over her shoulder in time to see Torleik standing next to the navigator at the ship's stern, a huge grin showing his pleasure at the stiff wind making their jobs easier.

Eilidh pulled up the hood of her cloak to cover her ears, wondering if it would be this cold on *Meganland*. Not that it mattered, as she had no real choice in the matter.

She quickly discovered that her hard plank bench was designed for big, burly men. Each time the ship rose on a wave and then the water receded and dropped them back down, her backside slapped against the wood. But if the men could endure it, so could she. Eilidh tore off a hunk of root ginger and placed it under her tongue, which should help her stomach settle a bit. Sea spray pelted her face like sharp needles. She held a kerchief in hand to wipe the moisture from her face, fearing she would appear a bedraggled mess by the time she arrived at her new home.

Torleik must have seen her burying her face inside her cloak to keep warm, for he suddenly appeared and brought a blanket to wrap around her. The blanket smelled of fish, but Eilidh chose not to complain.

"Are you warm enough? I can probably find another blanket."

"No, thank you. This should be fine." She finished wrapping the blanket around her so completely, it left only her face in plain view beneath her cloak's hood. She sat up. "That does help. Thank you for your kindness." She started to reach for Torleik's hand in gratitude, then caught herself when his ice blue eyes grew wide.

As an extraordinarily handsome man, he was not the sort she would have been comfortable with in a social setting. And though he hadn't shaved in a while, she wondered what his whiskered cheeks and chin would feel like against her soft and sensitive skin, while his darting gaze made him look like a Viking raider.

A few moments later, two men could be heard arguing loudly back near the rudder used for steering the ship. Torleik nodded politely at Eilidh, excusing himself as he hurried to keep a fight from breaking out. Once that was taken care of and the men calmed, Hallkel drew his attention by leaning close to whisper something in Torleik's ear. Torleik paused, a pained expression on his face. He responded to Hallkel but she couldn't catch what he said. Excusing himself, he headed towards the prow.

Sometime later, Eilidh was pleasantly surprised when Hallkel returned with a sack containing bread, cold beef, and hunks of cheese. He sat beside her and held out the meal offerings, causing Eilidh's stomach to rumble. It must be later than she thought.

He sat on the bench opposite and arranged his meal and then took a huge bite. After chewing thoroughly, he wiped his mouth with his sleeve.

"Torleik thought you might enjoy hearing some of the history of these islands you'll call home. That might take up some of the time."

Eilidh sat up, feeling a burst of energy. "Aye! That would be wonderful. Please, proceed."

He finished off his meal quickly, washing it down with a mug of watered ale. Then, with a sparkle in his eyes and his dimple showing in that rugged chin, he went into story tale mode.

It wasn't long before Eilidh discovered Hallkel was full of interesting facts regarding the many islands that made up *Orkneyjar*, and he seemed not to mind when Eilidh asked questions. He explained they were sailing on what the ancient Norse called *Petlandsfjörd*, meaning "the *fjord* of Pictland." He continued in a deep, soothing voice. "A Pict tribe inhabited the islands before the Norse came to settle here. The Picts called this the 'Sea of Orcs.'"

Eilidh leaned to the left as the ship changed direction to head into the wind. "What does '*Orc*' mean?"

Hallkel appeared thoughtful. "No one knows for sure, but the theory is that it comes from the old Gaelic name for Orkney, '*Insi Orc*', which means 'Islands of the Wild Boar'. Unfortunately, when Norse settlers first arrived, they translated '*Orc*' as '*Orkn*', the Norse word for seal. So, we have '*Orkneyjar*', the Seal Islands."

Eilidh enjoyed Hallkel's slightly accented Scottish Gaelic, and she had no trouble understanding him. She turned her head to peer in every direction. "Where are the ..."

"Seals?" Hallkel laughed. "You'll see them basking on the rocks when we get closer to the islands." He pointed northward. "Up ahead is the isle of *Háey*, which means 'High Island' in Norse.

From there, it is only a short distance to *Meginland*, your new home. You should start seeing seals from here on."

Eilidh felt a lightness in her chest to know how close she was to her destination. "Thank you for the wonderful explanations, Hallkel. You've made the time go quickly."

"It's a pleasure to have a good listener who's curious." He nodded politely, then unfolded his long legs and headed for the stern, where Torleik kept the navigator company as he scanned the horizon for trouble.

Eilidh was pondering all she had learned, and realized she'd already traveled farther than she ever had before. An exciting new world beckoned, causing her to smile into the wind. Eilidh had been left to her musings for a long while when Hallkel finally returned from the front of the boat where he had been speaking with Torleik.

"Is that where Torleik lives?" Eilidh asked Hallkel, once he was seated. She pointed to a small harbor town to their right.

"No. That is *Hannavoe*, the closest town to Torleik's farm."

"So if that is the closest landing, why are we not stopping there?"

"You will understand when you see Torleik's beach. I must help get ready to land." Hallkel hurried off to aid with the sails once again.

Torleik's beach? Would she like her new home? And would the people there like her?

Eilidh's chest tightened as they eased past *Hannavoe* and drew closer and closer to what would be her new home. For a few moments, she closed her eyes and inhaled and exhaled slowly, a technique her grandmother had taught her to calm herself whenever she became anxious. After five full breaths of the tangy sea air and wonderful new sea creature smells, she felt better. Darkness was still a ways off, allowing Eilidh to make out the tall cliffs carved from the sea. She knew from her geography studies the cliffs were formed over time into red sandstone, resembling tall warriors standing at attention.

Torleik crossed the deck and approached, a spring in his step. "We had good wind, so made excellent time." He stepped closer so Eilidh could hear his words. "We are almost to *Meginland*, where my farm is located. I can take the ship near the shore of my property, which is why we don't need to dock in *Hannavoe*. I know you must be anxious to arrive on dry land."

Eilidh had never heard Torleik speak with such eagerness in his voice. She felt a quick flush of warmth that he had considered her comfort. "Anxious" didn't come close to what she was experiencing at this very special time. If she lay down on a decent bed and closed her eyes, she just might sleep for days.

"I look forward to seeing your land and meeting your people," she said calmly to cover the awkwardness.

Torleik shrugged. "The farm and house may seem primitive compared to what you are used to, but you will have a solid roof over your head, good food to eat, and fire to keep you warm in winter." He kept an eye on his men. "I will make arrangements for the handfast in the morning, so we can get that out of the way."

Eilidh nodded, but winced at his words as the ship steered up onto the sand. As much as she wanted to trust this friendlier side of Torleik, he was still a complete stranger ... *and it will still be a marriage of convenience*.

14

ᚠᚱᚲᛋᛏᚷᚹᛗᛁᛟᚾᚾ

Torleik's Farm
Meginland (Mainland), Orkneyjar (The Orkneys)
Summer 1153

When Lifa heard the young boy's annoyingly high-pitched voice announce the arrival of Master Torleik's ship, she dropped a clothespin and shaded her eyes to scan the shoreline below. He'd been gone another week, and her stomach burned to not know what was happening with him. She watched as Astrid and her girls took Atli, the screaming brat, down the path to the shore to welcome Torleik – his father. Lifa stepped closer to the edge of the cliff that overlooked the ocean and watched as Torleik jumped down from the deck of his ship, then reached up to lift someone down to the sand. Was that a *woman*? When the new arrival lowered her hood and coppery curls cascaded down her back and glimmered in the sun's final hours, Lifa frowned.

Had Torleik finally found a bride?

Bile rose in Lifa's throat at the notion. Torleik was hers and hers alone. Fury settled like a stone in her stomach.

Lifa resumed hanging laundry, but jealousy reared up inside her, making her movements clipped. Hmm... How could she get rid of Torleik's new wife as quickly as possible? She grunted in frustration. She would come up with a way – because, whether Torleik realized it or not, he *did* belong to *her*. And someday he would come to understand it ...

***

Torleik led Eilidh up the steep path, Atli perched atop his shoulders. The boy chattered about all that his father had missed while away. Torleik listened patiently, pausing on the path occasionally to check that Eilidh didn't stumble. He hadn't introduced her to his son, deciding it might be better to explain things at the house.

Hallkel brought up the rear and conversed with Astrid, who worked in the main house and maintained their vegetable gardens. Her fair-haired daughters were older than Atli, but they seemed to get along well, thank God. Torleik's growing community needed more children playing about.

They reached the top of the cliff, where Torleik paused for a moment to admire the large, rectangular-shaped house he and Hallkel had constructed in the Norse longhouse tradition. He set Atli on the ground and was greeted with a wave from Kelda, his housekeeper, who stood on the porch and wiped her hands on her apron. She was joined by Siv, the cook, who wore a dour expression that rarely changed.

Torleik leaned down and whispered in a dramatic voice to Atli and Astrid's girls, Dagny and Ilse, to get their attention. "I want you three to go around to every worker's home and knock on the door. Tell them to come to the house, as I have a very special announcement to make."

Atli and the girls shared a surprised look then ran off to do his bidding.

Once they were gone, Torleik turned to regard Eilidh, who looked a bit overwhelmed in her heavy cloak. He forced a smile, knowing he'd avoided her long enough.

"I'm just going to make a quick introduction, then invite everyone to our handfast in the morning."

Eilidh nodded, but no words followed.

"We will have supper, and then I'll show you where you will sleep tonight." He hoped she didn't see his mouth twinge, as he hadn't thought this part out yet.

Eilidh's face drew a blank and she appeared wan, as if a stiff wind could knock her over. Then it dawned on Torleik that they'd all spoken in their Orcadian dialect, which she didn't understand. Something else to address when he had more time.

"Did you say we're having a handfast ... *tomorrow*?" Kelda inquired of Torleik, sharp gray eyes narrowing.

"*Ja*. Can you perform that for us? We didn't have the time in *Alba*. Her father wants our marriage recognized as legal until the time we can arrange for a priest."

Kelda was chewing on his words as if they contained something she didn't like.

Torleik turned his back to the yard to address her without anyone hearing what was said. "Kelda, I know when you don't approve of something, so spit it out."

The older woman heaved a heavy sigh. "What if everything goes well for a year-and-a-day, then she leaves? Your son will be devastated. Have you thought of that? And you'll be searching for a replacement again." Her eyes shifted suspiciously to Eilidh, who was petting a goat in the center of the yard.

"We settled on a marriage of convenience." Torleik crossed his arms over his chest. "That's what I want and she wanted, according to her father, and I agreed. If we are satisfied with each other, we plan a church ceremony. Otherwise, we go our separate ways."

"A marriage of convenience? Ah, Torleik." She reached for his hand. "I understand you still have great love for your late wife, but this—"

"We can discuss this later." Torleik looked at the gathering crowd. He didn't like his decisions being constantly challenged, as his pride wouldn't allow him to admit he didn't have all of the answers.

He took Eilidh by the arm and brought her to the middle of a circle formed by Torleik's workers. After a few moments, he raised his hand for silence.

"Everyone, this is Eilidh, of Clan MacAoidh near the town of *Tunga* in *Alba*. Tomorrow morning, you are all invited to attend a handfast ... as she becomes my wife."

Many of his workers must have known how long and hard Torleik had worked to find the right wife for him and a mother for his son. But as they turned to regard Eilidh's lovely face and hair burnished by the sun in a shade of copper Torleik had never seen before, it occurred to him how young she appeared. What had her father told him? Almost seventeen winters?

Torleik straightened to his full height and wore what he hoped was a confident expression.

This must work.

"Eilidh has endured a long journey, so save your well-wishes for tomorrow." He put an arm around Kelda's shoulder, attempting to coax her into a better mood. "Our very own Kelda will conduct a handfast ceremony at noon, and following that, we will celebrate with good food and drink. Everyone here is invited."

Much teasing greeted his ears regarding the end of his bachelor status, followed by shouts of congratulation for their master's long search ending in success. And he felt a certain satisfaction when women and children immediately gathered around Kelda, asking for assignments to help prepare for the event. Then he caught a glimpse of Kelda smiling at him. He bit back a grin and turned away.

When he turned to speak to Eilidh, she was no longer there beside him. For a moment, he panicked, but then spotted her sitting on a porch bench set against the wall of the longhouse, the hood of her cloak pulled up to cover her hair.

Relieved, Torleik turned his attention to the front porch. He had built it on a whim, as it wasn't a typical Norse feature. However, the magnificent view of the great Atlantic Ocean and the rising sun each morning, created a perfect beginning to greet each day.

As he approached the porch, he hesitated to tell her what he'd announced to his people about the celebration. He tip-toed closer and discovered her eyes were closed and her breathing steady. Perhaps, it was just as well she slept.

The slender young woman didn't even stir when he picked her up and entered the longhouse. For a tall woman, she felt as light as the gossamer veil worn by Ulla at their wedding. They'd both been so young and naïve. He frowned. Why had he conjured up that image? It had been a long time ago, and he felt angry with himself that he had compared the two.

He placed Eilidh on his bed – *their* bed, after tomorrow. Gently, he removed her shoes and cloak, then pulled the covers over her. He set her traveling bag where she could find it later, and quietly left her alone.

Siv, their cook, was working on the evening meal and turned at the sound of his boots on the stone floor. "Poor thing. Must be exhausted after a journey like that and all alone. I was thinking she would be hungry, but perhaps sleep is better." She paused and glanced his way. "She seems so young, master."

Torleik shrugged. "She *is* young – sixteen, almost seventeen. But she'll quickly get used to things here."

He headed back outside to collect his son and quietly explain how things were about to change for them very soon. He only hoped that change was for the better.

Part II: ALGIZ

(Protection & Healing)

15

ᚨᚱᚲᛋᛏᚷᚹᛖᛚᛟᚱᚢ

A dull headache greeted Eilidh when she awoke. Disoriented, she glanced around the room and tried to remember where she was located. She lifted the bed covers and sat up to discover she still wore the same clothes from the previous day. As she pushed aside the deer hide covering the window, memories of traveling on water returned bit by bit. The crossing had been invigorating and, thankfully, without incident. Still, she was very grateful to be on land once again.

Her growling stomach immediately reminded her she was hungry. Had she missed a meal? She must have slept the whole night through, because the sun was shining and a rooster crowed with enthusiasm close by.

She was taking in her new surroundings when an unfamiliar voice came from the other side of the door.

"Mistress, are you awake?"

Eilidh glanced down, glad she was already dressed, though feeling somewhat groggy.

"Aye. Come in."

A tall, thin woman entered, her head down as she placed a tray on the bed. Torleik entered right behind, appearing refreshed and in good spirits. A little blond boy clung to his father's muscular thigh, shyly glancing from behind to take a peek at Eilidh.

"Forgive my intrusion ... Eilidh," said Torleik. "But I wanted to let you know what we have arranged for today. Did you sleep well?"

His Scottish Gaelic was spotty, but Eilidh was pleased he tried. She eyed the wrinkled skirt of her gown. "Aye. I slept through the night, but how did I get here?"

She glanced around and saw only manly furnishings, though personal belongings were neatly arranged or folded on shelves or put away in the wardrobe. Her eyes grew wide at the animal skins on the walls, floor, and bed.

Torleik's chamber.

"You fell asleep before we came inside last evening. I didn't want to wake you, so I carried you here. I slept in the hall. The handfast is scheduled for noon. A special celebratory midday meal will follow."

Eilidh forced a smile. "I see. Thank you for bringing me here last night. I guess I was more tired from the voyage than I realized."

He appeared tall and confident as he motioned toward the older woman, who stood waiting. "This is our cook, Siv. She has brought you something to break your fast. If there is nothing else you require from her this morning, she would like to return to preparing the meal for the celebration."

"Of course. I look forward to the festivities," she added to show enthusiasm. Eilidh eyed the tray and smiled at the sprig of meadowsweet someone had thoughtfully added for decoration. She could use the sprig to scent the bedding – if she could lift off the heavy bear fur covering. Distracted by the steaming mug of tea with the familiar aroma of borage, she took a sip. "*Borage for courage,*" her grandmother used to say. The tea only reminded her how much she already missed her grandmother and home. She reached for a piece of sliced apple on a plate, then sat on the bed to keep from grabbing the bread and cheese and quickly inhaling everything on the table like her brothers did when they were starving.

"This is just right. *Tapadh leat*. Thank you," she said, nodding to Siv.

Torleik translated and Siv gave a polite nod before leaving.

Atli had spotted Eilidh's two trunks in a corner and went to quietly inspect them, though they were closed and locked. After several moments, he turned and asked Torleik a question.

Eilidh already regretted that she hadn't had time to learn at least a bit of Norse. Atli seemed to be a well-behaved and curious lad. He was also adorable, like a smaller version of his father. Same scraggy blond hair and pale blue eyes.

Torleik regarded his son and suppressed a smile. "Atli wants to know if you brought him a gift in one of those big trunks."

Eilidh jumped up. "Oh! Of course." She hadn't known it was expected, so she had no gift. But she thought quickly. "Tell Atli I will give him my gift ... tomorrow. After I've unpacked my trunks."

There must have been something in her eyes that Torleik recognized as a stall for time. He spoke to Atli, who appeared disappointed, but then turned and skipped out the door. Torleik shrugged. "Children have such short attention spans."

"Especially boys," she commented.

He smiled slyly, blue eyes narrowed. "Is that so?"

Was he teasing ... or flirting?

She shifted her thoughts to something else. "Well, my four older brothers *were* hard to manage, except for Padruig, who loves his studies as I do. The others were always off somewhere."

Eilidh turned away, feeling terrible that she hadn't thought of a gift for the boy. She hated to disappoint Atli at the very beginning. She sipped her tea, hoping Torleik would leave so she could devour her meal in private.

Unfortunately, Torleik stubbornly remained standing in the middle of the chamber. Eilidh crossed her arms over her chest and tried not to stare at the food on the tray. "Is there something you wish to discuss further with me?"

He shook his head and glanced at her storage trunks. "Do you have a gown to wear for the handfast ceremony? If so, Astrid may have time to smooth out the wrinkles and help you dress. Would you like a ... bath first?"

Eilidh knew she likely reeked of the sea. Her hair felt sticky as she smoothed it back, while her insides fluttered at the whole notion of being bound to one man. Even if it was only for a year and a day.

She pushed her troubled thoughts aside. "Ach, aye. Please. A bath would revive me considerably."

Torleik nodded. "I will have the tub delivered and filled. Astrid can help you dress, then bring you outside when you are ready for the handfast." He rubbed his whisker-covered chin and shrugged. "I guess it wouldn't hurt me to clean up a bit, as well." He inclined his shaggy head. "I'll see you shortly before noon."

She started to respond, but found that her voice failed to work. She smiled apologetically, to which he gave a short nod and left.

With his departure, she turned to nibble more of the food on the tray. Moments later, two burly servants appeared with a large wooden tub. They made several trips to the kitchen and back with pans of hot water. When Astrid arrived, she took over and sent the men on their way. Opening her sack, she pulled out sprigs of lavender and rose petals, and added those to the bath water. She placed clean linen and a large bar of homemade soap on a chair near the tub. Eilidh curiously sniffed the soap and detected an aroma that reminded her of her heather-covered land, with a hint of vanilla.

"Interesting combination. Do you make your own soap here?" Eilidh inquired, then remembered Astrid couldn't speak Gaelic. She closed her eyes in pleasure as she gave an exaggerated sniff to the soap bar, her lips turning up at the corners. "Soap?" she said, holding out the bar for Astrid to enjoy the aroma. "It smells nice, aye?"

Astrid sniffed the bar and grinned. "*Ja*, is nice soap!"

"You speak Gaelic?" Eilidh felt a flood of relief.

"Only little. Hallkel teach me some words. Are you ready for handfast?"

Eilidh felt her spirit deflate. "I guess." She unlocked the trunks and pulled out two new gowns, laying them across the bed.

As Astrid made everything ready for the bath, she glanced at Eilidh with a sad smile. "You do not ... um ... wish to marry Torleik? He is pretty man, don't you think? And good man."

Eilidh held up her arms so Astrid could undo the ties of the gown she wore. "He is kind of 'pretty', I must admit."

Astrid chuckled. "I use wrong word? How to say man is beautiful?"

Eilidh thought for a moment, not wanting to blurt out the correct answer so quickly and hurt Astrid's feelings. She seemed to want to please Eilidh and calm her fears at the same time. Eilidh could use a new friend in this strange new land.

"I would probably describe a man as *handsome*. I have four older brothers who all think they are the most handsome son in the family. They never let me forget that I am different because of my red hair and freckles."

"Your brothers are mean. You are most pretty woman. But ... what are freckles?"

Eilidh disrobed and started to ease into the fragrant, hot water. "Ach, this is wonderful." She got comfortable and then pointed to her face. "See those little brown spots across my nose and cheeks?"

Astrid peered closely, her face somber.

"Those are freckles. They come from the sun. My mother says a true lady does not race around outside and leave her fair skin unprotected." She picked up the soap. "Clearly, I haven't been a well-behaved lady ... so far."

"I see." Astrid stepped back and started to fold the clothes Eilidh had dropped on the floor. After a few moments of quiet contemplation, she asked, "Did Master Torleik say he chose you to be fine lady?"

Eilidh laughed heartily when she regarded Astrid's serious face. "No. He knew all about my flaws from my father." She washed her elbow slowly, thinking back. "But Torleik doesn't know *all* my flaws. He has a few surprises coming, I think."

Astrid nodded, again taking her mistress seriously. "Sometimes, man not like surprises."

"I'm hoping he will find they are good surprises." Eilidh smiled and laid her head back against the tub rim.

She heard the whisper of fabric as Astrid held up the two newest gowns.

"You wear one of these for handfast?"

Thank goodness for Hilda. Mother would be pleased.

"Aye." Eilidh selected the sage green gown with ivory lace trim, saving the luscious raspberry linen gown for something special. Torleik's people might think she had terrible taste in clothes, and as a redhead, on top of that, if she wore pink. She didn't want anything else to make her stand out.

"Is good choice. Shows you are good woman who comes to live with Torleik and Atli. Practical." She fingered the pinkish-purple gown one last time before hanging it in the wardrobe next to Torleik's clothes. "Besides, you must wear the colorful gown for big party sometime."

Eilidh relaxed until her head slid down to the water level. "Astrid, I have a feeling you and I may prove to be good friends one day. And a big party we shall have, when the time is right."

"*Ja*! I like that."

Astrid placed the green gown on the bed and used her hands to smooth the wrinkles.

Eilidh savored the bath to help her work out the kinks and bruises of her journey. But then, she began to worry. What if Torleik expected her to sleep with him after the handfast? He'd avoided her eyes this morning, while his right hand would clench open, then closed, at his side. It was as if he was confused ... or angry.

Was Torleik already regretting the impulsive agreement he'd made?

She felt the water cooling and stepped out of the tub, then reached for a warm towel.

"Astrid, I must come up with a gift for Atli. He thinks I packed one in one of my trunks. I don't want to disappoint him."

Astrid hung the new gown on the wardrobe door, and Eilidh had to admit it looked as wonderful as she had hoped.

"Oh, Atli is easy. Talk to Hallkel. He makes toys for all the children. I am sure he has something Atli would like."

"That's a wonderful idea, Astrid. I will do that ... after the handfast."

"Come, we get you in new gown, brush your freshly-washed hair, and when Master Torleik sees you like this, you take his breath away."

Eilidh smiled. She didn't know why the sudden urge, but that was exactly what she wanted to do.

Was *she* the one who was confused?

16

ᚨᚱᚲᛋᛏᚷᛈᛗᛚᛟᚾᚢ

Eilidh's body had turned numb at some point, and she couldn't decide if it was from the cool morning as she waited on the porch, or from what she was about to do. She pulled her shawl tighter around her shoulders, feeling awkward with nothing to do while everyone else seemed to be bustling about, laughing and enjoying the preparation for the handfast.

Kelda had sent the youngest children to hunt for wildflowers. They returned with baskets filled with cheerful daisies, pale pink dog-rose blossoms, the abundant wild yellow irises, combined with the airy stems of meadow cranesbill in a rich periwinkle. Under the guidance of the blacksmith's very pregnant wife, Valdis, the older children and women arranged and wrapped the flowers in small bunches tied together with red ribbons. These small bouquets were then placed in anything that could be used as a vase. Wooden mugs, bowls, even baskets lined with cloth to keep the blooms damp, decorated makeshift tables for the celebration meal.

At the sight and sounds of people who clearly enjoyed each other's company, Eilidh felt a pang of homesickness and loss. Consequently, when Astrid's youngest daughter, Dagny, shyly stepped forward and offered Eilidh a crown of flowers for the ceremony, Eilidh felt tears at the corner of her eyes as she graciously accepted them. She knelt down and let Dagny place the crown atop her loose coppery curls, white ribbons trailing down her back, and thanked the little girl who could not have been much more than six.

With the crown in place, albeit crooked as it dipped over Eilidh's right eye, Dagny grinned a gap-toothed grin and raced back to Astrid, who'd taken charge of Atli for the morning.

When Dagny wasn't looking her way, Eilidh adjusted her "crown." She couldn't help but smile as all sorts of people gathered in front of the longhouse. Some brought their own stools or chairs from home.

A palpable anticipation wafted in the air. Eilidh supposed it was due to the fact thatTorleik's people saw him finally settling down, marrying, and bringing stability to his home and community. But she did wonder what they would think if they knew Torleik had agreed to a one-year marriage of convenience only, that she had no wish to stay and raise a family with the man they clearly admired and respected.

Eilidh peered around. She had yet to see Torleik or Hallkel, but Kelda had started quieting the crowd and telling them to sit. Kelda appeared transformed, her drab brown service gown of the day before replaced with what must be the typical Norse gown, for the other women wore the same style, but in different colors. It appeared to be an apron-like gown with open sides, secured at the top where the front of the apron met the shoulders. Shoulder straps were held together by two large matching round brooches made of metal and engraved with Norse designs, which hung from a beaded necklace. A plain, long-sleeved undergown of contrasting color was visible underneath the apron, with a skirt that reached the floor.

Eilidh suspected the design was practical for the women who worked in the kitchen or outdoors. However, she couldn't see herself ever wearing one of those gowns. It wasn't that the gowns Hilda made were better, necessarily. It was just that the Norse gowns were just so very "foreign" to Eilidh. She didn't know if she wanted to get used to Norse clothing if she was to return home after a year and a day.

Eilidh spotted Torleik and Hallkel as they appeared from behind the longhouse. They had clearly washed up and donned clean clothes. She felt a fluttering in her stomach, something she hadn't experienced before. In fact, she wasn't sure she liked it, for it made her feel faint and dizzy as she came forward and took her place next to Torleik, as Kelda had instructed her.

Torleik gave her a quick nod as he stood straight and tall beside her. His pale blue, fine linen tunic reflected the ice blue of his eyes. But Eilidh thought his eyes seemed cold. And he hadn't noticed the new sage-colored gown made in the French style that Hilda had created for her. She chafed at her realization. She'd always told her brothers and parents that she didn't care about fancy new gowns. Yet now that she was wearing something new and feminine, she wanted the man she was tying herself to – quite literally – to notice.

She scolded herself silently and frowned.

Before Kelda got started, Eilidh's attention was drawn by movement near the southern side of the longhouse. A young woman with dark hair looked as if she was trying to hide behind a rowan tree flush with red berries. Why wasn't she sitting with the other invited guests?

Torleik followed her gaze for a brief moment, then focused on Kelda, his expression blank. "I believe we are ready, Kelda."

Upon hearing Torleik's words, Eilidh forced a smile.

"The term handfasting is derived from the Norse word *handfesta,* meaning to strike a bargain by joining hands." As Eilidh and Torleik faced each other, Kelda bound their wrists together with a smooth leather cord, then tied a knot to hold it loosely in place.

Eilidh felt a tug when Torleik moved to rake his hair back. She panicked, and wanted to throw off the cord. Instead, she stood obediently, as she'd promised her mother and grandmother.

"As I tie this knot, your lives are now bound." Kelda's deep voice reached everywhere.

Eilidh felt Torleik's glance, but could not sense his thoughts.

"By tying this knot, I bring together all of the dreams, desires, love, and happiness that is wished for you by your family and friends gathered here today."

Eilidh gulped, but was able to stifle a sob as a lone tear rolled down her cheek. She had no family nor friends in this place. She swiped away the teardrop so Torleik wouldn't see her as weak.

"By the joining of hands and by the knot that is tied, so are your lives now bound, one to another. May this knot remain tied for as long as love shall last. May it draw your hands together in love as a couple, as partners, and as parents."

Eilidh flinched. *Parents?*

Kelda had moved on. "Torleik, will you share the burdens of each of you so that your spirits may grow in this union?"

For a moment, Torleik appeared startled as he glanced at Eilidh, then at Hallkel, who stood by his side. He looked down and shifted his feet.

"I will."

"And Eilidh, will you always be open and honest with Torleik, for as long as you both shall live?"

Eilidh's heart skipped a beat. She hadn't expected the handfast to be quite so serious. She swallowed and straightened her shoulders.

"I will."

"Torleik, will you honor this woman?"

"I will," he said with no hesitation.

"And Eilidh, will you honor this man?"

"I will."

Kelda took a sip of water from a mug she kept nearby. "The knots of this binding are not formed by these cords, but instead, by your vows. Know that either of you may drop the cords, for always, you hold in your hands the making or breaking of this union."

She removed the cords and handed them to Siv, who'd been standing off to the side of the couple.

"By this handfast, you each commit to marriage for a year and a day. At the end of that time, you will choose to remain together or to go your separate ways." She looked closely at Eilidh, then Torleik, her blue eyes watery. "A handfast is understood as a promise to marry in the Christian church at some later date, which may occur before the year and a day end."

Again, Torleik seemed uncomfortable as he turned his gaze to the sea.

Kelda addressed the guests. "We celebrate this new union and wish Eilidh and Torleik a long life together." She smiled at Torleik with a twinkle in her eye. "You may kiss the bride."

Eilidh felt strangely rooted to the ground, not quite sure what had just happened, but when Torleik leaned down and his lips captured hers, she went still. She'd closed her eyes, surprised she hadn't panicked nor fought him off as she'd done with Bennett Sutherland – the only other man to kiss her on the lips.

17

ᚨᚱᚲᛋᛏᚷᛈᛗᛚᛉᚾ

As a small child, back on Stronsay, Lifa had learned how to blend into the background and make herself invisible when she needed to hide from her father or his friends. She used this skill now, standing back and quietly sneaking a small hunk of cheese and a slice of bread, then slipping them into her pockets. With Siv issuing gruff orders to poor Astrid and Kelda, an idea popped into her head.

"Siv, since this is the first midday meal you have prepared for Master Torleik and his new bride, I would be happy to help with the cleanup. An extra pair of hands might come in handy."

Siv turned and glared for a moment. "You never volunteer for anything. Why now?"

Lifa was intent on learning everything she could about the new woman warming Torleik's bed. By helping with the meal, she would have an opportunity to listen in on Torleik and his bride's conversation without them even noticing she was there. Lifa worried her hands together. She knew he had been searching for a mother for Atli and was having no luck. What made him choose this one so quickly?

"I can appreciate how hard you have worked on the handfast celebration, Siv. Everything looked, and I'm sure, tasted lovely." Lifa cocked her head. "Surely, extra hands would help get things cleaned and under control, meaning the sooner you could rest up."

Lifa would never admit it, but she'd held onto the hope that Torleik would marry *her* one day. She refused to believe he wouldn't marry a lowly servant such as herself. Besides, Lifa had been told by many men that she was beautiful, and she had been taught at a young age how to best use that knowledge, along with her considerable charms. She'd smooth-talked Torleik into hiring her two years ago when she clearly had little skill or interest in keeping a house running. The first moment she'd set eyes on Torleik, she knew he had to be hers. Never had she seen such a tall, handsome, well-muscled man. How dare this interloper think she could take Lifa's intended place by his side.

Siv, who had been scrubbing dishes, looked up. "I don't recall seeing you at the celebration."

"Come to think of it, neither did I," Kelda commented, looking at Astrid, who merely shrugged her shoulders.

Lifa pressed her lips together. "I ... wasn't feeling well. But I'm fine now and offering my help. How about I help serve dinner, and you can take the evening off, Siv. You do look a little pale and tired. Kelda and I can handle the evening meal."

"Hmph," Siv responded.

"Are you all caught up with the laundry?" Kelda inquired. As housekeeper, she supervised Lifa, so she had the final say.

Lifa paused for a moment, trying hard to keep her temper hidden. She gazed out the open doorway, knowing Torleik and Hallkel sat talking on the porch.

"*Ja,* the laundry is hanging to dry. I can bring it in before helping with dinner."

Kelda placed a gnarled hand on Siv's shoulder. "You know darn well you've outdone yourself and could use a rest. We'll be serving leftovers from the celebration, so no need to cook or bake. Take advantage of Lifa's generous offer."

Siv regarded the three women suspiciously, then lowered her shoulders. "I *am* exhausted, truth be told." She swiped a damp hand across her forehead and regarded Lifa. "Alright. But you do what Kelda asks you to do, and don't cause trouble for anyone."

Lifa tried to keep her enthusiasm tamped down, knowing she'd won this first round.

She picked up an extra linen towel and started drying dishes, excited to ponder how she might dispose of Torleik's redheaded wife -- who definitely stood in her way.

***

Eilidh enjoyed the evening meal immensely, especially with Torleik sitting beside her at the end of the huge table. It was only her second meal with them as a family, and she had to admit that Atli was a handful. Torleik was a good father, and seemed to know how to wrangle his son, so she dismissed the idea of saying anything to the little boy unless Torleik was preoccupied. She and Torleik would need to have an important conversation about her role in disciplining Atli – soon. But Eilidh was also wise enough not to do anything until they had come to an understanding.

"The handfast was lovely," she commented, wishing Torleik would say something.

"Umf," he grunted, digging into his meat.

"Is Kelda ordained as a ... person who can perform the handfast?"

A moment of silence.

"Umf."

Eilidh tried not to heave a huge sigh.

"More vegetables?" Lifa stood by her side, a huge smile plastered on her face.

Eilidh glanced up. Lifa's smile was without a doubt fake. In fact, she looked like she was trying not to scowl. For a moment, she caught Lifa's eyes shifting to Torleik. Eilidh suddenly had the strangest feeling that the two had been intimate at some point. When Lifa turned her full gaze on Eilidh, her eyes flashed with fire.

Eilidh's scalp tingled as if she could see something terrible on the horizon. Torleik hadn't even bothered to glance up, as he was too busy shoveling Siv's good food into his mouth.

"Master Torleik, may I bring you anything?" Lifa addressed him, her voice low and husky. She then turned to Atli and winked.

Eilidh almost gagged on her bite of turnips. Could Lifa be any more obvious?

"Umf." Torleik was still chewing. "More meat?"

"Of course."

Atli muttered something to Torleik in Norse.

"What's that?" Torleik asked, putting down his utensil and leaning in closer while lowering his voice. "What makes you say Lifa's only pretending to act nice?"

Atli shrugged as Lifa returned to the table. She held out the whole platter to Torleik, not bothering to offer any to Eilidh. His son's words forgotten, Torleik took what was remaining on the platter and resumed his meal.

"Anything else ... master?"

Torleik finally looked up, his brows raised. He glanced at Eilidh, as if in afterthought. "Anything you would like?"

Eilidh shifted and lowered her eyes. At least he'd remembered he had a wife – even if it took a while. "No, thank you. I'm full."

Atli smiled at Lifa and mumbled something about dessert as he pointed his finger toward the kitchen.

"Finish your vegetables before dessert," said Torleik.

For a moment, Eilidh felt like an outsider looking in.

"I will leave you to finish your meal." Before Lifa returned to the kitchen, she gave Eilidh one last final look, clearly triumphant that she had won over the boy and full of confidence that she would prevail in winning over Torleik, as well.

Eilidh shivered and watched the woman's back as she retreated to the kitchen. Was this going to be an ongoing battle between the two of them from now on?

18

ᚨ ᚱ ᚲ ᛊ ᛏ ᚷ ᚹ ᛗ ᛚ ᛟ ᚼ ᚢ

Eilidh had tossed and turned the previous night, going over and over in her head what she wanted to say to Lifa. *Eilidh* was the mistress and wife. Not Lifa. It was as simple as that. There was nothing Lifa could do about it.

Eilidh let out a deep breath and pasted a smile on her face, determined to have a good start to her day.

When she entered the dining area the next morning, she was surprised that neither Torleik nor Atli was seated at the table. Kelda appeared and set a plate of food in front of her to break her fast. Up close, Eilidh could see that Kelda was not nearly as old as Eilidh's grandmother, Marsaili, but she still reminded her of *Seanmhair* when she nodded a greeting and gestured towards the food. Eilidh had assumed the older woman didn't speak Gaelic, so she smiled and wondered how quickly she could learn Norse so she could interact with people.

Pleased to find familiar food items to choose from, Eilidh reached for a small bowl of porridge, adding a few plump raspberries. She then leisurely enjoyed a strong tea laced with milk while recalling how she and her grandmother had often used local berries in their potions and treatments. Eilidh would put foraging for berries and herbs at the top of her list for things she must learn here in a new environment. She quickly finished her meal, then grabbed a few extra berries for later and wrapped them in a cloth. Tucking them into the leather pouch she wore around her middle when searching for herbs, she rose but hesitated to speak, suddenly unsure of herself.

Eilidh had slept later than usual, but knew she needed it after the long journey. However, not wanting to cause the servants any extra work, she scooped up her empty dishes and placed them near the sink, where Siv and Kelda spoke in low voices. They turned in unison, the same startled expression on their faces. Siv grunted and said something in Norse as she grabbed the dishes, then she shook a finger at Eilidh.

"Did I do something wrong?"

Kelda shrugged and began to hum while she dried dishes.

A perfect moment presented itself when Astrid entered the longhouse. "I heard that." She grinned at Eilidh. "Siv teases. She says new lady of house should not lift one finger. That is our job and why Master Torleik pays us." She arranged a headscarf to tuck her lush honey blonde waves out of the way while she cleaned, then turned to address Kelda. "Today is garden day. I see pea vines starting to face sun. I think good winter for vegetables, *ja?*"

Astrid had spoken in Gaelic, clearly for Eilidh's benefit, then translated for Kelda. She was quick to interpret the older woman's Norse response.

"Kelda tell me to weed around cabbage. And then I should ask stableboy to use chicken wire to keep animals away."

Eilidh was so touched that Astrid seemed happy to be her translator. When Kelda spoke up again, another big smile lit Astrid's face.

"*Ja*, I will do that." Astrid finished tucking locks away from her face and gestured to Eilidh. "Come, mistress. Kelda wants me to show you water well, and bring back a full pail before I am all covered with dirt in garden."

Astrid reached for an empty pail and urged Eilidh to follow her. Eilidh was glad to leave the kitchen behind her and to step outside where she discovered a lovely summer day. A soft breeze off the ocean made her sigh as she tried to guess where her husband might be.

"Here is well for water."

Not far from the longhouse door, Eilidh stopped to watch Astrid draw water. "It's good to know you don't have to carry it too far."

"*Ja.* That is what I tell Lifa when she complain. And she complains a lot."

Eilidh gave a brief thought to the scowling woman she'd seen in the distance during the handfast. Curious, she wondered about her history and why she kept apart from the others.

"Is the water ... fresh?" Eilidh peered into the well to gauge how far down it went. From what she could tell, the well was very deep, and water appeared not that far below, so there must be plenty.

Astrid lowered the bucket by rope into the well, then gave Eilidh a strange look, her blonde brows rising. "Master Torleik and Hallkel made well themselves. Of course water is good."

"Ach, I didn't mean to criticize anyone. We've had times when something from the soil tainted our water back home." She wrapped her arms around her middle and watched as Astrid pulled up the now-full bucket, her arm muscles an indicator she had worked hard all her life.

Astrid set down the water and placed her hands on her hips, nodding. "We no tainted water here, but Master Torleik always checking to be sure it safe to drink."

"He sounds like an excellent master."

"He cares for his people."

Eilidh gazed off into the distance and took her first good look at Torleik's land. No homes nor towns marred the exceptional view of the sun rising in the east. As sheep and frisky spring lambs made their way through the green grass that covered the small hills to her right, she thought of home.

She'd noticed that few large trees were present, which could make finding her Wisdom Tree a difficult task if she wanted privacy. It had never occurred to her that the island would be so flat and almost treeless. She'd have to ask Torleik why that was.

She inhaled deeply, thinking her situation could be so much worse. She smiled with gratitude as the scent of sea salt and brine tickled her nose. "The land here is beautiful, so close to the sea."

"Norse men do not do well if they live too far from sea." Astrid leaned down to grab the bucket. "It is nice, sunny day. I thankful for that."

When Astrid lifted the bucket of water and set it down, Eilidh shaded her eyes as she looked all around the property.

"You wouldn't happen to know where Torleik is? And Atli?"

Astrid wiped her hands on a clean rag she then tied around her neck. "Master Torleik always like to start with horses. Hallkel too." Her cheeks blushed a pretty pink as she pointed east, towards the main road that passed by Torleik's farm.

If Eilidh wasn't mistaken, Astrid appeared to blush each time she spoke Hallkel's name, which could explain her earlier defense of his work on the well. She smiled and looked to where Astrid pointed.

"You walk toward road. First, you stop and see my lovely vegetable garden. Then, you see stables on left. Atli most likely with father, but Master Torleik will send him to come help me and the girls ... keep him out of trouble. You go find husband, Mistress Eilidh," she added with a sly grin, awkwardly lugging the heavy bucket toward the longhouse.

As Eilidh stopped to briefly admire Astrid's vegetable patch, she thought about showing her how to make a mixture that would make plants a bit perkier in this climate. She looked towards the large stable and barn area, and could hear the familiar neighs and whinneys of a busy stable.

Eilidh's heart began pounding at the idea she would see Torleik again and with any luck, her horse's filly, Arabel.

It's a marriage of convenience, she reminded herself.

Properly chastised, she set out to see the stunning horses that were visible behind pasture fences and to enjoy the sunny late spring day as well.

Still no sign of Torleik or Hallkel, Eilidh entered the stable and glanced around. Perhaps he was dealing with an ailing horse. She slowly walked down the stone corridor, trying not to make a sound as she peeked over the stall doors.

After a few moments, she lit up as she came across the young chestnut filly Torleik had purchased from her father in *Thjorsá*, as she would now call it in Torleik's world. The filly nickered and poked her head over the stall door.

"Ach, Arabel, *mo chridhe*, how are you?"

She placed a hand on either side of the chestnut's face and gleefully kissed her forehead, so glad to see a friend from home. But when Arabel backed away and began to rear up, Eilidh took her time and softly whispered Gaelic words that eventually calmed her. Eilidh had never understood why the filly would behave the way she did. Had she'd experienced some type of trauma in her past that no one knew about.? Thank goodness she hadn't been purchased by a monster, like Bennett Sutherland.

"I'm so glad you're here with me to keep me company." Eilidh reached into the herb pouch around her waist and retrieved the berries she'd saved. When she held out her hand and offered the berries, the filly hesitated, then took another step closer. Clearly curious, she stuck out her nose to get a good whiff of the berries. When she finally stood at the stall gate once more, Arabel reached for the berries, her muzzle as soft as velvet against Eilidh's palm. Content with her dessert, Arabel nudged Eilidh's arms, causing her to laugh.

"I see you have a way with animals. I believe your father mentioned this, but I ... forgot."

Eilidh stopped laughing and whirled around at the sound of Torleik's deep voice. She swallowed and deflected his attention. "Have you made any progress with Arabel?"

He placed a hand on the filly's head, rubbing gently – which Arabel surprisingly allowed.

"She's been a good challenge for Hallkel. But he is a patient man." Torleik settled his eyes on Eilidh and frowned at the gown she wore.

Had she missed one of the gown's ties under her arms? That's what happened when she didn't have Muire to keep an eye on her. She turned her head away so she didn't have to deal with the cause of his dour expression. Perhaps it was the color he disliked.

"Are you alright?" he inquired politely.

"I apologize. I keep remembering things from home. And people I may never see again." She swiped at her eyes. "Don't worry. I'll get over it shortly. I'm neither a weak nor fragile woman." She'd added the last part because she had the feeling Torleik was regretting his choice of a bride. Perhaps he even thought she'd be more trouble than she was worth.

Torleik said nothing for a few moments then gave the filly one last pat, a smile making him appear as if a different man. It must be the horses who gave him satisfaction.

Not me. Never me.

"I planned to give you a tour of your new home this morning. Since we're here, I'll start with the stables if that's alright with you?"

Eilidh forced a quick smile. "I would like that very much."

***

Eilidh's pale green gown reminded Torleik of one Ulla used to wear that last year of her short life. With his former wife's fair skin, white-blonde hair, and gentle manners, he'd thought she looked like an angel as she silently glided across the floor of their home back in *Nidaros*. She would be *with* the angels now, bless her. That's what he'd told Atli, anyway.

He heard Eilidh clear her throat and turned.

"Mmm, Torleik, may I meet your other horses?"

Eilidh's clear voice brought him back to the present, stirring up even more guilt for his rudeness and brooding. It wasn't Eilidh's fault Ulla had died in his arms. He ran a hand through his hair, which needed a trim. But he must keep his guard up ... for Atli's sake.

"*Ja*. The horses." Torleik started down the corridor. Eilidh followed, her worn leather shoes making no sound on the stone floor dusted with hay.

Peering into the next stall, he found his mood lightened considerably. "This is Bera. She is two years old, born here in *Meginland*."

"A pretty name. *Bera*. What does it mean?" She gazed with wide eyes at the reddish-brown filly, its contrasting flaxen mane and tail lovely in the still of the day.

Torleik liked how Eilidh's Gaelic accent caused the name to lilt, slightly.

"*Bera* means 'spirited' in Norse."

"Ach! That seems perfect!"

Torleik found himself unexpectedly pleased with her approval. And proud that his hard work in breeding had paid off so handsomely with this filly. "Like Arabel, Bera is still young and can be willful, so we've just begun her training."

Eilidh enticed Bera to come closer, and the two young females stood eye-to-eye, red hair and reddish coat catching a ray of sunlight slanting through the stable doors and into the corridor. Bera swished her tail.

Torleik shook his head, trying to banish the odd vision before him. It seemed as if the pair were communicating ... in some secret language. He rubbed his whiskered chin, having forgotten to shave after Atli and his dog, Runi, a huge Norwegian Elkhound he'd brought along to Orkney, jumped on him and made enough noise to raise the spirits around them, as Kelda would say. Wide awake after that, Torleik had observed Atli and Runi playing, and felt thankful they were so devoted to one another.

Torleik stretched his arms above him and smiled at Eilidh. He'd slept poorly in a corner of the longhouse generally reserved for friends and visitors. He would have to come up with something more comfortable if this was to be their new way of life.

"Come. We must move on. Many horses to see."

"Of course."

He'd seen enough of Eilidh to know she appeared to be optimistic and pleasant most of the time. She rarely complained, which surprised him. They both knew Eilidh had "married down," as far as society was concerned. But Torleik had hoped it wouldn't matter here in *Meginland*, where everyone worked hard. He considered it a good sign that she hadn't shown disappointment in the rustic accommodations and what little he had to offer.

Torleik finished with one row of stalls and crossed the corridor. "When we finish here, you will meet the rest of my people, many who attended the handfast."

Eilidh said nothing, likely overwhelmed by so much that was new. And missing her family. He hadn't seen his parents or brother, Kol, in almost three years. He should make time for that. Atli had still been a baby the last time they saw each other.

Slowly, but surely, Torleik introduced Eilidh to all of his horses. She appeared delighted with each, and praised Torleik's fledging horse farm business. She said all the things a supportive wife would say, but Torleik sensed she was not quite revealing the real Eilidh. He liked it when she teased and stood up to him – not an easy thing for a young girl to do in a faraway land. And she was smart and asked good questions. But, for now, she seemed to be keeping him at arms' length in terms of emotions – just as he was doing.

When they came to the last stall, Torleik found the bearded man he'd known most of his life. He was tending to a pregnant mare standing in a corner, listless. He stood and nodded at Torleik, exhaustion written all over his face.

"Eilidh, this is Isolf, who understands some Gaelic. He tends to sick or injured horses and other farm animals when he has time, and works with Hallkel on training the yearlings."

Isolf nodded politely.

"And this is my wife ... Eilidh." Torleik had almost said Ulla's name, and he could tell by the grimace on Eilidh's face, she knew it. He glanced away.

"Very nice to make your acquaintance, Isolf," she responded, her voice confident.

Torleik was impressed with her quick recovery. However, by her expression, he clearly had not given the transition in his family enough thought before he brought home a new bride. He'd assumed Eilidh would just quietly slide into place like a piece in a puzzle and make life easier by watching over Atli. A business transaction.

"How is Maeva doing?" inquired Torleik, stepping into the stall and gently touching the belly of the white mare.

Maeva gave a small snort, eyes wide as she struggled to get comfortable.

Isolf shook his head. "I don't think that foal is turning in the right direction yet."

"Breech birth?"

"Maybe. I've never seen anything like this before. They usually turn by now. There's still time, but each day that passes makes the birth more likely to be a dangerous one, for both mother and foal."

Although Isolf's Gaelic was a bit rough, Eilidh seemed to understand. She stepped inside the stall to draw their attention. "May I take a quick look? Perhaps there is something I can do to help. In addition to healing, I also have midwife skills – for people *and* animals."

Isolf stepped out of the stall to make more room, but Torleik remained where he stood and patted the distressed mother. "I don't want to upset Maeva any more than we have to. She doesn't know you yet, Eilidh."

Again, Eilidh's face fell, her cheeks blushing a deep pink. "But I ..." She muttered "bogfeathers" and stepped out of the stall. "Of course. As you wish."

She appeared to be trying to hold her emotions in check as her eyes darted around the stall. Once she'd collected herself, she addressed Isolf. "If Maeva becomes distressed to the point that she may hurt herself or the foal, please come get me. I do have experience with these kinds of things." She briefly glanced at Torleik, lips pressed together. "It would be no bother, truly."

Isolf gave a nervous nod. "Thank you, mistress."

Torleik said nothing further, his mind made up as he crossed his muscular arms over his chest.

***

As Eilidh and Torleik left the stables, she peered over at Torleik who appeared deep in thought. She certainly didn't know Torleik well enough to determine if he was angry with her for intervening with the struggling mare, or just being plain stubborn.

She suspected both. But why make a creature suffer when it was so unnecessary? She vowed to return and check on Maeva after the midday meal.

They continued walking at a brisk pace around the farmyard and past buildings designated for specific tasks, such as cheesemaking and butter churning, a granary for storing barley and oats, and a large building devoted to wool processing.

Eilidh could see Torleik had built up quite a self-sustaining operation in three short years. The workers appeared content and well-fed. At twenty-one, it seemed that Torleik was already showing great promise as a leader. She observed quietly as he listened to complaints and asked questions, demonstrating his interest in finding solutions whenever possible.

At each stop, Torleik performed brief introductions between Eilidh and his workers: Stigr, the blacksmith, and Brusi, his eldest son, who had bright red hair and freckles. Eskil, Stigr's young nephew, who had just started working for them. Lastly, Torrad, the foreman in charge of the farm's various crops and head of their guard, who provided security on their land. Eilidh was surprised to learn Torrad's wife, young Ola, was the ale-brewer. And, with enough seamen to fill two ships, Torleik's men helped transport goods of all kinds to ports in the north.

Eilidh couldn't help but note that Torleik's community had no separate chapel or priest to marry them. Eilidh's mother would be upset if she only knew. Despite that, Hallkel had mentioned on the long voyage that a massive cathedral church was under construction in the largest island town, *Kirkjuvagr*. Surely there would be a priest, maybe even a bishop, there who could marry them when the time came. *If* the time came. She wondered if Torleik hadn't said anything on purpose ... waiting to see which way the wind would blow between them.

Finished with the tour, Torleik led them back towards the longhouse. Eilidh sensed someone watching her and turned to see the dark-haired young woman from last night hanging laundry. She never seemed to smile, but when her gaze shifted to Torleik as he approached her, she paused and straightened her back. When Eilidh's gaze locked on Lifa, Eilidh experienced a strange crackle in the air.

Torleik put an arm around Eilidh's shoulder as he made formal introductions. Taken by surprise, she felt a measure of satisfaction when his hand then slid down and settled around her waist, letting Lifa know by his actions that he was claiming Eilidh for his own. He peered down at her with a sly grin and she breathed in his natural scent of horses and leather, mixed with a clean breeze off the sea that carried a hint of spice. Inwardly, she thanked him, as she felt certain Lifa could be a worthy adversary if she wasn't careful.

"Eilidh, this is Lifa, who is in charge of our household laundry." He returned his gaze to Eilidh. "You will want to familiarize yourself with our routines and change any that are not as efficient as they could be. Or, you may reassign Lifa to something else ... if you find her work is not satisfactory."

To Eilidh's continued amazement, Torleik gave Lifa a pointed look. Relief washed over her for his thoughtfulness.

"Lifa, this is my wife, Eilidh, and your new mistress. You will treat her with respect. Is that clear?"

Lifa's eyes shot hot fiery daggers, but she voiced a moody, "*Ja.* I understand ... *master.*" She gave a half-hearted curtsy to her mistress, not hiding the smirk that followed.

With a pained expression, Torleik turned away from Lifa and suggested he and Eilidh refresh themselves with a mug of cool well water before they finished the tour.

Eilidh was grateful for the brief respite, for the day had become quite warm.

Torleik led Eilidh to a shady spot on the side of the longhouse where two rustic wooden chairs and a small table situated in between acted as an invitation to sit. Neither spoke for a while, and Eilidh felt she must say something encouraging.

"I can see all of your hard work has paid off. This is quite a business you have. Actually, you have several businesses. The horses. Your wool processing. Crops and food you can sell at market." She smiled. "I'm very impressed. I can't wait to write to my parents and describe everything. I think they will be quite relieved." She looked down at her empty mug. "You seem an ambitious man, Torleik. That pleases me."

He nodded, and his lips formed a small smile. "Thank you. It's a lot of work."

After a few more moments of silence, she brushed off a piece of hay from her skirt, and summoned her courage. "The laundry woman ..."

"Lifa?"

"Aye. I find her demeanor unpleasant. Does she always speak to you in such a disrespectful way? My mother would never tolerate such behavior."

Torleik heaved a great sigh and hesitated before responding. "Lifa is very troubled, and I suspect she ran away from a hard life on a small island. That doesn't mean she can act the way she does, but I've tried getting her to treat others with more respect."

"Mmm. I wonder if Lifa has no respect for herself, therefore, she has none for anyone else, either."

Torleik gave her an odd glance. "You may be right. But you must not allow her to make your life miserable."

When he rose and set their mugs on the small table, Eilidh's instincts told her that perhaps there was a lot more to Lifa's story. Enough to cause Torleik to warn Eilidh about her.

The way Lifa looked at him made her wonder. Had Torleik been in a relationship with this girl? Or had it merely been a one-sided obsession?

The truth was usually somewhere in the middle, Grandmother Marsaili used to say.

19

Eilidh felt refreshed after drinking the cool water on a warm day, so felt more like asking questions as Torleik took her by the two rows of identical workers' homes made from local stone. They paused to admire contented sheep grazing in lush green pastures beneath the hills to the south of the longhouse.

"Astrid told me it's called 'Torleik's Hill'. Why is that?"

Torleik rested a hand on his hip, gazing off into the distance. "I have no idea. I guess because it's on my land." He shrugged and raised his brows.

The sight and sounds of a four-year-old boy yelling at the top of his lungs as he rushed over to see his father startled Eilidh. She hadn't seen Atli for a while, and she felt a bit guilty that she'd forgotten about him.

She watched as Torleik lifted him high in the air. Atli shouted – a high-pitched noise that made Eilidh's ears hurt.

"It's time for you to get cleaned up for the midday meal," said Torleik. "I will ride!" Atli stated, holding out his arms to sit on his father's shoulders.

Eilidh was surprised to hear Atli speak Gaelic, and even more surprised that Torleik had been thoughtful enough to have the boy speak it when she was around.

"Hallkel taught him a few words so that he would be able to speak to you when you arrived," Torleik explained.

Eilidh's heart warmed at the idea.

Torleik paused, glancing at Eilidh. Then to Atli he said, "How about we all walk together so you can get to know Eilidh better?"

When Torleik placed Atli back on the ground, the boy regarded Eilidh for a few moments as he clung to his father's leg.

"Modir?"

Torleik looked up, light brows furrowed as his eyes met Eilidh's.

"*Ja*. Remember, we talked about a new mother coming to live with us?"

Eilidh studied Atli's somber little face, and suddenly experienced her first sense of doubt. What if Atli refused her as a mother and she couldn't fulfill her part of the agreement? What would she do then? But when she saw a tear glisten in one eye, she felt horrible.

Poor thing probably feels lost without a mother.

Atli shook his head and reached for Torleik's hand. "She *not modir*."

"Be nice, Atli. She's trying, and so will you."

Torleik gave a sidelong glance to Eilidh, who felt as if she'd been stabbed in the heart. Most children followed her around as if she was a mama duck. Had she lost her touch?

"Don't worry about it," he said. "He'll get accustomed to you soon enough." Torleik shrugged and reached for Atli's hand. "This is all new for him."

Eilidh nodded that she understood, but she didn't. Not really. It was new for her, as well. In fact, she'd had only a few weeks to consider her impending motherhood.

They washed their hands at the well, using Kelda's strong oats soap and entered the longhouse, Atli skipping ahead of them. The delicious aromas wafting through the door immediately made Eilidh's mouth water, despite her current worries.

To her dismay, Lifa was there, setting plates and eating utensils out for them while Torleik settled Atli on a stack of linen cloth he placed on the bench to bring him closer to the table. "Lifa, why are you serving again today? Is Siv still ill?"

Kelda studied the platter of sliced pork, wiping her hands on a towel. She said something in rapid Norse, mentioning Lifa's name. Based on the tone of her voice, Eilidh suspected there was a problem.

Torleik nodded and glanced at Lifa, who's sullen face broke into a big smile. He looked away and rubbed the back of his neck before leaning in toward Eilidh.

"It seems Lifa convinced Siv she needed yet another rest, and that Lifa would fill in serving today. Unfortunately, Lifa said nothing to Kelda ahead of time." He shook his head. "Lifa is often up to no good, so people don't trust her." He shrugged and tickled Atli, who screeched and laughed out loud. "But let's talk about something more pleasant."

Eilidh saw what a good father Torleik was to Atli, but he'd been right when he said the boy needed consistent, yet firm guidance. She mustn't give up so soon. Eilidh was no quitter. Her brothers had seen to that.

The food arrived and Eilidh's mouth watered as she tried to wait patiently for everyone to serve themselves. Roasted chicken with an enticing garlic and mushroom sauce. Green beans with onions and chunks of pork. Fresh garden greens from Astrid's garden, and plenty of Siv's fresh-baked oat bread, ready to be slathered with butter churned that very morning.

Torleik didn't say grace before his meals, so Eilidh assumed he was not as dedicated a Christian as her mother. It seemed a bit strange not to pray before a meal such as this, but Eilidh sometimes felt closer to her grandmother's Old Ways. It seemed right that Nature was at the center of Druid life. Eilidh said a quick thank you to the Goddess of the Moon, thanking her for helping Eilidh escape both Geirolf and Bennett Sutherland's grasp. Now that all that was behind her, she had a new life to build.

As Torleik chatted with his son, his light eyes crinkled at the corners. His devoted attention to Atli made it obvious to anyone how much he loved his son. Unfortunately, Lifa made a point to stop by his side several times during the meal, being sure to ingratiate herself with Torleik's son before asking Torleik if he needed anything else.

Eilidh bristled at the idea that Lifa was trying to create a wedge between her and Torleik's son. But Torleik must have recognized what she was up to because he looked up, his smile disappearing.

"You can leave now, Lifa. We will finish cleaning up with Kelda."

Lifa's dark eyes grew wide, her mouth dropping open as she stared at Torleik, then her eyes darted to Eilidh for the first time. She had clearly never been dismissed in such a manner. An orange fire raged within, flames licking up to sear Lifa. Eilidh reeled at the image, which was surely not real, instead a throwback from her Druid heritage. Did she have the gift of second sight, like many Druids before her, starting with Great Grandmother Saraid? Grandmother had told her of such things, but until now, she had thought it unlikely, or she would have been aware of it by now. Eilidh started to rise, as if she needed to pour water on the flames. But then, she recalled the flames were on the inside. Lifa was hiding something terrible, and the menacing look she aimed at Eilidh made it clear that Eilidh was now her sworn enemy, despite never saying a word.

"Stop glaring, and do as I say, Lifa. Do you wish to be dismissed permanently?"

Torleik's voice sounded gruff, his shoulders tense as he waited to see what the servant would do.

Atli calmly stared at his father, but then he reached for a piece of bread on his plate and casually spread the butter onto the slice. "No, Fàdir. Lifa stay."

Atli's voice came out assertive and confident ... for a four-year-old.

Lifa glanced at Atli with a false smile that Eilidh could read by the color of the aura that surrounded her. Then she turned and left the longhouse.

Eilidh felt the tension in the air dissipate. And then a cold chill settled over her. She clutched her shawl tighter around her. How did Torleik expect her to handle someone like Lifa? Didn't he sense how dangerous she could be?

Perhaps even more so than either Geirolf or Bennett.

Eilidh shivered at the realization. She had jumped from one set of dangers only to end up no safer here than back home in *Alba*.

***

Torleik sat on his front porch chair, shading his eyes against the lowering western sun while Hallkel sat on the bench next to him, eyes squinting as he focused on the wood toy he was carving for Atli at Eilidh's request. Then he nodded toward the stable, where the mare was attempting to give birth.

"She's a strong mare. Maeva will get through this, even if it's a breech-birth."

Hallkel's voice had a lazy quality that made him appear so calm to everyone else, no matter what was happening. At times, Torleik wondered what he really thought and felt, but he never dared ask. Hallkel had his own demons to fight. Torleik's eyes shifted to the stable. No sign of Isolf waving frantically.

"She's not doing well. No change." Torleik looked down at hands, feeling helpless.

"You said Eilidh offered to help? Why not summon her? I'm sure Isolf would appreciate her assistance."

Torleik grimaced. "She is a brand new bride who has only been here one day. I would hate to throw her into something bound to upset her when it all goes bad."

"Sounds like you don't believe she can turn things around ... save Maeva and her foal."

Torleik shook his head, then ran his hands through shaggy hair. "I don't know what she can do, honestly."

Silence ensued for several moments as they both sipped their mugs of cool ale.

Setting the mug and wood carving aside, Hallkel picked at wood shavings that clung to his tunic. "Without help, they're both going to die, Maeva and the foal. Why not give Eilidh a chance to see what she can do? What's the worst that can happen?"

Torleik stood and stretched. "I'll see."

"Don't be so stubborn that you lose two good horses."

Torleik pressed his lips together at Hallkel's reminders. He was absolutely right, of course. Torleik *should* give his wife an opportunity to help the horses. Why was he hesitating?

"I'm heading back over to the stable now to reassess the situation." Torleik whistled once, and a few moments later, Runi came flying towards him, all fur and muscle as he leaped up and placed muddy paws on Torleik's chest. Runi yipped once, and his master gave him a good head rub before making him sit.

"You're spoiling that dog, you know." Hallkel grinned.

"I should probably give my new wife at least half this much attention." Torleik gave the dog one more pat.

Before he departed, Torleik paused, remembering the other matter that niggled at him. "Lifa's behavior has gotten worse since Eilidh arrived. Although she hasn't done anything overt, I don't trust her not to cause trouble. Eilidh has enough to deal with, getting to know who does what, learning the language, adjusting to Atli's ways. Do you have any ideas what to do with Lifa?"

Hallkel picked up the wood carving of a horse and examined it briefly. "It may be time to send her on her way, my friend. If she's more of a liability than an asset, she should go."

Runi stood still, except for his curly tail that swished from side to side, eyes never leaving Torleik.

At the thought of sending Lifa packing, Torleik swallowed. He didn't like confrontations, and one with Lifa would be ugly. Perhaps if he gave her a solid reason based on her inappropriate behavior ... He must pay more attention, for Eilidh's sake if not his own.

"I'll give her one more chance, and tell her exactly why her behavior needs to change."

Hallkel nodded. "If it were me, I wouldn't even grant her that. She's been trying to wiggle into your bed since she first arrived."

"And I've managed to avoid her for two years." Torleik heaved a sigh and gave Runi another pat when he leaned against Torleik's leg. "She makes me uncomfortable when she tries to corner me, and I don't want Eilidh to worry there's something going on when there's not."

He frowned. "I'll give her one more opportunity to behave herself. That's it."

Hallkel reached for his mug of ale, his dimples on display as he smiled at his friend. "You're a fair man, Torleik. Lifa doesn't deserve such fairness."

"I guess we'll wait and see."

Torleik set his empty mug on the table and strode off to the stables to see how Maeva was doing.

As he scuffed his boots in the dirt, he hated to admit it, but perhaps Hallkel was right. Maybe he should just send Lifa packing.

20

ᚨᚱᚲᛋᛏᚷᛈᛖᛚᛟᚱᚢ

After she'd finished her midday meal, Eilidh considered defying Torleik and insisting she help with Maeva. He was out in the fields checking on his crops, and would likely be training horses after that. For a few moments, Eilidh wondered if she could accomplish the task before Torleik even noticed. She could see it in Isolf's eyes that he didn't know what else to do for the mare or her foal.

It rankled that Torleik didn't appear to trust her skills around animals. She'd never been treated in such a way before.

"Remember, ban-ogha, these people do not yet know you. Be patient."

Eilidh twisted around, searching the room for signs of her grandmother. The words had come to her as if her grandmother stood right behind her and spoke into her ear. It seemed so real. It was true then. Her Druid roots had indeed taken hold just as Grandmother had predicted. A chill raced down her spine. But why was *she* the only one being told to be patient? She took one final glance around the bedchamber she'd assumed she would share with Torleik, once he got tired of sleeping on the floor in the great hall.

Eilidh walked out onto the porch, worried that if she offered her assistance, and Torleik accepted, she had to figure out how to get the foal turned into a natural position for delivery that Isolf hadn't already tried.

Smaller hands, granddaughter.

Again, she felt a tingle, her grandmother's words as clear as if she'd spoken out loud. Grandmother Marsaili had taught her to feel confident as a healer and as a midwife. So confident, others would immediately step out of her way and allow her to do what she must. Now Torleik was keeping her away from the animals. Would he do the same with his own people, as well?

She shook her head in frustration and went back inside. She'd wait a bit longer and find something to do so she could work up her courage to confront Torleik. After two days of mostly sitting, she felt the urge to do something that used her muscles. If only Nairna was here. They'd ride for hours along the pristine sand, and into the green rolling hills, losing track of time until one of her brothers, usually Gregor, came to bring her home.

And yet, she'd signed an agreement with Torleik to become a wife who would manage his home and be a mother to Atli. She would have no more time for things she'd enjoyed back in Alba. She had adult responsibilities now. She only wished she knew what they were.

She returned to her bedchamber and eyed the trunks she'd brought with her. Now seemed as good a time as any to put things away. She lifted the cover of the first trunk. Her new gowns had already been readied by Astrid, but she knew there must be other items of clothing to put away. When she glanced around the bedchamber, she saw that the room was immaculate. Torleik was either very neat, or else Kelda cleaned up the minute he left. Eilidh tossed the rest of her clothes onto the bed to sort and fold, not one of Eilidh's favorite things to do. She wondered if she could ask Astrid to help. She really *did* want to get outside and check on Maeva.

When she heard the swish of the animal skin covering the doorway, she looked up to find Atli staring at her.

He said something in Norse. And while she couldn't yet understand the language, his facial expression made it obvious he thought she was leaving already. Eilidh couldn't help but smile at his disheveled hair, and the knees of his braies covered in mud. She gave him a welcome smile and beckoned him inside. "I have trunks to unpack today. Would you like to help?" She made a digging motion at the trunks. He nodded shyly, then stepped further inside the chamber.

When he asked another question, Eilidh decided to pretend she understood. "What's inside? Oh, mostly clothes and household goods, I think. My mother and grandmother did the packing before I left home, so I'm not quite sure. Do you want to see if they packed my horse, Nairna in there?" She made a galloping motion with her hand followed by a brief "neigh."

His eyes grew huge. "*Hest?*"

"Does *hest* mean horse in your language?"

He nodded, clearly not yet sure what to think about Eilidh and her claim of storing a horse in her travel trunk. He peeked into the first trunk, filled mostly with ladies' clothes, and made a face. *"No hest."*

Eilidh sighed. "I would have liked to bring my Nairna. I miss her already. But this is no time to be sad." She pulled the other trunk away from the wall and lifted the lid while Atli sat on his knees next to her, peering inside. She removed a few more serviceable gowns on top and set them on the bed.

After a few moments, Atli asked another question, disappointment showing on his youthful face.

"I know. Clothes are not very exciting, are they? Let's check the very bottom."

About halfway down, she felt the hard edges of her sword, wrapped tightly in several layers of linen to protect both the blade and her clothes. With reverence, Eilidh pulled it out and unwrapped it.

"You might like to see *Fitheach*."

Atli jumped up and clapped his hands together. "*Ja!*" And he said something else while holding out his sweet dirt-covered hand.

Eilidh carefully held the weapon out of reach. "This is not a toy weapon, Atli. It can do a lot of damage if you're not careful. I'll hold it and you can look, while I tell you a little story."

He seemed spellbound, so she encouraged him to sit on the floor while he stared up at her with curious blue eyes.

"My grandmother, Marsaili, was just a wee bit younger than I am now when she left her home with the Druids and traveled north to marry my grandfather Niall MacAoidh. The head Druid gave her the sword and called it *Fitheach*, which means 'raven' in Scottish Gaelic." Eilidh showed him the pommel up close. "Do you see the wings of a bird there on the hilt?" She made a flapping motion with one arm.

He peered at the design intently. After a moment, his eyes grew wide. "*Ja!*"

"That's called a raven. Do you have ravens here?"

Atli scratched his cheek for a moment, then nodded his head slowly up and down. "*Ja. Hrafin. Fadir ...*"

He chattered in Norse, for which Eilidh deduced that *hrafin* was the Norse word for raven.

Then Atli peered closer at the etched silver hilt, and pointed. "*Fadir – tveir hrafin*," he held up two fingers, then pointed to his left upper arm.

"Your father has two ravens on his arm?" Eilidh scratched her head. "I need to learn Norse soon if I want to talk to you, don't I?" She carefully wrapped *Fitheach* and set it on the bed as she wondered what Atli meant about Torleik having two ravens on his arm.

Raven had always been Eilidh's spirit guide, just as he was her grandmother's. However, she hadn't seen nor heard from him in a very long time. These recent images of ravens must mean something magical was about to happen.

The boy continued to talk for a few more moments, and Eilidh admired how at ease he was with her and her with him. More than she'd thought possible in a strange land.

With the sword covered and out of the way, Atli spied nothing else of interest in the trunk as Eilidh removed each item. When it was completely empty, he bent over the trunk's edge with a wistful sigh. "No *hest*?"

"*Ja, no hest.*" Eilidh felt miserable that she had nothing for him yet, but Hallkel had promised to whittle one and should have it to her soon. They had both decided a toy horse would be perfect for the boy. "Perhaps I can ask Hallkel if he has any horses looking for a home?" she added with a wink.

Atli jumped up and waved his little arms. "*Ja!*" He spoke rapidly, his enthusiasm obvious as he then pointed outside.

"You want to go outside and play?"

Atli pointed towards the window, and said something in Norse. She recognized the names of Stigr's young sons, Hodur and Einar. Surely, that would be okay, as she'd seen him playing with them when she first arrived. Still, she and Torleik really needed to discuss rules and guidelines for his son, both for his safety and for her peace of mind. Soon.

Eilidh nodded and pointed towards the window. "Ach, you go ahead and go, Atli." She had a feeling Atli understood more than he let on as he quickly scampered off.

Eilidh's feelings weren't the least bit hurt, as she was well aware that little boys sometimes had very short attention spans. She removed undergarments and night clothes from the first trunk and set them on the bed. Then she checked for room in the wardrobe Torleik had provided for her. Had it been his late wife's? Or was it new, intended for whomever he brought home as a new bride? As she gazed at the dancing foxes and leaping rabbits carved on the outside of the wardrobe doors, she felt a strange sense of contentment wash over her to think he'd made something so personal.

She unfolded several gowns intended for a variety of functions and set them aside, along with two pairs of what she called her "dancing shoes," though she rarely danced at festivals or other clan celebrations because of her unwillingness to learn the steps and the requirement to stand close to a male stranger. The shoes were made of soft leather, one pair in brown, the other in black. Now that she'd had a good look at her new home, she doubted she would ever need those shoes here, so stuffed them onto the floor of the wardrobe.

When she reached the bottom of the trunk, she found one last item wrapped within a soft green shawl that she knew had belonged to her grandmother. She held the wool shawl to her nose and inhaled the strong scent of roses. Eilidh couldn't remember packing this. She gingerly unwrapped the shawl to reveal two objects wrapped within another brown linen cloth. Inside, she found the strange book her grandmother had shown her before she left. The book the Goddess of the Moon had charged her with rewriting in a more sustainable format that could be passed down through the ages to Eilidh's female descendants. In a language she'd never seen or heard spoken. Bound books were extremely rare to come by, and each page needed to be copied by hand, a task usually performed by a monk, since few people could read and write. Consequently, the only books available tended to be religious in nature. Although she could read and write just fine, what could she, Eilidh, know about producing such a thing as a precious manuscript?

As she reached for the large volume and tried to maintain order with the many loose pages, a note slipped out from between the book's pages. She recognized her grandmother's familiar scrawl across a stiff piece of dried birch bark. It was written in Greek. Eilidh knew that Druids sometimes used Greek in business transactions, and so it appeared Eilidh's grandmother had done the same, perhaps as a way to keep the message private. Eilidh felt her pulse quicken as she held the note up to the light, grateful she had studied Greek with one of Padruig's tutors.

My Dear Granddaughter,

By now you will be a married woman with a ready-made family. I know that yours will be a good life full of love and contentment.

The women of our bloodline have served the Goddess of the Moon with honor.

Beginning with Saraid, my birth mother, the Goddess has asked for our assistance in forging a path that leads to improving the plight of women. She believes that once women have easier access to education, they will have greater choices in their lives, as well as having a voice in society. You must embrace and share this amazing concept: KNOWLEDGE IS POWER.

While Saraid was imprisoned, the Goddess appeared and issued her the charge of developing a language to be used solely by women to facilitate communication between women, without drawing the attention of men or others who pose a threat to the Goddess' vision. This language is the first step to educate women.

Granddaughter, it is now your time to receive a charge. The Goddess has determined you shall copy the book's contents so that it may be easily read and shared. It should be constructed of sturdier materials that will withstand the ages. In the future, our goal will be facilitated by an invention that will change the world dramatically by making printed materials more accessible to the general public, not just for the rich and privileged. For your charge, you will be allocated twelve cycles of the moon from the day you read this note, in order to produce the new book. By the time you complete your charge of copying, you will be conversant in the new language. You will utilize this new skill by teaching the language to other women in your community. They will in turn, teach it to more women, and so it continues on. You will set this project into motion, and you will have proven yourself and our bloodline to be loyal and dedicated Daughters of the Moon.

Your female ancestors will celebrate your triumph as you pass the book along to your own first female descendant to be used in conjunction with the charge given to her by the Goddess. You will know when the time is upon you.

Be advised that should you choose not to participate in this endeavor, or you do not complete it by the twelfth moonset, the original manuscript will disintegrate into dust – never to be seen again. That tragedy will deter the progress for women everywhere, and would remain a heavy weight upon your shoulders.

My dear Eilidh, please remember to be patient, kind, and creative. You have a challenging task ahead of you, but I have great faith you will succeed. I will be there by your side whenever I am needed, even if my physical body is no longer of this world. I will always have a very special love for you, ban-ogha. You are my heart.

Your Grandmother, Marsaili MacAoidh

A thickness built at the back of Eilidh's throat as she fought back tears. Only two days had passed since she'd last seen her *seanmhair*. And yet, it felt like three long winters. Eilidh refused to believe this could be her grandmother's time to move on to the Otherworld.

She gazed around at the plain bedchamber devoid of anything that could be considered cozy. No colorful rug to warm her feet when she stepped out of bed in the morning. No tapestry hanging on the walls to soften or warm the cold stone that surrounded her. The window had no glass nor shutters, just a fur covering to lift and lower. There was nothing present to even hint at a lady's presence in the home, neither personal objects nor lingering feminine scents. She guessed she shouldn't be too surprised at that, since Torleik's wife hadn't lived to see *Orkneyjar*.

The ache of loneliness continued to block her throat. "I will not cry. *Seanmhair* would be so disappointed."

She re-read the contents of the message, her stomach muscles clenching. "I must complete this project in one year. Oh, my Lord." She thumbed through the cumbersome volume and shook her head. "How am I to do as she asks? I know nothing of this language. How can I faithfully reproduce words I do not understand? How can I find paper that will last?" She placed the message on the bedside table, then sat and slumped in her chair.

After allowing herself a few moments to feel miserable, Eilidh sucked in her breath and started back to work with her trunks, certain the answers would come to her eventually. She set the empty trunk at the foot of the bed for now, as it could be used for extra blankets and pillows, or clothes that could be folded. She then focused on the second trunk, which she knew her mother had packed. When she opened that trunk, a waft of meadowsweet teased her nose, making her smile. Her mother loved having all the linens smell clean.

By late afternoon, Eilidh had unpacked and put away everything she'd brought with her. Her clothes, shoes, cloaks and shawls filled the wardrobe nicely, leaving room in the trunks for the few personal items she'd brought, a hand mirror and a small box for hair clips and her brooches. Her mother had also packed a few rugs and wall hangings, which came as a pleasant surprise. Eilidh set those items on the trunk at the foot of the bed, wanting to think about how she could use them to enhance the chamber for another time – when she was feeling creative.

She hugged herself and smiled at her accomplishments. Her eyes slid to the large, down-filled bed.

It would do Eilidh no good to dream about a life with Torleik as a happily married couple. He'd stated his terms, and so had she.

There was no turning back now.

Just then, she heard footsteps racing toward her room. She stuck her head outside the opening in time to see Isolf huffing and puffing as he came forward.

"You must hurry, Miss! Maeva is about to deliver but something's wrong. You must come now!"

21

ᚨᚱᚲᛊᛏᚷᚹᛗᛚᛟᚺ

As Eilidh raced towards the stable with Isolf in the lead, she came upon Astrid, who was busy weeding the kitchen garden.

Astrid straightened and stood with a spade in one hand as she brushed back strands of blonde hair escaping the scarf she wore. "You want to see garden?"

"I must check on Maeva first," she told Astrid. "We can talk about the garden later."

"*Ja*, Hallkel says Maeva not doing well." Astrid waved a hand. "You go now. Poor Maeva."

Eilidh huffed a sigh. "I don't understand why Torleik hasn't let me help her before now." She paused for only a moment to catch her breath. "He's so stubborn. I can't seem to make him understand I would never harm his brood mare."

"Some men insist they do everything themselves. Then no one else to blame when they are wrong."

"You mean, not because he doesn't trust me?"

At that, Astrid grinned broadly, her smile lighting up her whole face. "I think not. He must get to know you, then all will be good. You go and help Maeva." She pointed towards the stable where Isolf was waiting impatiently.

With a nod, Eilidh raced to join him but he had already entered the stable. She spotted Isolf standing outside of Maeva's stall, hands on hips as he stared ahead with a grim expression. As Eilidh approached, she sensed tension.

"Maeva still hasn't delivered? She's been in labor since this morning. If it's a breech birth, every moment counts."

Isolf nodded and let out a huge breath, clearly relieved she was there. In contrast to Torleik, Isolf sported a short dark beard, unusual for Norsemen, but not unattractive on Isolf. However, the poor man looked like he hadn't slept in a long while. Dark smudges beneath his eyes let Eilidh know just how serious he was taking this.

She watched Maeva struggle to get up, the poor mother heaving for a few moments. She then lay down again, as if her strength was waning.

"She's suffering," Eilidh said, biting her lower lip.

"*Ja*. I think so as well."

After a few moments, Eilidh asked the obvious questions. "Have you tried to reposition the foal with your hands?"

Isolf pressed his lips together and shook his head. "My hands ... too big. Maeva not appreciate that attempt." He glanced down at Eilidh's hands, then rubbed his chin.

Eilidh knelt by Maeva and gently ran her hands over the horse's distended belly. The mare grunted, but didn't move. Eilidh could feel the foal moving inside, but its movements were sluggish.

"There's not much time left, Isolf. The foal is getting tired, and so is Maeva. She put her ear against the horse's chest for a moment. "Her breathing is becoming more labored." Eilidh stepped back, pondering what could be done. "I know Torleik said he didn't want me to do anything for Maeva, but if we wait, he will lose both mother *and* foal." She held out her hands. "I can turn the foal. I've done it before."

Isolf nodded, new hope showing in his eager expression. "*Ja.* That might work."

"Where is Torleik? Why isn't he here?" She looked around, hands on hips, as anger built inside for her husband. Would he truly allow such suffering? If so, he wasn't the man she hoped she'd married.

Isolf shrugged. "He was called to help fix water trough in the far pasture. I sent Brusi to fetch him, but they not yet returned. Should wait?"

Maeva struggled to stand once again, her stomach heaving.

Eilidh made a decision. "No, we can't wait. If something happens, Torleik can blame me. I'm going to turn the foal with my hands. You may need someone to help hold her still."

"I will go find Eskil, Stigr's nephew."

"And send someone to bring Kelda – just in case."

"*Ja.* I will do that, mistress." Isolf took off, leaving Eilidh alone with the mare.

Daily sounds of horses' whinneys and other passing voices slid into the background as Eilidh ran her hand down Maeva's neck, crooning soothing words into her ears. The mare seemed to calm a bit despite the pain she must be experiencing. Eilidh began singing in a low voice and Maeva turned her head to gaze at her, her eyes no longer wide with fear. She snorted softly.

"I will help you with your little one, Maeva. And both of you will be fine. I promise."

The straw rustled. "You shouldn't make promises you may not be able to keep." Torleik stood behind her.

Eilidh didn't bother looking up, just continued caressing Maeva's head and neck. "Isolf went for help. I'm going to turn the foal around to the proper spot so Maeva can have a regular delivery. I refuse to watch her suffer anymore."

Torleik stepped into the stall and knelt, running his hand over Maeva's belly. He straightened, then sighed. "I agree. We cannot wait any longer. This is not going to fix itself like I'd hoped it would."

Still miffed from his treatment earlier, Eilidh had to ask the question. "Did you tell me to stay away from Maeva because you don't trust my skills with your horses? Is that why you wouldn't accept my help the first time?"

Torleik stood on the other side of the horse from Eilidh, head down. "It's not you. I—"

"I brought help!" Isolf appeared with Eskil and Kelda, who thankfully carried supplies she may need.

"Thank you. I think it's best you stay back for the moment. Too many people in her stall at one time may frighten Maeva."

Torleik glanced at Eilidh and gave an abrupt nod that she should continue to take charge.

She knelt beside the horse and resumed softly singing a Gaelic tune from her childhood. After a few moments had passed and Maeva had stopped struggling, Eilidh washed her hands and arms up to her elbows with soap in the basin of water Kelda provided. She dried them on clean linens, then spread butter on her hands and forearms to help them slide inside the horse easier.

"All right," she said, inhaling deeply. "Let's get this baby delivered."

Isolf remained kneeling at Maeva's head. He held her, keeping up a low stream of soothing Norse words. Torleik steadied the mare's hind end as he watched Eilidh slowly and gently work her right hand up into the birth canal. Maeva gave a loud snort, her eyes growing huge. Eilidh paused to give the mare a moment. She tried inserting her hand, and as soon as Maeva settled, she pushed on further, searching for the foal. Shocked when a sudden contraction clamped onto her arm, Eilidh yelped at the stabbing pain that gripped her arm like a vice. Maeva, typically a pleasant light gray mare, turned her head and made a loud, lowing sound, like a cow at milking time.

Eilidh felt her eyes cross at the pain. Maeva produced a deep moan that vibrated everywhere. When she looked the mare in the eye, Eilidh could see the terror. Or was it her own fear mirrored through glassy eyes? She removed her hand, and gave her arm a quick examination as she checked for bruising. Satisfied that her arm wasn't bleeding, she spoke to the mare quietly. "We don't have much time now. I have to get your baby out with the next contraction. Will you help me?"

She cleaned her hand and arm once more with soap and water. After using another clean cloth to dry her hand, she stuck her arm inside to determine where and how the foal was presenting. Once again, a huge contraction gripped her and locked her in place. For moments, nothing happened. Eilidh squeezed her eyes shut, refusing to complain. But this contraction went on and on.

"Aaaaaaa!" Eilidh lashed out and gripped Torleik's hand. "I can't move until she relaxes her muscles." Eilidh began to sweat as the pain lanced through her arm.

Torleik ran his hands down the mare's back, sleek with sweat, and murmured something. Maeva responded by perking her ears forward, a good sign she was listening to his voice because her contractions began to relax.

Dismissing the pain in her arm, Eilidh tried to move further inside, still searching for a leg to get her bearings. After several moments had passed, she felt beads of perspiration gather on her forehead.

Nothing.

A hoof, a nose, anything. Then, she had the horrible sensation of Maeva's heart beginning to slow. Eilidh grimaced and tried again.

"Eilidh?" Torleik's voice broke the silence. "Her breathing …"

"I'm aware."

Maeva panted heavily now, eyes bulging as she struggled with a contraction that again pressed down on Eilidh's arm with great force. After a few more moments with no success, Eilidh's shoulders slumped as she began to doubt her abilities.

A rustle of clothing announced Kelda had come to sit behind her shoulder.

"The foal's head is facing the wrong way," Eilidh said, grunting in effort. "I need to push the baby back into the belly, so I have room to turn it into the proper position for delivery. But every time she has a contraction, I'm stuck and can't move my arm."

Torleik translated her words for Kelda and Isolf, and Eilidh felt grateful for the old woman's calming presence and vast experience.

"You're doing fine," said Kelda, her voice reminding Eilidh of Grandmother Marsaili.

Renewed, Eilidh focused on her task, trying not to cause more pain for the mare or herself as she whispered words of encouragement. And for herself, *Goddess, please help me perform this miracle.*

All of a sudden, Eilidh braced herself against Maeva's flank and took slow, calming breaths. Maeva had just finished a strong contraction and Eilidh couldn't move her arm any further.

"Keep trying. You're almost there," Kelda whispered over her shoulder.

"I can't move my hand, and I'm stuck," said Eilidh, trying not to panic.

"Can you pull your hand back out?" asked Torleik, reaching to steady her shoulder while Isolf and Eskil held on tightly to Maeva to lessen her struggle.

Eilidh's chest tightened, her head began to spin. "I don't know. I'm not sure."

"Don't risk harming yourself," said Torleik, his voice replacing Kelda's right behind her. "If I must choose between you or the horses ... I choose you."

His words felt strangely comforting. Torleik and the others might be encouraging, but Eilidh knew she was in trouble, causing her to scream when Maeva's eyes rolled back in her head.

If only her grandmother were here to make her feel strong. *Seanmhair, guide my hands*.

Kelda had returned to hunch down just to Eilidh's right, while Torleik sat behind her, holding Eilidh around the waist and acting as a physical support. That way she wouldn't need to lean on Maeva unnecessarily, and would be there to help her pull the foal out if it suddenly emerged. Her arms trembled from the effort, and sweat dripped down into her eyes. Suddenly, the contraction ended, and Eilidh's hands found more space to move.

In her head, an hourglass of sand trickled down the moments left of Maeva's life.

Kelda wiped the dampness from Eilidh's forehead with a kerchief. "Can you feel the position of both legs now?"

After a few moments, Eilidh felt her head clear and her breathing slow. "Aye! I've got one."

Kelda's voice was soothing, a balm that eased the tension Eilidh had been fighting.

"Make sure the legs are relatively close together. As Maeva's belly contracts, you will have a bit more room to work. Pull gently on one leg, rotating the foal's body. Eventually, the foal's hindquarters should appear, and then you should be able to perform the delivery. Maeva will work with you," Kelda said with an edge of finality. "Hurry now. We're out of time, Eilidh."

Maeva's grunting and groaning, much like a human mother, broke the tense silence.

Eilidh tried not to think about her arm and the bruising that would be left behind. Nor to think about the fact that her stomach felt heavy, like a giant, hard pit rested in the center. She could not fail at this, or no one would trust her as a healer or midwife in her new home. *No room for mistakes or disasters.*

Slowly but surely, Eilidh felt the foal turn into a more natural position on its own. Even Maeva seemed to heave a big sigh of relief as Eilidh removed her hands and reached for the cloths Torleik had moistened with fresh water and handed her.

"She's ready now," said Eilidh, wiping her hands and arms thoroughly. "Isolf, could you please take over? My arms are trembling." She stepped out of the way, fatigue setting off her emotions. She was beginning to feel moisture gathering in the corners of her eyes, but it was for a happy reason this time.

"I would be glad to," said Isolf, looking eager now. He took her place next to the mare's hind end, with Torleik assisting.

Using arms much stronger than hers, Isolf completed the delivery with no further complications. "A filly!" he announced as he pulled out a light gray, speckled foal.

"Welcome to the world, wee one," said Eilidh, reveling in the warmth that spread throughout her at the presence of new life. "Now, Eskil, you just had the most wonderful opportunity to see how life is ... Eskil?"

She found him in the far corner, passed out in the straw from the sight of so much blood.

"Oh, dear. I guess Eskil didn't handle that birth as well as I'd hoped," she said to the others. "Maybe next time."

Eskil stirred and sat up. "There won't be a next time. He rubbed his head where he must have hit it on the floor. "I mean no disrespect, mistress, but if you ever need help in delivering a baby ... of any sort ... please ask someone else. I will remember that image for the rest of my life."

Laughter filled the stall at Eskil's expense, but he took it well. Then, Eilidh shooed out those who had no need to remain. Torleik, Isolf and Hallkel, who had just joined them, spent several moments congratulating each other on the filly's birth by backslapping each other.

Men. Eilidh would never understand them.

As she stood admiring the new mother and foal, she happened to glance at her husband. She wanted to ask if she'd proven herself to him, if he would trust her in the future. This was a perfect example of things that mattered to Eilidh – very much. Torleik needed to understand that, if they were ever to become true partners in life.

"Could you walk with me for a few moments?" Torleik held out an arm for her to take. While Atli and the girls tiptoed into the stall to see the foal under Maeva's watchful eyes, Eilidh joined him in the corridor that separated the stalls.

Before he could speak, Eilidh asserted herself. "I'm glad I was here to help. Maeva and I will be good friends now."

Torleik grinned. "I'll bet you're right. She may be the one bringing *you* carrots as treats."

Eilidh laughed, feeling the release of her previous tension. "So you're not mad at me for disobeying?"

"I wanted to finish my apology from before." Torleik stopped near the deserted kitchen garden and looked down at his boots. "It's true that I place a great value on the horses I'm raising and breeding, but it was *you* I was trying to spare. I didn't wish to put you through a difficult birthing so soon after the handfast."

Eilidh shrugged. "But that's the sort of thing I do on a regular basis. I'm not a weak and frail woman, Torleik. I'm a skilled healer and midwife. My grandmother made sure of that, so I could carry on the family tradition ... wherever I might end up."

His face remained impassive, but his voice indicated emotion as he cleared his throat. "I understand that now. I'm sorry I doubted your strength of will. I worry about losing even one horse, not just because of its potential value if sold, but because

I raise them from the time they are born. They are my children, I guess you could say."

Eilidh wanted to lay a hand on his too-somber face and kiss his warm lips. Instead, she placed her hand on the side of the water well outside the kitchen door. "There is one thing I would like to say. This event made me realize I need to learn Norse more quickly. Could you teach me, so I can communicate easier with Atli, Kelda and the others?"

Rather than show surprise, Torleik appeared thoughtful. "I would be a terrible teacher, and we could end up hating each other."

She couldn't help but laugh. "I'm sure that's not true."

He shrugged his well-muscled shoulders. "I wouldn't want to take that chance. However, I will ask Hallkel. He is excellent at that sort of thing. He has taught Atli quite a bit of Gaelic. I will ask Hallkel tonight about providing you with Norse lessons."

Eilidh considered his suggestion. "Hallkel does make a good storyteller, and appears to have a great deal of patience. Aye, I would be pleased to have him teach me Norse, if he is willing. Thank you."

"I shall arrange for your lessons the next time I see him."

She slapped her forehead as she recalled her other priority. "Hallkel! I must talk to him right away. Do you know where he is? I must ask if he has finished carving that wooden toy horse I promised Atli."

For once, Torleik gazed at her as if she were the most amazing woman in the world, his eyes appearing a much darker shade of blue.

Eilidh felt her legs quiver.

"I'll take you to his quarters and you can ask him yourself."

He held out his hand, and she slid hers inside his, happier than she'd been in a long time.

22

ᚨᚱᚲᛋᛏᚷᚹᛖᛚᛜᛒᚢ

Still feeling emotional after the arduous birth experience, Eilidh was glad Torleik asked Hallkel to join them at their midday meal where he secretly handed her the wooden horse he had been carving for Atli. She tucked it into the folds of her gown, waiting for the perfect opportunity to present it to him.

In the meantime, Hallkel joined them in celebration of the birth of a healthy filly. Her body sagged in relief knowing that she'd had a hand in saving the mare and its foal. If she had failed in her mission, she would be enduring the unbridled enmity of everyone here. Instead, she was enjoying the dry humor in Hallkel's responses to Atli's many questions. For Hallkel's part, he exhibited not only a great sense of humor, but extreme patience. As Hallkel spoke in his unhurried style, she studied his craggy features and mannerisms and came to the conclusion he seemed more like an older brother or uncle to her husband than simply a friend. Torleik may not have other family members in *Orkneyjar*, but it appeared he considered Hallkel a member of his family, which pleased her considerably. Hallkel was clearly a good influence, with his calm demeanor and ability to address her husband's stubborn streak without raising his voice. She could learn from him.

Excited at the prospect of giving Atli the *hest* he had so wanted, Eilidh then turned her attention to the meal set before them of roasted salmon, a bowl of vegetables that included chopped turnips, peas, and onions mixed together. All of it roasted with butter and seasonings. Another bowl was filled with fresh uncooked cabbage and carrots from Astrid's garden, accompanied by a special sweet sauce made from honey and ginger. As always, fresh bread and butter graced the table on two platters. The men dug in, as they typically worked hard outdoors, and needed to be fortified for the afternoon.

After adding selections to her plate, Eilidh took a bite of salmon and groaned with pleasure. She couldn't recall ever tasting anything quite so delicate and flaky or so wonderful. Hopefully, the meal would give her the energy to attack the Goddess project. As the two men conversed in low tones about grain crops, her thoughts drifted to her need to become better acquainted with the workers. Before that, she should address the cook, Siv, and complement her on a truly fine meal. Salmon was common in *Alba*, so it felt like a bit of home, but she'd never tasted salmon prepared quite like this.

While the men continued their discussion, Eilidh entertained herself and Atli by playing a word game. She would point to an item on the table and say the word for it in Gaelic. Atli would respond by repeating her word, then saying the equivalent word in Norse. Every now and then, Atli would giggle at her Norse pronunciation. Torleik would look up and smile, then return to his conversation.

At the end of the meal, Eilidh rose from the table, stuffed. She lifted Atli down from his perch atop the stack of cloths. "I have something for you," she told Atli, "but first, you need to close your eyes."

He did as asked. "What is it?" he said, bouncing up and down on his toes.

"You'll see." She removed the horse from the large hidden pocket within the folds of her skirt and laid it in his hands. "Okay, you may open them now."

When he saw what lay in his hands, his eyes went wide and his mouth formed a huge smile. "Can I show it to Einar and Hodur? Please, please?"

By now, Eilidh knew he meant Stigr's two youngest boys, but she didn't feel comfortable telling him what he could and couldn't do with Torleik sitting right there.

Thankfully, Torleik glanced at his son. "*Ja*. But behave and come in when I call, and don't come inside covered with mud. Understand?"

Atli nodded emphatically, then raced outside.

Eilidh sighed as Torleik turned back to continue his discussion with Hallkel, but not before he offered her a wide smile. Happy to see both son and father content, she turned her attention to the food and her idea to complement Siv. Spoken words might be minimal between them, but wasn't the language of food something they should all have in common?

Eilidh rose from her seat and approached the kitchen, smiling brightly. "Siv, excuse me, but I wanted to tell you how much I enjoyed your meal."

Siv paused at the sink at the sound of her name. Her head swiveled and a frown made her look old and mean, her body tensed, as if for battle.

Shocked by Siv's reaction, Eilidh froze as she took stock of the short, stocky woman. She tended to wear dark and somber colors, making Eilidh wonder if she was a recent widow. But she would never ask about such a personal matter, having just made someone's acquaintance. Eilidh forced a smile she didn't feel, attempting to appear friendly. "I also wanted to ask which spices or seasonings you used with the roasted vegetables?" Eilidh spoke slowly in Scottish Gaelic and gestured as she had with Stigr, hoping Siv would get the idea. Eilidh pointed to a bowl holding leftover vegetables and pointed to her own wide smile to demonstrate her appreciation. When the cook held up her palms and shrugged, Eilidh realized she didn't understand.

A movement in the corner caught Eilidh's eye, and she turned her head to find Lifa scraping a pot. She didn't remember seeing Lifa enter the house, but she supposed Kelda or Siv had asked for her assistance in cleaning up after the meal. Although Lifa's head was down, Eilidh knew she was listening.

Siv then said something in Norse to Lifa, causing her to look up from her chore and regard Eilidh with a sullen expression, eyes narrowed.

In broken, but serviceable Gaelic, Lifa translated. "Siv say onions, garlic, marjoram are seasonings for vegetables."

"I see." She nodded to the cook. "Thank you, *taak*, Siv."

Although she couldn't see Lifa's aura in the dim light, Eilidh sensed something about the dark-haired young woman that felt sly and dishonest. Like she was hiding something dark and evil. But until Eilidh had proof, there appeared to be no point in disciplining or firing her – as long as she performed her job adequately. It was very likely Lifa needed the job, like everyone else on the island.

Eilidh started to ask Siv another question, but the woman of perhaps fifty winters stared at her with a hostile expression. She whispered something to Lifa, who didn't respond right away.

"What did Siv say?" Eilidh disliked that she had to ask for Lifa's help.

Siv set down the linen towel she'd used to dry a pot, carefully folding it into a square, while muttering more words in Norse. She was clearly upset about something.

Lifa gave Eilidh a smug look. "Siv say she has too much to do, so go away."

Eilidh's brows shot up at the defiance in Lifa's voice. But before she said the first thing that came to mind, she caught herself, not wanting to give Lifa the satisfaction of letting her emotions spin out of control. "Somehow, Lifa, I very much doubt those were Siv's exact words." She regarded the older woman and gave a brief nod. "I will leave you to your work. Again, *taak*, Siv. Your efforts are greatly appreciated. I will speak with you at another time that is more convenient for you."

Siv seemed to understand that well enough, as she didn't look to Lifa for translation, and bobbed her head. Maybe Astrid could tell Eilidh why the head cook had treated her with such disdain.

Eilidh didn't bother to glance at Lifa as she headed out the back door. She immediately spotted Astrid in the kitchen garden and headed straight for a friendly face.

Astrid looked up from her hoeing. "Good afternoon, mistress."

Her Gaelic was more precise today, making Eilidh curious. "How did you learn Gaelic, Astrid? Did someone teach you?"

The other woman's beautiful skin, tanned and glowing from time spent outdoors, actually turned a rosy color.

Eilidh bit her lip. Had she asked something improper?

Astrid shrugged and leaned on her hoe as she struggled to stand. "Hallkel lived in *Thjorsá* for a while, few years past. He learned Gaelic while there. When he came here, he taught Torleik and me, when I ask."

Eilidh nodded. Things started making sense. "But, why was Hallkel living in *Thjorsá*? I thought he came with Torleik from *Nord Vegr* to settle *here*."

Astrid knelt once again, digging at weeds that had popped up with all the rain they'd had recently. "Ah, *ja*. That is true. But

Hallkel marry a young woman who lived in *Thjorsá*, so he go live there. They have pretty little girl."

Eilidh inhaled deeply. This was not going to have a happy ending. "I didn't know that. What happened to the wife and daughter?"

Astrid straightened and stared down at her hands covered in dirt. "A sickness came. Both mother and child died. Torleik find out, and he go to help his friend, Hallkel – bring him back here." She gazed off in the distance, exhaling a sigh.

It was obvious that Astrid had feelings for Hallkel. So, why were they not together?

Astrid turned to Eilidh and shrugged. "Hallkel is better now, not so much pain, I think. But some days, not so good. My girls and I ... we try to cheer him with other things, like music and dancing when there is something to celebrate, sometimes offer him a good meal in return for his songs on fiddle. He is good storyteller, too."

Eilidh nodded. That explained some things she'd noticed. Hallkel could be alert and engaged in a conversation one moment, then seem to float off into another world the next. And, oddly, she felt proud knowing that Torleik was looking out for his friend.

Perhaps she could help move along Hallkel and Astrid's relationship.

"Mistress Eilidh? Did I say something funny? You smile so big," said Astrid.

Eilidh caught herself and waved a hand, embarrassed. "Ach, just thinking about life – the good and the bad we all experience." She started to turn away but then recalled her reason for seeking Astrid's company. "Do you know why Siv is so...?" She paused, unsure what to say without sounding rude.

"Big grump?" Astrid inserted.

Eilidh's shoulders drooped. "Precisely!"

"She has a grown son she not see for many, many months. He is off on Crusade with Earl Rögnvald until who knows when?

He may be our jarl, but why take Siv's boy so far away? It be three years now. She worries something happens to son. He could die of sickness, of which there is much of in those lands. There are also many bad men in that part of world." Astrid shrugged her shoulders. "Lifa is constantly in her ear, which does not help. I don't know what she says, but I think it bad."

Eilidh digested that news. She paused and considered being nicer to Siv. "And how about you, Astrid?" Eilidh realized immediately this may be a sore topic. "Oh, I am so sorry. If you don't want to talk about it ..."

Astrid shrugged again, her mouth turning up at the corners. "Is okay to ask. It be many years now. She counted on her fingers. "Three years. When Dagny was three, her father was working on the new cathedral in *Kirkjuvagr*. There was accident, and he died." She waved her hands around her, as if he'd slipped into the air. "I wander all over town, looking for work, and Torleik see me and girls. He hired me right there, and we be here many years now. *Ja*, Hallkel took pity on me and teach me Gaelic to keep me distracted from my grief." She chuckled. "Every once in a while, I meet someone like you, and I can practice my Gaelic so I don't forget."

"Well, I'm the lucky one. You can practice on me anytime." Eilidh pressed her new friend's forearm gently. "I am so sorry to hear about your husband. On the other hand, I'm so glad you're here."

Astrid nodded once. "I am grateful to be alive, and grateful to have met you, mistress."

Moved by her heartfelt honesty, Eilidh glanced around the clearing. From where they stood next to the garden plot, the farmyard was surprisingly empty and quiet, except for squabbling ducks and geese over at the small natural pond. The usual.

Eilidh gestured toward the house. "I have a project I must work on this afternoon, so I need to go inside. Thanks for ... the useful information," she added in farewell.

As she approached the main entrance, she stopped and scratched her head. How awful for Astrid and the girls. Perhaps that was why Hallkel was going so slowly. They both had a lot to overcome. It reminded her that time was precious. It also reminded her that time was slipping away for any translation of her grandmother's book.

Eilidh couldn't suppress the long sigh at the thought of spending more time going over her great grandmother's *Book of Delsiran*. She'd already spent a morning examining each page, from beginning to end, but still had trouble with the strange words.

Eilidh shivered at the thought of disappointing the Goddess. Or worse, her grandmother.

23

ᚠᚱᚲᛊᛏᚷᛒᛗᛚᛟᚾᚢ

As the days passed since the handfast, Eilidh settled into a routine, starting each day by trying to make sense of Saraid's strange book. She had spread everything out on the dining table in the center of the longhouse and closest to the community fire pit so she could see where the pieces might fit, when Torleik entered the longhouse. Since it was well before the midday meal, she wondered if something else had happened with Lifa. Eilidh still wasn't certain why Siv had treated her so badly. After all, Eildh wasn't responsible for the danger Siv's son was in. Perhaps she hadn't slept well and was just having a bad day. Or more likely, Lifa had been telling the cook lies about Eilidh in an attempt to win Siv to her side. No, surely even Lifa wouldn't stoop that low.

Eilidh reached up to work out the knotted muscles in her neck, noting the grim expression on her husband's face as he approached. She instinctively shuffled the pages so they couldn't be seen, recalling her grandmother's instructions. Although, not that many here seemed able to read, from what Eilidh could tell.

"What are you working on there?"

She had anticipated the question, so had prepared an answer that was truthful – more or less. "I'm working on one of my grandmother's projects ... regarding herbs. I told her I would do this if I had time."

Oddly, she wondered how Torleik could appear more handsome than usual, his hands in the pockets of his work clothes, his face smudged with dirt.

"I see," he said politely. "Looks like a lot of work. Perhaps you could use a break? Come walk with me ... please?" Torleik held out a hand, so she couldn't refuse.

Why was he acting so strangely? He'd been avoiding her since they arrived on the island. She'd actually become comfortable with the arrangement.

Although she didn't take his hand, she nodded her agreement to walk with him. "Let me just put this out of the way so Kelda can set the table." Thankful that Torleik seemed preoccupied and didn't ask more about her "project," she placed the pile of pages made from dried bark carefully inside a trunk in the bedchamber and then followed Torleik outside.

As they chose a worn path that took them beyond the north-facing workers' huts, they came to a pleasant spot situated at the foot of gently sloping hills and graced by three mature aspen trees. She'd spotted the small grove from the yard below, but Eilidh hadn't found the time to climb the hill. She looked up and shaded her eyes. The tallest and oldest aspen *could* make a fine wisdom tree, and it was close to the longhouse. *Seanmhair* once told her that any spell of protection could be enhanced if performed near an aspen tree. Eilidh reached out to touch the white bark with reverence, her heart singing with the acknowledgment of a whisper.

She came to attention when Torleik cleared his throat.

He looked down and shuffled a foot. "I need to speak to you about something I was told recently."

Eilidh felt her bubble of happiness burst, quickly followed by a sick feeling. "What were you told?"

Torleik didn't look at her. "I received a complaint from Siv and Lifa that you were rude and interrupted Siv's work after the meal the other night. Siv was so busy that she became flustered by your appearance in the kitchen, and had to ask Lifa to translate."

Eilidh felt like she'd been punched in the stomach, her cheeks growing hot. Careful not to lose her temper, she straightened her shoulders and looked him in the eye. "Who complained? Lifa or Siv?"

"Does it matter?"

"Of course it does." She looked out to the expanse of sea and thought back. "I was trying to compliment Siv on the wonderful meal she'd prepared, thinking it a good approach to become better acquainted. I made the assumption she understood a little Gaelic, but if she does, she didn't let on. Lifa stepped in and translated for her. As I'm sure you know by now, anytime Lifa is involved, the situation winds up a mess." Eilidh looked up at the quivering aspen leaves above. "I don't know what Lifa told Siv, but according to Lifa, the cook was busy and she wanted me to leave her kitchen. They were both quite rude to me. And you have the nerve to confront *me*?"

Torleik gritted his teeth. "That sounds like Lifa. Siv would not normally be so rude." He exhaled and placed a hand on a tree trunk. "Kelda told me Siv was nervous about making a perfect meal for us on our first night together. In addition, her son is in harm's way. Perhaps that's all it is.

"I was trying to show her my appreciation for all her hard work!" Eilidh shook her head, then winced at the pain that had started in her temples. "To be sure I offended no one, I ended the conversation by telling Siv I was sorry for interrupting her, and that I would speak to her when she wasn't so busy. She seemed to understand that part just fine because she curtsied before I left." Eilidh trembled at the accusation and wrapped her arms around her middle. "Your servants are not too keen on people who are different from them, are they? Is it my fault my father is clan chief?"

Torleik heaved another sigh. "*Nei*. Of course not. It sounds like a miscommunication with too much Lifa mixed in to stir things up."

"What can we do about Lifa?" She bit her lip, uncertain whether she should broach the subject of Lifa's behavior toward Atli. "I was alarmed when I saw her trying to befriend Atli the other day. I worry that she's trying to drive a wedge between us."

Torleik's ice blue eyes narrowed. "I don't want you to worry. It's funny, Atli never mentioned running into her. I wonder why."

Eilidh swallowed, recalling how Torleik's son had responded to Lifa's overtures at the dinner the other evening. And she had seen him playing with the new kittens in the barn when she had delivered the foal the other day. "Lifa appeared, but Atli wanted nothing to do with her. He came to me right away when I entered the stall."

Torleik came to attention. "That is good. He may be young, but I think my son has fine instincts about people and animals."

Frustrated by Lifa's attempts to oust her from the community, Eilidh focused her attention on the rustling leaves and clear blue sky of a bright summer day.

Only moments later, the silence was broken by the sound of Eskil, the new stable lad, racing towards them, hands waving. "Mistress! Mistress! You must come right away!"

Any thought of spending time with her sacred wisdom tree today vanished when she heard Stigr's nephew call out.

"What's the matter?" Eilidh asked, heart pounding. The last time she'd received such an urgent plea, Maeva had been in danger of a breech birth.

Eskil leaned his hands on his knees and blew out a series of short breaths for a few moments. Back in control, he straightened.

"Brusi was kicked by a horse in the blacksmith's shop. His leg is hurt, so Uncle Stigr sent me to find you. Can you come now?"

Although her heart continued pounding like a drum inside her chest, Eilidh forced herself to remain calm. "I'll need to get my medicine bag, and then I'll be right there."

Eskil nodded and returned to the blacksmith shop with Torleik, while Eilidh made a dash for the longhouse. She quickly retrieved her sack, added a few fresh herbal mixes, then dashed across the farmyard.

As Eilidh approached Stigr's shop near the back of the barn, she recalled the last time she'd seen young Brusi. He'd been playing a stick game with his two younger brothers, Hodur and Einar. All three boys had been blessed with their father's vibrant red hair and freckles. Just the thought of Brusi injured and in pain forced her to focus her attention.

She made her way through a small crowd of workers and their children, who'd come to see what had happened. Off in a corner of the blacksmith's workshop, she saw Torleik holding the reins of a skittish horse that must have been the culprit. Stigr, a big and burly man whom she'd seen playing with his boys on occasion, knelt beside Brusi on the ground, who moaned and squeezed his eyes shut at the pain.

Once he spotted Eilidh, Stigr moved out of her way and pointed to the boy's shin. "The horse kicked Brusi in the leg. Is it broken?"

Eilidh knelt to take a closer look at the wound. As she ran her hands gently up and down the leg between knee and ankle, Brusi tried not to cry out. A deep purple bruise had already formed, accompanied by a large bump. Eilidh sat back on her knees.

"I don't think it's broken. I feel no bones moving where they shouldn't be, and the skin looks like a deep bruise, which may take a while to heal. I can help reduce the swelling with a poultice, and then we might have a better look." She glanced back at Torleik, wondering why he didn't take the nervous horse outside to give them more room. "I must return to the house to assemble what I need for the poultice. Meanwhile, take Brusi to your home and make him comfortable. I will come there as soon as the poultice is ready. Do not allow Brusi to walk on that leg, for now."

Torleik repeated Eilidh's instructions in Norse to make sure Stigr understood. The worried father nodded, and was carefully lifting the boy when a very pregnant woman pushed her way through the crowd.

"What happened to Brusi?"

Stigr said something to calm her, then motioned to Eilidh. Valdis seemed to take in what her husband was saying, and nodded to Eilidh as they quickly left with the boy.

Torleik took the horse outside, then returned and watched as Eilidh put away her medical tools.

The onlookers had disbursed, thankfully. She paused in the doorway, noticing that Torleik's thoughts seemed far away as he gazed into space.

She looked around and saw the horse that had done the damage tied to a railing outside the stable. "Was that one of your horses that kicked Brusi? The horse doesn't look familiar."

Torleik raked a hand through his blond hair. "No. That's the first thing I checked. I have no idea where he came from or how he got here and into the blacksmith's work area, but he's not one of mine. I haven't had a chance to ask Stigr how he ended up here." He glanced out the door. "I can put him into an empty stall for now. Maybe someone will claim him."

Eilidh had a feeling no one would dare, if mischief had been the goal.

She hurried to the longhouse to make sure she had all the ingredients for the poultice. Unfortunately, she would need to use the kitchen. She breathed a sigh, thankful neither Siv nor Lifa were there. Instead of thinking bad thoughts about either woman for the complaints to her husband, she turned her frustration to assembling the necessary ingredients. First, she chopped comfrey roots and leaves, combined them in water for heating, then created a paste she spread onto a clean linen cloth. She stored the extra paste in a jar and placed that in her medicine bag, along with a jar containing dried willow bark. When she felt satisfied with the thickness of the paste, she rolled it up and wrapped it inside a cloth, securing it tightly.

Kelda, who had stayed in her hut to rest that morning, shuffled into the kitchen from outside, her eyes widening when she saw Eilidh.

"Kelda! I'm glad to see you're up. I hope you're feeling better?"

Kelda smiled weakly and nodded. "I am fine. Just getting older every day and in need of more rest. What are you doing with that poultice? I smell comfrey, *ja?*"

Eilidh suddenly recalled that Kelda had been Torleik's healer. Still was. "Aye, comfrey. Brusi was kicked in the leg by a horse. His shin is badly bruised and has a large lump, but I don't think he's broken any bones. I thought I'd start with this poultice. I can leave a jar of salve containing calendula with Valdis, as well as willow bark for tea, to manage the pain."

Kelda nodded again. "It is good to have another healer here. I fear my remaining days are not many. I will rest peacefully knowing Torleik's family will have you here to take care of them."

A pang of guilt shot through Eilidh. Would she still be here?

Kelda turned and walked slowly by the fire pit to warm herself.

Eilidh whispered a prayer to the Goddess to watch over Kelda while she placed the wrapped poultice in her bag. She then made sure the jars were packed so they wouldn't spill or break.

As Eilidh hurried out to find Stigr's hut, she vowed to check in on Kelda when she returned. Surely there was something she could do to help alleviate the woman's aches and pains.

***

Torleik was greeted at the door by Valdis, who had one of her hands resting atop her large belly. She appeared relieved to know Eilidh was on her way, and motioned for him to enter. As he glanced around the room, it occurred to him that the hut was much too small for five people, soon to be six. Perhaps he and Stigr could either expand their home or relocate them to another spot on the property where he'd have more room to build and for the children to play. He was surprised he hadn't thought to do it earlier, though Stigr would never complain. Torleik made a mental note to revisit the idea. Perhaps Eilidh would have some good suggestions. *Eilidh.* She seemed to be on his mind a lot lately.

Brusi lay on a pallet near the fireplace, eyes squeezed tightly closed. Stigr quickly scooted the two younger boys outside, and Valdis asked her husband to keep them from getting in the way. Torleik considered Stigr a good father, and occasionally consulted him when he had an issue with Atli. With three boys between ten and five winters, Stigr had a wealth of experience raising boys.

Eilidh appeared soon after, and immediately got to work, washing the leg carefully with soap and water, then unrolling and applying the poultice to the deep bruise. Although she was gentle, Brusi stifled a whimper or two. His wide eyes drifted up to Torleik's, and it was clear he tried hard to show how brave he could be in front of the master. Torleik gave him a reassuring wink.

"This poultice smells pretty bad, doesn't it?" she said, clearly trying to put Brusi at ease. "It's made from *meacan dubh*, comfrey leaves." She turned to Valdis once she'd finished wrapping the poultice over the injured area. "Leave this on until Brusi goes to sleep tonight. Check to see if the bump is getting smaller. If not, I've added another poultice ready to use. Again, wrap it around the leg, like I've done here. Leave it on until morning, then remove the poultice and wash the wound gently. If the bruising and lump have decreased, apply this salve made from *lus Máiri*, calendula, and apply twice a day for five days. I'll return after that, and see how the leg is doing." She ruffled Brusi's hair. "If you stay off that leg for those five days, it should heal quickly." She turned and addressed Torleik as he stood in the doorway. "Can you or Hallkel make a crutch for Brusi to use while the leg heals?"

"Oh, must not go to trouble," said Valdis, clasping her hands in front of her huge belly.

"It's no trouble," said Torleik with a shrug. "I'll bring them by tomorrow." He caught a surprised look from Eilidh and grinned.

Eilidh held out a linen-wrapped pack containing dried herbs. "Valdis, if Brusi is in a lot of pain, this is for making tea to help him sleep. It contains *saille*, willow bark. Simmer in water and let it steep. You can allow Brusi as many as four cups per day."

"Thank you, mistress. You so kind." Valdis accepted the poultice materials, salve, and tea package for Brusi.

Eilidh then reached for another package in her sack. "And this is a tea blend I made from *camobhil*, chamomile, and raspberry leaves – to help *you* get more sleep as you prepare for the delivery of your child." She held out the package, and when Valdis didn't take it, Eilidh set it on the table anyway. "It won't harm the baby, as long as you don't use too much." She squeezed the other woman's free hand. "When it comes time to deliver your baby, please send Stigr to come get me. I want to help make your experience as safe and pleasant as possible. Will you do that?"

Torleik translated to make sure Valdis and Stigr understood the instructions.

Valdis's forehead wrinkled. "But we cannot pay for medicines, mistress." Her dark brows created a deep furrow between her soft brown eyes.

Eilidh stepped back and clutched her sack. "We would never expect you to pay us." She glanced at Torleik. "Isn't that right?"

Torleik felt a moment of breathlessness, gazing back into Eilidh's incredibly bright blue-green eyes. He then got a grip on himself. "My wife is correct. You and Stigr work hard for us and our community every day. For that reason, it is our duty to care for you and your family, when you need help."

Eilidh sent Torliek a wide smile, and he thought he caught a sparkle of tears.

Valdis thanked them again and followed them to the door. When Torleik glanced back at the lad, his eyes had already closed.

Eilidh and Torleik walked slowly back to the longhouse. Somewhere in the west, beyond the great Ocean-Sea, the sun was beginning to set as the day drew to a close. Eilidh seemed quiet, and Torleik wondered what she was thinking. All he could think about was kissing her until she was dizzy.

"You must be exhausted," he said. "Already you've resolved a mare's difficult delivery, and now, a boy kicked by a horse. And it's only your third full day here."

Eilidh smiled weakly. "Aye. It has been a long day. A long week, for that matter. But I am glad I can help make a difference here."

Torleik wasn't used to handing out compliments, but felt that was the very least he could do. Everyone needed encouragement. He'd learned that much from his son. "You're very good with your patients – horses *and* humans. You seem to have a special touch that puts them at ease."

"Ach, I don't know about that."

"Definitely magic," he mumbled to himself as he stepped closer. Her hair and cloak smelled a bit like her wildflowers and herbs. Unique, like the woman herself.

"I wanted to add to the conversation we had earlier," she said, staring up into his eyes.

His breathing grew shallow. What he wouldn't do to reach out and kiss her on her full deep pink lips. But he had promised to take things at her pace. That it would be a marriage of convenience only. Now, he was beginning to regret that decision. Something was happening between them. What would she say or do if he asked for a Christian ceremony now ... and she said no? She was so very different from Ulla. Hard to predict. And there was no denying Atli's eyes lit up when she approached. All of this was floating around inside his head when he recalled the matter with Siv.

Eilidh sighed heavily. "After the misunderstanding with Siv and having to rely on Lifa for translation, I think I should begin learning Norse as soon as possible. Can you arrange for Hallkel to teach me, starting right away?"

"I will do that." He grinned down at her, realizing what a fortunate man he was to have had Eilidh burst into his life. He took her hand, and this time she let him hold onto it until supper was called.

24

ᚨᚱᚲᛋᛏᚷᛈᛗᛚᛟᚦᚾ

Eilidh was excited about the challenge of learning a new language, but in her opinion, Norse sounded much harsher than Latin or Greek. She felt comfortable meeting with Hallkel following the midday meal each day. She found him to be a patient teacher, who, thankfully, possessed a healthy sense of humor. When she'd worked with her brothers' tutors, Eilidh had been considered a good student who learned things easily. However, her first attempts to speak Norse were tentative, sometimes causing Atli or others in the vicinity to laugh, although she knew it was meant to lighten the moment, not ridicule her. Nevertheless, Eilidh decided she must be diligent so she could learn quickly. So that she could converse with Torleik in his own language. Her heart still fluttered at the sensation of his touch, his hand in hers. Did this mean he was thinking of her as more than just a business arrangement? Part of her hoped so, while another part of her was terrified by the thought. In the meantime, she planned to focus on her work here, and she could only do it properly if she knew the language.

The first hour passed quickly, but she still felt discouraged as they came to an end of that day's lesson. "Hallkel, I will never get this right. It's hard to reproduce those sounds."

As he sat at the dining table in the center of the longhouse, he leaned forward. "The more you hear it spoken by a variety of speakers, the easier it will become. I once said the same thing about learning your Gaelic."

She looked up at that. "Really?" She wanted to ask if he learned Gaelic from his wife, but thought that too intrusive. Still, her curiosity stirred.

"*Ja*. It's true," he continued. "I was terrible at speaking Gaelic in the beginning. But I learned it takes more time and effort for an adult to learn a language than for a young child, so I didn't feel so bad."

Hallkel glanced across the room, eyes landing on Atli, who sat in the kitchen with Siv and Kelda, playing with his horse and making soft neighing sounds. Sadness engulfed Eilidh as she wondered if Hallkel was thinking of the daughter he'd lost.

***

Torleik held the damaged wheat sprout sample and examined it for a few moments before glancing up at his farm manager, Torrad, who had brought it to his attention. They stood just outside the barn, where Torleik had been enjoying the sight of Maeva and her frisky foal in the enclosed pasture they used for training.

His thoughts returned to Eilidh. Since she came from a wealthy clan, Torleik had expected his wife's healing skills to be more along the lines of skinned knees, broken bones, and stomachaches, and perhaps assisting with routine baby deliveries. He hadn't expected anything like the courage and skill he'd witnessed when she used her hands to move Maeva's foal into position to reassure a successful delivery. With Eilidh's help, what could have been a financial disaster had been averted, not to mention a devastating personal loss. He'd put his heart and soul into those horses and their well-being. And then she'd immediately followed that feat with her confident treatment of Brusi's leg injury. Torleik could hear the whispers making the rounds already. His people were impressed with his new wife.

But as he gazed at the ruined shoot of wheat he held, Torleik felt the bottom of his world drop out once more. He frowned and handed back the sample to Torrad. "Why did the leaves turn yellow? We did everything right."

Torrad scratched his beard. "My guess is a disease that comes from the air, not an insect. It could easily be from those dry, sunny days we experienced earlier in the spring, or the heavy rain that came later. Either one can do damage if there's too much."

Torleik nodded. "I know we took a chance trying to grow wheat in this climate, which is why I planted a small crop this year." He gazed off into the distance. "It's a good thing we can count on oats and barley this winter."

"*Ja.* That is good." Torrad, who also served as a guard of sorts for Torleik's property, didn't stand as tall as the typical Norsemen, but his build was of solid muscle that more than made up for his lack of height.

"What should we do?" Torleik's cheeks warmed to have to ask such a question, but this was one of those things he was learning along the way.

"We must burn the crop, so it doesn't infect the oats and barley. Then leave that field fallow until next spring, maybe longer. If you like, I can take a couple of men along and organize the burning. As you said, it's a small crop, and shouldn't take long to get under control."

"It's nearing dusk, too late to burn today. Can you take care of that first thing tomorrow?"

"Consider it done, master." Torrad dipped his head and exited the barn to make arrangements.

It had been a long time since Torleik had felt such a complete failure at something. Perhaps since Ulla's death. People had warned him about trying to grow spring wheat here. He saw now he'd been foolish and arrogant not to listen. On the other hand, perhaps he could redeem himself by finding a solution that would ensure they had plenty of grain to get them through winter.

Torleik snorted in disgust with himself and returned his focus to Maeva and the gray filly he'd named Saga. After several moments, Maeva moved slowly, head down, as she approached him at the railing, Saga trailing behind her. The white and gray mare nudged his hand, and he couldn't help but smile.

"Looking for something?" He patted her soft nose and produced a carrot from his pocket.

Torleik had ceased being surprised at how animals could sense humans' moods. Maeva gently took the carrot from his hand, and when she finished chomping it down, she took another step closer and nuzzled his arm.

He stroked his hand down her forehead and over her shoulders and back, and laughed at Saga's frisky antics until the sun started its slow descent. When Eilidh called Torleik from the porch to come inside for the evening meal, he reluctantly took Maeva and Saga to their stall for the night, making sure they had fresh food and water. Closing the stable door behind him, he crossed the yard to wash at the well before going inside the longhouse.

The meal was dominated by Atli's chatter and Eilidh recounting her funny mistakes with the Norse language, making him smile. She was trying. That's all he could ask. As he brought a spoonful of lamb stew to his mouth, Torleik felt a contentment he hadn't experienced in a very long time. But each day kept him busy with a new crisis.

Torleik returned to the barn after the meal, needing time to think about this new grain supply challenge. After a short while,

Isolf appeared and waited as Torleik stepped outside of the stall where he kept his personal mount, Rig.

"Maeva and the foal both continue to do well, *ja?*" asked Isolf.

"*Ja.* I think so."

Torleik paused at the mother and child's stall again, pleased the filly had inherited a light gray coat with a sprinkling of dappled spots from her sire, Vàli, as well as Maeva's dark gray mane and tail. She came from good bloodlines and temperaments, so he had high hopes for her.

"The foal is going to be one strong little filly with a mind of her own. She stands on those quivering little legs and pokes her nose into every corner of the stall while her poor *modir* rests." Isolf shook his head, but he was smiling.

"Maeva will recover?" Torleik needed to be reassured.

"I am sure. Your wife did a fine job. I don't think Maeva will have problems breeding again."

Torleik crossed himself and looked up. "Thanks be to God and Odin, the allfather. Eilidh is like having a shieldmaiden here to watch over us."

"Mistress Eilidh appears very skilled for one so young. I heard about what she did for young Brusi. We are fortunate to have her here."

That thought was beginning to settle firmly in Torleik's mind, in more ways than one. He grunted his agreement.

Isolf brushed some straw off his hands. "Well, I'm off to have supper with Asse and Frida. I will see you in the morning."

Torleik wondered what it would feel like to have a daughter. Frida was a chubby little girl, just learning to walk. She had inherited golden hair from her mother, and tight curls, like her father. She looked as if she would keep both parents on their toes.

Grateful that at least one crisis was over, Torleik left the horse stalls and found he'd rather not think about the ruined wheat crop just now. Things had been going well, especially where Eilidh was concerned. He had watched how she interacted with Atli. The boy was quickly coming to adore her, and he felt certain the feeling was mutual. Now, if only he could allow his own feelings to take root, but every time he did, he pictured his wife, Ulla, and all she had meant to him. He sat atop a bale of hay, allowing himself to feel the exhaustion in his very bones.

He was thinking about how small and delicate Eilidh's hands were when he heard a rustle of clothing. Expecting her to appear, he turned his head in time to see Lifa at the stable entrance. Disappointed, he avoided her eyes.

Lifa approached, a slow smile directed at him. "You look tired, Torleik."

She sashayed when she walked. He wondered if she'd always walked that way and he'd just never noticed before now. Lifa had perfected the art of using her body to tempt a man with her every move. And yet, her female ploys were wasted on Torleik, especially now. He stood and took a step to pass by without speaking.

Her hand shot out and grasped his arm.

"I'm glad you're here. I need to speak with you – alone," said Lifa, her dark eyes blinking rapidly.

The alarm bell that sounded inside his head seemed too real. "As you say, I am very tired, Lifa. I must go inside and see to Atli … and my wife, Eilidh." He frowned at the idea that he had needed to remind her yet again that he had other responsibilities now. He turned to walk away, tired of this flirting game of hers.

"Wait! I have things to tell you … about the new mistress. I was present when she upset poor Siv something terrible. I saw–"

Torleik's lips pressed into a thin line as he held up his hand. "You've already stated your case for Siv. I don't want to hear any more tales or lies from you, Lifa."

Lifa's chin jutted out. "I do *not* make up stories nor lie."

Torleik couldn't believe he'd ever considered Lifa attractive. Thank God he'd never fallen for her constant attempts at seduction. On the other hand, she'd already disturbed his peace.

"When I say I do not wish to speak with you, you must desist with your games. I am not a foolish man who believes everything that comes out of your mouth." He gritted his back teeth. "And I should not have to remind you that I am a *married* man. Do your job, and you'll be fine."

Lifa crossed her arms over her impressive bosom, her expression darkening. "I don't know what you mean."

"You purposely misled Siv about what my wife was saying. All she intended to do was compliment the cook on her meal."

Lifa turned her head and stared over his shoulder, a frown deepening the lines in her forehead. Anger making her movements brusque, she brushed back loose strands of straight dark hair that hung limp and oily.

"You are mistaken, Torleik. I have no wish to cause trouble." She smiled sweetly. "But if you are truly married, as you say, I must make the assumption that you and the mistress have consummated the marriage?"

When he didn't answer, she smiled and placed a hand on top of the gate to Maeva's stall, pretending to appear thoughtful. "Just as I suspected. After all, I wash your bedsheets, Torleik. There has been no sign of virgin blood since she arrived. In fact, you've been sleeping in the great hall. Why is that?"

He crossed his arms over his chest and towered over her with what he hoped was a menacing scowl. He started to silently count to ten – but only made it to three – when he felt the urge to explode.

"But then, perhaps Mistress Eilidh is no lady. I've heard talk of why she ended up here. It makes sense." Lifa moved a step closer.

Torleik took a deep, cleansing breath so he wouldn't strangle her right then and there.

"What my wife and I do is not only none of your business, but completely inappropriate to discuss in polite society. If you open your mouth and spew that kind of trash to others, you will be dismissed and sent packing with no reference. From this day forward, you will not approach Eilidh or Atli, nor will you enter the longhouse unless you have been summoned. Am I clear?"

She regarded him for a moment. "Well, it's obvious you are in a very bad mood, so I'll just leave you alone."

"Lifa..."

"I understand. Good night, *Master* Torleik."

She turned and, straightening her shoulders, headed in the direction of her small hut, but Torleik was quick to note that her chin was raised in defiance.

He could only hope she'd taken his words to heart. Eilidh didn't deserve that kind of treatment in her new homeland. Torleik would make sure that no one would treat her badly in the future.

25

ᚨᚱᚲᛋᛏᚷᛈᛗᛚᛟᚾᚢ

Eilidh had discovered that Torleik was a man who liked his routines. Mornings were spent dealing with farm chores or building maintenance, while he reserved afternoons for working with the horses. He returned briefly for the midday meal, then was off again. Consequently, she had learned to fill her days with activities to keep herself occupied. With a boy of four running in and out of the house all day, it was at times a challenge to get things done and yet, she was quickly coming to love Torleik's son. When he fell asleep for a nap after wearing himself out playing, she worked on the Goddess Project, as she'd come to think of it, on the table set in the middle of the great hall, or in her bedchamber if she wanted to be alone. She stared at the pages, knowing she would need to find something durable on which to transcribe it. That's when Torleik entered the longhouse in the early afternoon.

Eilidh glanced up from where she'd spread her materials on the dining table, surprised to see him. "Is something wrong?"

Torleik shifted his weight, glancing quickly at Kelda and Siv, who carried washed pots from the outside kitchen they'd used for the midday meal back into the staging area.

"May we step outside so we can speak in private?"

Eilidh's brows furrowed. "Am I in trouble again?"

He chuckled and placed a hand on her arm. "No. Not at all. Please, come."

Once they stepped outside and settled on the bench that faced the ocean, Torleik took a moment to gather his thoughts. "Since you arrived, my people have had nothing but praise for how you've cared for them." He paused. "I'm sure the animals would say the same – if they could talk."

They both laughed softly.

"That's good to hear," Eilidh said, feeling immense relief. "It's hard to tell sometimes, because I still don't understand Norse all that well."

He nodded and glanced down at his hands, avoiding her eyes. "Hallkel says you're learning quickly."

"He's a good teacher."

"Atli talks about you, as well. I think he's quite taken with you."

Surprised, Eilidh smoothed the skirt of her gown. "I'm happy to hear that. He's a fine boy, though active, like my brother, Gregor, who rarely sits still."

Torleik nodded and she studied his features.

"*Ja*, Atli is a handful for anyone." He was quiet for a moment, gazing out to sea. "You've done a good job with him. That is why I thought we might take some time off to celebrate, just the two of us, so we can get to know each other better."

Eilidh's heart stilled. She hadn't expected that. In fact, she'd come to the conclusion her husband was intent on making it through the year-and-a-day, then moving on if he decided they didn't suit each other well. She wished she could discuss *them* – their relationship. She'd signed the agreement for a marriage of convenience, but there were times when she caught him studying her in a certain way that caused her heart to beat faster.

"I know what you're thinking." He rubbed his chin and the accumulating dark stubble. "But I think we can afford a break this afternoon. I thought we'd take a ride to a peaceful place ... and talk about Atli."

Eilidh had two fleeting thoughts. Discussing Torleik's expectations for raising Atli would be much appreciated if she was to play her part of wife and mother well. However, the idea of being completely alone with Torleik in an unfamiliar environment caused anxiety and her stomach made a grinding noise. Though she knew he was different from Bennett and Geirolf, the memory still jarred her, made her distrustful even when she needn't be.

"We won't go far, but you'll have a chance to see more of *Meginland*."

Clearly proud of his new homeland, Torleik's enthusiasm was contagious, and truth is, she'd felt isolated on the farm since she'd arrived.

Eilidh removed the apron she'd donned over her gown, while working on the dusty old pages, and set it aside. "You make it almost impossible to say no."

Torleik grinned. "You might want to bring a warm cloak, in case the wind picks up. I'll get the horses ready and speak to Atli so he knows we'll be gone for a few hours." He turned and said something to Siv, who glanced briefly at Eilidh, then waved him out of her kitchen, a smile tugging at the corners of her mouth.

As Eilidh returned to the bedchamber and reached for a warm cloak, she couldn't help but wonder what specifically had prompted this unexpected surprise. Not that she wasn't grateful, but she couldn't help but be suspicious of his motives. She arranged the cloak over her shoulders and fastened the MacAoidh brooch, taking a quick look in the polished mirror. Her hair was tucked into one long braid, so there wasn't much she could do, which was just as well. As she turned away from the mirror, something niggled at her.

Take *Fitheach* – just in case.

Quickly, she retrieved the sword in its scabbard and hid it beneath her cloak. If Torleik said anything, she would deal with it. She needed the reassurance, even if it might wound his male pride. After all, he couldn't protect her from everything ... But what if he thought she didn't yet trust him? She would cross that hurdle when she came to it.

Eilidh had grown up in a place where she could wander outside and ride the hills at any time, away from her brothers' prying eyes. But things were different now. Images of Geirolf lurked in her thoughts, making her afraid to venture out alone, no matter what Torleik said. On top of that, as the new mistress, each time she entered the farmyard, she felt the eyes of an entire community watching her in expectation. She had a great responsibility to Torleik's people, and hopefully, someday she'd be one of them. Although she'd only been there two weeks, she still felt that burden settle onto her shoulders. She thought of her mother and suddenly felt guilty for not understanding the strength and courage it must have taken for her to raise five children to adulthood, manage a castle household efficiently, and to respond to complaints or disasters for the clan members when necessary.

Eilidh wished her mother was with her now. She would value her advice about the marriage bed, which had been firmly on her mind as the second week passed and Torleik said nothing. Did he not find her pleasing enough to bother with? Her shoulders drooped as she walked outside and found Torleik and the horses in front of the longhouse.

"I apologize for being so abrupt," she offered. "I'm just tired, I think."

He held Rig's reins and that of another horse she'd not yet met.

"That's not a problem. The ride back should regenerate you." He shrugged good-naturedly. "This is Skadi, a mare I brought from *Nord Vegr*. She will be gentle and obedient."

"I don't need a gentle horse. I've been riding my whole life." Eilidh frowned, puzzled by his quick judgment of her. She knew her words were coming from a place of deep frustration, but for some reason, she let them fall on Torleik's head rather than take a moment to gather herself.

Torleik rubbed his neck and glanced around. "I apologize. I should have asked about your skill level." He ran a hand over Skadi's dappled gray and white back while Rig nudged the hand holding his reins. "But I think you will appreciate her smooth gait on our journey today."

Eilidh took a deep breath and forced herself to remain calm. "She *is* a beautiful horse, and ... she *is* saddled and ready to go."

"That she is."

Although she couldn't tell if Torleik was angry or not, this *was* a trip away from Torleik's farm for the first time since she arrived. She would be a fool to pass up this opportunity.

"I do miss my rides with Nairna."

"Well, at least let me help you mount."

She put up a hand, but controlled herself this time. "No, I can do it." She boosted herself up onto the saddle quickly, before he could see or feel the shape of her sword beneath her cloak.

Torleik stood there, hands on hips. "You are indeed self-sufficient around horses." With that, he mounted Rig and turned left from the yard to the road north.

"Where are we going?"

"It's not far."

The mystery actually added to the joy of getting out on a gorgeous summer day with Torleik. Eilidh decided to savor the time alone with her husband and forget about dealing with a sullen Lifa or an inquisitive Atli. She may be having difficulty learning

Norse or making significant progress on the Goddess Project, but at least those things distracted her from the constant fear that Geirolf would reappear. Still, something niggled at her.

Skadi settled into a comfortable gallop alongside Torleik's horse, and Eilidh enjoyed the warm sun on her face and the wind passing through her hair, though it made the strands of her braid come loose. As she stole glances at the big black horse that Torleik rode so effortlessly, she admired the striking flaxen mane and tail. And while the horse's slender legs did not appear as sturdy as a Highland Pony, they demonstrated good strength and speed. The ponies her father bred were reliable for hard work and easily kept their footing when managing rough Highland trails or rocky soil. For generations, the clans had bred a similar type of pony to be used as a warhorse that could handle heavy weaponry. Perhaps that was what Torleik was studying in his breeding operation. A new breed with endurance and looks.

After a while, they left the road north and veered off to the east. Eilidh followed Torleik onto a narrow dirt trail. A flat green grassland surrounded them, a few low hills visible in the distance. Thin smoke lazily drifted up from an occasional stone hut, leaving a hint of earthy peat in the morning air. Clumps of heather dotted the grassland, interspersed with summer wildflowers, which she took note of for her herbal potions and salves. The delicate blush-tipped dog-rose offered considerable nutrients to stave off colds and coughs. Eilidh felt some of the old excitement returning. She would return to get clippings later, as Torleik made no indication of stopping until they reached their destination.

When she spied something unusual in the distance, she slowed then sat up in her saddle and pointed. "What is that big lump sticking out of the ground?"

Torleik saw where she pointed and slowed Rig to a walk so they could speak. "It's an ancient burial cairn. A tomb where the original inhabitants buried their dead. The Norse call it

Orkahaugr. Not much is known about the natives who once lived here, but I enjoy the stories."

Eilidh tried to recall if Hallkel had mentioned this place during her voyage here.

"We're not far from our destination. When we get there, you can ask all the questions you like."

She nodded, sensing his eagerness, then they urged their horses to a canter.

Sure enough, they came to a flat land situated between two lochs. Bright yellow daisy-like flowers stretched for the sun and waved in the soft breeze. When Eilidh looked up, however, she had to gulp. A high mound had been built up with dirt to create a raised platform. Upon that flat-topped hill loomed the remains of a circle of huge standing stones, resembling ancient warriors.

Torleik dismounted and untied the sack. "Come, take a closer look."

Eilidh jumped down before he approached and absently patted Skadi, who was suddenly more interested in the plush grasses that surrounded them.

"The Norse call it the Ring of Brodgar, but Hallkel is not sure what the name refers to."

"*Brodgar*," she repeated, savoring the new word. "I wonder how long ago those people lived here. The stones appear to be in relatively good shape. There must be a reason they built it on a hill and surrounded it with a ditch."

Torleik ran a hand through his wind-blown hair. "*Ja*. Hallkel thinks the people used several monuments in conjunction with *Orkahaugr*, to view the sky, stars, and moon."

After a few moments of studying the ancient objects, Eilidh began to feel a slow vibration pulsing against her side, closest to the tallest stone. Her curious nature got the best of her, and she placed a hand on the stone and closed her eyes.

As Torleik continued walking slowly away, the vibrations became more insistent and frightening, when suddenly, Eilidh realized it was *Fitheach*, her sword, that vibrated. The Standing Stones must possess some kind of power that could be transmitted to other objects, such as a sword already imbued with Druid magic. Or was the sword alerting her to some danger? She put her hand on the sword's grip and opened her eyes. The sword now emitted a sound that she could hear. As though unaware of both the vibration and low-pitched sound, Torleik walked ahead, his strides putting a distance between them.

Uneasy about her strange circumstances, Eilidh heard the word, "Raven," coming from her mouth. Why did she say that? She'd never called upon Raven before.

Immediately, her spirit guide appeared and perched atop one of the Standing Stones with a rusty caw in greeting. Eilidh was so relieved to see him, that she had ignored the rush of cold air surging in from behind her until it was too late. She tried to cry out, but two rough hands pressed against her throat and pulled her backward. She couldn't see the man's face, but she recognized the stench of sweat that clung to Geirolf like an old cloak. Once again, she tried to scream, but this time, the blade of a sharp knife against her throat stopped her. Although she tried to remain calm, he growled like a bear and pushed her up against one of the standing stones.

"Do not make a peep, Miss Eilidh. If Torleik comes to save you, he will die slowly, in great pain, and so will you." Geirolf laughed and took away *Fitheach*, tossing it in the dirt. "Actually, I look forward to that."

She shuddered and glanced at Raven. He was her protector, wasn't he? Why didn't he do something? As if he read her mind, Raven shot forward and began pecking Geirolf on the face.

He said a few cuss words Eilidh had never heard and let go of her to fight off the large bird. Eilidh raced to get away, but

Geirolf freed himself of the bird and grabbed her from behind before she could escape, once again dragging her to the stone. As Eilidh struggled for air, she felt a niggling of betrayal. Grandmother Marsaili had always been able to count on Raven's help. Sharing the same spirit guide, Eilidh couldn't help but wonder if Raven was ignoring her now because she hadn't taken the time over the years to understand and know him.

Raven will come, no matter how small the complaint or request. She recognized her grandmother's voice and felt a tingle of hope.

"Why are you ... doing this?" she managed to whisper to Geirolf.

Again, he laughed, and his rancid breath caused her stomach to turn.

"Because it will make Torleik angry and ready to fight." He yanked on her cloak and shoved her away from the Standing Stone, while still holding her tight, both now facing Torleik's direction.

"Where is the big coward?" Geirolf demanded. "I thought he would have returned for you by now."

Eilidh felt the need to defend Torleik, but it occurred to her that she really didn't know much about him. Had he abandoned her on purpose, then used her as bait?

Geirolf's hands again circled her throat. She jerked away but he kept his hold on her. She swallowed, trying not to lose her apple and oatcake from this morning. Torleik would return for her ... wouldn't he?

"Well, he's certainly making this easy. Come. You are mine now. You will be *my* wife."

Eilidh's head pounded, her vision becoming foggy. It was happening all over again. But no older brother would dash to her rescue this time. And after all she'd left behind in order to be safe. She couldn't let it happen again.

Between Geirolf's body odor and something equally as evil that she couldn't quite name, she knew she had to act. Eilidh took a deep breath, then kicked backwards, like her brothers had taught her, aiming for his shin. She made contact, and was pleased at the hissed sound of his breath inhaling as he tried not to call out. The pain must have caused him to release his grip. Just then, she saw something coming at them from the corner of her eye, so she used that moment to turn and push Geirolf away. Eilidh called out and ran in the opposite direction.

"Torleik! Geirolf is here! Help me!"

It seemed only moments had passed when she heard a scramble followed by horse's hooves, and then felt a strong set of arms engulf her. She yelled and fought with all her strength.

"No! I will never go anywhere with you, Geirolf. Let me go!"

"Eilidh, it's me, Torleik."

It took a few moments for his words to sink in. He placed his hands over hers to still their beating against his chest.

She swallowed and her eyes darted about. "I don't ..."

Torleik turned to glance over his shoulder at a horse and rider already in the distance, dust stirring in their wake. Still holding her by the shoulders he attempted a weak smile. "You are safe, *min kjærlighet*." He gently kissed her lips until her trembling stopped.

A whimper escaped her mouth as she stared back at him, wanting to ask what those words meant. Shame burnished her cheeks. She pushed against Torleik's chest and stepped back to gaze up at him. "I am *not* safe. And I will never be safe until Geirolf is out of my life."

"I don't understand. Why would *Geirolf* be here?" Torleik stood very still, as though trying to wrap his mind around what she'd said as he glanced in the direction of the retreating figure.

"I take it you don't believe me?"

"Of course I–"

Torleik started to reach for her but she ducked under his arm and raced to the spot where Torleik had returned with the horses. She snapped up *Fitheach*, not waiting for Torleik's reaction. She spotted the reins trailing on the ground, so scooped them up and hoisted herself into the saddle on the first try.

"Wait, let me explain," Torleik said. "I didn't mean —"

But all Eilidh could see in her mind's eye was Geirolf and his grasping hands while Torleik had been nowhere in sight. She gave Skadi a swift kick to her side, and set the horse on the path that would take her back to the main road and in the opposite direction than Geirolf.

Torleik doesn't believe me.

As she settled into a smooth canter, she was well aware of the sound of Rig's thundering hooves as Torleik tried to catch up to her on the way toward home.

His home.

26

ᚨᚱᚲᛋᛏᚷᛈᛗᛚᚢᚱᚢ

As Eilidh pressed Skadi to reach Torleik's farm, she couldn't help but recall her last ride on Nairna in the hills back home. She typically set all worrisome thoughts aside and focused on the ride, the wind whipping her hair into a frenzy. In the past, she had always looked for any new sign of Nature's wonder when out, a particular tree or flower in bloom, or a secluded stream and lush green haven when exploring a new glen.

On this day, however, her heart mirrored the frantic hoofbeats of her horse as she urged it onward. After all, Geirolf might still be out there, watching her, even now, from behind a tree. She swiped at the falling tears. Though she heard Torleik in the distance, she didn't want to face him just yet. She knew she had overreacted, that he was only trying to help, but with her emotions so raw, she had mistakenly taken his surprise that Geirolf might be out on the glen for a challenge to her honesty. She knew she would need to apologize at some point, but after the frightening experience at the Standing Stones with Geirolf, all Eilidh wanted was to have a good cry and hide beneath the bedcovers. She most definitely had no desire to greet the strangers talking to each other as they stood beside a large wagon in the middle of the farmyard.

As she drew closer, however, she realized those strangers were her brothers, Gregor and Leith. Her mouth dropped open as she approached.

Despite the shock of seeing family members once again, it was the familiar nicker that made her heart pound. She jumped down from Skadi and rushed to her beloved mare tied to the back of the wagon.

"Nairna!"

"It seems our sister hasn't changed much. She still greets her horse before her own flesh and blood," teased Gregor, holding out his arms.

Her day improved considerably as she stepped into her brother's embrace. After several moments, she stepped back to regard Leith, who leaned casually against the wagon, appearing his usual handsome self. He beckoned her for another hug, and she felt the love down to her toes.

"Mistress," came a soft voice behind her.

Eilidh whirled around to find her former servant, Muire, gazing at her with loving brown eyes ... and holding her grandmother's white cat, Fenella.

"Muire! This is all such a surprise!"

"You didn't expect to see us again?" Muire teased gently.

"I ... didn't know. But I had hoped I would." She smiled and caressed the patient cat. "Why did you bring Fenella all this way? And for a visit? She doesn't like water."

"It's not a visit, mistress."

As soon as Muire quietly uttered those words, Eilidh's heart stopped.

"Is it Grandmother Marsaili? Is she ..."

Muire held out the cat, which Eilidh immediately cradled in her arms like a baby.

"*Seamnhair* is still giving grief to anyone who gets in her way," said Gregor with a chuckle.

"But she thought you might be homesick and suggested we bring Fenella to comfort you," added Muire. "She couldn't stand the thought of sending her sweet darling alone in a cage on a ship, so she asked me to ... escort her." She glanced around the yard with wide eyes.

Eilidh looked from Gregor to Leith. "And so you brought Nairna, Muire, *and* Fenella here to help out?"

The two young men exchanged a look just as Torleik entered the yard atop Rig, heading towards them slowly. He gave Eilidh a brief glance, then dismounted. "To what do we owe the honor of a visit from the MacAoidhs?"

The men shook hands and stepped back to regain their sense of space. It seemed clear to Eilidh that her brothers had news of some import, but were reluctant to say anything in front of her. While Leith was typically close-mouthed, Gregor did the talking.

"We need to speak in private," Gregor said, peering nervously around him.

"Come to the stables. We can talk there," Torleik said, taking charge.

Eilidh watched them walk away. Still holding Fenella, Eilidh sighed and addressed Muire. "I'll feel better if we keep her inside until she's used to her new environment. Then, you and I will have tea, and you can tell me everything." She entered the longhouse and let down the hide covering the front door.

Muire reached out a hand. "Are those tear stains on your cheek? Have you been crying, mistress?"

When Fenella started squirming, Eilidh set her down on the stone floor and swiped the remaining evidence from her eyes and cheeks. "Ach, I will be fine." She led the way to the dining table, inviting Muire to sit. "You should feel free to call me Eilidh. They don't stand on ceremony here."

Kelda appeared out of nowhere, the same stealthy way that always startled Eilidh when she was focused on something. When the housekeeper caught sight of Fenella, Eilidh was surprised to see a smile appear on the old woman's face. She bent down and ran a hand over the thick white coat. In response, Fenella rubbed against Kelda's legs and made a chittering sound in pleasure. When Kelda straightened, she glanced at Muire with curiosity, but addressed Eilidh.

"Do we have guests for the meal, mistress?"

Eilidh glanced at Muire, not sure of the proper way to introduce a former servant and companion. Fortunately, that didn't prevent Muire from jumping in to explain.

"I'm Muire, and I used to be Mistress Eilidh's personal servant, as well as companion."

As she heard the words, Eilidh nodded. "Aye. But, mostly, my friend as I grew up among all those men. Two of my brothers are with Torleik in the stables. They have come a long way. So I imagine they will stay for dinner."

She watched Fenella explore the longhouse and began to worry about the older cat's reaction to meeting Torleik's exuberant hound, Runi. To distract herself from thinking about Torleik at the moment, she patted Muire's arm. "Muire is about to tell me why she and my grandmother's cat have journeyed this far."

Kelda looked from Eilidh to Muire and back. She must have understood the close bond, for her features revealed no judgment about social structures as she held out a hand to get the cat's attention.

"Then you two must sit and have tea before the meal, and meanwhile, while I boil fresh water, I will find something tasty to feed this lovely beast." She peered down at the cat. "Hmph. I hope Master Torleik warns Master Atli about not playing too rough."

Eilidh nibbled her bottom lip at that thought. "I may need to prepare them both."

While they waited for their tea, Muire glanced with interest at the longhouse. "This is nice, but ... sparse. Your husband is not much for decorating, is he?"

Eilidh snorted. "Ach, not at all. I'm glad *Màthair* packed a few small rugs and things to soften and warm the floors and walls. I just haven't done anything with it."

"Well, she sent another trunk with even more lovely things your *màthair* and *seanmhair* chose for you."

"How is Grandmother Marsaili, really? You'd tell me the truth, wouldn't you?"

Kelda arrived with two steaming mugs of borage tea.

Borage for stress ... and for courage.

Eilidh almost chuckled at how appropriate that tea might be. Tension seemed to touch on everything around her since the attack, and now that her brothers had arrived.

Once Kelda was through delivering the two mugs of steaming borage tea, she left them alone again. Eilidh leaned over and patted Muire's hand. "Grandmother Marsaili?"

Muire sipped her tea and nodded. It no doubt soothed her parched throat from the sea voyage. "Gregor wasn't wrong. She acts as if she's hale and hearty, but she seems to be getting weaker each day. I'm afraid that cough may never go away." She blew on her tea to cool it. "I have a feeling that's why she wanted to be sure Fenella came to you."

Eilidh brushed at a wayward tear and looked away. "I understand she may not have much longer to live. I just ... I should be there. This whole situation is my fault. If I had married a suitor back home, I could still be tending to my grandmother's health."

Muire patted her hand and shook her head. "No, not everything. You had nothing to do with that crazy man who tried to grab you off the street in *Inbhir Theòrsa*."

Eilidh heaved a heavy sigh. "Bennett? Aye, but it was the man I mistook for my rescuer that I saw again. Just this morning. Torleik took me riding to a place with Standing Stones. That man, Geirolf, he's the devil, himself. He came out of nowhere and attacked me, tried to get me to go with him. To marry him. I broke free, and when Torleik arrived, Geirolf was gone." She gazed across the great hall. "I thought Torleik didn't believe me when I said it was Geirolf. Now I realize he was merely confused about what I was saying. I have made such a mess of everything." She felt a sob rise up and placed a hand across her mouth.

Muire took Eilidh's hands in hers. "Everything will work out. You'll see. You have to give it time."

Eilidh shook her head and sniffed.

Muire patted her hands, then reached out and took a sip of her tea. "Actually, Geirolf is the real reason we're here."

"What?" Eilidh straightened her shoulders.

"He was seen leaving *Inbhir Theòrsa* recently. But Leith had his suspicions that Geirolf was after something. So he looked into the matter and discovered Geirolf had bragged in a local tavern that he was coming after you, to make you his wife and to get even with Torleik for something he did." She reached and squeezed Eilidh's hand. "When Leith spoke to your father and brothers, it was decided they would find a good excuse to come visit you so soon after your handfast to make sure you're okay."

"He's here. I was right about seeing him at the Standing Stones at Brodgar." She clutched Muire's sturdy hand and leaned towards her. "I'm so glad you came to warn me."

Muire flashed a smile. "And I'm glad, as well. Because your father knew how miserable I was without you, and Nairna wasn't eating properly. She missed you desperately. So he asked me if I wanted to come and start a new life with you here in the Northern Isles. And I said yes!"

Eilidh blinked and remained silent for a moment. "That's good to hear about my father's generosity, but I'm not sure what your job will be. People here don't appear to have personal servants. And I want to add, you are free to go anywhere you wish, Muire. You don't need to take care of me."

The tea was gone and voices could be heard as Torleik, Leith, Gregor and Hallkel entered the longhouse and began seating themselves at the table.

Muire jumped up and waved to Eilidh. "Perhaps I can make myself useful by helping with the meal."

Eilidh nodded her agreement, but something didn't feel right as she watched Muire approach the cook, Siv. A shiver of anxiety crept down Eilidh's back. She turned to see Lifa hovering in the doorway, uninvited to enter unless summoned. She stood just long enough to overhear what Siv and Muire were discussing. Too late, Eilidh realized she hadn't warned her friend about very few people speaking Gaelic. However, it appeared Muire was having no trouble "speaking" with Siv, as they both laughed.

Lifa's gaze moved to Eilidh. To her surprise, the girl wore a gloating expression. Did she know about Geirolf luring her into his trap? Had Lifa fed him information about Eilidh and Torleik? Eilidh's scalp prickled.

Lifa threw Eilidh one last threatening look then flounced out the doorway and into the yard, where laundry awaited her. Eilidh clutched her skirt, balling it into a fist. If she was correct, Geirolf and Lifa had teamed up to bring down Torleik and her. But why?

27

ᚨᚱᚲᛊᛏᚷᛈᛗᛚᛟᚱᚢ

Although Eilidh didn't pout or speak sharply to anyone after their abrupt return from the Standing Stones, Torleik felt certain she was angry with him for questioning her about Geirolf being here on *Meginland*. At every turn, she avoided meeting his eyes when he was in her presence.

Perhaps, he should have let her know how much even the *idea* that Geirolf had followed her to Orkney unnerved him. And when he spoke alone to Leith and Gregor in the stables, he felt even worse. They confirmed the news that Geirolf was on the island. They had recognized him at the docks in *Hannavoe*, the small port village south of Torleik's farm.

"We came as soon as we learned what he was planning," said Leith, leaning against a bale of hay, his face surprisingly calm.

"Seems Geirolf's developed a habit of gathering gossip when it pertains to one Torleik Sorensson. He's been spending a lot of time in the Gray Goose Tavern in *Thjorsá*. Apparently, he has been speaking to one very chatty bar owner." Gregor flicked a piece of straw from his tunic.

The men were ruminating on those details when Saga, Maeva's new foal, came trotting down the corridor on spindly legs. She snorted, then stuck her nose out to sniff Gregor's hand.

Gregor laughed and rubbed Saga's nose. "You're already looking for a treat, little one?"

Torleik shifted his weight. "Saga must have escaped out the stall gate." He quietly led the filly back to the stall she shared with her mother, who was being groomed by Isolf.

"We may have a new little escapee," said Torleik, gently pushing the filly towards her mother.

Isolf turned in surprise, then glanced at the gate. "I could swear that gate was latched shut."

Torleik grunted. "We may have another Draupnir on our hands, a little escape artist. Best to put something else to secure the latch tighter so she can't wiggle her way out."

"I'll do that."

Torleik wasn't angry at Isolf, who was a dedicated and loyal worker in charge of the animals' welfare. Torleik was merely exhausted, his head full to the brim with problems that required his attention. Eilidh's safety. Geirolf. The crop failure. Almost losing Maeva. Way too much to tackle all at once.

He closed the gate behind him and returned to Eilidh's brothers. For a few moments, he didn't speak, simply gazed through the stable entrance, crossing and uncrossing his arms. "Saga turned out much better than I could have hoped for." He paused, shoving his pride aside for the moment. "Eilidh saved Saga and her mother during a difficult breech birth. I don't know how your sister did that."

"I'm not surprised," said Leith, his lips twitching. "She's a very intelligent woman with a unique way of calming the most desperate of beasts, be they man or animal." He offered a brief smile. "It's wise to never doubt her when she says she can do something."

Torleik felt his cheeks flame hot. "I'll remember that."

Of similar height and the muscular build of a warrior, Leith exuded strength. But here, he offered comfort by patting Torleik's back as they headed towards the house. "You'll figure her out … eventually."

For a few moments, Torleik resented the handsome older brother. Privileged and clearly well-educated, he dressed well for a warrior, as opposed to Gregor's casual style of muddied boots and tunic. But then again, he supposed Leith was a decent sort, like Eilidh herself.

As they approached the water well just outside the longhouse, Torleik considered whether revealing that he and their sister had agreed to a marriage of convenience might explain a few things they were about to find out anyway. Such as why he slept alone in the hall.

"How long can you stay?" Torleik casually inquired.

"As long as Eilidh's safety is in doubt," Leith replied, his expression neutral as he stared back at his brother-in-law.

Torleik knew he must be extra vigilant for the time being. However, it was *his* responsibility to protect Eilidh, not theirs. But then his thoughts reeled back through the day and he flushed with heat. He hadn't protected her, had he? Never suspecting that Geirolf might be stalking them.

"I and my men will protect Eilidh from here forward, now that you have warned us. Feel free to stay a day or to visit with your sister. I'm sure she would like that." He glanced around, then as if an afterthought, he raked a hand through his hair. "You are welcome to sleep in the barn or inside the hall. There's plenty of floorspace." Torleik suddenly experienced a stab of inflated male pride. He didn't want to have to explain why he and Eilidh were sleeping apart after only a few weeks together.

"The barn is fine by me, as long as the roof doesn't leak," said Leith with a grin.

"We haven't had much rain this summer." Torleik felt immediate relief wash over him, knowing he wouldn't have to worry about the men seeing and hearing things said in the hall. He shrugged casually, as if it made no difference to him. "Shouldn't be a problem."

Gregor, who had been standing off to one side of Leith, hands in his pockets, glanced around at the farm and studied its buildings, strangely silent.

Torleik knew what Eilidh's brother was thinking. That Torleik was just a poor farmer with aspirations of raising his position in society by marrying Eilidh and then starting a successful and sought-after horse breeding business. His success would then support Eilidh in the manner in which she'd been born. To both her and her family, Torleik must demonstrate he was worthy of her.

Before he could dwell on it further, a flash of scraggly blond hair suddenly crashed into Torleik's legs from behind. Used to Atli's ability to appear and attack at any moment, Torleik indulged him by reaching down to lift him high into the air. Atli screeched and then glanced shyly at the two guests, Hallkel not far behind. Torleik set Atli down on the ground and the boy scuttled behind his father to peek out at the two strangers.

"Slow down there, mister. You're not a racehorse." Torleik gestured towards the two visitors. "My son can be shy in the beginning, as you can see, but that disappears quickly." He took Atli's hand and brought him from behind to stand facing the brothers. "These men are Eilidh's brothers – your new uncles from *Alba. Onkel* Gregor and *Onkel* Leith."

"*Alba? Onkels?*" Atli's blond brows drew together at the unfamiliar words.

Gregor and Leith appeared to be taken by surprise with the idea that their baby sister was now a mother. They both took an awkward step back. Torleik had hoped to distract attention from himself, but this worked almost too well. Eilidh's brothers recovered their wits and both made a point to bow politely to the young boy who's thumb now occupied his mouth while he considered his *onkels*.

"We'll talk about this later, Atli."

Hallkel left to take care of something, so Torleik waved the brothers over to the well, where they found a fresh bucket of water and towels to wash off the travel dust.

As they washed, the two brothers laughed and bantered back and forth. Torleik admired their closeness, and wondered what they would say if they knew he'd hurt their little sister that morning by questioning her about Geirolf.

Either way, he and Runi may be sleeping in the barn if he didn't make things right with Eilidh ... and quickly.

***

Although thrilled to have her two siblings visit her in her new home, Eilidh felt an underlying anxiety for what they'd discussed with Torleik at the stables. Had Torleik mentioned her claim earlier about seeing Geirolf?

Consequently, she expected their gazes to fall upon her often during the midday meal, asking her to join in on the conversation. Instead, the men, including Hallkel, laughed and drank ale, and acted like it was a routine day with nothing better to do.

Frustrated, Eilidh darted glances at Leith, who smiled back on occasion. Why had he come and not Padruig, who was Gregor's typical companion on the road? Her thoughts took her back to the encounter with Bennett in *Thjorsá*, and upon accidentally seeing the brand on Bennett's bare arm, still red and ugly, almost as if it were a new wound. She hadn't had a really good look, but she thought it might have been the brand the MacAoidhs used to identify cattle and sheep so they could easily tell them apart from their marauding neighbors – a simple "Mac-I" symbol, as the clan name was once spelled. She shuddered to think Leith may have purposely gone after Bennett to seek justice for attacking her three years ago. Her second oldest brother had seldom stayed around the castle, even on special holidays, so there were times she felt she didn't really even know him. Like now. She frowned to think he might be capable of hurting someone on her behalf. On the other hand, in three year's time, Bennett still hadn't demonstrated he'd changed for the better. And then there was Geirolf! That he would even consider her as a bride to get back at Torleik caused her to set down her fork and stare at her plate. But why? What did he have against Torleik? Could Muire have been right about Geirolf's real reason for being here?

Astrid and Muire were helping serve the meal, and their constant smiles and good cheer were a balm to Eilidh's bruised ego as she contemplated all that had happened. She knew her brothers were not here to deliver Muire, Nairna, Fenella, and another storage trunk full of who knew what. No, Eilidh's instincts tingled too strongly for that. Something was going on, and the men refused to discuss it in front of Eilidh or Atli, who listened closely to everything, and appeared quite the mimic when it came to learning new curse words in either Gaelic or Norse. She'd have to be careful around the little ball of fire that was Torleik's son.

No longer hungry, she sipped her ale and thought about what to do next with the Goddess Project. She needed something to write on. Something that wouldn't crumble any time soon, and would absorb ink for a smooth, long-lasting appearance. Where to start? Stalled before she even started, she watched how happy Astrid appeared each time she came near Hallkel. And he, who did not often break into a smile that displayed the dimple in the center of his chin, was in fine form this afternoon.

Eilidh sighed and folded her hands in her lap just as Torleik caught her eye. She tried to look away, but then his eyes settled on her with such intensity, she couldn't help but gaze back, wondering what he was thinking.

Not long after, the meal ended and Atli raced back outside to play. Torleik and the three men remained at the table. When Eilidh rose to see if she could help in the kitchen for something to do, Torleik placed a hand on her arm.

"Eilidh, please stay. Your brothers bring news you should hear."

She stared at his hand, and felt warm sparks from his touch. She shook her free hand and rose. "You waited until Atli went outside. What is it? What has happened?"

"It's important you hear this from us," said Gregor.

She couldn't imagine what all the drama and tension was about, but she sat obediently, and was glad Kelda brought her a fresh mug of hot tea for something to hold onto, then quietly vanished, along with the other servants.

Leith cleared his throat. "The last time we were in *Thjorsá* on business, we happened to come across Geirolf several times. He was staked out in the same tavern, the Gray Goose."

"The owner of the Gray Goose is a good friend of mine from *Nord Vegr*," Torleik responded thoughtfully. He indicated Leith should continue.

"That makes sense. Apparently, Geirolf must have known that fact, for he kept bringing your name into the conversation with the bar owner to see if there was any gossip about you." Leith paused and reached for his mug. Torleik hesitated and poured himself more ale, offering the pitcher to Gregor. "I knew Geirolf in *Nord Vegr*. But I wouldn't say we were friends." Torleik stared across the room. "From an early age, Geirolf picked fights with guys twice his size, for just about any reason. He would steal, lie or cheat his way out of any situation. Eventually, he murdered a man when he was sixteen. He spent a short time in prison, but he always returned to the streets somehow." He regarded Eilidh for a moment, then folded his hands on the table. "I knew he ... had problems, that he wasn't well. His mind was twisted and full of hatred for anything and anyone – especially me. I testified in court for his first conviction. I'd been called as a witness, and just told the truth – that I'd seen Geirolf strangle a man with his bare hands. His parents disowned him. He blames it on me ... and that was twelve years ago. I didn't want to scare you, Eilidh, nor should you worry much. He is probably targeting you just because you married me ... and are so beautiful. He has always wanted what I have that is good in this world." Torleik paused to gaze at her with an expression she'd never seen before. Tender. Vulnerable. Intense.

"We will eliminate his threat as soon as we capture him and turn him over to the authorities in *Nord Vegr*." He scratched his chin with a thoughtful expression. "I tend to be a cautious man, Eilidh. I wish I'd seen him right away when you claimed to have seen him this morning at the Standing Stones. I was sure I could protect you from him, and that he wouldn't be bold enough to follow you here. It's clear, now, I was wrong. I'm so sorry, love."

Eilidh's lips quivered. He'd called her "love" as his voice fell to a whisper. She clasped the skirt of her gown beneath the table. "*Tapadh leat*, Torleik. Thank you. I accept your apology." She took a deep breath and looked at her brothers. "What do we do now to keep Geirolf away?"

Leith leaned his forearms on the table. "It might help if we knew why he's obsessed with you, as well, Eilidh. Had you spoken to him before, and he somehow mistook that for interest?"

Eilidh thought back to the encounter with Bennett attacking her, then Geirolf coming to her rescue in *Thjorsá*. After a moment's hesitation, she told her brothers ... *almost* everything. She'd been waiting to walk her father home to their inn a few blocks away, knowing he'd need help after so much drink, though it was still daylight due to Midsummer. Then she recounted how

Bennet had spotted her and had grabbed her by the neck and pulled her into an alleyway. How Geirolf came to her rescue and had tried to calm her. At the time, she had found Geirolf charming and respectful, so she had no reason not to converse with him to pass the time.

She ended by telling them how Torleik had warned Eilidh to stay away from Geirolf, that he was an evil man, which didn't sit well. Eilidh lowered her head. "I'll admit I made some bad decisions recently, but I'm older and wiser now. I can take care of myself."

Leith cocked his head. "That wasn't the case this morning at the Standing Stones, though, was it?"

She glanced at Torleik and ground her back teeth together, attempting to remain calm. "I was taken completely by surprise. Like Torleik, I didn't think he would be foolish enough to show up again ... now that I'm married."

Gregor stood and gazed into the fire for a few moments. "So, Torleik, do you think Eildih and Atli are both targets of Geirolf's delirium?"

"And if so, how are we going to stop him?" added Leith.

Torleik heaved a great sigh and set his empty ale mug on the table with a loud thump.

"I don't know why he's so obsessed with revenge. It all began when I was summoned to court. I had no choice but to testify to what I'd seen. Sure, we fought when we were children, but then we grew up and went our separate ways." He ruffled his overly long blond strands that framed a square masculine square jaw. "I must be missing something."

"Geirolf wants what you have," said Eilidh, speaking for the first time. "And that includes me ... and Atli, I presume."

He hesitated for a moment, his ice blue eyes sparkling suspiciously.

"But he doesn't know we —"

"He doesn't need to know the details. He just wants to steal you from me." Torleik gave her a stern look for almost revealing their marriage would not be filled with love.

The back of Eilidh's throat ached. How could she ever live a life without love?

28

ᚠᚱᚲᛋᛏᚷᚹᛖᛚᛟᚾᚢ

Despite the scare with Geirolf as well as her brothers' concerns, Eilidh insisted she make herself useful in her new home but she still wasn't certain what was expected of her.

With Geirolf still at large, Torleik asked Eilidh to be especially watchful of Atli. By mid-morning, Eilidh was so grateful that Astrid offered to take the rambunctious boy, which allowed her more time to focus on the Goddess Project. This morning, over the morning meal, Torleik had asked Eilidh to be especially watchful of Atli, with Geirolf still at large, so she was grateful when Astrid had offered to take him this morning so she could continue her work on the Goddess Project, which she had just completed for the day. When she'd cleared the table for the midday meal, she then stepped outside and stretched her weary back, eager to take advantage of the sunny weather, but she knew Geirolf could be out there, just waiting for his chance to abduct her, so it only made sense to stay close to home.

As she left her bedroom and headed for the front porch she thought of Torleik. She suspected he had said something to the other workers about keeping an eye out for Geirolf. Now, with

Atli at Astrid's place, the peace and quiet helped her concentrate, though she still didn't know what was expected of her.

Eilidh went outdoors and found a seat on the bench with Fenella at her side. She was an observer of people by nature, so she spent considerable time getting to know the folks around her and trying to understand their Norse. In this way, she noticed Kelda was slowing down day by day. Eilidh was coming to think of her as the Norse version of her grandmother, Marsaili, in some ways. Naturally, Eilidh wanted to help in any way she could. Based on the fact that Kelda tended to bump into things, Eilidh suspected her eyesight was failing. But she couldn't bring herself to ask her housekeeper if she would submit to an exam. That would be stepping over the line.

Eilidh often sat on the front porch, Fenella asleep and purring contently on her lap. She was silently counting her blessings when Leith appeared. He surprised Eilidh by leaning down to pet Fenella, who raised her chin and opened sleepy green eyes just a crack.

"It seems Grandmother's cat has settled down quite nicely here." Leith sat beside Eilidh on the bench, then reached for an unfinished wood carving Hallkel must have left behind last night. "He's good. Torleik's carver."

"Aye. And a good friend to Torleik."

"Torleik asked when Gregor and I plan to leave. I wanted to talk to you about that."

Eilidh ran her fingers through the white cat's soft fur. "Did he say he wants you to leave?"

"Not exactly. But we've been here for two weeks. We will be expected to return home soon."

She stopped caressing Fenella, who turned her head, narrowed her eyes in what appeared to be displeasure and jumped off Eilidh's lap. Tail in the air, she ambled slowly toward the small pond where the geese and ducks spent the bulk of time in summer.

"Ach, I just remembered I haven't gone through that trunk you brought with you."

"Grandmother said to be sure and go through it thoroughly."

Eilidh looked at her brother directly. "What did you wish to speak with me about? I should be helping in the barn ... cleaning out stalls or ... something."

Leith laughed easily, his deep blue eyes sparkling. "I never thought I'd see the day when you would say words like barn and chores in the same sentence. There must be others who can perform those jobs, surely?"

She shrugged. "I'm a farmer's wife now. Everyone must pull their own weight around here. I have new and different responsibilities."

Leith allowed the silence to grow, then stood abruptly and held out his hand. "Let's walk down to the shore, little sister. We can talk more freely there. I'm sure your barn chores will still be here when we return."

Eilidh swallowed the lump in her throat, nervous about why he wanted to talk to her away from the longhouse. As they passed through the yard, she noted Lifa watching them from the doorway of her hut, dark eyes narrowed. Eilidh hurried to catch up with her brother's long strides.

They walked in silence until they descended the steps that ended at the sand. As they continued towards the water, she wished she'd brought her summer shawl, as a cool breeze had kicked up.

Leith strolled with his hands behind his back, taking in the day in all its glory. That is, until he cleared his throat in the same way her father used to do when he had a hard time telling her or her brothers news he knew they wouldn't like.

"How are you and Torleik getting along? Are you content?"

Eilidh watched little crabs scuttle back under the sand as waves broke up and dribbled back to the sea. "We're fine. Why do you ask?"

"I rarely see you alone together. When I do see you together, you act as if you barely know each other."

She glanced away and followed the flight of gull-like birds up toward the cliffs. The black markings on their wingtips and short black legs identified them as kittiwakes – Eilidh's favorite seabird. She was glad so many inhabited the island. Their "ki-ti-wak" call reminded her of home so intensely, she had to wipe the corners of her eyes on her sleeve.

"It's true. We still don't know each other well," she said softly. "He has his customs and I have mine. He's also stubborn and set in his ways. It's been difficult, but I'll manage."

And yet, she wasn't being totally truthful. There had been those moments when they had connected, when she'd felt a spark between them, and then he would quickly pull back, like those crabs she'd just seen, pulling into their shells any time danger lurked.

Leith stopped to pick up a large shell and inspected it closely. At last, he looked up. "You haven't consummated your marriage, have you? You do know this is dangerous for you?"

"What business is that of yours?" She felt a twitch begin beneath her left eye. "You're one to talk. You told Torleik what happened three years past, didn't you?" She wiped a big fat tear rolling down her cheek. "You promised." Her voice trailed off.

Leith's eyes softened to a gray-blue. "Aye, I promised you, and I kept that promise. But you used that incident as an excuse to turn away dozens of men, and never explained to our parents why you behaved as you did. They would have understood and granted you more time, I'm sure."

"You don't know that."

Leith shaded his eyes and watched several yellow-headed gannets dive from an impressive height above the sea to catch their dinner. They reappeared above the surface moments later, a wiggling cod or herring dangling from their mouths.

"Little sister, though I didn't say anything to Torleik, I suspect if he knew about what happened to you, he'd be supportive and patient. That's the kind of man we've found him to be."

Eilidh swallowed and glanced over her shoulder to see a dozen or so of Torleik's seamen preparing his empty cargo ship to sail back to *Thjorsá*. Would Torleik sail with them? When Geirolf was in the vicinity?

"Why are you discussing this with me *now*?" she demanded.

He shrugged. "I've seen how you and Torleik circle around each other, not quite trusting the other. I think he finds you interesting because you are so different from Norsewomen he knows, and yet, he appears to be frustrated and unsure about how to approach you. You've been as prickly as a thistle these past few days."

"I have not." She pouted for effect.

Leith reached out and gently pushed a lock of wavy red hair behind her ear. "If you keep these secrets hidden, it may result in consequences that affect both of your lives. An unconsummated marriage can be challenged by parties such as Geirolf. He has no scruples. He can claim you and Torleik are not a truly committed husband and wife if you continue to let this drag on."

Eilidh blanched and felt her legs quiver.

"Gregor and I are leaving on the morning tide," Leith continued. "Torleik insists he doesn't need our help in protecting you from Geirolf. You must trust him. But send for us if anything changes. And think about sharing what frightens you about the past with Torleik. Once you are done holding so tightly to that event, you will be free to heal."

"You sound like you have experience with secrets."

"Perhaps that's why I don't want you to regret them."

A vision of the scar on Bennett Sutherland's arm popped into her mind. This was the perfect time to ask her brother if he'd had anything to do with that mark.

However, before she could say anything, Leith wrapped her in his arms and hugged her, then set her away. "You will get through this and be stronger than ever. I believe that."

After Leith's show of faith in her, Eilidh couldn't bring herself to ask him about Bennett. Instead, they returned to the longhouse to await her brothers' departure. Leith was right. She had a decision to make regarding Torleik, and she must make it soon.

***

Eilidh's appetite had returned by supper. The men ate quickly, then walked down to the ship to check preparations, with Atli and Runi trailing behind. Eilidh used that time to wade through the third trunk. What had her grandmother thought she needed so badly that she had sent it all this distance?

"Perhaps your *màthair* or *Seanmhair* wanted to surprise you with something for the house," Muire suggested, joining Eilidh where she knelt on the floor before the opened lid of the trunk.

For a while they worked in silence, unpacking small household items that would add a woman's touch to their home. Delicate table linens edged in lace. Her grandmother's matching comb and hairbrush with the clan's bulrush carved on each piece. Eilidh paused, goosebumps rising on her arms.

"Muire, tell me truly. *Seanmhair* is dying, isn't she?"

Muire looked down and fingered one of her worn service gowns. "She thinks she is."

Eilidh remained silent for a few moments, then resumed sorting through the trunk. Her grandmother would remain an unsolved mystery in death as she had been in life.

Then Eilidh came to the middle of the trunk where Muire's things were neat and folded. Muire quickly grabbed what appeared to be a man's tunic on top and held it to her chest, then set it behind her. Eilidh brows came together, wondering why her friend carried a man's shirt in her trunk, but she thought better of asking.

"Your mother knew I didn't have my own trunk," Muire explained. "She said it would be acceptable for me to include my belongings with what she was sending to you. I hope that's alright?"

Eilidh pulled out the other items and handed them to Muire. "Of course. You would have had trouble keeping your things together on that journey with several small travel sacks to keep track of ... and Fenella, as well."

Muire's forehead smoothed in relief. "Exactly. Even though she was in a cage Gregor made for her, I was worried about her the whole way. I was distracted before we even left *Inbhir Theòrsa*. I'm so grateful for your parents' kindness in allowing me to come here. I also hope you are glad to see me?" She picked up Fenella and began to pet her nervously. Fenella meowed and scampered away.

Eilidh stopped her sorting and reached over to give her friend a hug. "You brighten up my day like a ray of sunshine. I'm thrilled I won't be all alone now."

"But surely you're getting to know the people here. Are they not friendly?"

Eilidh poked at the next layer in the trunk. "Most don't speak Gaelic. The Norsemen moved in and made it a Norse settlement long ago." She held up a rug that caught her eye and ran her fingers over its soft, rich wool yarn. "The only way around the communication problem with our workers is for me to learn Norse. So, I have lessons with Hallkel almost every afternoon." Eilidh shrugged. "I'm not very good at it."

Muire chuckled, then held up the man's shirt she'd packed and breathed in its scent. "That would be a first. You were always better at languages than your brothers."

Eilidh frowned and regarded the shirt Muire now set aside. "Where did that man's shirt come from?"

Muire sighed. "I couldn't leave my husband, Fearchar, behind completely. So I brought the one last tunic that still carries his scent from when he was alive."

Eilidh felt a chill. "Ach, I am so sorry for not thinking about your poor husband. Of course you must bring his spirit essence with you." She rubbed Muire's arm as the servant crushed the tunic to her nose a final time, tears gathering in her eyes.

When Muire finally had her emotions under control, she said, "I think Fearchar would be glad I came to be with you, mistress. I wasn't handling things well after you left."

Eilidh hugged her tightly. "I'm glad to have you by my side. You're like a sister to me. I'll introduce you to everyone tomorrow. In the meantime, let's finish this, then I can have Torleik take the trunk back to the ship."

The summer light was still visible, though the hour was late. Fenella had found the last warm sliver of light peeking through the open window and had curled up on the bed to take advantage. Eilidh examined several colorful ceramic pots and woven baskets from the trunk, wondering if her mother thought they would have nothing as fine here. When she re-examined what appeared to be the relatively new wool rug, she speculated Grandmother Marsaili had been busy – despite her poor health. Soothing shades of deep blue and rich green stripes were separated by thin stripes of gold that crisscrossed the fabric, creating small squares.

"This is beautiful. Do you know if *Seanmhair* made this?" Eilidh stood and spread it on the floor near the bed.

"I didn't think to ask where it came from. But it's perfect for this room, and definitely adds some needed color." Muire rose and came to stand beside her.

Eilidh placed the rug where her feet would welcome the warmth on a cold winter's morning when she exited her bed each morning.

"This must be from your grandmother, as well." Muire pulled out something near the bottom of the trunk wrapped loosely in an old gray shawl. Her nose wrinkled as she sniffed and quickly handed the package over to Eilidh. "I swear, there's something dead in there."

As soon as Eilidh's fingers made contact with the cracked leather cover, a strange feeling washed over her. A sense of longing for the Old Ways, a time long before her birth, when the ancient lore was handed down through generations of Celtic tribes.

She swallowed the unexpected pain that lodged in her throat. "This is Grandmother Marsaili's *Book of Herbal Wisdom.*" She paused in silence for a few moments of reflection. She took a deep breath. "I'm surprised this didn't go to Great Aunt Davina's family. She was the one who used it most. And yet, she left the book for me." She sniffed and reached for a kerchief.

"Didn't Davina have twin boys?"

"Aye. Donnchadh and Cormac. They both married and had families of their own. They live in MacDonald country, I believe." Eilidh smoothed her palm over the leather. "Perhaps they had no interest in learning the Old Ways of healing."

As Marsaili carefully leafed through the pages, Muire looked over Eilidh's shoulder. "And now, it comes to you." Muire turned back to the almost empty trunk. "Oh, there's something else at the very bottom!" Her eyes widened in surprise. "And there's a note attached."

Eilidh peered into the trunk and spied something wrapped in linen stuffed at the very bottom. Carefully, she lifted out the heavy, awkward package and unwrapped the linen to see what was inside.

"What is it?"

"I think it's ..."

Eilidh parted the linen to find blank pages made from vellum. Pages that would be perfect for her Goddess Project.

"Is that a book?"

Eilidh blinked and took the note Muire held out.

"Not yet." Eilidh read the note and felt a smile stretch her lips wide. "Grandmother Marsaili thinks of everything. These are for a project I'm working on. *Seanmhair* must have purchased them from the local monastery. And she included the instructions for how to make more, if needed."

Muire gaped at her mistress. "And why is this making you so happy? It's just a book."

"Ach, it's more than that. It's an answer to my prayers." She set the package on her bed. "I must find a place to keep this trunk. For my projects."

Muire shrugged and helped Eilidh close the empty trunk and drag it to a spot in the corner and out of the way of traffic.

Once in place, Eilidh crossed her arms over her chest and stood contemplating its presence. "I wonder if I should keep it locked? From curious little boys."

"Might not be a bad idea. Atli does seem an active little dear. He reminds me of your brother, Gregor, when he was younger."

Eilidh chuckled. "I was thinking the same thing. 'Prone to misbehaving,' as *Màthair* would say."

"And prone to sly mischief." Muire made a funny face. "I had three younger brothers just like that. Always getting into trouble." Muire winked. "And aren't you just the smart mother? You must learn quickly."

Eilidh rewrapped the gifts from her grandmother and set them back in the trunk, wondering how best to ask Torleik for her own lock and key. She still didn't know him well enough to gauge if he might be offended that she thought his son unworthy of her trust.

Aware that Muire was sending inquiring glances her way, she tidied up the gifts from home and placed them on top of the trunk for now.

"Are you and Master Torleik getting to know each other, now that you've had some time together?" Muire grabbed her belongings from the trunk and set them on the bed.

Eilidh didn't want to discuss her complicated relationship with her husband, even with her closest friend. "He works long days between the stables and in the fields. We converse at meals to catch up on what's happening each day."

Muire considered Eilidh's words and pressed her lips together for a moment. "Does that bother you?"

Eilidh looked away and swept invisible lint from the skirt of her gown. "If I didn't know better, I'd think you were spying for my mother." Though she'd meant it only as a joke, she caught the immediate sense of hurt in Muire's soulful brown eyes and took a step back, hoping to smooth things over. "It's only that I have no time to think about Torleik and me. I have other duties and responsibilities now, with my major responsibility being Atli." She ironed out the bed covers with her hands. "Let's go see if Kelda has some nice clean bedding to use for a pallet for you tonight. You may find a spot in the great hall to your liking. There's plenty of room."

Muire's eyes took in the bedchamber. Eilidh knew the servant was sharp enough to note none of Torleik's items lay around the room.

Muire fingered her belongings one last time. "Of course. I would be grateful for whatever is available, mistress."

Eilidh didn't feel as relieved as she might have expected. Muire wouldn't have expected to sleep with her mistress now that she was a married woman. However, Muire would clearly see Torleik sleeping alone on a pallet in the hall and know they didn't share the same bed. Still, Eilidh could not break her promise to herself or to Torleik by revealing they had secretly agreed upon a marriage of convenience.

If only she'd told Muire about The Incident long ago, she wouldn't be in this messy situation.

Eilidh was beginning to understand the impact of her brother Leith's words.

She must confess all to Torleik before long, or things just might become impossible to fix between them.

***

Torleik needed to clear his head, so took a leisurely walk along the shore with Runi. He felt better knowing he'd posted two guards right outside of the longhouse, so he had a few moments to himself where he need not worry about Eilidh and Atli. What was he going to do in the long run? He disliked having men around he hadn't vetted himself, but these were tough times, and he would not sacrifice his wife and child.

Waves were relatively calm this day, and one slowly made its way as far as Torleik's bare feet. He'd forgotten where he'd left his shoes, which wasn't like him, but decided they'd turn up eventually. The wave receded back to the loch, and with it, dozens of small crabs. He squatted to watch the tiny beings in shells scrabble to bury themselves before the next wave. Sometimes, that's what Torleik thought about himself. He was so cautious, he would bury his head in the sand and wait for a new season. *Wait and see*. Atli said that was his favorite phrase.

As those words reverberated in his head, something caught his eye. Leaning forward, he reached for a stone that had been buried until now. The shape was almost identical to a human tear, and his scalp prickled. Did this mean something important was about to happen? He turned it over and over, studying the surface.

What he needed, for his own sense of security, was a talisman aimed at protecting Eilidh – from herself, if necessary. "Eilidh's Tear," he said. "It looks like a teardrop. And it's for my Eilidh." He didn't know what he would do if he lost her to someone like Geirolf. Life without Eilidh would be dull, indeed.

The stone was dry now, so he slipped it into his pocket, gave Runi a whistle, and headed back to the house to see if he could find Hallkel.

29

ᚠᚱᚲᛋᛏᚷᚹᛖᛚᛪᚾᚢ

The longhouse had an empty echo once Eilidh's brothers departed. However, as much as she missed her family back home, she was determined to make the best of her situation and not feel sorry for herself. Hallkel came every afternoon to tutor her, and she thought she might finally be making progress when she greeted Kelda one morning in Norse. Surprised, Kelda smiled and bobbed her head that she understood. She didn't laugh, nor was Lifa present to ruin Eilidh's moment. She felt like she was floating on a cloud when she returned to her room.

Eilidh still hadn't found the right time to talk to Torleik about her past. Most of the time, he appeared to be preoccupied as he came and went, splitting his time between the horses and the crops, and if he'd seen Geirolf, he gave no indication. Consequently, after a few weeks of isolation had passed since the day at the Standing Stones, Eilidh's fears began to subside a little. She was dying to get out and explore the nearby hills for much-needed herbs, and though she was frightened by the prospect, she couldn't put it off any longer. Not if she was to care for Torleik's people adequately.

"You may *not* go alone." Hands on hips, Torleik glowered at her in the middle of the yard where she had waylaid him.

Eilidh clutched her empty garden basket to her chest and summoned all of her patience. "I've gathered herbs alone since I was a young child. I need to discover locations for herbs here on *Meginland*, and build up a supply for winter if I am to nurse the sick and wounded. And Astrid is watching Atli." She frowned, knowing this was an awkward request. Although she'd earned her independence with her brothers a long time ago, Eilidh was not one to take unnecessary chances. And truth is, she couldn't help but feel a twinge of fear that Geirolf and his ilk might still be out there. "Torleik, I appreciate your concern for my welfare. Surely, we can come up with a reasonable solution that makes us both comfortable."

Torleik stood staring at her. After a few moments, he produced a shrill whistle between his teeth that brought Runi running from the direction of the workers' huts. As the hound approached, he slowed to a casual lope, curly tail wagging.

"Hey, boy. You have been bothering Hallkel again, haven't you?"

The large Norse-bred hound sat and regarded his master with an intense look, but then Eilidh spotted his curled tail twitching, and couldn't help smiling at the two of them.

"Runi, you know Eilidh, *ja?*"

As Torleik gestured to her, Runi gave a short bark and then sidled over and sat close enough to lean against her thigh. Used to her father and brothers' various hunting dogs as she grew up, Eilidh put her hand down to allow him to smell her. Satisfied, Runi let his tongue loll as he breathed heavily and waited for Torleik's command.

"You're going to be Eilidh's companion on a short walk. You will protect her just like you do with Atli, *ja?*"

Runi jumped up, as if excited, and yipped.

"He understands you." She didn't know why she was surprised.

Torleik scratched Runi behind the ears. "We have a long history together, Runi and I." He looked up briefly. "He will keep an eye on you and will come for help should anything happen. I have extra men guarding the perimeters of our property, so there should be no surprises if Geirolf shows his face."

Eilidh wondered when Torleik had made those arrangements, but didn't bother to tell her?

As if reading her mind, he gave Runi one last pat. "I was waiting until you were ready to go for walks again to speak to you."

Eilidh forced a smile. "Well, today is the day. Runi, come along."

She thanked Torleik, then hustled toward the hill before he changed his mind.

Runi served as perfect company, not wandering far, not minding the gradual climb.

Eilidh, on the other hand, grew disappointed when she didn't find a greater diversity of plants on the island. She carefully took a few plant cuttings to bring back to the farm to plant in a pot or in Astrid's herb garden. How would she do her best healing if she didn't have access to fresh herbs?

Eilidh realized she'd been gone longer than she'd anticipated when Runi lifted his snout and sniffed the air. She rose and put the latest cuttings in her basket. The sky had turned an unnatural gray, and for a moment, she thought she smelled smoke. It was then she spied smoke coming from the direction of the farm.

One of the fields is on fire!

Runi began howling and turning in circles, but he refused to leave her side.

Eilidh gathered her things and placed a hand on his neck for reassurance. "Good boy. Let's go see what that smoke is all about."

Runi yipped and started down the hill, stopping every few steps to wait for Eilidh. When they reached the bottom, people were running every which way, shouting and gesturing, lines of men, women and even a few of the older children racing with buckets of water towards one of Torleik's grain crops.

Eilidh searched for Torleik or Hallkel, her heart thumping loudly. When she came across Astrid trying to carry a heavy bucket of water without it spilling, Eilidh stopped her with a hand.

"Astrid, where is Torleik and Hallkel? What happened here?"

Astrid set down the bucket and tucked loose blond curls back into her headscarf, leaving behind a smear of ash on her forehead. Her eyes appeared red from the smoke as she pulled out another headscarf from a pocket to moisten with water.

"I'm not sure what exactly started the fire, but Torleik thinks it was purposely set. He said if I saw you, to tell you to stay inside the longhouse with Atli so Torleik can focus on getting the fire put out."

Eilidh gritted her teeth. "The arrogant man thinks I'm useless and that I have nothing to contribute."

Astrid was about to resume her dash with the bucket of water, but instead, she cocked her head. "He wants you and Atli to be safe and unharmed. He cares about both of you, mistress." She tied the moistened scarf around her mouth and nose and lifted the heavy bucket. "I must get this water to men. And you must go check on Atli and wait for your husband to advise you when it is safe to come outside."

Although Astrid's words were muffled beneath the scarf, Eilidh understood them all too well. Torleik wanted to protect her, but couldn't he see that he was treating her like a rare flower that was only meant to be admired? She felt as if she was suffocating and glanced around for Runi. He must have thought he'd completed his job of escorting her up and down the hill, because he barked and seemed to be searching for Torleik. After a few moments, he must have caught a glimpse of his master because he took off and vanished into the smoke.

The smoke.

It had become so thick in such a short time that Eilidh coughed and tried to gauge where the longhouse was situated. She closed her eyes for a moment, chaos all around her making it hard to focus. When she opened them, she thought she spotted Lifa riding a dark horse into the yard and in the direction of the huts, which oddly enough helped Eilidh regain her sense of direction. Whose horse was that? Eilidh shook her head, intent on getting back to Atli. She'd figure out what Lifa was up to later, when things had calmed.

Eilidh stumbled up onto the porch ... and into Kelda's waiting arms.

"We were so worried and didn't know where you went."

Kelda pulled her further inside the house where she found a clearly upset Siv, who held onto Atli as he screamed for his father. His face was covered in tears as he struggled with the cook. It was apparent Siv had no skill with children.

Eilidh dropped her basket of wilted herbs on a large work table and reached for Atli, who came running and jumped into her arms. He was so taken aback, he stopped crying and stared with wide blue eyes, his legs wrapping around her waist.

"Let's go sit over here and I'll tell you what I know about your father."

"My *fadir*?"

"*Ja.*"

She made herself comfortable in the chair typically occupied by Torleik, as it was the largest and roomiest, definitely the most comfortable. Settling Atli on her lap, she said nothing when his thumb drifted into his mouth. Deal with one issue at a time, Grandmother Marsaili always said.

Kelda brought Eilidh and Atli a cool mug of water and she drank thirstily to relieve her parched throat. When Atli held his mug, but didn't drink, Eilidh wondered what he was thinking.

She didn't know what to say or do in a situation like this, so she'd have to rely on her instincts. "Does your throat hurt?"

Atli was strangely quiet as he reached a hand up to rub his eyes.

Eilidh nibbled on her bottom lip, wondering how to explain the chaos outside so it wouldn't frighten him even more. She encouraged him to drink by holding his mug up to his mouth.

"If you drink water, your throat will feel better. I promise. I can put a cool cloth on your eyes so you don't rub them. Would you like that?'

Eilidh spoke slowly in Gaelic, but like Runi, Atli appeared to instinctively understand what she was saying. When he leaned his head against her chest, a spark of something she'd never experienced before shot through Eilidh with intensity.

What is happening?

"*Fadir?*" Atli reminded her, then rubbed his nose on her sleeve.

Eilidh stifled a laugh. "You take after your *Onkel* Gregor. He would have taken my whole sleeve and turned it into a kerchief." She squeezed his small hand. He was so vulnerable. "Now, your *fadir* is outside trying to stop the fire that started in the barley field."

"Bygg?"

Eilidh turned to ask Kelda, who had resumed her seat nearest the unlit fire.

"*Bygg* is barley. *Logi* means fire."

"Thank you, Kelda. I learned two very important words today."

Eilidh sat forward and recalled from Astrid and Kelda what she'd heard and seen with her own eyes. "I was just coming over the hill with Runi ... I brought back lots of berries for us." She tweaked the boy's chin, hoping to distract him. "Berry pie for you tomorrow – if you're really good." She coaxed a tiny smile from the boy with those words. "I smelled smoke from the other side of the hill, and when I ran toward the village to find your father, the fire billowed out and quickly gobbled up all the *bygg*." She made a gobbling motion with her hand, causing Atli to giggle before stuffing his thumb back in his mouth. "Your *fadir* is directing everyone to help put out the fire. I'm sure he'll come home to give you a hug as soon as things are under control again. He wanted us to stay right here so we'd be safe from harm. Do you understand?"

Atli removed the thumb from his mouth and gazed at her with wide blue eyes. She wondered if he feared he would lose his father as he had his mother.

Eilidh wrapped her arms around him. "Your *fadir* will be alright, Atli. He loves you, and would never leave you alone."

"You will stay, too?"

Somehow, his words rested heavily on Eilidh's young shoulders. Would she, or could she truly abandon the child at the end of a year-and-a-day? Eilidh searched for something that would be true and positive, whether she stayed or left. "As long as I am able, I will always be here for you, Atli."

"And for *fadir?* You be here for him?"

"If he will allow me to, *ja.*"

Atli grunted, a smaller version of his father's famous answer to everything when he didn't know how to respond.

Eilidh felt her throat throb painfully. If Atli didn't receive the proper nurturing and love he needed as he grew to manhood, Eilidh suspected the boy would not only lack in communication skills, but lack in confidence as well. She had a brief thought of how her four brothers may have turned out had they been raised in a home that was cold and uncaring, rather than one filled with love and laughter.

She gently wiped Atli's tears from his face with a kerchief and pulled him close. In moments, the boy was fast asleep as he nuzzled against Eilidh.

Now, she just had to hope she'd told Atli the truth about his father coming home unharmed.

30

ᚨᚱᚲᛋᛏᚷᚹᛗᛚᚬᚢᚾ

Torleik stomped the ash and mud from his boots, then pulled them off and set them on the porch to dry. Anxious to check on Atli and Eilidh, he entered the longhouse to find an eerie silence. Kelda was snoring softly in a chair before the cold fire, her sewing forgotten for the moment. She must have sent the servants not helping with the fire to their huts, for it seemed much too quiet. When he didn't immediately see Eilidh or his son, he experienced an unfamiliar moment of panic. Surely his headstrong wife couldn't still be wandering the hills? And why was he not receiving a typically exuberant greeting from Atli? His stomach churned, already sensitive from the smoke.

Torleik heard a noise and turned to see Runi entering through the door flap behind him, face whiskers singed and his thick fur coated with ash. His old hound would need a trip down to the shore to remove the worst of it. When he sat on his haunches and didn't demand food, Torleik suddenly realized Runi was staring intensely at the back of Torleik's chair ... which appeared to be occupied.

Torleik slowly tip-toed around the front of the chair and was astonished to find his son asleep in Eilidh's lap. Her arms were wrapped around the boy in a possessive manner, and she slept deeply as well.

Runi barked softly at the big white cat curled up on the floor next to the fire. She opened one green eye and glanced up, then sniffed the air. Satisfied she was in no immediate danger, Fenella yawned, stretched out her front paws, then resumed her nap.

Runi barked softly and lunged at the cat. Torleik quickly grabbed onto the dog's collar.

"That's enough, Runi," Torleik whispered. "Sit. No barking, or you go back outside." He waited for his hound to settle down, which he did so reluctantly, his eyes never leaving the huge white cat who'd crossed a sea to be with her new mistress.

It was no secret to those who knew Torleik well that he didn't like cats, based on a strange cat that acted as his great aunt Truda's companion for many years. He found the black cat with gold eyes too sure of getting his own way. Not only was Grimkel sly in how he went about things, there were times Torleik could swear he had the human habit of manipulation down to an art.

But as he turned to regard Eilidh and son sleeping so peacefully, his heart skipped a beat. Wasn't this exactly what he'd hoped would happen? That Atli would find a new mother who loved him and would carefully guide him into becoming a respectable and kind man someday? Even if she did bring a huge white cat with her.

The intimacy of the two in the chair sent him back in time, had him recalling a similar scene back in *Nord Vegr.* Atli hadn't quite passed his first winter. Even then, Torleik saw how closely Atli resembled his mother, with Ulla's bright blue eyes that sparkled when she was happy. And she was always happy with her child, her smiles turning a bad day into something remarkable.

For several moments, Torleik relived the pain of her young life cut short. She would have been about Eilidh's age when she succumbed to a fluke accidental death. He grunted, and Eilidh stirred, then opened her eyes.

"Ach, you're back," she whispered with a smile. She put a finger to her lips to indicate he should let Atli continue sleeping.

The boy appeared so innocent when he was asleep and dreaming of the things boys dreamt about. Horses? Games to play with new friends?

As he often did, Torleik felt a deep well of gratitude resonate inside his chest that his son was a major part of his life. However, he had to ask himself seriously, did he have the emotional room on his ship for anyone else after Ulla, even someone as beautiful and kind as Eilidh? He opened his arms and gently took Atli to his bed without waking him. After carefully removing his son's clothes, he laid him in his bed and pulled the covers up to his chin. Just as he was about to leave the room, Atli opened one eye.

"*Fadir. Logi* all gone?"

Torleik smiled into the dark. "*Ja*, all gone. Sleep well."

He lowered the door covering and returned to find Eilidh folding the blanket Kelda must have provided.

"Thank you for caring for Atli. I know he can be a handful at times." Torleik realized he'd said and done little to show his appreciation these past weeks, despite Eilidh's efforts to fit in and learn about his world. Even if it was a marriage of convenience, he could do better.

"He's a sweet child ... with a lot of energy." She ran her fingers over the old quilt and set it aside. "Were you able to save your crops?"

Unable to look her in the eye, Torleik turned away, his mood plunging. He was sure she'd judge him a bad bargain for a husband. He'd failed spectacularly.

On the other hand, perhaps it was best to get it over with and move on. "I lost all the barley, and some of the oats. We will have no excess grain to store or sell over winter."

Eilidh paused, taking in this new information. "But I thought I heard Hallkel say you planted winter wheat?"

He muttered something she shouldn't hear, then reached for a pile of blankets in the corner where he'd made his pallet for several weeks now.

"Do you suspect anyone of setting the fire?"

Eilidh would not give up. She was tenacious.

He shrugged, not wanting to alarm her. "Geirolf, I suppose. I haven't seen him, but I have this feeling he's been watching us. Waiting for his chance."

Eilidh shivered and rubbed her arms at the mention of Geirolf's name. "He's ... still here? In *Meginland*?"

Torleik spread his blanket on a straw mattress and reached for his old saddlebag to serve as a pillow. "Geirolf will be dealt with immediately. I'll take some men and ride out tomorrow to find out if he's left the island already, and to warn the authorities here, so he won't come after you again to take out his vengeance on me."

"You have yet to tell me, why would he want to do that?"

"He's a sick man who was indulged by his parents as their only child."

"What does he think you did to him?"

Torleik shrugged and raised his hands. "That is for another time. I bid you goodnight. We can discuss the fire when we are not both exhausted."

"But first," she said, holding up a hand, "let me put something on your hands to help the burns."

***

Eilidh reached for some salve on a high shelf in the kitchen and returned to where Torleik sat at the table, his head in his hands.

"Torleik, I feel bad that you're still sleeping out here in the hall. If you like, you could move back into your bedchamber. The bed is huge for just me, alone."

He glanced up and regarded her with icy blue eyes that seemed puzzled as he watched her work magic with his hands. He was so close, she could feel the heat emanating from his body in waves. A strong whiff of ash and smoke, mixed with a working man's sweat, almost knocked her down as she tried not to grimace or take a step back, for surely he would take offense.

"That is important for you, I realize," he finally responded. "To change our marriage agreement from one of business to one of ... what? What do you want, Eilidh?" He pushed aside a stray loose curl on her forehead, twirling it around his finger. "As much as I would like to know what lies at the end of our year-and-a-day contract, we should have that discussion sooner rather than later, for Atli's sake." He glanced at the hallway that led to Atli's bedchamber.

Eilidh felt her skin begin to warm under his intense gaze. She wiped her hands on her old gown. "Oh, I think you may have misunderstood me. I didn't mean we'd ... be intimate right away. I wanted to offer you a more comfortable place to sleep. In the meantime, we could talk of your plans for the farm and the horses, and do so in private. This is your home, after all."

He let go of the curl, but she could see the disappointment evident in his eyes. "Of course. Well, now's as good a time as any to give you an update on the farm." His shoulders sagged. When he ground his jaw, Eilidh could see the feeling of helplessness wash over him.

"And now, the barley was destroyed by fire. I should have listened to my neighbors about taking a risk on wheat so soon."

"Perhaps, we could..."

"Thank you for the hand salve. That does take away the sting."

It was clear by the frustration playing across his face that he didn't want to hear her cheerful chatter. Like her brothers, Torleik seemed determined to wallow for a while before deciding what to do. After all, as Eilidh knew only too well, he was the man responsible for the success of their community. That meant he'd need to find the solution for how they'd survive the winter – even if it meant selling some of the horses much sooner than he'd planned. Eilidh felt a deep sadness for Torleik as he returned to his makeshift bed. How had her talk with him gone so wrong?

She watched as he pummeled his saddlebag into a bulky pillow shape and lay down, turning his face to the great hall wall. She had to find a way to make this up to him. But how?

31

ᚠᚱᚲᛋᛏᚷᚹᛗᛚᚢᚾᚢ

On the day after Torleik's barley crop was destroyed by fire, Eilidh rummaged through her trunk and pulled out her grandmother's *Book of Herbal Wisdom*. Much like Saraid's *Book of Delsiran*, it was a loosely bound collection of crude, thick pages made from dried bark that had formerly belonged to her great aunt, Davina. Eilidh couldn't quite figure out who had started compiling the catalog of herbs and plants used for healing purposes in northern *Alba*, but she found the dried samples, detailed illustrations, and brief notes invaluable to help identify and locate the correct plant she might be seeking.

Torleik and Hallkel had left the longhouse earlier, so she suspected they were surveying the damaged field and conferring with Torrad, their security guard and crops manager. With Atli playing outside, and the longhouse vibrating with the sounds of Siv attempting to sing as she worked on berry pies, Eilidh sat at the dining table with the herb book, finally able to focus on finding a solution for recuperating their losses with the ruined crops.

As she scanned through the pages, she wondered why yesterday was the first she'd heard about the ruined wheat crop. Didn't Torleik think she would want to know? Her father had always kept her mother apprised of concerns both within and without the keep. With that knowledge, he or she could make important decisions if the other had to be away overnight or for whatever reason. It didn't take much for Eilidh to understand that she and Torleik needed to communicate better if they were to be true partners.

The morning passed quickly as Eilidh worked through the herb book. However, she experienced guilt that she wasn't working on the Goddess Project, which she'd vowed to spend time on each day. Compelled to show Torleik that she could be a part of the solution for the crop loss and make important contributions, she poured through the book. As she reached the end of the book, she discovered newer pages had been added, and recognized *Seanmhair's* distinctive form of writing. Spotting something vaguely familiar, Eilidh's heart leapt.

"*Bere barley*," she read. "Why does that sound familiar?" As she read through the notes, her scalp tingled. "This is it!" She jumped up and hugged Kelda in the kitchen, who blinked in surprise.

"What has you so excited, mistress?"

Eilidh didn't want to get anyone's hopes up. "I may be able to help. I'm off to the south field."

"It's almost time to serve the midday meal, mistress. Send the lad, Stigr's nephew." Kelda made a hand gesture in the general direction of the farmyard.

"Of course. I will do that."

Eilidh dashed out to find the stable lad. Having completed her task, she returned to the longhouse and gazed down at the book her grandmother had thought to pack for her. Perhaps this would lift Torleik's spirits.

Eilidh cleaned herself up in her bedchamber, and briefly checked herself in the small mirror that Torleik had hung for her inspection. When she realized she now owned several gowns in various shades or green, her favorite color, her smile in the mirror grew in size.

Eilidh walked over to the long dining table where Atli was playing with Runi as Torleik was seated next to Hallkel, engaged in lively conversation. He paused to face her as she neared. "Torleik, I wish to speak to you in private about your grain crops ... but first," she said, lowering her voice so that no one could hear, "we need to communicate better. I need to know what you know so we can make the right decisions when the time comes."

"As you say, we will discuss this later, *in private*." Torleik resumed his conversation with Hallkel, who shot her a glance of sympathy.

Frustrated and embarrassed by his easy dismissal of her, Elidh plopped down next to him on the bench seat. Did Torleik always have to be the one to come up with the best solution just because he was a man? That was certainly not the impression she'd gathered when she met him in *Alba*. She had found him thoughtful and caring. Maybe that had all been an act because he'd been desperate to find a young and willing woman to move to the middle of nowhere, and who didn't know any better.

But I do know about how cruel men can be.

Eilidh winced, for a brief moment, comparing Bennett Sutherland to Torleik.

No. Torleik was a good man. He would never have allowed such a personal invasion of her body. She jumped up and to help serve the noon day meal.

The meal of fresh roasted lamb, peas and onions, and fresh-baked oat bread had stopped all conversation between the men, so this was the time when Torleik typically allowed Atli to ask his many questions for the day. By suppertime, the boy was often asleep on his feet, so Eilidh respected this routine by giving it time to run its course.

As the meal progressed, Eilidh took comfort in all her grandmother had sacrificed, and yet, still managed to accomplish in her lifetime, despite the obstacles. That brought a smile to Eilidh's face, and her enthusiasm for sharing her grandmother's idea with Torleik returned. What did she have to lose? If she succeeded, perhaps Torleik would soften towards her. If she failed, their life would continue in cold silence between two strangers.

When the table was finally cleared, Atli asked to go outside to play. Eilidh worried about residual smoke and ash still hanging in the air, but Torleik seemed unconcerned, waving to his son outside with the other children.

Eilidh bit her lip, knowing she couldn't dare question him. Not when he was in such a foul mood.

She watched as Astrid cleared the table and carried platters to the kitchen, Hallkel's eyes following her every move.

Eilidh grasped that moment to speak to Torleik. She leaned in. "I have an idea that may allow you to get a crop in before winter."

When Torleik glanced at Eilidh, his eyes appeared red from the smoke. "I don't recall your father saying anything about you having experience with farming. Your job is to manage the household. I will deal with this."

Hallkel coughed softly and looked away as Eilidh felt the heat rise on her cheeks.

Shocked that her husband could speak to her in such a brusque manner in front of others, Eilidh's shoulders slumped. She was glad Lifa wasn't there to witness her humiliation. It seemed like every time she spoke to Torleik, he turned into a different man.

Do not be afraid to share your thoughts, ban-ogha.

Eilidh lifted her head at the sound of her grandmother's voice nearby.

Ach, Seanmhair, just when I need you.

Moments of silence passed, when it dawned on Eilidh that *Seanmhair was right*, she must take a risk to achieve something better for her future. Her gut instincts were seldom wrong. She took a deep breath. "Torleik, let me show you something in my grandmother's herbal medicine book. She includes information about seeds and growing unusual crops. There is an entry of particular interest I want to show you." Eilidh fetched the book and returned to place it in front of Torleik. "Please take a look at what my grandmother said about growing bere barley." She pointed at the page she'd left open. "Bere has a short growing season, but has typically done well in these climes."

"Hmph. Bere barley. I've heard of it. Never knew anyone who grew it."

Eilidh jumped at that opening. "Let me show you what my grandfather, Niall, and *his* father accomplished. "The book is very old, so please take care."

Torleik glanced in the direction of the front door as if dying to go back outside. "I don't read Gaelic all that well. Perhaps you could summarize the contents of your grandparents' notes?"

Eilidh's stomach fluttered, grateful for the opportunity as she searched for the words that would compel her husband to listen with an open mind. She glanced at the open page on the table as she tried to still her racing heart. "My grandfather, Niall, perfected a process for how to grow a crop of bere barley in three months. He told my grandmother about his strategy, and she wrote instructions in her book for future generations. It's a kind of barley that requires only ninety days from planting until it's ready to harvest. It's an ancient grain that goes back for eons, so many native inhabitants of the isles have relied on it, as it is considered nutritious and easily substitutes for failed crops within any given year."

Torleik's arms were crossed, but he listened.

Eilidh knew she may be overstepping her bounds, but she had to make him understand this could be an easy solution to their collective problem. *Stubborn man.* She clasped her hands in front of her. "We still have several weeks ahead of us with long hours of daylight. If you planted seeds *now*, you could have a crop ready to harvest by early November. You'd have a later than usual harvest, but if we all work hard to finish ahead of the autumn rains, we will have grain for the worst part of winter. It may not taste like the barley we're used to, but it would be better than nothing."

"Hmph," Torleik grunted. "I suppose I should look into this."

She couldn't tell if that was a "Yes, you are brilliant, my love," kind of grunt, or, rather, "We need something that grows even faster."

Eilidh licked her lips. "Do you know of anyone in *Meginland* who grows bere barley? Perhaps you could ask him questions."

Torleik studied the floor and shook his head.

Hallkel rose from the bench. "I may know of someone out by *Kirkjuvagr*. A young farmer named Onund Haakansson. He does a lot of experimenting, so he may know more about bere barley. I think it's been grown in *Nord Vegr*, as well."

Torleik looked up and nodded. "Then, it seems wise that we speak with this Onund Haakansson and see what he has to say."

Eilidh wanted to clap her hands at this small victory, like the happy girl she'd once been. But as Torleik and Hallkel quickly departed on horseback, she felt the tiniest pinch of annoyance that Torleik had only made up his mind to look into the crop after Hallkel spoke up. Still, if it worked, that was what was most important. Wasn't it?

***

Torleik had just returned from meeting with Onund about the bere barley only to discover the door to one of the stalls open. Hallkel appeared behind Torleik and peered over his shoulder and through the door of the empty stall, where a mother cat had set up residence with five brand new kittens.

"Now, there's a sight you don't see every day," Hallkel whispered.

Torleik grunted his assent. He would never have expected to find Eilidh and Atli snuggled against each other fast asleep, a tiny kitten in each lap. He felt his gut tighten while his thoughts bounced around in his head. Atli had taken to Eilidh like a pup to a bone, making Torleik a wee bit jealous, if he were being honest with himself. As far back as the boy could remember, it had been just Atli and his father. How could Torleik have not realized how desperately his son needed a mother?

Anxious to share his good news about the bere barley with Eilidh, he debated waking her. The farmer they'd visited had been very helpful, enthusiastically sharing all he knew about bere barley. Torleik could have another crop by winter.

As he observed his son at rest, Torleik leaned down to rub Runi's head.

"Looks like Atli is happy with your choice of wife and mother," Hallkel said, peering at him with a sly glance.

"It would seem so," Torleik agreed with some relief. He'd had his doubts, and yet seeing her there, all curled up beside Atli, he had to admit that he felt not only jealous that Eilidh had formed such a tight bond with his son, but that she had done the same without returning any of the overtures Torleik had made toward her.

Eilidh must have heard the men's low voices because she slowly came awake. She started to stretch her slender body, hair tumbling over her shoulders in a coppery cascade. Atli burrowed like a little squirrel against her, and she suddenly registered the child's presence for the first time upon awakening.

Torleik felt his whole world flip upside down when she turned her gaze on him. Her eyes were glittery from having just awoken as she calmly reached out for the yawning black kitten in Atli's lap.

She smiled at the men standing in the doorway. "Oh! You're back."

She lifted the white kitty from her lap, then the yawning black kitten from Atli's lap, and returned them to the mama cat while mumbling something. Mama cat blinked, then gave her tail one serious shake, as if she understood whatever it was Eilidh had said, but was not in the least disturbed.

When Atli awoke and saw his father standing there, his face lit up like a sunbeam. He smiled in a way that tugged at Torleik's heartstrings.

"*Fadir*!" Atli stood and raised his arms like he used to do when he was much smaller.

Torleik lifted Atli into his arms, a grin spreading across the boy's face as Torleik felt the reassuring weight of his young son. "Looks like someone needed a nap today."

"Nun-huh." Atli ducked his head but Torleik just laughed.

Eilidh rose and brushed straw from her skirt and hair. Torleik had never seen anyone so beautiful. She had a tall, elegant way about her, and yet, she could just as easily show up with straw in her hair, like now, or mud on her skirt from chasing geese in the yard. She made little effort to primp and do those feminine things other women did to keep their complexions smooth or their hair styled in the latest fashion. She'd made no demands for new gowns or jewels. Her eyes were her jewels, such a bright blue-green, they reminded Torleik of a serene pool of water.

"Were you able to find that bere barley farmer Hallkel mentioned?" she asked in a sleep-husky voice.

Although Eilidh appeared calm on the outside, Torleik sensed how important this topic was to her as those beautiful eyes darted between him and Hallkel.

"Let's go inside and we'll talk."

As they crossed the yard, Hallkel veered off in the direction of his hut, giving them privacy, while Atli shadowed his father, imitating his every move until they were inside the longhouse.

Torleik smiled at the familiar scents clinging to his son as he carried him to the longhouse. He'd spotted the smear of raspberry jam on Atli's face, and noticed the smells of hay from playing in the barn, wet dog, and now, the hint of squirming little furballs with sharp claws. Redirecting his thoughts to the woman who walked beside him, Torleik's stomach burned. The sun made Eilidh's long curls appear burnished with golden highlights. Torleik felt a knot form in the back of his throat and had to look away. He had been most fortunate to find Eilidh. While away, Hallkel suggested he needed to tell her that ... soon. Before she gave up on him and Atli, and returned to her own village.

He stopped and gently lowered Atli down onto the porch. "Atli, why don't you go take a bath. Kelda will call you when it's time for bed."

Atli grinned. "Can Runi come, too?"

Torleik ran a hand through his son's hair, then signaled the dog. "Just make sure Runi doesn't jump in your bath water. We'll wash him later."

Excited, Atli shrieked playfully and scampered off with Runi in hot pursuit.

Torleik regarded Eilidh as she shaded her eyes and watched the boy and dog head in the direction of his room. He was surprised and happy that she appeared almost content.

They entered the dining room and made themselves comfortable. In a few moments, Astrid appeared with a mug of ale for Torleik and raspberry tea for Eilidh. He took great pleasure in watching how she sniffed the delicate aroma, as if trying to identify the flavor. She then seemed to nod that the tea was acceptable, before taking a sip. He'd already noticed his new wife had funny little quirks in her routines. He liked that. Somehow, her presence was becoming familiar and ... necessary. As he observed her deep pink lips blow gently on the tea to cool it, he suddenly felt a rush of desire.

He needed a distraction. Torleik cleared his throat and set down his mug.

Eilidh looked at him as she sipped. "The barley? Will you make me wait much longer to find out what you learned?"

He glanced down, detecting her interest. "We located the farmer, Onund, just as Hallkel remembered. He knew all about bere barley, and agreed that might be a good solution for replacing this year's crop. I bought some seeds from him. We can begin right away to prepare another field next to the field that burned."

"That's good news." Eilidh smiled sweetly and took another sip of tea.

A spark in her eyes told him he'd missed something. He racked his brain to recall what. As her silence continued, it finally dawned on him. She'd been the first to make the suggestion for planting bere barley. He'd been terse in his response, frustrated beyond reason about the whole burned crop situation. It was only afterward, he realized he was the cause for the glint of wet tears in the corners of her amazing blue eyes before he and Hallkel departed to meet with the farmer. Torleik had been so disgusted by his failure with the wheat crop that he'd forgotten to take her feelings into consideration. *"You behaved like an ogre,"* Ulla would have scolded him. She never let him get away with anything.

As he gazed at Eilidh, it occurred to him that she may be more like Ulla than he would have guessed. Their personalities and appearances seemed opposite. And that's what he'd wanted. No reminders that made both he and Atli sad and lonely. They had enough to deal with.

He inhaled deeply, then exhaled. *Get it over with.* "Thank you for suggesting the bere barley. That may make a huge difference to all of us this coming winter."

Eilidh nodded briefly, then rose, taking her tea mug to the kitchen.

***

A week later, Eilidh hugged herself as she gazed out onto the newly planted field of bere barley. Her husband had listened to her, after all, and had even apologized for his previous treatment of her. And he admitted that, because of her, they may not starve that winter. Despite everything, his continued vacillating behavior towards her still hurt, making her long for home, where people loved her for just the way she was, flaws and all, and rarely failed to speak their minds.

As she walked toward the cliffs that faced the sea, the man assigned to guard her took several small steps toward her, too close for comfort. She stopped abruptly, and so did the man.

Now, what is his name? Torleik told me just a while ago.

"Ma'am? You don't want to get too close to the edge."

She pulled her cloak tighter at the stiff breeze that had risen, annoyed that the man seemed to think she had no common sense. "Thank you. I understand." For a moment, she took in his patched clothing and hat, which he'd pulled down over his ears. He was considerably old for this time and place. And yet, he seemed spry as he smiled, most of his teeth missing.

"You do a good job of keeping an eye on me ..."

"Aye, I am Eyvindr, son of Hallr, from a long line of guards. Ancient names, those are, back in *Nord Vegr*."

She smiled, feeling a bit better now that she knew his name and that he was an agreeable old man. "Thank you again, Eyvindr, son of Hallr." She held her hand above her eyes, squinting into the distance. "I must return to the house. My husband should be back soon."

The man stepped out of her way as she turned on her heel and walked back toward the longhouse. Eilidh had been gone from *Alba* not quite a month, but felt she was finally beginning to make progress. The Norse lessons must be working, for already, she found it easier to understand others. If her pronunciation was bad, people at least seemed to appreciate her efforts – except for Lifa, of course.

She and Torleik had discussed Eilidh's ongoing problems with their laundress. Eilidh advised him that Lifa was obsessed with Torleik. Although it made him uncomfortable to admit it, he agreed, and they focused on Lifa's job performance. Eilidh's instincts warned her to be alert, that Lifa's destructive tendencies could put them all in danger if she was planning something. People like that didn't just change overnight, which made Eilidh wonder what had happened in Lifa's past to make her so cynical and mistrustful.

Leaving the bere barley field behind, Eilidh once again walked to the cliff edge, inhaling the sea air to banish thoughts of Lifa lusting after her husband. Her eyes settled on the white-capped waves crashing against the rocks below. Gathering gray clouds indicated a storm on the horizon.

When she stepped back from the edge and walked toward the path to the longhouse, her guard a good twenty paces behind, her thoughts turned to Torleik. He had seemed sincere in his apology for treating her idea about the barley with such skepticism. And yet, the man still didn't understand how deeply he'd hurt her by naysaying her idea in front of others.

Then, when she'd awakened in the stable that afternoon, she'd been baffled by the expression on Torleik's face. She couldn't quite read what he was feeling. Longing? Uncertainty? Anger? Shouldn't she know her husband better by now? Or was she expecting too much from herself? How she wished *Seanmhair* was there to share her wisdom. Which only reminded her she must establish a strict routine to work on Saraid's book each day if she was to complete her "mission" in a timely manner. The twelve-month deadline weighed heavily upon her shoulders and she'd made very little progress to show for it.

As Eilidh strolled past the pasture where Torleik's yearlings grazed, she spotted a lone figure slowly walking the perimeter of the stone fence. The man was dressed all in black, the hood of his cloak covering his face. He stopped every now and then, approaching the fence to peer at a particular horse. Something about him made the hairs stand up on Eilidh's arms. Something familiar about how the man carried himself, proud and self-assured. He turned his head toward the sea and Eilidh ducked behind a rowan tree, the only tree in the vicinity of the house. A sudden stiff breeze lashed at her, causing the hood of the man's cloak to fly back, revealing his face.

Eilidh rocked slightly where she stood, her limbs beginning to tremble.

Geirolf.

Heart beating like a hummingbird hawk-moth in her chest, she called to Eyvindr, who trailed behind her, his old legs tired from the climb. Once he recognized Geirolf for himself, the old guard yelled, "Hurry! Go back to the longhouse, while I go in search of the intruder."

Panting heavily, Eilidh ran through the moors, constantly checking over her shoulder to see if Geirolf followed. When she passed Lifa, who was busy hanging laundry, she caught a sly smile from the woman as though she'd known what awaited Eilidh on the moor. More frightened than ever, Eilidh went straight to her bedchamber, speaking to no one, her whole body shaking. As she crawled into bed fully dressed, all she could think of was Geirolf's face. Even at a distance, his intense gaze had made her skin crawl.

When Geirolf had told Eilidh that she would be his "beautiful bride," that day by the stones, she thought she would be ill. She was handfasted to Torleik now. When Torleik returned, she should tell him that she had spied Geirolf skulking around the property.

But then Eilidh got a grip of herself. Why was she cowering under the covers? She certainly couldn't hide away forever.

She'd scarcely got her breathing under control when she saw Torleik raise the door covering of the bedchamber and step inside. He paused, glancing about, confusion written on his face. "Astrid said you had come this way and that you appeared shaken. What are you doing in bed? Are you ill?"

He took a step toward her, brows furrowed. She lowered the bedcovers and sat up, but her hands trembled.

"I saw Geirolf out near the horse pasture."

Torleik raked a hand through his long hair, then repeated the unconscious motion. "He must still be in the area then. I have scouts in *Thjorsá* who would have sent a message had he escaped via the harbor. I'll go after him."

Eilidh hated herself for her weakness, but couldn't stop shaking. "I will feel so much better when the authorities have him in custody."

Torleik sat on the edge of the bed and rubbed the back of his neck. "I'll tell Torrad, and Eyvindr and the others, to look around the property. If Geirolf is here on foot, we will find him." He grasped her hand, the look in his eyes so filled with longing that it took Eilidh's breath away. In that moment, Eilidh felt a similar desire to let go of her fears, to make a true go of their marriage. But before she could make sense of her emotions, he stood, walked over to the flap, and ducked out through the door covering.

32

ᚨᚱᚲᛊᛏᚷᛈᛘᛚᛉᚢᚾ

Torleik and Hallkel arrived in *Kirkjuvagr* while the morning breeze off the harbor made the humid air around them still bearable. They dismounted near the public stable, and Torleik tossed a precious coin to a young boy to keep an eye on the horses. Torleik must have been generous, for the boy sent a huge grin his way, and called out, "Thanks, mister!"

"Make sure they get some fresh water," said Hallkel, handing the reins to the lad.

As they walked the main street of *Kirkjkuvagr*, Torleik's tired eyes missed nothing.

"The sheriff, first?" Hallkel inquired.

"*Ja*, I want to know if Geirolf is even a suspect here in town. I want a clear explanation about why he's still a free man, able to stalk young women."

"Agreed" Hallkel said.

"If anything had happened to Eilidh ..." Torleik glanced around, determined to find the scoundrel and to make sure he never bothered her again.

Hallkel chuckled. "You're starting to sound like a married man."

Torleik stopped abruptly, and stepped off the side of the street that was being converted from dirt to stone. He reached out and grabbed Hallkel's arm. "I don't know what happened. One minute, I was sure that all I wanted was a marriage of convenience, but now ..." He shook his head, thoughts swirling. "I swear, she's bewitched me. I want nothing more than to hold her in my arms until the end of time."

Hallkel grinned, the dimple in his chin showing. He leaned back against the wall of the apothecary. "How do you propose to get her to the church?"

***

That night, Eilidh followed Torleik and Atli to the boy's bedchamber to say good night. As they walked down the corridor, she realized they'd been speaking Norse most of the evening, and she'd understood quite a bit of it.

Eilidh made a quick decision and tapped Torleik on the shoulder as they walked through the doorway to Atli's bedchamber. "May I join you and Atli for your story tonight? I would love to hear it, and it would be good practice for learning Norse."

Atli jumped up and down. "Ja, *Fadir.* Can she?"

After a few moments of studying her, Torleik nodded. "Ja, that *would* be good practice to listen to a story."

Eilidh marveled at how thorough and gentle her husband was with his child, and yet he was no-nonsense, at the same time. She felt a tiny flutter in her stomach to think that could be her someday, tucking in Atli, and perhaps other children they had created together.

With room for only one chair, Torleik offered it to Eilidh while he settled on the edge of the bed. Eilidh had observed Atli's bedtime routine from the hallway before, but hadn't wanted to intrude. Consequently, she knew that Torleik told a different Norse myth each night, using varied voices for each of the characters, delighting Atli in the process. Every once in a while, she crept closer to the doorway, and Torleik would look up and nod. He never made her feel as if her presence was unwanted. But tonight was a first for her to join them in this tiny room and experience the power of Torleik's personality up close.

"Tonight, I will tell a story about how the beautiful Goddess *Freyja* helped the mighty Thor retrieve his giant, magical hammer, *Mjolnir.*"

Atli clapped his hands in anticipation. He lay back, eyes sparkling.

"Although Thor was the strongest of all the gods, he still relied on three treasures in his quest to kill giants. The first *Megingjord*, a belt that doubled his strength. Next, came his gloves made of iron, called *Jarngreip*. When Thor wore those gloves, he could get a better grip on his hammer and swing it with more accuracy. And lastly, of course, was his hammer, *Mjolnir*, created by the brother dwarves, Brokk and Sindri."

Torleik moistened his lips and glanced at Eilidh. For a brief moment, she thought his icy gaze hinted of desire. She looked away, uncertain how to react.

"One day," Torleik continued, "Thor looked everywhere, but couldn't find *Mjolnir*. 'This is a disaster!' Thor roared. 'Without Mjolnir, I cannot hunt giants. And I, along with the other gods, will be an easy target for whoever has my hammer.'"

Atli held his breath, eyes wide.

"And so, not knowing what else to do, Thor turned to Loki for help, even though Loki couldn't always be counted on to do the right thing. He was called the Trickster for a reason. Loki and Thor went to visit Freyja to ask if they could borrow her falcon-feathered cloak. She agreed to loan it willingly, as retrieving the hammer was to everyone's benefit."

For once, Atli listened closely and didn't interrupt with dozens of questions. As the story progressed, the sleepy boy was unable to keep his eyes open, and by the time Torleik finished the story, Atli was fast asleep. Torleik settled the covers over him and kissed his forehead. "Goodnight, Little Trickster." He brushed back the boy's straight blond hair away from his forehead, and again, Eilidh felt that painful longing, that desperate need to be a part of a family once again. To truly belong.

Eilidh didn't wish for Torleik to see the tears that gathered at the corners of her eyes, so she retreated to their bedchamber, but left the door covering open. She hoped Torleik would make the first move. A few moments later, he filled the doorway and paused.

Eilidh swallowed and tried to smile as if she didn't feel the tension in the air. "I enjoyed your storytelling, Torleik. Especially when you changed the characters' voices."

He shrugged his powerful shoulders and entered. "Atli is easy to entertain. But wait until you hear Hallkel tell a story at *Yule* time. He is a fantastic teller of tales. He has all the children under his spell."

Torleik stepped further into the room and regarded Eilidh for a moment. He then settled into a chair by the window. "I should have paid better attention to your concerns. That won't happen again. The same goes for your suggestion regarding the use of bere barley. As I said before, it will make a big difference this winter." He looked down at his hands, and she could see the furrow deepen between his eyes. "You are an extraordinary woman, Eilidh MacAoidh. I learn something new about you every day."

Eilidh felt her cheeks grow hot.

Torleik shifted in his chair. "I overreacted about the bere barley crop. I felt foolish that I couldn't take care of you." He licked his lips, as though uncertain whether to say more. "When I spoke to your father, he reminded me that you would be marrying beneath your station. You are the daughter of a great clan chief and deserve more than I, son of a Norse shipbuilder. That weighs on me." He tried to smile, but it was tentative. "I promised your father I would give you a good life, no matter what."

Eilidh slid off the bed and onto the floor, kneeling before him. "*Beneath* my status? Do you think I would come all this way for just *any* man? I came because, with you, I felt I had a chance at love." The moment the words left her mouth, she knew they were true, despite the blossoming warmth of her face. She took his big hand and studied his palm for several moments. She kissed it gently. "Torleik, we will be fine and have a very good life, once these current challenges are behind us."

Torleik placed his big hands over hers, looking grim. "As long as these challenges are not deadly. We think someone set the fire intentionally. Someone who may be here."

"Geirolf?"

"That was my first thought. But I was told by someone I trust that Geirolf was still in *Thjorsá* when the fire broke out."

"Someone he hired?"

"Most likely."

Eilidh squeezed his arm. "We'll figure this out ... together. But we must listen to each other and trust each other."

He took her hand between his large palms. "I will do my best to honor you and trust your judgment, to never let you down again."

"Ach, no more holding back!"

His hands gripped her shoulders lightly as he leaned forward. "I made a vow to protect you and keep you safe. Always."

He climbed into bed and pulled a sheet over his lower body, then glanced sideways with an amused grin. "Now, I must know what happened in your past to make you frightened of men?" He indicated the spot next to him.

Eilidh reluctantly settled by his side, using the moment to cuddle for warmth, and took a deep breath. "I've never told anyone this story. It happened about three years ago at a clan gathering near *Inbhir Nis*."

He fingered the tendrils of hair at the side of her face. "Your whole family was present?"

"Ach, aye. My brothers loved those gatherings. Grandmother stayed home."

She felt her skin blush as she tried not to stare at his naked chest.

"What happened that year?"

Eilidh glanced at the window, surprised to see the light still visible. "There were some lads there."

Torleik frowned. "What were their clan names?"

"Oh, I don't recall ..."

"You must remember."

Torleik's intense blue eyes held her gaze. "Someone hurt you?"

She let go of the breath she'd been holding. "Sutherland. Bennett Sutherland, and two of his henchmen." She shivered and pulled her warm shawl tighter. "I was bored at the clan gathering without my brothers at my side. I found a nice, quiet spot to rest, under a small stand of pine trees. I knew who Bennett was, but had never spoken to him before that day. I had grown quite a lot that spring so I felt awkward and clumsy. Other lads and lasses taunted me and called me ugly. I had to get away. I wandered away from the clearing, and I lay beneath a pine to take a quick nap. I thought no one would even notice me."

Eilidh reached up to loosen her burnished curls and then tied her back hair severely, as if she wished to cover up her true features. She tugged on the loose ends, still trying to think what to say. "When I awoke, Bennett was lying on top of me, kissing my neck and fondling me under my clothes."

Torleik gritted his back teeth. "What did he say once he realized you were awake?"

Eilidh tried to recall the scene, but it was too painful. "I don't quite remember. He called me a dirty whore and a faithless tease. He was intent on making his conquest."

Torleik stood and his whole face and neck suffused with red. "That little pissant! He was the same man in *Thjorsa,* the one that Geirolf stopped. He gazed at her with an angry expression.

"That meeting was a fluke. Bennett led me to believe that my father had put me up for sale to the highest bidder, and he planned for *Àthair* to reward *him* by making me his bride. And it's true, my father had spread the word far and wide, hoping to attract new suitors. Bennett happened to show up, hoping to be the one. But ... when he put his hands all over me, and inside me, and told me he was going to buy me for his bride, I ... I ...vomited all over him. I didn't do it on purpose, but he was furious, and demanded recompense." She lifted her chin. "I didn't know I had a power. I love my grandmother, Marsaili, but I couldn't blindly accept her Old Ways and be faithful to our family's religion at the same time." Eilidh shook her head, recalling the bumps along the way.

"I can understand that. I have experienced much the same in *Nord Vegr*." He caressed her brow and whispered. "Tell me the rest."

Eilidh sighed and took another deep breath.

"I had flicked my hand, like this," she said, demonstrating. "At the same time, I mumbled some nonsense words." She looked out the window. "Suddenly, there was a bright light that lasted about five counts. When I opened my eyes, Bennett's shirt was cleaned up. No sign of my ... breakfast. Bennett and his friends were frightened. Apparently, without my knowledge, a curse that promised to shrivel up their man parts should they ever force a woman against her will was brought down upon them. He has hated me ever since."

Torleik was laughing softly now, his arm around still holding her close.

"There are times when I don't know what to think of you, Eilidh. But today, I am proud of you for standing up to men like that. And for your fellow women. I like that." He pushed back his long hair. "Why do you think Bennett Sutherland resurfaced now?"

Eilidh shrugged. "I saw a wound on Bennett's forearm. It looked like a brand that we used to use on cattle. It's the letters, MacKY. I don't know for sure, but I think Leith chased him down and branded him. It still looks new. I ... couldn't ask Leith. I didn't want to know the answer." She settled against her pillow. "Once I saw that, I suspected Bennett wanted revenge for that. Even though he attacked *me*, I think he's rather afraid of me because of what I did with magic. I'd never done anything like that before. At the time, I didn't even realize that my thoughts would have such consequences. I should have discussed all of this with my grandmother. It may be too late now. Are you horrified with what I've done?"

Torleik slid his arms around her from behind. "Not in the least. As I said, I admire what you were able to accomplish without having been trained." He gave a wry smile. "Did I ever tell you I had a great aunt, Truda, on my mother's side who was also a great healer and seer? I remember she had a sly black cat with gold eyes, named Grimkel." He shook his head and gazed across the room. "Times have become very difficult for those who have more than one belief. I understand better than you think." He pulled her head towards him to lean against his bare chest.

He suddenly let go of her and fished for something in his pockets. "I asked Hallkel to make this for you, as a special gift." He handed her a stone with a black leather cord inserted through a hole.

Eilidh turned the stone over and fingered the etched symbols painted red. "A gift? It looks like it's tear-shaped. How unusual."

"A talisman is for maximum protection. Those carved markings are runes, which were used long ago by Norse peoples to communicate or divine the future." He gazed down at her. *Raidho*, The Journey; *Algiz*, Protection and Healing; and *Laguz*, A Gathering of Spiritual Powers and the Natural Flow of Love. When you combine runes like those three, it becomes a powerful binding stone."

Eilidh slipped the cord holding the talisman over her head, and when the stone rested against her chest, she held it near the candlelight to read it. "I love this. And it's true. I've already had a long journey. And I like the part about increased gathering of spiritual powers, although I still have some confusion about those. And then, there's ..."

"Love?"

"Hallkel is the true expert on runes and their magical powers, so you'll have to ask him for specifics."

Eilidh fingered the stone, admiring it.

"Ach, like my heart stone."

"Your what?"

"The light pink heart stone my grandmother gave me assists with matters of the heart, as well as being beneficial to a number of health conditions. I'll show you another time. You were saying about the runes?"

He stood and reached out for her, pulling her tight against him. "Hallkel was once a well-known rune carver for kings, so he has infused this rune stone with great power to keep you safe – as long as you wear this around your neck."

Additional magic – to give me strength – like Fitheach.

"I will be sure to thank Hallkel for this beautiful talisman. And I thank *you* for such honesty, Torleik. I hope we will always have honesty between us."

Eilidh felt the tension in the room decrease noticeably, leaving a clean, pure light surrounding them. For several moments, their gazes locked and neither of them moved. When she wrapped her arms around Torleik's waist and rested her cheek against his chest, she felt a low hum that seemed to awaken her inner core, her center of being. The hum grew stronger and stronger, sending a pulse surging throughout her body, a force she'd never experienced. Torleik's heart seemed to answer with a similar drumming. Was it magic?

Perhaps *Seanmhair* had been right all along. Perhaps Torleik *was* part of her destiny and she'd needed to travel her path in this roundabout way.

Eilidh was content standing still, her arms wrapped around Torleik's solid body, absorbing his warmth and taking courage in his strength. He must have bathed recently, for her nose detected Kelda's oats and honey soap.

"Eilidh ..."

Clearly, all common sense had abandoned her as Torleik whispered her name and shifted his grip so he could lean down. She braced for the kiss, but could never have anticipated what came next. As soon as their lips made contact, she felt his kiss heat up. His whole being embraced and surrounded her, and after a few moments, the kiss created a tight cocoon with him at the center.

He nibbled on her lips, and she stopped breathing. When she parted them for air, his tongue darted inside, and she felt a shiver of pleasure like a tingling that shot from her fingers to her toes. When his hands began exploring her body, his touch was confident and knowing the human form. She raised her chin and he brushed his lips over her neck, his beard stubble waking her from what seemed like a long slumber.

"Torleik," she murmured. "Does this mean we will consummate the handfast? And remain together?"

"I don't need to wait a year-and-a-day; *I want* you *now*, Eilidh. I never realized until now how much I need you in my life. And I want to take you to the new cathedral dedicated to St.

Magnus under construction in *Kirkjuvagr*, where I will marry you in front of God and the whole world! Should I continue?"

She smiled up at him, feeling dazed, as everything else slid away.

"Ach, *ja, taak.* Please continue."

Torleik lifted her and placed her gently on the bed. His hands were steady as he slowly undressed her and set aside her clothes so he could caress her bare skin, so soft and white. He captured her lips as if they were a pirate's prize, making Eilidh more than a willing prisoner. She returned the kiss with a passion that shocked her. Her muscles felt warm and tingled as her breath quickened. Torleik's hands ran up and down her arms, her back, his lips causing goosebumps wherever he planted kisses.

She made a little desperate sound and pulled his face towards her once again. "Don't you dare stop now."

"There will be no games between us," he whispered.

She felt the truth of that as his whiskered chin rubbed the sensitive spot behind her left ear. The spiral birthmark.

He wasted no time lifting his tunic over his head and tossing it on the chair. After he threw his final garments onto the chair and stood in the middle of the bedchamber completely naked, grinning in all his spectacular male glory, he climbed under the covers and held the bedclothes up for her. She ducked her head as she slid in under the smooth sheets.

"Come here, little wife." And Torleik then proceeded to show her the spectacular world of love-making in such a way, she could never doubt him again.

For the first time, Eilidh felt as if she was truly Torleik's wife.

***

Eilidh stood at the water's edge and laughed when Atli chased a gull into the air. He then squatted in the wet sand to trace something that caught his eye. Nearby, Eilidh could see Lifa standing at the top of the shoreline, watching them, arms crossed.

Eilidh tossed her wild red curls over her shoulder, pretending she was no longer bothered by the woman. Torleik was *hers*. After the previous night's magic, she knew she belonged to Torleik. And he to her. There was no room for another woman in his life. The night she'd spent in Torleik's arms had done wonders to gently heal the wound she'd carried around for years. Fear of men. How odd the way it all came about. And Torleik's fear to love again.

"*Modir*! See big yellow bird?"

Glad for Atli's distraction, Eilidh followed where his finger pointed. "I do! That's a gannet. Watch how high he dives when he's trying to feed his family."

As much as her body shook with anger whenever she was faced with Lifa, she'd promised Torleik to let him deal with her. Gladly. If only Lifa would leave them alone.

"What's that you have, Atli?"

Eilidh walked over and put her hands on her knees to examine his find.

"Words!" said Atli, pointing in the sand.

She inhaled fresh briny air and noted his name was written in the sand, small, imperfect letters eroding away with each wave that washed back over it. Eilidh studied the script and glanced over her shoulder. Lifa was no longer there.

"Aye. This says your name, Atli. Was this here before?"

Atli used his foot to erase the crude lettering. "I don't know. Maybe."

"Did Lifa come anywhere near you?"

He didn't turn his head this time. "No. I would not let her come close. My *Fadir* told me to stay away from her."

Eilidh forced a smile and patted his shoulder. "You're a good boy, Atli. Your father would be proud."

When she sent a final look behind her, she saw something that made her heart stop beating. A white furry lump lay on the sand near where Lifa had been standing. A very familiar white lump. And it wasn't moving.

"Fenella!" she screamed.

Eilidh raced down the coastline, but Atli beat her to the creature. Squatting, he listened to her heart. He looked up as Eilidh settled beside him, his eyes huge.

"What's wrong with her?" Atli wanted to know.

"Don't touch Fennela! I will take care of her."

When Fenella began convulsing, Eilidh tried not to panic as she turned to Atli. He should never be exposed to this kind of evil. She wanted to strangle Lifa.

"Let's go find Kelda. She may be able to help. You go ahead and find her." She hurried toward the longhouse, her face close to the cat's as she smelled her breath. Lifa's hut faced the farmyard. She stood in the doorway, a smug look telling Eilidh all she needed to know.

"If this cat dies by your hand, Lifa, I swear to you—" Eilidh called out. If she could have, Eilidh would have set the cat somewhere safe and lit into Lifa with her fists. But, at that moment, she didn't have the luxury of time.

Atli exited the longhouse, hanging onto Kelda's hand as he pulled her towards Eilidh.

Kelda reached for poor Fenella. "What happened?"

"I think Lifa fed her poison of some kind."

"Oh, my. That's a strong accusation, my dear."

"Yes, it is. For once, Lifa has gone too far."

Eilidh placed Fenella on the ground, exposing her stomach to Kelda who examined her.

"Did she eat something bad?"

"Most likely. Hold her by her legs, like this. If she'll allow it, we want to press on her tummy."

Fenella struggled to get away. After waiting as long as she could, Eilidh watched as the slick white cat sat back on her haunches, and surveyed the whole scene as if it were beneath her. But then, Fenella dry-heaved for several moments until she hawked up something, which Eilidh grabbed, holding onto a stem still containing three distinctive leaves.

"Hemlock!" Eilidh tried to control the tremor in her voice. "Does that grow naturally here in Orkney?" She gave Fenella a deserved caress down her neck.

"Not that I'm aware of."

With a loud, "Yeow," Fenellla gave up the last of her midday meal, sat up on all four paws, and strode off towards the longhouse.

"Fenny," said Atli, trying to pet her, but with little success.

Fenella twitched her long white tail and preceded Atli through the side door.

"Is she going to be all right? Hemlock is deathly poisonous to humans and animals." Anger simmered in Eilidh's chest at the idea that anyone could be so cruel. "I'll let Torleik know someone around here is using hemlock. Lifa must be stopped."

"I suggest you give Torleik the evidence, then let him do the dirty work." Kelda rose. "The cat should recover. However, I must tell Astrid and Siv not to give her any table scraps tonight."

Kelda chortled. "She is a bit like a dog. At least she doesn't beg. She just waits until I notice her – the queen – and then she receives what she thinks she's entitled to."

"Like someone else we know."

"I thought we weren't going to mention Lifa's name anymore?"

"I didn't. I just hinted at it." With a sigh, Eilidh released the fear she'd been holding onto until now.

Kelda tucked her wrinkled chin and pulled her warm winter wool sweater closer. "I know you and Torleik are truly one now. That man has wasted too much time since his wife's death." She reached into a pocket of her sweater and produced a smooth red stone, which she placed in the palm of Eilidh's hand.

"What's this?"

Kelda smiled, a bit of whimsy showing through. "It's a red jasper heart stone similar to the pink one your grandmother gave you. Next time Torleik gives you reason to doubt him, you can use this stone. Keep it close by so you can use it at a moment's notice."

Eilidh turned the stone over and over. "This is beautiful, Kelda. Where did you find this?"

"A gift ... from another strong woman. When she gave it to me, she said, "When you hold onto this stone, you will have the courage to speak up, and put sensitive topics on the table, topics that cause you fear. Let go of those fears and live your life."

"But it must be ancient. It's ..."

Kelda wrapped her hand around Eilidh's, locking the stone there, in her palm. "I knew the first time I laid eyes on you, you would need this stone to continue your work here."

For a brief moment, Eilidh felt lightheaded. She took a step back.

"What work?"

Kelda gave a gentle smile, a rarity for her. "The work you do for the benefit of all women."

"You know about –"

The old woman put a finger to her lips. "We Daughters of the Moon must stick together."

Eilidh pocketed the red jasper heart stone, hoping she would never experience such difficulties that she would require its use.

33

ᚨ ᚱ ᚲ ᛊ ᛏ ᚷ ᚹ ᛗ ᛁ ᛟ ᚾ ᚢ

When she entered the barn, Eilidh was still thinking about what Kelda had said about Daughters of the Moon helping each other. Did that mean she was a Daughter of the Moon? The thought made her smile, but it soon fell when she saw several workers gathered around Torleik and Isolf, all wearing grim expressions.

Eilidh felt the prick of tension finger up her spine as Torleik stood with his arms crossed. Everyone seemed to be waiting for him to speak. Even the horses in their stalls were unusually silent.

A sense of foreboding made the hairs on the back of Eilidh's neck stand up as well. "Torleik, is something amiss?"

He cleared his throat and looked up. "Arabel is missing."

"Wh-what?" Eilidh gasped and rushed over to the horse's stall, just to be sure. Her hands gripping the top of the gate to Arabel's stall, Eilidh could clearly see the chestnut filly with the black mane was missing. In the stall beside her, Nairna, Arabel's mother and the normally unflappable mare, stirred restlessly back and forth from the food bag to the water trough, as if she couldn't make up her mind what to do.

Eilidh knew by now how much these horses meant to Torleik, but this horse was special to *her*, because it was the yearling filly of her own horse. She had helped raise it, care for it. And now, to find it missing left a giant chasm where her heart had been moments earlier. When she came to stand beside Torleik and saw the slump of his shoulders, she knew he felt the loss just as much as she did. She reached out and put a hand on his arm. "Are you sure she didn't get out again and is playing a joke on us? She does that at times."

Torleik shrugged. "It's always possible. But I don't think so."

Eilidh shifted her gaze to Isolf, Hallkel, and the stable lads. "Who might have seen her last?"

"Probably me when I locked up last night," said Torleik. "I guess it's possible I didn't secure her gate tight enough."

"Don't beat yourself up," said Hallkel. "She's a clever girl, and has outsmarted all of us."

"She's definitely got a mean streak," added Eskil with a frown. "She bit me the day before yesterday. No reason. Just reached out and bit my arm."

Eilidh said nothing to that, as she suspected Egil had teased the young filly.

Torleik shifted his shoulders and his facial expression became more determined. "I have sent men out to search all of *Meginland*, if necessary. As you say, Arabel is quite a clever filly. She can open stall doors with her teeth. Did you know that? She prefers not to be confined in the stables, so she sometimes slips out. It's possible she escaped and is leisurely wandering around, in which case, we should find her soon."

Despite her fears, Eilidh bit back a smile at the tale of the filly's antics, then sobered. "You're probably right. She just found her own way out." Yet a passing worry nudged the thought she tried to quell. Could this be the work of Geirolf? He couldn't be blamed for everything that went wrong, could he?

Torleik wore a strange expression, as if he was asking himself that very same question.

"Did you not have guards posted on the horses?"

"*Ja*, of course. That's why this makes no sense."

Eilidh put a hand to her throat, wishing she could help. "I would assume Arabel would have made some noise if a stranger approached her, let alone removed her from her stall?"

"That's true." Torleik's response carried his frustration. "Unless someone here knew how important she was to you and was involved."

Lifa.

A chill in the air caused Eilidh to shiver.

"If we don't find the filly within the hour, we'll head for the ports to search for Geirolf. If he's still here and has Arabel, he is likely planning to take her to *Thjorsá*." He scowled. "Or worse, *Nord Vegr*, to capture the king's gold, and win his freedom. But first, we need to find Geirolf and the horse before we accuse him of theft. Horse theft is a serious crime, even if he claims to be taking Arabel to the king."

Eilidh wanted to squeeze his hand in reassurance, but didn't want to embarrass him in front of his men. "What happens if they find Geirolf in time and he *does* have the horse?"

"If they find Geirolf with Arabel, there would likely be some type of criminal trial in *Nord Vegr*. The king, or an assembly of men, would decide what to do with him."

Eilidh dropped her hand to her side, feeling a tightening of her chest. "Would you be required to attend?"

Torleik ran a hand through his hair, looking tired. "I will go, if I must. Let's see what the others can discover first. We should know more by suppertime." He dismissed the men and they dispersed to their various duties. Once they were alone, Torleik lifted Eilidh's chin, a gentle expression on his face. "I know how much Arabel means to you. Someone else may have figured that out. I'm so sorry you had to have this happen." He brushed a finger against her cheek. "I want you to stay here where I know you'll be safe. The men and I will turn over every rock to find Arabel."

Eilidh didn't say anything as the back of her throat had closed up. After a few moments, she looked up into Torleik's eyes. "You know how ornery she can get. Be sure to take some apples with you. She's much likelier to come with you if you have something sweet."

"I will take care of that right now." He kissed her on the cheek, grabbed an empty bucket, and went to saddle up Rig.

Eilidh glanced at the stall where Arabel usually rested, then took a few more steps to check on Nairna. Lying down in the straw, the dun-colored mare had her head down, as if she knew her daughter was missing. Eilidh entered Nairna's stall and crouched down next to the mare. Gently, Eilidh ran her hands over Nairna's sides, crooning to her in Gaelic for a few moments. Others might not believe she could "talk" to animals, and yet, that's just what she had done with Maeva. Nairna was poised to listen, her ears back, the better to hear her mistress.

After several moments, Nairna had given Eilidh an idea to pursue. If only Grandmother Marsaili were here, then she could be certain a *frith* would work.

***

By midday, Eilidh knew that Arabel was nowhere to be found. Torleik had received no word on the missing horse, not even a ransom note. Consequently, Torleik and Hallkel returned to the barn that afternoon and asked Eskil and Brusi, recovering from his leg wound, to feed and water Rig and Vàli so they could go out again.

As Eilidh waited at the longhouse, her hands felt oddly clammy, but she assumed it was from worry about Arabel and Torleik. Now that Eilidh and Torleik had consummated the marriage, she felt different towards him. More in tune with his thoughts and feelings. More protective.

"Where will you go first?" she inquired in the yard, trying to stay focused on the problem at hand.

"We'll try *Kirkjuvagr*, in case he's headed for *Nord Vegr*." Torleik's response was tight, as if chomping at the bit to be off. "If Geirolf is to be found, I expect that's where we will find Arabel, as well."

"But, won't he be hanged if he returns to *Nord Vegr*?"

"That will be *his* problem."

Eilidh couldn't recall Torleik ever sounding so cynical. But she supposed Geirolf had brought bad things upon himself.

"What about Lifa?" she inquired. "She may have had something to do with this. She may be sly and smug, but she *does* seem to have a way with horses."

"We'll be on the lookout for her, as well. Chances are, she's not coming back here if she's the one who poisoned Fenella. That was personal. And what's personal to you is *very* personal to me. Geirolf and Lifa know that. "In the meantime, I'm leaving Torrad in charge here while we're gone. I'll try to get word to you if anything comes up."

He stepped over to her and surprised her with a hug that rattled her bones. Then, he hopped up onto Rig, and was gone.

First, her cat had been poisoned, and now, Arabel's disappearance. But Eilidh knew this was about more than just her. Events seemed to be happening much too quickly. Clearly, someone was out to destroy Torleik, if that explained setting fire to their food sources. And stealing their horses could mean eliminating their back-up resources for food or cash resources this winter to buy grain. She must contact her grandmother to find out what she could discover in time to help Torleik save himself and his people.

Eilidh glanced in the direction of Lifa's hut. If she wasn't there now, there was no reason Eilidh couldn't go take a good look – maybe even clean out her hut–in preparation for Lifa's replacement.

34

ᚪᚱᚲᛋᛏᚷᚹᛗᛁᚷᛉᚾ

Eilidh slept deeply, her dreams vivid and real. She was trying to talk to Grandmother Marsaili. She followed her around and around her father's stronghold, trying to get her attention, but Seanmhair had so many needy patients. It seemed to Eilidh that every young woman in the province of Srath Nabhair, and some, who were no longer so young, were about to go into labor at any moment. Eilidh had never embraced the midwife part of the job as readily as her grandmother. Instead, she'd discovered she preferred searching for herbs and discovering which worked best together in combinations. But now, Kelda's poor eyesight was keeping her from delivering babies. It was the perfect opportunity for Eilidh to hone her midwifery skills.

"Alright, *ban-ogha*, I see you. What is so important it can't wait?" Her grandmother whirled in place and pinned her granddaughter with one blue eye. Eilidh gasped at the sight. She was aging so quickly.

"*Seanmhair,*" she breathed into the cold morning air. "I have many questions for you. You said you could help."

"Hmph. Well, all these babies can't wait forever. What is your first question?" Eilidh tried not to peek into the dozens of baskets her grandmother carried as she went about her day. Baskets? Was she delivering babies in plain old baskets?

Eilidh shook her head to clear away the images. "I'm here because I need your help."

When she turned her head, she realized her grandmother had disappeared.

"It's about time you came and asked for help," said the large scruffy raven sitting on her grandmother's chair. "Why have you waited so long?"

"I have a hard time believing in you, Raven." She gazed at the large black bird preening before her, realizing that Raven and all the pagan practices that came with him scared her. "Can anyone else see and hear you?" she whispered.

Raven glanced at Astrid and her daughters working in the kitchen garden. "I should take offense at that. Remember, you called me. I'm *your* spirit guide, not theirs. Of course they can't hear or see me." Raven lifted his feathers and settled on the soft chair. "I hope you were not planning on asking me about all those dowdy baskets?"

"Uh, no." The baskets had gone the way of her grandmother and disappeared. "How can you help me?"

"I was spirit guide to your grandmother once. And now, I am here for you. You must call me, '*Fitheach*'."

"Like my sword?"

Raven looked disapproving, his beak flat. "That sword is not really yours. It will be passed on to your first daughter when the time is right. It is simply on loan to you."

Eilidh digested that, not liking the answer. *Fitheach* was *hers*. She'd earned it.

The Raven fluffed his feathers, and it took some time for them to settle into place. He preened one or two, then turned back to face her. "We must not waste time. What is your most pressing question?"

Eilidh bit her lip, the decision already made. "Where can my husband find his missing horse, Arabel?"

"A horse is missing? How can a man misplace something that large?" Raven ruffled his feathers.

"You should not judge him. Torleik is a hard-working, busy man. He's had several new ventures go bad lately. I don't know if he can keep his community safe if he doesn't find Arabel. He needs every crop and every animal he has to keep them going."

Raven flexed the toes on his left foot and began picking out something with his beak that had stuck between them. "You wish to help him with this?"

"Absolutely. I want my husband to trust me with everything. His secrets, his longings, his fears. I can help him, but not if he's hiding something."

"I see." Raven tilted his head, as though considering her request. After a few moments, he re-fluffed his feathers, which were looking plumper and sleeker right before her eyes. "Have you ever performed a *frith*?"

Eilidh blinked. "A locator spell?"

"It's not just a spell. It's how we find things that may have eluded us in this lifetime, but are ready to reunite with us now, if the time is right."

Eilidh clasped her hands in her lap, feeling much younger than her almost seventeen years. "I've never performed an actual *frith*, but I've watched my grandmother locate extraordinary things for others."

Outside the window, Eilidh was aware of the farm animals settling in for the night. The chickens nestled inside the chicken coop, their clucks audible every now and then. She realized how much she'd grown to love the chaos of farm life, with so many animals and children about. It was beginning to feel *real* to her. A place she could call home.

Eilidh waited, eyes closed, desperately hoping for a sign telling her what she was supposed to do. Although the air still retained a bit of warmth from the summer day, she shivered at a slight breeze and pulled her shawl tighter over the new sleep gown she wore for Torleik. To perform the *frith*, Eilidh would need to step outside and circle the house in bare feet. However, she didn't dare risk being seen performing a pagan ritual out in the yard. It would be just her luck that Lifa would be sitting at her window, spying on her. She had already seemed suspicious when she found Eilidh "talking" to her grandmother the other day.

In her dream, Eilidh checked to be sure that Atli still slept soundly. He'd been muttering in his sleep on his stomach, his favorite position. Fenella had finally settled down, and was curled up at the foot of Eilidh's bed. Enough moonlight showed the rise and fall of her breathing, which comforted Eilidh, somehow. A few feet away on the new wool rug, Runi was stretched out on his back, bubbles escaping his slightly open lips.

"I'm sorry to say I must get on with my task of delivering babies. Are you sure you won't join me?" Raven had transformed back into Grandmother Marsaili, as she darted about, a finger to her lips to remind Eilidh to make no excessive noise.

Eilidh shook her head. "I think I would enjoy delivering those baskets, but I need to find Arabel first."

"Then you must do as Raven asks. Perform the *frith*. Then, you will know the truth about Arabel."

Eilidh had never considered herself a skilled *an da shealladh*, or seer, able to see future events before they happened, or have the ability to locate missing persons or objects, like her grandmother could. She'd had the occasional vision, but she never possessed her grandmother's ability for second sight. Still, she'd listened carefully and learned all that she could over the years, sometimes crouching hidden in the background as she watched

Seanmhair work her magic. That's how she had learned of the *frith*, yet she'd never performed one.

"I understand," Eilidh responded. She closed her eyes for a few moments, and when she reopened them, both the Raven and her grandmother were gone.

As she inhaled, then slowly exhaled three times, she felt her head clear and her body prepare for the work ahead. To avoid suspicion, she would perform the *frith* from inside their dwelling. It may not work, but anything would feel better than doing nothing at all. She removed her shawl and stood barefoot and bare-headed. She darted a glance around the farmyard once more, memorized the moon's location, then shuttered the window so as not to be seen from outside. Quickly, she lit a candle and set it on a side table.

To begin the *frith*, she closed her eyes and took slow, measured steps around the chamber, moving her feet in the direction *Seanmhair* called '*deisiol*,' left to right. Fenella opened her eyes a fraction, but didn't twitch as she watched Eilidh's every move. It took longer than Eilidh had expected to complete her task with eyes closed. Her hands guided her, and she felt fortunate she didn't stub her toe on one of her trunks. At long last, she had successfully touched each corner of the chamber, arriving back where she started.

Eilidh's eyes popped open and she held up her hands to form a circle made by her fingers and thumbs as she faced the direction where she'd seen the moon beyond the shuttered window. Gazing through the circle of her hands, she focused on "seeing" an image of the missing filly. Eilidh had chosen Arabel as a whimsical, sunny-day name for the sleek-coated chestnut filly. Her father had indulged her choice, as well as appreciating her constant attention to the animal. That attention made it quite easy now for Eilidh to visualize the filly's physical manifestation, as well as her spunky personality. Next, she concentrated on a physical image of Torleik. Tall, well-muscled, long, blond hair. His crooked smile. His image was easy to envision, as well, thank goodness.

Use your powers, ban-ogha!

Feeling her grandmother's presence at last, Eilidh felt a chilly breeze on her bare feet. Her arms grew weary from holding them up, but still she pressed on. She began to murmur in Gaelic, speaking directly to the young horse in her mind. She had no idea if this would work, but she had to try.

Unsure if the wavering image in the circle of her hands was caused by simple fatigue or an actual vision, she couldn't help but gasp as she recognized the dark-haired man.

"Geirolf," she whispered into the night.

So, Geirolf *had* taken Arabel. She cringed to see the man and horse struggling at a stable outside of an inn near a ships' landing. The filly obviously didn't want to go with Geirolf, who tried yanking her forward with the rope tied around her neck. Again and again the filly reared up, hooves dangling dangerously close to Geirolf's face as he tried to break free while harsh words continued to tumble from Geirolf's lips. Eilidh couldn't distinguish what was being said, but it didn't matter, now that she knew where they were located. She'd never been to the port town of *Kirkjuvagr* on the north-eastern shore of the island, but she assumed that's what she was seeing, as it would be closer to sail to *Nord Vegr* from there if that was his destination, rather than from *Hannavoe* on the western side of the island.

Remaining as still as possible, she squeezed her eyes shut and tuned out all night noises – the waves gently breaking against the shore, animals shuffling in the barn or pens, a rope flapping on a post near the pasture. The scent of rosemary wafted from the kitchen garden that Astrid tended so lovingly, lending a softness to the night.

Eilidh considered her words carefully.

"Arabel, hear me. Do not be afraid. We, your family, love you very much, and wait anxiously for your return. Find Torleik. He is on the way to bring you home. Be brave. Don't let that dark man frighten or bully you."

She ignored the cold fingers that gripped her spine at the thought of Geirolf. Having completed the locator spell, she knelt before her bed and prayed to the Christian God. She needed to be sure she'd done everything she could. When finished, Eilidh rose and noticed the crick in her neck from holding her arms up for so long. As she stretched and rubbed until her neck felt better, she tried not to lose hope that both her husband and the horse were safe ... somewhere.

***

With Torleik gone to search for Arabel, Eilidh slept through what was left of the night, but was suddenly awakened by Kelda's voice and touch in the early morning hours.

"Mistress Eilidh, you are needed right away. Valdis' family has waited as long as they could to wake us, but Valdis' baby is coming. You must go. My eyes are useless this early in the day."

Eilidh jumped out of bed. "Ach, you rest those eyes, Kelda. I can go. Send someone to tell them I'm on my way. I just need to dress and grab my medicine sack."

Suddenly, she felt wide awake and aware she had a duty to deliver this child, especially if Kelda was no longer able. Someone had to take over her duties. It might as well be Eilidh. Wasn't that what her grandmother had hinted at? At peace with her decision, Eilidh quickly washed her face and dried it as she eyed the plain fern green gown Kelda set out for her.

"There's a Bannock cake on the table for you," said Kelda, heading for the doorway. "This may be the fourth child that Valdis has borne, but we should always be prepared for a lengthy delivery."

"*Taak.*" Eilidh nodded her agreement and quickly dressed while Kelda bustled off.

As she donned the work gown with help from a sleepy-eyed Muire, Eilidh wondered whether Torleik and Arabel had found each other during the night. Pleased with the distraction of bringing a new life into the world, she left Atli in Astrid's care, knowing when he awoke in a few hours he'd be okay. She grabbed the Bannock cake, and rushed towards Stigr and Valdis' hut. The sun had not yet risen in the sky, as Eilidh picked her way carefully towards the family's home.

She knocked on the door, and heard Valdis let loose with a loud lingering scream as a strong contraction gripped her. Stigr invited them inside, where Eilidh could immediately tell that Valdis appeared pale and exhausted in between the pain as she lay on her sleep pallet.

Stigr quickly shooed the three boys outside and followed them, closing the door behind him.

"Haven't you been drinking the raspberry and chamomile tea I left you?" Eilidh inquired as she rummaged for something in her medicine sack. "You look like you haven't been sleeping enough." She examined her patient's extended belly, relieved that everything appeared as it should.

"I've been so busy with the boys. Brusi's injured leg took a lot of time and attention. It's hard to keep boys in bed." She looked up. "But he's all healed now, thanks to you, mistress."

Eilidh nodded, glad to note her first patient's recovery. She checked the young mother's pulse by pressing her fingers against her wrist. She then placed her ear against her chest to listen to her heartbeat. "Everything looks and sounds good, Valdis. Is this delivery taking much longer than the previous three?"

"*Ja.* It started yesterday evening." She inhaled a deep breath, clearly in pain. "Do you know why my baby isn't ready to come out?"

Eilidh sat back on her haunches before the pallet. "Were any of your boys born late?"

Between contractions, Valdis scrunched her face as she tried to think. "Let's see. Brusi was a few days late, but I never felt this exhausted. Hodur came early, and Einar was right on time, thank the Lord."

Eilidh reached inside her sack and pulled out a package of herbs. "I can brew some tea that should promote contractions and shorten the labor. Unless you wish to wait?"

Valdis brushed back a dark wavy strand of damp hair then let out a cry of pain as a new wave of mild contractions began, and yet Eilidh knew that these were only the precursors to the real contractions that would come later. When Valdis was finally at rest again, she said, "No, I want to get this over with." She shifted on the pallet. "I just realized that I can understand your Norse!"

Eilidh grinned as she set a pot of water to boil over the fire. "*Taak*, Valdis. Hallkel ... *and* Atli make excellent teachers."

After the tea had steeped, Eilidh asked Valdis to drink the whole mug. She then encouraged her to rest so the tea could do its job and Valdis could store up some energy for the final push.

Eilidh didn't speak, as she watched Valdis' breathing become slow and steady. Eilidh knew there was always the possibility that something could go wrong, something she couldn't foresee. So, as Valdis slept, Eilidh prayed to Brighde, Goddess of Motherhood, to give both she and Valdis the strength for what they must do. Of course, she threw in a little prayer for the baby's well-being too. Feeling content that she'd done all she could to prepare, she sat back and dozed off, but she came to full wakefulness at the first cry of pain from Valdis.

Eilidh placed a hand on her stomach, and could feel the baby working hard, having entered the birth canal. She took a look underneath the sheet and grinned. "Not long now. The tea seems to have done its job. You can push any time."

"Thank God." Valdis made the sign of the cross.

Eilidh made sure to keep the pot of heated water going and set aside more herbs that might be needed to stop any excessive bleeding. Stigr entered the home at the sound of Valdis' renewed screams, and then hurried to retrieve clean cloths for Eilidh. They both washed their hands thoroughly, at which point Valdis experienced a particularly long contraction causing her to try to sit up, eyes wide as she bellowed. Stigr tried to comfort her, but his wife waved him off when she could catch her breath.

Eilidh nodded after peeking once more beneath the sheet. "All is ready. It's time to push again, Valdis. The baby is coming ... and fast."

After several moments of pushing, Valdis grunted as the baby finally slid into Eilidh's waiting arms. She then handed the baby to Stigr to wrap and clean while she cut the umbilical cord.

"Girl or boy?" asked Valdis, her voice a whisper, as if afraid to ask.

Stigr unwrapped the blanket to show them. "A *girl* ... at last!"

Valdis sank back and cried tears of joy.

After both mother and daughter were cleaned up and ready to be presented, Eilidh invited the boys inside to join their parents.

"A girl," Valdis breathed. "The boys have a little sister."

Stigr leaned down and kissed his wife's cheek, tears glistening at the corners of his eyes. He then kissed the baby's tiny little forehead. "What will we call her?"

Valdis held her baby girl to her breast and peered inside the blanket wrapped around her. "Gida. For my mother."

"Gida it is," said Stigr. "Boys, come meet your sister, Gida."

Eilidh treasured moments like this. However, on this particular day, she was seeing the miracle of childbirth and the challenges of parenthood through new eyes. Maybe her destiny was as a midwife after all.

Part III: LAGUZ

(Gathering of Spiritual Power; Love's Natural Flow)

35

ᚱᚱᚲᛋᛏᚷᛈᛗᛚᛟᚦᚢ

Lifa glanced out the window at an alley that reeked of skunk, and considered Geirolf's choice for an inn. The temperature outside was sweltering, and she felt her best wool dress cling to her. Since Geirolf was willing to pay for a roof over her head, she shouldn't complain. When this matter with Torleik was concluded, they'd be in much better financial shape, she was sure.

A knock at the door startled her. As she opened it carefully, she was surprised to see Aevar standing there, looking awkward as ever.

"What are you doing here, Aevar?"

He reached past her and shoved his way inside. "Plans have changed." He stepped to the window and held back the curtain. "The town is swarming with Torleik's men. They're not leaving anything to chance. Geirolf says if they are this involved in finding the horse, he's taking no chances that anything else can go wrong."

Lifa took a step back. "So what does he want to do?"

"Geirolf says you are to move quickly and nab the boy, Atli." Aevar reached into the pocket of his shirt and pulled out a cloth dipped in valerian and cowslip. It was a heady sedative, and Lifa looked up at him in question.

"What will you do with that?"

"*I* will do nothing." He placed it in her hand and closed her fingers over it. "*You* will use it to grab the boy."

Her first impulse was to decline or complain, but then she warmed to the idea quickly. "I suppose he *would* make a good hostage if we need one."

"And if Geirolf is correct, Torleik and Eilidh will do just about anything to protect that boy. That ensures their cooperation."

Lifa nodded, liking the plan more and more. Making Eilidh miserable was sure to cheer Lifa up. "So where do I grab the boy?"

"Torleik has a big announcement later today, so we have to act quickly. Geirolf wants you to return with me to Torleik's farm right away. Geirolf wants you to act agreeable, talk to folks in the crowd in a light manner, so they'll remember seeing you there. You will then approach the boy and do whatever it takes to gain the boy's trust enough to follow you. Once you get close enough, when Torleik isn't looking, use the cloth over the boy's mouth and nose to sedate him. I'll take you and the boy to the Standing Stones where Geirolf will be waiting with the kidnapped horse. Geirolf confronts them and makes some kind of deal. We return to our homes, and that's the end of that."

"There are a lot of moving parts to that plan," Lifa said. "Anything can go wrong."

Aevar narrowed his eyes. "Are you up to the task? If not, Geirolf said you ..."

"I'm up for the job. But if everything goes smoothly, I will expect some kind of bonus. You can tell Geirolf, since I'm taking the greatest risk."

Aevar smiled. "That you are. Can you pack quickly? I'll wait downstairs. We leave well before midday."

Lifa produced a genuine smile. At last they had a plan, and soon they would put that plan into motion.

***

As Torleik spoke to the crowd, Lifa stood toward the back, pondering how she would kill Eilidh, with so many possibilities available to her. She loved the world of poisons and figuring out the right mix for each person. She supposed it might come down to how Eilidh acted towards Lifa, at the end of the day. Would she beg? Would she curse Lifa? Whatever Eilidh did, Lifa needed to remember how she'd been treated as a lowly laundress by the pair.

Torleik stood in front of the stable and continued the speech he'd begun. "We have the bere barley harvest celebration in two weeks to look forward to. On the other hand, I'm sorry to report that our horse, Arabel, has been missing the past twenty-four hours. We must find the filly and bring her home. She is of special personal interest to my wife. Hallkel made posters, so I'd appreciate it if some of you would show these to folks in nearby towns and villages. Hallkel and I will ride for *Kirkjuvagr* now, and will return in the morning ... unless we have another lead. Please pray that we find the filly and unite her with her mother, Nairna."

Lifa's gaze sought Eilidh one last time. She couldn't help but admire how natural and slender she appeared in a fine pale green gown she'd no doubt brought with her from *Alba*. She must think she was too good to wear the Norse apron gown the other women wore, as was the custom. She licked her lips and watched Eilidh and Torleik stand beside the stable, hands entwined. Inside, Lifa seethed, the fury causing her chest to ache. Let them think that she would simply go away quietly. But they would be wrong. Dead wrong. This plan had to work.

People seemed excited about the upcoming party to celebrate the very late, but special, harvest, and she listened in as people talked about what food and drinks should be served. What music and dances they'd enjoy. With all that racket and intensity, Lifa found it easy to glide through the crowd, smiling at this person and that, until she found Atli on the longhouse porch by himself.

"You're so quiet over here, Atli. Aren't you excited about the party?"

Atli looked up at Lifa. "I'm not s'pose to talk to you."

Annoyed at his whiny little voice, Lifa frowned, then caught herself and smiled. "Now, who said that? I just work here, like Kelda and Astrid. You talk to them, don't you?"

"I guess."

"And when they want you to go someplace, you go with them?"

Atli looked at her with a suspicious glance. "Maybe."

Lifa whipped out the cloth from her pocket. Glancing over her shoulder to make sure no one would see what she was about to do, she quickly grabbed the boy and placed the cloth over his mouth and nose. He struggled for a moment, but quickly lost consciousness. Relying on Aevar for the next part, she took Atli around the side of the house where two chairs and a small table were placed in the shade. With Atli spread out on her lap, she waited. She looked down at the small child, a replica of Torleik, and grinned. He really was the spitting image of his father.

The slow clip-clop of two horses approaching caught her attention. Aevar rode Walnut, but in his free hand, he held the reins of another horse. A huge horse that danced nervously.

"I'll ride Walnut. You ride that dancing giant," she said before he could speak.

"But ...."

"The boy needs a calmer, gentler horse." *And so do I, you fool.*

Aevar appeared to accept that excuse, for he dismounted and tied the larger horse to a chair. Taking the boy in his arms, he watched Lifa hoist herself into Walnut's saddle, then Aevar handed the boy up to her.

He surprised Lifa when he quickly mounted the big horse and turned him towards the gate at the front. "Wait for my signal," said Aevar.

Lifa thought the "signal" was a bit dramatic, but she waited in a spot where no one could see her, regardless. She glanced back at the dispersing group where she saw Torleik and Eilidh with their arms around each other. It was then they walked over to the porch and found Atli missing.

She could hear them call the boy's name over and over, but … no Atli. Fortunately, at that moment, Aevar gave the signal and she rushed to greet him, before the couple's eyes turned to her and the boy.

No doubt by the time they thought to ask others of Atli's whereabouts, Aevar and Lifa would be long gone … Atli withstanding a very bumpy ride to the Standing Stones.

36

ᚨᚱᚲᛋᛏᚷᚹᛖᛁᚲᛟᚾ

The scene kept playing over and over in Torleik's mind, making it impossible to come to any other conclusion. As he sat atop Rig, accompanied by Hallkel on Vali, he tried keeping his eyes on the road ahead. He would have to adjust to the fact that because of Eilidh, Atli had disappeared – practically in front of his eyes. How could he have been so wrong about her? Eilidh had one job, and he thought he'd been clear about that. Keep an eye on Atli at all times, or place someone in charge of him when they had something to do that took them away from the longhouse. He growled at the very idea. He would never have allowed Atli to run around on his own like that with someone like Geirolf on the loose. Did she have no common sense? Of course, it niggled at him that he had been guilty of the same thing, but not to that degree. But first things first.

"I can't get over Eilidh failing me at such a time."

Hallkel cleared his throat. "I wouldn't blame Eilidh for any of this."

Torleik's emotions quickly shifted from desperation to anger, and still his friend kept his eyes gazing ahead.

"She's been trying to make sense of things since the beginning. You know how much she loves that boy. I really don't think she'd intentionally let any harm come to him. You know that, as well."

Torleik was still pondering his thoughts and emotions when Egil Hromundsson, his neighbor to the south, stopped him along the road to *Kirkjuvagr*, riding a spent and braying donkey, his daughter Ashilde seated on a white horse. Torleik nodded politely, then did the same to the young woman beside him.

"Greetings, Egil, mistress Ashilde. How goes your day?"

Torleik had heard the tale of how Egil had survived a horrible accident that crippled him many years ago. If he rode a horse or donkey, he could conduct business as usual. The rest of the time, he was a foul-mouthed peasant who had few good words for anyone. Once considered a wealthy landowner, Egil had lost his fortune, his mobility, and blamed the accident for everything that went wrong following that awful day.

However, Egil was blessed with three beautiful daughters, two of marriageable age. He'd tried to convince Torleik to marry his eldest, a tall, thin woman named Brynja, who rarely seemed to smile or laugh. Torleik had talked himself out of taking *that* on almost as soon as the idea passed Egil's lips. Dark-haired and of an uneven temperament, with little interest in child-rearing, Brynja hadn't won Torleik's heart. Egil didn't bother to argue, so it could be that her personality was even worse than what Torleik had heard at the community store. The second daughter, Ashilde, a pleasant-looking girl closer to Eilidh's age of sixteen, rode beside her father, a deadly-looking crossbow sitting across her lap in contrast to her quiet demeanor.

Egil stopped the donkey and glanced around at the gray day. "How goes my day?" he repeated, then frowned. It didn't take much to imagine him a self-pitying man. "I have accomplished nothing today. And you? You look to be in a hurry to reach

Kirkjuvagr." He pulled a slip of paper out of his pocket and straightened it on the donkey's back. "A complete stranger gave me this message to give to you. More like a map than a message, don't you think?"

Torleik was aware that Geirolf likely had never learned to read, like many people. For that reason, he could appreciate the small map Geirolf had produced on the back of a brewhouse napkin. Torleik stared at the objects and handed the slip of paper to Hallkel to examine.

"What do you think? Look familiar?"

"Brodgar's Standing Stones, is my guess."

They had passed the giant stones a quarter of an hour earlier. Torleik ran a hand through his hair. "Let's get going. Our paths must have crossed, somehow."

"Did you see this?" On the back of the same small map, Hallkel indicated what appeared to be a child's stick figure drawing of a blond boy, standing in front of one of the giant stones that towered over him.

"Damn, is that supposed to be Atli?" Torleik ground his teeth together, fury causing his hands to shake. "How could Eilidh be so careless!

"We're almost there," Hallkel reminded him. "I would suggest we hold the blame until we have more information."

Though Torleik felt chastened, and knew in his heart that what his friend said was true, he wasn't ready to let go of his anger. He nodded his thanks to Egil, while pondering Hallkel's words. He so wanted to believe she was innocent in all this.

Egil gave a considering nod. "You need some help? I can't do much myself these days, but I can volunteer my second daughter here, Ashilde. She's a cracker shot with that bow when you need it."

"That's good to know, but I think—"

"We can always use help," said Hallkel, overriding Torleik while smiling at Ashilde.

She had long straight blonde hair, a slender build, and rode upon an all-white horse–conveying the look of a disciplined female warrior all in white. Local talk, Torleik knew, claimed that she conducted various mysterious matters requiring muscle and finesse for her father or anyone else who was willing to pay. She gave Hallkel an abrupt nod, bypassing Torleik altogether.

Irked at first that Hallkel had countermanded his response, Torleik gave a grudging nod to Ashilde. "Alright. This may be a hostage situation with a man who's not quite in his right mind, so there's a possibility things may get physical. Are you willing to take that chance?" He looked to Egil first, who regarded his daughter with a sparkle in his eyes.

"I'm prepared," she said. "I work fast. Who is being held?"

"My horse, Arabel, and my four-year-old son, Atli, I see now," he said, looking at the map. Fury sparked his words that Geirolf would have taken Torleik's son. And yet how had he entered the farmyard in such a crowd? No, this smelled of Lifa's intervention. Why hadn't Eilidh posted someone to watch the boy while Torleik spoke with the crowd? No matter what Hallkel said in Eilidh's defense, he would never forgive her if anything happened to Atli.

Ashilde turned to her father. "You need to go home and get some rest, *Àthair*. I will tend to this matter."

Egil picked up the donkey's reins. "Let me know how this all turns out in the end, eh?" Egil nudged the donkey, who gave a feisty kick or two before moving along home.

Still seated atop Rig, Torleik held tight to his reins as he watched Egil make his way home.

Ashilde, too, regarded her father's departure. "I like to give him little skirmishes to savor. It keeps him from becoming difficult."

Hallkel offered a tight grin. "And you're not afraid to jump right into something so dangerous?"

Torleik put his hat on and straightened in the saddle. "We don't know yet how dangerous this will be, but we could use someone watching our backs." Torleik pocketed the drawing of Atli and nudged Rig back the way they'd come. "We'll pay you for your services, of course. Now, I want to see if there's an approach to the Standing Stones that Geirolf doesn't know about."

The two men took off at a gallop, their horses' hooves clip-clopping on the dirt road, Ashilde, trailing the pair.

All Torleik could think about was how ironic it was that he and Eilidh had finally come together, declared their love for each other, and now, the disappearance of one little boy made everything they'd accomplished a matter of life or death. Heading back the way they'd come, Torleik swore softly in Norse.

***

Exhausted after the long search for Atli resulted in no wiggling little boy to embrace, Eilidh retreated to her bedchamber. Torleik and Hallkel had saddled up and were heading beyond the property boundaries. To distract herself from the fear and worry, Eilidh folded a shawl and thought about her accomplishments with the Delsiran project. She'd created and compiled dictionaries in Norse, Scottish Gaelic, and Delsiran, yet it felt as if any successes she'd made in that regard had been negated when she realized she may now lose everything precious in her life. Eilidh fought back tears. Torleik was so angry, and rightly so. No wonder he felt betrayed by her lack of oversight. Atli was missing. Arabel was missing. Everything that had come to mean so much to her happiness had come to a crashing halt.

And Torleik blames me.

She accepted that blame, but she wasn't sure what to do about it. For a short while, she pondered what would happen if Torleik sent her away. Would her family take her back? Or, would

311

they simply find another man to marry her, even though she was no longer a virgin?

Why had she not paid more attention to Atli? Her oversight hadn't been intentional. She'd been distracted, so worried about Arabel being stolen, on top of the trouble with Lifa and Geirolf. Then this morning, Torleik had asked her to join him while he made a brief announcement that had grabbed everyone's attention. It had all happened so fast, she'd had little time to think. And just when she'd become Torleik's woman in every way. She shook her head and swiped at the tears that fell in earnest now. Eilidh was not one to feel sorry for herself, but this was a mistake she might never be able to undo. How had things gone so terribly wrong in such a short time?

And what bothered her most was knowing Atli may be alone, or worse, Geirolf might have tied him up and, even now Atli might be at his mercy. He was a sick man. She could only hope he wouldn't do something to give a small child nightmares for life.

She poked around her bedchamber and eyed the empty trunks. Should she begin packing, assuming Torleik would send her back to her father's home? She needed to do something to help the situation. She couldn't just stay here, worrying.

At that moment, Kelda stepped inside, her hands clasped in front of her. "I know you never meant any harm to come to Atli. Torleik is so attached to that boy that he can't think straight." Kelda opened her arms and enveloped Eilidh. After a few moments, she stepped back. "I think you should go and try to find them. They will need your help, I am certain. Last night I had a dream of you and Torleik at the Standing Stones. I would wipe those tears and start there."

Suddenly feeling a newfound purpose take hold, Eilidh dried her eyes and nodded her agreement. *The Standing Stones.* Could it be that this is where Geirolf had taken the boy? And yet it seemed only fitting after the last time she had seen him there. Her thoughts turned to Torleik. She loved both Torleik and Atli and would do whatever it took to save them both. Then, she would abide by Torleik's decision. If he asked her to leave, she would go, but not before she had done everything in her power to protect them.

"You're right, Kelda. I must do something productive." Eilidh reached for a light summer cloak. "Be ready with herbs and supplies. Willow bark, and so on. I may need them. Have them waiting for me in the barn."

Kelda's brows rose. "You have seen something?"

As Eilidh secured the family brooch on to her cloak, she shook her head. "Not really. But it makes sense to be ready. I'll try to rescue Atli and convince Torleik I had nothing to do with his son's disappearance."

"Just remember, Torleik is a stubborn man. It may take a while to change his thinking and regain his trust." Eilidh's throat tightened, knowing Kelda was right. He might never forgive her. She reached in her pocket and found the red jasper heart. She gave it a squeeze as she glanced at Kelda. "Maybe it will help if you keep reminding me of that. I don't want to leave here if Torleik determines I can't be trusted ever again, yet I will go if he says I must. My heart will be broken, however." Eilidh offered her friend a watery smile.

"We don't want to see you go, either." Kelda stepped over and gave Eilidh a big hug, then stepped back. "May God go with you. And the Goddess guide your steps."

As she walked quickly toward the stable, Eilidh hoped it was all a serious miscommunication. That, in the end, Torleik would understand that she would never do anything to purposely jeopardize her relationship with either Torleik or the boy she was quickly coming to regard like a son.

***

The wet road had dried already as Eilidh pondered her situation. Grandmother Marsaili had been such a steady influence her whole life, that now, Eilidh had trouble letting go. In truth, as much as she liked learning about the Old Ways of the Druids, it took up time and effort. This just proved she needed to be focused on her family. She felt a need to be tethered to the ground, her feet firmly placed in reality. That meant her mother's Christian religion. She had gone back and forth for so many years, it sometimes felt like it was the most natural thing to do. Perhaps, it was as simple as giving all her attention to Torleik and any children they may have.

Just before she arrived at the Standing Stones, Eilidh was approached by a woman dressed in white, sitting on an all-white horse. Eilidh stopped to give Nairna a breather, her eyes immediately drawn to the large crossbow on the other woman's lap.

"Greetings. I'm Ashilde Egilsdottir, one of your closest neighbors, about three miles south of here." She gestured behind her. "You must be Torleik's new wife?"

Eilidh looked around them, not liking this strange interruption. She smiled tentatively. "Aye, I'm Eilidh."

"Torleik and his friend saw you from atop the hillside and sent me to be your backup." She pointed toward the hill. "They're coming from the other side of that hill, hoping to take Geirolf by surprise. She gestured at the longbow lying across her lap. "I seldom miss. If there's someone who needs killing, I can help."

Eilidh let a few moments pass as she considered the woman's proposal.

You need her. Raven's voice in her ear was not the least bit subtle.

"Can you tell me what happened?" Ashilde inquired. "What brought us to this day?"

Eilidh didn't want to lose time, but she needed the woman to understand what she might be getting into. "I attracted a stalker from my husband's former life in *Nord Vegr*, a man named Geirolf. He came here, with the intention of killing Torleik for some perceived insult. I'm here to ..." Her voice caught. She paused for a moment to collect herself. "To save my husband and stepson." Eilidh looked off in the distance. "If this is too much of a complicated mess, I don't blame you. I appreciate your assistance, but I would feel terrible if anything happened to you."

Ashilde touched her crossbow once more, her fingers caressing the deadly trigger. "Do you wish to see Geirolf dead by the end of the day?"

Eilidh blinked twice, the thought shocking her. "Dead?" If she were really honest with herself, she knew they would never be free of the man as long as Geirolf walked the earth. She brushed back a loose strand of damp curls. "No, I will take care of Geirolf. And if I don't, Torleik will."

For several moments, Ashilde sat and digested all Eilidh had told her. She pulled out a water bag and took a long drink. Putting it away, she faced Eilidh squarely.

"You're a very brave woman. I'll be honored to help out in any way."

"I have nothing to pay you."

"I expect nothing."

Eilidh thanked Ashilde for her kindness, but before she could say anything further, she saw movement at the Standing Stones. If Torleik and Hallkel were going to try and attack Geirolf from higher up, she must hurry! It was now or never.

"Let's go and get this over with." With a flick of her reins, she galloped off, Ashilde keeping pace beside her. "By the way, that's a beautiful animal. What's his or her name?" Eilidh called out.

"Her name is Ghost."

Eilidh felt a chill race down her bones. If that wasn't an omen, Eilidh didn't know what was. "Good name. Good omen." She flicked the reins harder. Once they arrived at the Standing Stones, Eilidh caught a glimpse of Torleik and Hallkel's horses hidden and tied to a small tree at the foot of the high mound that supported the massive stones. But she didn't see the men. Eilidh hopped down and glanced at Ashilde's wordless vanishing form as she climbed a path that led upward into some tree cover. With no sign of Torleik or Geirolf, Eilidh let out her breath and sat, waiting, hoping to draw his attention to give the others time to attack.

Her greatest hope was that Torleik would let her say what needed to be said ... and that between them, they would be able to save Atli.

37

ᚪᚱᚲᛋᛏᚷᚹᛗᛐᚾᛟᚢ

Eilidh rested near the Standing Stones for what seemed like hours, but could have only been a short time at best, every nerve tingling and on edge as she waited for Geirolf. She heard a noise and turned, her heart thumping in her chest, but it was only a red bushy-tailed squirrel native to the area. Relief flooded through her, but no sooner had she begun to relax when Geirolf appeared, wearing all black, like his soulless heart. Furious at him for taking Atli, and for ruining her chances of happiness, she jumped to her feet.

Geirolf appeared smug when he saw her. "Greetings, my dear. How are you, this fine day?"

Eilidh shook, fists balled. "You piece of dung. Where is Atli and where is Arabel?"

She was careful not to look for Torleik. If his plan was a surprise attack, she didn't want to give him away.

"My, my, what a surprise to find you here." Geirolf looked her up and down. "I had expected to see your husband, not you."

"I want my son ... now."

Geirolf shook his finger at her. "He's not really *yours*, though, is he?"

For a moment, Eilidh wondered if Geirolf was aware Torleik was nearby, and could hear everything being said. At least, she hoped he was nearby.

"He's mine as much as he can be, Geirolf. Bring him to me, and we can talk."

Lifa appeared off to the side, arms crossed, a smug look on her face. Geirolf looked her way briefly, and flicked his wrist for her to fetch the boy. Glaring one last time at Eilidh, Lifa disappeared behind a group of boulders and returned a few moments later, dragging a reluctant four year-old.

"Atli!" Eilidh called out. "Are you injured?"

He shook his mophead in a distinctive "no."

Just then, Eilidh detected movement out of the corner of her eye and saw Torleik standing behind the pair, but slightly to the left, a finger to his lips to win her silence. Even then she could tell he was still very angry with her. Hallkel appeared to the right, both men in the ready.

Eilidh tried to appear calm, forcing her eyes on Geirolf and Lifa. "Geirolf, you've made your point. Now allow Atli to approach me." Her voice was not as strong as she would have liked it, but the words were clear.

Geirolf glanced at Atli, who stood in front of Lifa. Her hands gripped his small shoulders tightly, and Eilidh caught his wince.

"You speak with so much confidence, my dear. Is that new?" Geirolf asked in an oily tone that made her cringe.

Eilidh wondered what he was talking about, but that was for another time, if ever. "Again, I want you to send Atli over to me. *Now.*"

Out of the corner of her eye, she saw Torleik nod, as if to say "good job". She had only moments to retrieve Atli so that the men could swoop in on the pair. But before she could put her plan into action she heard Atli cry out.

"Ouch! She pinched me," Atli cried, big tears forming.

"Lifa, he's just a little boy," Geirolf said, clearly angry at Lifa. He stepped forward and handed a treat to the boy. "There you go, laddie. This should make things smoother."

"He's *our* prisoner," she said in a tight voice.

"What was that you gave Atli?" Eilidh called out, when she saw the anger boiling over on Torleik's face, his emotions raw.

"Just a honey treat. Although, it might be a tad messy," said Geirolf with a low laugh.

Geirolf seemed to be enjoying the show. But then he sobered, as if in afterthought. "You have made your point, Lifa. Now, let the boy go and point him toward his soon-to-be exiled mother."

Lifa obeyed, but Eilidh could see her silent rebellion.

All of a sudden, all hell broke loose. Just as the boy started to toddle off to Eilidh's waiting arms, Torleik and Hallkel rushed in. But not before Lifa grabbed Atli and pulled him toward her and the closest Standing Stone, while Geirolf rolled out of the way. Everything happened so fast that Eilidh had little time to react as Ashilde appeared from a copse of trees and released an arrow that whizzed by with a whirring sound, narrowly missing Geirolf's shoulder. It landed in the grass with a thud, but its menace was clear. That had been only a warning shot.

"You have reinforcements, I see," said Geirolf, gritting his teeth as he eyed the arrow that barely missed him. He shaded his eyes and quietly drew a dagger and palmed it at his side. Looking into the hills, he searched for the unseen archer, while also keeping close watch of Torleik and Hallkel.

Eilidh had a feeling Ashilde knew what she was doing, so she forced herself to remain calm as she glanced over at Atli. He was crying now, and visibly fighting Lifa's attempt to drag him away.

"Atli, don't cry," said Torleik, his jaw clenched, his eyes never leaving Lifa and Atli. "*Fadir's* here. I won't let anything happen to you."

"Nor will I," Eilidh echoed. "We aren't leaving this place without you, Atli." She glared at Geirolf and Lifa, making her point clear. "I would die before I would let you hurt that boy," she added, her chin held up in defiance.

At that moment, hearing how Eilidh had offered her life up for the boy, Lifa seemed to snap out of her stupor. She shook her head, and peered over at Torleik with a pleading expression. "I didn't purposely do anything to harm your son, Torleik. You have to know that. I love him just as dearly as you. Don't you see? We were meant to be together, you and me. I love you."

Torleik started visibly at those words. "You don't know the meaning of the word love, Lifa. You never have."

"I left everyone and everything behind for you," Lifa shouted, tears filling her words. "I was all alone here because of you!"

"Now, children," said Geirolf, rushing over to Atli and pointing the dagger at him in order to keep the others at bay. "We must all get along." He waited a moment for that to sink in, then glanced at Atli, who was beginning to tire. Eilidh watched in distress as Atli wiped his tears and rubbed his eyes, looking like a little boy who needed his mother and a nap, in that order. She reached out her hands, wishing desperately to envelop Atli in her arms and reassure him all would be well.

"*Modir!*" Atli cried.

"Lifa, please let Atli go. He's tired and it will only make matters worse for you if you take our son."

"Atli is *my* son." Torleik's tone left no doubt.

Eilidh felt the sting of his words, but refused to let it show. "He's a small child, Torleik. I am sorry I didn't watch him more closely. You must know that." Atli only cried harder as he reached out for them, calling for each in turn.

"That's enough!" Geirolf raised his arms and gestured towards Atli. "You won't get Atli back until we are assured safe passage."

Torleik looked as if he wanted to strangle Geirolf. He turned to Lifa. "Please, Lifa. I never meant to hurt you, but I could never love you. And it wasn't because of our stations in life. You deserve someone who can offer you love. True love."

Lifa grew still, her chest heaving even as Eilidh's heart ached. For one brief moment, Eilidh had thought she'd found true love, both as a wife and as a mother, but she realized now that she would never be forgiven. That one mistake would cost her everyone she had come to love in such a short time.

"Please," Eilidh begged. "Let Atli go. If you do, I will leave here forever. You have my word on it."

Lifa paused, as though considering, then pushed Geirolf out of the way and released Atli. To both Eilidh and Torleik's surprise, he hurried over to ... Eilidh. She reached to pick him up, and he immediately wrapped his legs around her middle as he had countless times before. Eilidh felt a rush of love settle in her heart.

"Where *were* you, *Modir*?" Atli scolded her.

"I was looking for you, my sweet boy," Eilidh said, tears staining her cheeks. "We looked everywhere, but couldn't find you."

Torleik leaned in, his hands on Atli's arms. "Who brought you here?"

Atli scowled and pointed at Lifa. "*She* took me. And a man named Aevar."

Eilidh glanced around. "Is Aevar here?"

Atli set his jaw like his father did when he was particularly angry. "I don't know. He was on a horse."

"Ah, that would be Geirolf's brown horse he shares with Lifa?" Torleik asked a question that didn't require an answer.

Emphatically nodding his head up and down, Atli reached for Torleik's arms, but Eilidh was ready. He was getting so big all of a sudden. She glanced at Torleik, her brows raised in question.

Torleik took Atli in his arms then turned to Geirolf, who now held both the dagger and a sharp-edged hunting knife on the four of them. "Geirolf, just tell us what you want."

Eilidh knew enough to know that Torleik's temper was on the edge. She had to do something soon to end this peacefully. "I have a slightly different question. Why did you take Arabel? She's not exactly fit for a king ... yet."

Geirolf shrugged, as if he hadn't given it much thought. "I grew fond of the little nipper. She reminds me of you, my dear. Sweet at times, but full of sass and vinegar at other times. She's a fighter. He turned to Torleik. What is her heritage, if I may be so indelicate as to ask?"

Eilidh answered for Torleik. "My father bred and raised her. As you probably know, breeders are more concerned with function rather than pedigree. Arabel is half Highland Pony and half standard riding horse. That means she's hardy enough to climb around the Highlands, but smooth enough to provide a comfortable ride to any gentleman." She glanced at Torleik. "Isn't that why you purchased Arabel?"

Torleik raked a hand through his hair, as though unsure if Eilidh was serious about having this conversation right then and there. The flash in her green-blue eyes told him she was quite serious. He set Atli on the ground and kept a hand on his shoulder. "*Ja,* Eilidh is correct. I like to breed different traits and characteristics into my horses from those on neighboring islands and see what I come up with."

Geirolf put a hand to his chin, as if considering.

"I want to go home!" Atli announced with a huge yawn.

Torleik started to lift him in his arms again when the sound of a thundering of hooves caused Eilidh to turn, just as several deer crashed through the bushes and stumbled on to the platform that held the Standing Stones. One deer careened off a horizontal slab and ended up right where Eilidh had stood a moment before.

"A deer!" Atli shouted, falling out of Torleik's arms and onto the ground, close enough to stare the frightened buck in the eyes.

Eilidh was eying the buck's horns, and debated whether it would spook the critter to try and scoop up the boy before the deer could gore him.

Raven. Tell me what to do, she pleaded, terror causing her hands to shake.

She couldn't have saved the boy only to lose him to a large roe deer. For several seconds, neither moved, when suddenly Raven appeared on one of the upright slabs of the stone nearest her. "Tell me what to do, Raven."

She watched with horror as Atli tried to get closer to the deer. "He wants to be friends with me," said Atli. "Can I hug him?"

"No!" Eilidh and Torleik responded in unison.

Atli paused just as the stag prepared to lunge at the boy, head-first. For one brief moment, she imagined her life without Torleik or Atli. Or Kelda, Astrid, Hallkel, and Isolf. All those people who had become dear to her in such a short time. Her life would be stale and without love. Could she live her life that way?

Eilidh threw herself in front of the boy. Torleik yelled. The deer, frightened by all the quick-moving humans, tried to dash out of the way of the stones. But before he found the way out, he put his head down again. In a flash of pain, Eilidh felt the horn pierce her shoulder, and then the blood began to flow. She heard a shout and a thud as the animal plowed its way through the gathering. After that, she started to lose consciousness. It wasn't until later, when she came to, that she realized Geirolf was also down on the ground, lying very still, blood staining his tunic. Lifa rushed to take a look, but was clearly upset by what she saw, for she took off at a run, leaving the borrowed horse behind.

Eilidh could hear Atli's small, frightened voice, sobs breaking up his words. "*Mo-dir? Mo-dir?* Are you d-dead, too?"

How she wanted to answer that question for the boy. But her body felt so heavy.

"Is Torleik still angry with me?" she murmured, pain making her head swim.

"You're going to be fine. Just relax. I've got you ... love."

In answer, Torleik swept her in his arms. Hallkel helped him arrange Eilidh in front of him on the horse that remained, after which he gathered Atli in his arms and placed him on his horse. Then they headed for Torleik's Farm. For home.

Just then, Ashilde appeared from her place in the copse. "Go ahead," she said. "I will keep watch on Geirolf."

"Thank you for everything," Torleik called to her, while holding Eilidh tight against his chest. Behind him, Atli held the reins of Arabel while Hallkel looked on.

All Eilidh could think, as she felt the jostling of the horse's movements, is that she was heading home with her family. Maybe for the last time.

38

ᚠᚱᚲᛋᛏᚷᚹᛗᛚᛟᚱᚾ

Once Eilidh was under Kelda's care in their bedchamber, Torleik called for a bath for Atli, then he and Hallkel tiptoed to the bed where Eilidh lay. A while later, clean and no longer sticky with honey, Atli entered the bedchamber wearing a fresh tunic. In the meantime Kelda had given Eilidh something to help her sleep, and Eilidh had drifted off, mumbling words they couldn't understand or even recognize.

"What's *Modir* saying?" Atli's brows rose.

Torleik realized he'd never asked questions about the huge project she was constantly working on. Feeling ashamed, he combed his son's damp blond hair with his fingers. "I don't know, Atli. That's something you should ask her when she's feeling better." *If she lives, that is.* Tears welled in his eyes. From now on, he would pay more attention to Eilidh.

Kelda left to work on a poultice with Atli trailing her and asking questions. That left Torleik and Hallkel.

Torleik shook his head and leaned it against the bedpost. "Everything seemed to be falling into place at last. We'd just confessed our love for each other. I had even asked her to marry me in the cathedral in *Kirkjuvagr*. In spring."

Hallkel reached out and patted Torleik's arm. "Congratulations. You can still do that. Kelda will tend the wound the best she can. Eilidh should be as good as new by then."

"What do you think will happen to Lifa, with Geirolf dead?"

"She may still be here. I saw her leave the Standing Stones and head in this direction. She may have come for her belongings. Perhaps she has money to help her find someplace new. London might be far enough away," Hallkel added with a laugh.

Torleik turned to regard Hallkel for several moments.

Hallkel heaved a great sigh. "You want me to go look for her? And if I see her, what would you have me say?"

Torleik shrugged. "Tell her I never meant to get her hopes up. That what she did to me and Eilidh was wrong and that she's no longer welcome here. I'd say more, but she'd no doubt take it the wrong way."

"No doubt."

Torleik stepped close to the bed, his hand reaching for Eilidh's. "With Lifa and Geirolf gone, things will finally be normal. No more looking over our shoulders."

"You and Eilidh can get out and live your lives the way God intended."

Torleik gazed down at Eilidh, who thrashed and mumbled in that strange language he couldn't identify. When he touched her forehead, it felt like fire. Alarmed, he alerted his friend. "If you see Kelda, tell her Eilidh is burning up with fever."

"I will certainly do that." Hallkel hesitated a moment before turning to leave. "You've been hard on her, Torleik. While she is healing, take the time to think about all the good she has done for you and Atli. I'm sure you will come up with much more on that list than things she did wrong." Hallkel regarded his friend for a moment. "Eilidh hasn't been around small children in a long time. It's easy to lose sight of how quick they move and how easily they escape. Especially an active child such as Atli. How many times has he escaped *your* supervision?"

"Is that your way of saying I'm not a perfect parent?"

"*Ja.* Just think about it."

Torleik followed Hallkel out of the bedchamber and stopped to pat Runi, who hadn't barked and was especially well-behaved since they had brought Eilidh inside. Atli was playing quietly near the unlit firepit. To Torleik, it felt as if everyone waited for Eilidh's fate. He returned to the bedchamber, then watched as Kelda applied a poultice to her shoulder.

"After all this, she may still die." Torleik gazed off into space.

"You can't think that way," Kelda chided him. "You and Eilidh have come a long way. She put her life on the line to protect Atli. What more could you ask of her? You owe her a second chance." With that, she exited the room, Torleik feeling firmly chastised.

Eilidh slept fitfully as her fever climbed. Torleik couldn't help but notice how young she appeared, her fair face almost the same shade of white as the pillow. Hallkel was right. She was still untried as a parent. It wasn't fair of him to expect so much of her so soon.

God, please don't let her die.

***

Eilidh's fever broke on the third day. She was able to sit up in bed and have broth, surprising both Torleik and Kelda. However, she grimaced as Kelda cleaned the wound. The older woman "tsk-tsked" as she worked on sewing the hole closed, now that the swelling was down. Eilidh averted her eyes, unable to stop shivering. That evening, she was surprised when Torleik appeared with Atli at his side. After Kelda refreshed the poultice and administered some willow bark tea to keep the fever in check, she left them alone. With a deep sorrow, Eilidh wondered how Torleik would approach the subject of sending her away. He quietly cleaned up around the bedchamber, as Atli walked over to the bedside. "I'm so glad you're okay," he said in a squeaky voice, his hair still damp from the bath. "You my *modir*."

Eilidh brushed back his damp hair, and favoring her right shoulder, pulled him into an embrace, tears moistening her eyes. "I'm so glad you weren't injured, and that you're home with your father ... and me." She kissed his soft pink cheek, cherishing the clean, little boy smell from his bath. Soon, she might never see Atli again, as she felt sure Torleik would want her gone. The fact that he wouldn't look her in the eye said everything. Well, so be it. And yet her heart ached at the thought of being separated from the two – father and son identical. She quickly looked away so he wouldn't see the tears she shed as he urged his son to come to him so he could put him to bed. "I love you so much, little man. But it's time for bed now." Eilidh glanced over and saw Torleik waiting by the door. She let go of Atli and watched them leave the room.

For a long while, she sat there, not ready to sleep, when suddenly, Torleik reappeared. He must be extremely angry, for his hands shook. Finally, he sat and his eyes roamed over her as if looking for other wounds.

"Tell me. Why did you jump in front of that animal? That was a foolish thing to do."

His voice was light, though not accusing. Eilidh sought comfort by burrowing down among the soft pillows. "It all happened so fast. All I could think was that I would never allow that deer to harm either Atli or you."

Torleik nodded and his gaze went to the window, where the rain pelted against the back side of the animal hide.

"You sacrificed yourself for my son ... and me?"

Eilidh was about to respond when Muire appeared with a glass of liquid in her hand and asked Torleik to come out to speak with Hallkel. He quickly excused himself, and then Muire came to stand beside the bed. "Drink up. You must sleep now."

"Kelda put cowslip in my wine, didn't she?"

"It will help you get a good, deep sleep. You'll feel much better tomorrow if the poultice is working."

"I hope so, because I feel miserable right now."

Muire reached out and placed a hand on Eilidh's good shoulder. "You saved Atli's life. You were very brave."

"Torleik says I acted foolishly."

"He'll come around. He's just a man who requires a bit more time to sort through things."

"I hope you're right." Eilidh glanced up at her friend. "I love him, Muire. I don't want to be sent away. I couldn't stand that."

Muire's smile was gentle as she tucked the blanket around Eilidh's neck. "I have a feeling Torleik would hate himself if that happened." Muire helped her scoot down.

Eilidh was asleep by the time Muire passed Torleik in the doorway on her way out.

***

When Eilidh opened her eyes the next morning, she was surprised to find Torleik sitting on top of the covers. "Finally. I thought you might sleep the day away." He gave a brief smile.

Eilidh rubbed her eyes, feeling somewhat heartened that he'd been watching her sleep rather than wake her to tell her it was time to leave. "Are you in a rush to tell me something?" she asked, her stomach in tangles.

He looked down at his hands. "I have things I don't wish to forget."

He arranged the pillows behind her back, and she couldn't stop the groan when he accidentally moved her shoulder. No use fighting the inevitable. She looked at him with sorrow. "You were saying?"

"I don't mean to speak lightly of this. I have so much to apologize for."

Eilidh released the breath she hadn't known she was holding at this turn of events. "Can you be more specific? I'm feeling too awful to guess what you mean."

Torleik raked a hand through his hair. "Your fever broke during the night. Kelda thought you might feel more like your old self today." He waved toward the spot where a door would eventually go. "I can wait, though, if you aren't."

Eilidh shook her head, her throat tight with emotion. "No, I'm fine. What is it you want to say?"

He settled his back on a pillow. "It started when we were in *Thjorsá*, and Geirolf and Bennett assaulted you. I'd never experienced such rage and jealousy before. I wanted them both dead for making your life miserable. Thank God, Hallkel talked some sense into me, or I might have ended up in jail." He took her hand in his. "And the other day, when I realized that deer was about to attack you, I thought I'd lost you ... and I had so many regrets, things I'd wanted to say. I'm sorry for doubting you and for not taking your concerns about Geirolf and the bere barley seriously. I'm sorry if I made you feel less than a partner, because that's what I've always wanted – a full partner in life. And I can't imagine my life without you in it. Last night made me realize ... I *want* you. I *need* you, and so does Atli." He leaned forward and gently kissed her cheek. "I'm not saying this very well, but I want to know ... I have to know. Will you marry me in the spring? Anyplace you want. Anywhere you desire. I want to be all yours. And you, all mine."

When Eilidh let out a giggle, Torleik's shoulders slumped. After a few moments, she finally stopped chuckling and covered her mouth. "Oh, Torleik. I'm not laughing at your words. I think that has to be the most words I've ever heard you speak at one time."

He sat forward, appearing relieved. "It's true. I'm not a man of many words."

She sobered. "I would never laugh at something so serious as our son." Careful of her shoulder, she tilted her head and gazed fondly at his rugged features. "I would never laugh when you declare your heart for me in such a way. It just so happens ..." She cupped his face in her hands and gazed into his beautiful blue eyes. "I love you dearly ... although, you *must* promise me you'll work on your communication skills in the coming year." She was sure he recognized the twinkle in her eyes. "But, in answer to your question ... aye, I will marry you in *Kirkjuvagr* at the cathedral. In fact, I will write to my mother right away and ask her to choose a day when they can all be here. Hopefully, Grandmother Marsaili will be well enough to make the trip."

Torleik leaned in closer, a smile transforming his face. "Then I will be the happiest of men to join with you for the rest of our lives, and be part of your family."

For the first time in days, she was deliriously happy, but something still bothered her. "Would it be possible to invite *your* parents and brother? Might they come to celebrate this happy occasion with their eldest son and their grandson, Atli?"

Torleik looked away, his face a mystery once more. "I can ask. But I doubt they will want to travel this far. They are both getting old, I'm sorry to say."

"What about Kol, your brother?"

"You provide me with a date, and I will ask. Kol just might sail down to show off his latest ship design and to see his nephew and beautiful new sister-in-law."

Eilidh started to clap her hands, but again groaned as her shoulder made her wince.

Torleik plumped her pillow then helped her lay her head back onto it, and for once, she didn't try to be strong. She accepted his assistance with a tentative smile. As she waited for Muire to appear with the soap and water, she savored the feel of Torleik gazing into her eyes with what could only be described as love.

And when she couldn't wait any longer, he put his hand carefully around her waist and pulled her in close for a kiss that melted all of the ice in his eyes, the warmth of their kiss turning them a deep sea blue.

Muire arrived and Torleik reached for the bowl before either woman realized what he was up to. "Muire, I'd like to bathe my wife. Might I have that soap, bowl, and sponge? I promise to do a good job and not disturb her shoulder."

Muire held a hand before her mouth. "How can I say no to such a thoughtful request?"

"You can't," said Eilidh. Her eyes went to Torleik.

Muire left quietly, hiding a secret smile for her mistress that all was as it should be.

***

They sat on the porch later that morning, waiting to see if it would be a warm and sunny day. Eilidh had wrapped herself in a warm shawl and enjoyed not having to get up and do anything while she recuperated. "How is my Arabel doing? Is she up to her old tricks?" she asked Torleik as they drank their morning tea.

Torleik snorted. "Your Arabel is her typical self. She *ate* the exercise toy Hallkel created to make her mouth easier to fit the bit. It's like she *knows* what we're doing. Is there such a thing as a witch horse?"

Eilidh laughed out loud, then held her stomach. "That is so like her. Maybe we should have trained her to steal treats from Geirolf."

Torleik sobered and leaned back to gaze across the sea at the horizon.

"There's something I've been meaning to ask you, Torleik."

"Ask away." He poured her more tea.

He seemed to be in a good mood, so Eilidh let down her guard a bit. "Why did you appear so upset when Geirolf offered Atli that honey treat?"

Torleik looked away. "I apologize to you and to Atli. Honey is made by bees. And bees love honey, so they stick around, looking for more pollen."

"And that's a bad thing?"

Torleik shook his shaggy head. "Not by itself, no." He rose and started pacing. "I told you how my wife died when she was young?"

"Of course, I remember."

"Well, there's more. We were visiting a beautiful city garden in Oslo. Atli would reach his second winter soon, so mostly, I carried him when Ulla got tired." He let go of a huge sigh.

"We weren't paying attention when all of a sudden, Ulla called out in pain. I went to her and realized she'd been stung by a bee. We didn't know it then, but Ulla was one of those people whose bodies can't handle bee venom. Her body went into shock and convulsed. It was terrifying to watch. I held her in my arms, but it didn't take long before she was ... gone."

"That's so sad. I'm sorry you lost your wife like that. No wonder you have real fears about losing another loved one."

"I yelled at Atli because bees are attracted to honey. I thought he might have the same affliction as his mother, if he was stung."

"I see. That might make sense."

"It's been three years since her life was snatched from me." He looked down at his clenched hands. "I think of her every day since then." He sat back and folded his arms across his chest as though seeking comfort. "And then, one day three years later, you crash into my life, Eilidh MacAoidh."

She smiled. "I would have said 'stumble' into your life."

"Stumble. Crash. Rush. Whatever the word, it was unexpected."

He was smiling, and Eilidh never wanted to see that happy look disappear.

"I wish to hear more about this, but I'm a bit chilled. May we go inside?" she asked in a husky voice.

He rose quickly and grabbed an extra blanket. "You should have said something earlier."

"I had great hope for the sun to shine."

"I like how you're always so positive thinking." He held the front door covering aside and mumbled. "That's another door to install. How can this small house have so many doors?"

Eilidh wanted to comment that it was not a small house, but she realized in Torleik's mind, doors connotated privacy. And she wasn't about to argue with that.

He offered to carry her mug of tea, for which she was grateful as Torleik led the way into the heart of the longhouse, stoked the fire, and paused to watch her settle into her chair with the blanket he offered. Torleik gazed down at his feet.

"Torleik, does the pain of your grief over Ulla ever lessen?"

He hesitated, and after a moment, crossed one foot over the other. "I still miss her every day." He paused again. "That is, I did until you came into my life. So, I guess, if one is fortunate to find love again, the pain does lessen." He gazed into the fire and shook his head, recalling with a laugh, "Ulla's anger was like a wild winter storm from *Nord Vegr*. When she got angry, it would simmer and stew until it blew its top like a volcano. Your anger is more like a spring squall. You get over it much quicker. I'm grateful for that. I hope you can forgive me for the ridiculous things I may have said or done in my moments of excessive male pride. Sometimes men think they have to have all the answers all of the time."

Eilidh nodded, able to understand from her experience with her brothers. "And yet, you don't. However, together, I think we can find our way."

"Since we're clearing the air, was your experience with Bennett Sutherland the reason you tried to avoid your suitors? Strange men frightened you ... including me?"

"I suppose so. For a long time, I felt so .... dirty. Like I wasn't good enough to even be in their company."

"Eilidh, that's ridiculous."

"Really? That's your response? And yet I suppose you consider me damaged goods now? Do you want my dowry money back?" Her fiery response surprised her to her core. Not one who typically showed her emotions in matters of the heart, she immediately reached for the pink heart stone that nestled in the pocket of her gown next to the red jasper heart stone.

Torleik's facial features began to soften. "Eilidh, no, I do not consider you damaged goods. And I don't want your dowry money back, either. Your experience was a horrible nightmare to have to endure. But you are safe now, and I will always protect you."

He looked down at Runi, snoring softly by his side.

"I'll ride into *Kirkjuvagr* tomorrow and report Geirolf's death to the authorities." Torleik sobered. "He was a wanted criminal in two countries." He shook his head. "You can come, if you like, but I doubt anyone will need to speak to you. He took a wrong turn when the deer got to him and finished him off."

"I never dreamed that he would die that way. From an animal attack." Eilidh covered her eyes with her hands.

"I don't think any of us could have seen that coming." Torleik reached for her tea mug and handed it to her.

Eilidh took several sips, a few of her own pressing questions still needing an answer.

"Torleik, do you know where Bennett Sutherland is? Is he in prison?"

Torleik lifted his head. "When I last spoke to the authorities, I was told he'll remain behind bars until they decide upon a trial. Do you wish to press charges for either attack?"

She paused for another sip of tea. "I don't think so. No. The Sutherlands, wield great power in our province. And I have no real witnesses who saw either attack, just the end of the encounter. It would be my word against his." She couldn't stop the tears rolling down her cheeks this time, and swiped at them angrily. "I don't think he'll try anything again, at least, not with me. I think I scared him off with my fake curse."

Torleik examined the back of his hands. "You're probably right. I plan to have a conversation with his father soon, just to let him know what his son has been up to. Bennett is not a particularly popular son with the ladies, I hear."

"I think when he drinks, his insecurities become worse."

He rose and placed his hands on his hips. "You're wise for someone your age."

Eilidh shuddered and wrapped her blanket tighter as she stood to follow him to their bedchamber. "Wisdom earned the hard way. I hope I never see him again."

Torleik put an arm around her good shoulder. "You must never feel the need to apologize to anyone, or that you must give up your natural personality, your sense of honesty, your passion. You almost sacrificed your life for me and for Atli. That's the most selfless act anyone has ever done for me. I love you just the way you are. The way you came to me and bared your soul."

Tears began running down her cheeks, but Eilidh felt the burden, the weight of a mountain lift from her shoulders. She sniffed. "You said you l-loved me. Is that t-true?"

His hands, his big, work-roughened hands came up on each side of her face and centering his gaze, he said, "How's this? Does this tell you what you need to know?"

His kiss was firm, yet gentle at the same time. She had the luxury of leaning against his muscled chest, and it held up well until he began exploring her other various curves. After a while, he stepped away, a look of regret replacing the passion of a moment before. "You need to rest your shoulder tonight. Kelda won't be pleased if it doesn't look improved by tomorrow."

"I have to agree." Eilidh took him by the hand and started for their bedchamber, even though it was still daylight. "I need rest, and I want you beside me while I nap.

"You're a bossy little thing, aren't you?"

"I'm a Little Squall, remember?"

He waited a moment. "That you are," he said with a laugh." As they passed beneath the deerskin covering the door, Torleik started to remove his clothes, then gestured behind him. "My Yule gift to you is to install a real door with a real lock."

"Ach, we will get much use out of that gift," she said with a twinkle in her eye.

"That, we will," he agreed. "That we will."

Epilogue

Christmas Day
AD 1153

Eilidh surveyed the Yule landscape around her. Snow had inundated the farm the night before, and the storm that should have ended by now showed no sign of slowing down. Because of the early snow, they had decided to put their wedding off until spring. In the meantime, Torleik was on a deer hunting trip with other men from the community, and was due home that evening. When he didn't arrive, she sent out two of his men to find out if they'd stopped for shelter somewhere.

Already anxious, Eilidh put her mind toward the Christmas Eve dinner Siv had prepared for their community as a way to thank workers this year, especially with the additional hustle and bustle of bere barley harvesting, which involved almost all of the community – even the children. It had been a smashing success, and took much of the pressure off Torleik.

Eilidh enjoyed the sight of his people fed and content, as winter set in. People back home would be shopping and baking, and sledding and skating. Now, she understood how important the bere barley really was if it fed more mouths so no one went hungry this winter. They'd survived.

The meal was a major success, with folks like Hallkel and Isolf taking over duties Torleik may have performed, had he been there, such as watching a pheasant roast perfectly on the spit.

"Don't worry," said Hallkel. "We sent out Torrad and Herdis. They will find Torleik and bring him home."

Eilidh smiled her appreciation, then glanced over to see Atli sitting with Astrid, Ilse, and Dagny. Knowing he was occupied and smiling, she turned to clean up the tables so they could be moved out of the way for dancing.

Before that, however, Hallkel took the stage set up at the front to tell a story to the children of Torleik's little community. He put up a hand, and immediately, silence prevailed. Hallkel set his fiddle behind him. "It's that time of year, folks. But, time for ... what?"

"Trows!" yelled the children, in unison.

"And who can tell us what's so bad about Trows?"

"Um, bad creatures with no souls who cause trouble at night," said Hodur, the blacksmith's middle son, in a quiet voice.

"And that means it's time for ..."

"The Wild Hunt!" Dagny shouted out.

Hallkel grinned at her. "*Ja*, that is absolutely what happens." He held up both hands, palms out, and the children listened in silent anticipation. "As you know, Odin, the allfather, was considered the leader of all disembodied spirits, like the trows. He was a gatherer of the dead. When he took on this role, he was known as The Wild Huntsman. He conducted a hunt known as ..."

"Odin's Hunt, or the Wild Ride!"

"Correct, Brusi. And this very special hunt was said to foretell misfortune such as pestilence, death, or war. Followed by the ghosts of the dead, Odin would roam the skies, accompanied by furious winds, lightning, and thunder.

"Now, as you also know, trows are at their most active on nights like Yule, Samhain, and the beginning of the new year, Hogmanay. Why do you think this is?"

Hallkel stood and started pacing the short space at the front. He looked driven, and didn't wait for an answer, probably to hold their interest.

"Because on those dates, the walls between the living and the dead is at its thinnest. The Trows search for mortals who have been blessed by the gods." Hallkel altered his facial muscles into a strange, gaunt frown.

"Odin rode across the sky throughout the nine worlds on his eight-legged steed named ..."

"Sleipnir," said Ilse, winking at Atli.

"So, every year, you may be able to see Odin and the Wild Hunt in the winter skies. But know this: if they see you first, you just might be snatched away from the living and become a part of that wild ride of dead beings."

He stopped and put his hands together. The children knew that was the end, yet waited.

"If the night is cold, the winter darkness unrelenting, and the silence desolate and broken only by the baying winds and galloping bodies of the undead, you may not wish to venture outside and ... join the Wild Hunt."

The adults clapped and whooped, and the children shouted and clapped as well. Eilidh glanced over at Astrid, and saw her clapping the hardest.

Torleik was right. Hallkel made a wonderful storyteller for the children. Eilidh was glad she hadn't missed this.

Just then, there was a commotion at the main door. A small group of men entered, shaking the snow off the fur coats they'd brought from *Nord Vegr*. Of the men, Torleik was the tallest and most handsome. He immediately spotted Eilidh and moved towards her.

"Torleik, what happened? I was so worried."

He grinned and lifted Atli as he pointed towards one of the men who'd gone in search of them. We were on our way back and just climbed the hill to *Okneyjaugr* when the snow came down even harder. We couldn't find shelter anywhere else, so we broke into a burial cairn to sit out the worst of the storm. There was a roomy chamber once we got inside."

"Did you find a treasure?" asked Atli, sitting on his father's shoulders.

"Not exactly."

"What did you find?" inquired Eilidh, brushing off snow on his arm.

"Runes! Lots and lots of runes. Some were from the modern day. Others went back hundreds of years." He set Atli down and glanced around the busy hall. "Atli, why don't you join Hallkel and the others clear the floor for the dancing. We'll be right over."

Atli made a chirping sound, like a satisfied baby bird, and crossed the room.

Torleik reached into the pouch around his waist and pulled out a stone. "I found this. And I knew it was meant for you, Eilidh, my love. My light in this world." He held out the stone and she studied what was written upon it.

"What does it say?"

"I'll check with Hallkel, but I think that's the symbol for *Laguz*. It represents water – the sea, a lake, or bay. It can mean a journey by water, like when you first arrived. Water is linked with the realm of emotion, feeling and flow, sensibility. A more profound journey signified by this rune is one inwards to the depths of the self. *Laguz* is most often associated with the process of discovering the hidden springs of our inner self."

He took it from her palm. "But see the other side. What do you see?"

Eilidh squinted and drew a breath. "It looks like ... to me, it seems to be a ... raven! How can that be? Was it added later?"

He shook his shaggy head. "I don't know. But that raven grabbed my attention." He took her empty hand and squeezed gently. "I think this will be a special year for us. Good business. New families bonding and connecting. And perhaps ..."

"A baby?"

His ice blue eyes sparkled for a moment, and she thought she saw tears gather.

"A baby would be nice. Very nice."

"I thought so too. Babies change everything."

When Atli returned from moving chairs, he hugged Torleik's legs, then turned and gave Eilidh a kiss that made her laugh.

"I love you, *fadir* and *modir*."

Torleik looked away, but his hands went to his son's shoulder.

Eilidh felt light-headed for a few moments, but then she pulled Atli towards her and gazed into Torleik's eyes.

"To think, I was once scared I would ever be a good mother."

"And look at you now."

Atli saw his friend, Hodur, who signaled for Atli to follow. He rushed off and the two boys climbed under a table to create mischief.

"Do you think we should nip that in the bud?" Torleik inquired.

Eilidh glanced across the room and noted how closely Hallkel held Astrid as they danced. Then she turned back to the boys and shrugged. "I don't think it matters. Let's leave them alone for one dance."

He glanced at the two boys. Not seeing any fire or other elements that could destroy the longhouse, Torleik relaxed and escorted his wife to the dance floor. She dropped the raven rune into the pocket of her evergreen Norse-Scottish gown and gladly put her arms around her man as the music flowed around them.

***

Before Eilidh knew it, the coastal Highland areas were spilling over with spring flowers, such as pinkish-purple sea thrift, and bright cheery yellow daffodils, later joined by the heavenly scent of old-fashioned aromatic roses from her mother's garden.

Thanks to the work of many hands, Eilidh was able to take her time with wedding arrangements, her main concern that her family would be able to attend. The responses came in slowly, each one making her grin in excitement.

Somewhere near mid-spring, she received a note from her mother. She'd been expecting it, but it broke her heart, just the same. Her grandmother had died quietly during the night, her breath stopping once and for all. For the first week, Eilidh scolded herself for not being there. By the second week, she couldn't stop the tears. The third week, she switched from one to the other while working through some of the more thorny quandaries between the Christian religion versus Druidism. Grandmother Marsaili had opened Eilidh's mind and heart and taught her the value of education for women. As much as Eilidh had tried and failed to communicate with her grandmother, she still felt comforted and watched over. Grandmother had whispered words of encouragement as Eilidh slept, so that upon awakening, *The Book of Delsiran* had taken on new meaning and context. It was as if, in the darkest hours of the night, she'd been available to communicate across the distance with Eilidh, explaining the meaning of *The Book of Delsiran*, and encouraging Eilidh to use the book when she was ready.

But now, Eilidh was on her own.

Before everyone arrived, she pulled out the odd volume and sat down with Ashilde's youngest sister, Eilidh's first student, Unne.

"Is this book filled with magic?" Unne inquired the first day.

Eilidh smiled and set the book aside. Around the corner, she could just see her brother Gregor, and her new friend, Ashilde, conversing on the porch, their laughter punctuating the silence. There wasn't a doubt in her mind that the two would be engaged to marry before Gregor left for Alba.

She placed her hand on the book to answer Unne's question. Although she could have been dismayed at how long it had taken her and Torleik to marry in the church, she wouldn't revisit that. Grandmother Marsaili would simply say that Eilidh's path was different.

She nodded towards the tome. "I'm sure the book will appear at times to contain magical properties. But for everyday purposes, no." She laid it in front of the blonde six-year-old with her hair fixed in a long, slender braid. "Now, let's start with the alphabet. What word can you think of that starts with the long A sound, such as 'ate'? I *ate* a rock."

Unne giggled. "You didn't eat a rock."

"Well, let's pretend it's one of those magical moments. I *ate* a rock instead of an *apple*." While she repeated the last sentence, she pointed to the first letter of the alphabet. Unne's big blue eyes grew wide as she understood the distinction in sound.

Eilidh felt a sweep of emotion race through her. She may miss her grandmother, but Marsaili would accompany Eilidh in spirit on her new path to educate girls and women. That way, they too may see how knowledge could facilitate their power in new and creative ways to help their families and to prepare their own voices to be heard. Of that, she could be sure.

Magic, indeed.

Acknowledgments

As always, thank you to my friends and family who were kind enough to ask when my next book was coming out. A special thank you goes out to Linda Arthur, the wonderful CIE tour guide who took the time to answer all my hypothetical questions about Orkney all those years ago. That was a magical experience in every way.

Author Notes

<u>Orkney</u>

It's been more than twelve years since my eye was caught by a travel guide that focused on Scottish island-hopping. I came across a story that caught my fancy. That supposedly true story involved a hunting party of Norsemen (they did not yet refer to themselves as "Vikings") who broke into Maeshowe, a burial cairn on Christmas Eve, to shelter from a snowstorm. Inside the cavern, they discovered graffiti written by other Vikings hundreds of years before them. The Orkney Islands, or Orkney, as the locals refer to it, consists of sixty-seven islands (sixteen are inhabited) located off the coast of Caithness, the northeast corner of the Scottish mainland.

Orkney was invaded and settled by the Norsemen beginning in the 8th century, with Viking influence predominating on the island until the 15th century, when Orkney returned to Scottish rule. Intermarriage with the local population eventually resulted in few speakers of Gaelic during that period of time. I have made attempts to introduce Scottish Gaelic and Old Norse words throughout the story to provide that "flavor." Any mistakes in usage are mine.

Author Bio

LAINE STAMBAUGH earned degrees in Russian, Linguistics, and Library Science. Her love of language and culture led her to a long career in academic libraries where she served as an acquisitions librarian and as library human resources director. Now retired, she lives with her "tuxedo" cat, Minka, and writes full-time from her home in the Pacific Northwest. *Raven in the Runes* is the second book in the *The Heart Stone Trilogy*.